BENJAMIN TWIGG

DAD MAGIC

THE MONARCH CHILDREN SAGA: BOOK ONE

CONTENTS

City of Spellford 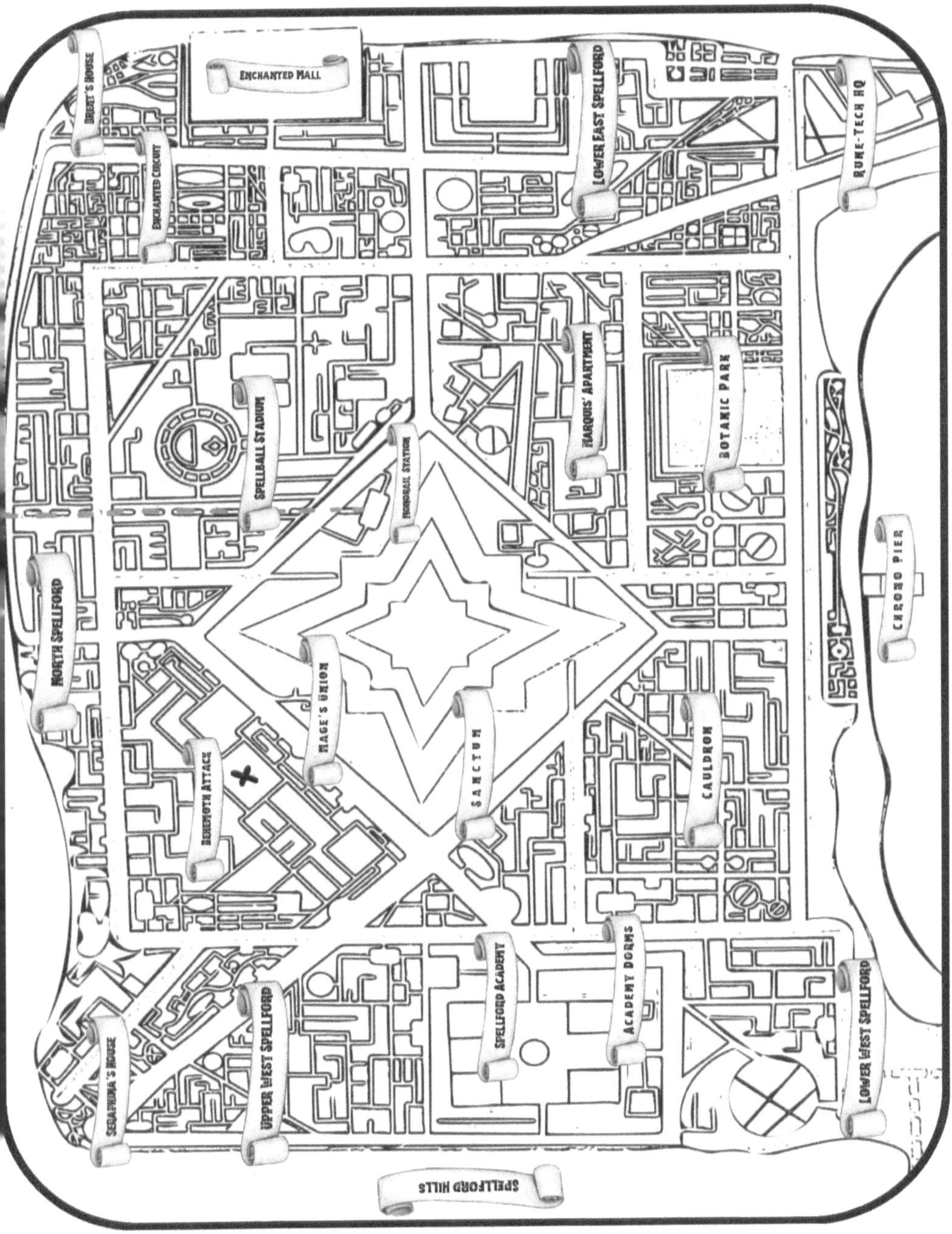
ENCHANTED MALL
BRENT'S HOUSE
ENCHANTED CIRCUIT
LOWER EAST SPELLFORD
RUNE-TECH HQ
MARQUIS' APARTMENT
BOTANIC PARK
SPELLBALL STADIUM
MONORAIL STATION
CHRONO PIER
NORTH SPELLFORD
MAGE'S UNION
BEHEMOTH ATTACK
SANCTUM
CAULDRON
SERAPHINA'S HOUSE
UPPER WEST SPELLFORD
SPELLFORD ACADEMY
ACADEMY DORMS
LOWER WEST SPELLFORD
SPELLFORD HILLS
MAP ILLUSTRATED BY DESMOND BELL © 2024

CONTENT AND TRIGGER WARNINGS

Whilst I have endeavoured to make the book not triggering, I recognise this book explores topics that may be sensitive or triggering to some people. Do take care when reading.

Topics include:

UNRESOLVED GRIEF
ADOPTION
LIGHT RACIAL TAUNTS TOWARDS MODERN DAY ORCS
FOOD CONSUMPTION
BULLYING
ABDUCTION
BETRAYAL
CATTY BANTER BETWEEN FRIENDS
SEXUAL CONTENT BETWEEN CONSENTING ADULTS
POWER PLAY (BOSS x EMPLOYEE)
POWER DYNAMICS
EVIL FORCES
CLONING

To my Dad! Thank you for all your lessons, your humour and all your *magic* you have passed on to me.

To Aleks and Venus. My two greatest loves of my life. You are both the missing pieces I needed to become whole.

And to anyone who's ever found family in the most unexpected places: This book is for you.

Tropes and Themes you will find in this book:

FOUND FAMILY
OLDER PROTAGNISTS – AGE 30+
SECOND CHANCE AT LOVE
MAGIC & TECHNOLOGY HARMONY
MODERN MULTICULTURAL FANTASY RACES
MAGICAL INVESTIGATION ADVENTURE
FANTASY TWIST ON MODERN COMMODITIES
QUEER JOY AND FREEDOM
BANTER BETWEEN FRIENDS
ANCIENT SECRETS UNCOVERED
DISABILITY REP – APHONIC AND APHASIA

DATES AND SEASONS
IN THE DAD MAGIC UNIVERSE

"The passage of time yearns to be recorded...All that graces our existence in this world, the moon, the sun and the stellar sky that turns..."

Arcanthus' Legacy - Passage of Time - Verse IX

The Dad Magic Universe has unique names for Months and Days.

Days of the Week

1. Runasday – 1st day of the week
2. Lunasday – 2nd day of the week
3. Wintasday – 3rd day of the week
4. Tutelasday - 4th day of the week
5. Flintasday - 5th day of the week
6. Shroudasday - 6th day of the week
7. Solasday - 7th day of the week

Lunars (Months) of the year

1.   Winterturn
2.   Gloomarch
3.   Stormtide
4.   Bloomveil
5.   Emberfell
6.   Luxenturn
7.   Brightmarch
8.   Heartbloom
9.   Duskmarch
10. Gloamturn
11. Nightveil
12. Frostmarch

Seasons and Corresponding Lunars

<u>Spring Equinox</u>
Stormtide
Bloomveil
Emberfell

<u>Summer Solstice</u>
Luxenturn
Brightmarch
Heartbloom

<u>Fall Equinox</u>
Duskmarch
Gloamturn
Nightveil

<u>Winter Solstice</u>
Frostmarch
Winterturn
Gloomarch

PROLOGUE
MARQUIS BEAUMONT

Darkness surrounded the ornate halls of the Suncrest Palace. Marquis Beaumont moved stealthily through the corridors, making his way to the grand chamber. His steps were silent along the blue quartz tiles, as if he were gliding along through the passageways. His presence, a mere whisper in the dead of night. The air was heavy with anticipation and a sense of impending doom lingered in the shadows. The shadows that Marquis clung to.

Marquis came to Suncrest for one purpose—to capture the queen and get his revenge for what she did to his wife. Dark sprites surrounded Marquis and whispered nefarious rumours in his ears, urging him on to capture her.

She must pay. She is to blame. She took her from you.

The queen would be a powerful adversary. Marquis was aware of the powers she possessed. As Sun Queen, she controlled magic like no one else in her land. He was determined to harness her powers for his own. Anything he could use to bring them back to him.

He skulked around the corridors until he came to a set of guards stationed outside the queen's bedchamber. Marquis slithered in silence amongst the shadows cast by the pillars for further inspection.

He watched for a pattern in their movements and then, with precise timing, he slinked into the shadows and slid across the floor. One by one, he emerged and knocked out the soldiers, a reddish dark hue left behind. He bound the soldiers together and covered them with a disillusionment spell. Where they lay, they would appear as an ornate sofa, one that fit the surroundings.

Marquis turned sharply and sped forward. He reached the doors and took a moments pause. He knew the risks of facing the queen head-on.

But he was prepared to do whatever it took to achieve his goal. He flicked and turned his hand, silently picking the lock.

As he crept through the room, his eyes darted around searching for a sign of the queen. Finally, he spotted a small alcove above the main chamber. Soaring upwards like a bullet Marquis came to land before her bed. Positioning himself above her, he licked his lips eagerly. He was finally about to enact his revenge on the world that had wronged him.

He looked down at the woman sleeping before him, casting an incantation with his mind. Slowly and gracefully, his hands weaved and formed a shadowy web of dark energy. The web crackled as it expanded. The queen stirred causing Marquis to look down. She was still asleep. *Good*, he thought, *stay asleep*. Marquis licked his lips once again. He savoured the moment, taking enjoyment in knowing he had been successful. With a last flourish of his hands, he gave a silent snap with his fingers and the web was ready.

As the queen turned in her sleep, she awoke with a start, her eyes wide with fear and confusion. Marquis smirked triumphantly, hastily wrapping the bindings around her like a spider catching its prey. He watched her struggle against them, her screams muffled.

She levitated above him in mid-air, but as he turned to take his prize, he realised he had been fooled.

"I knew it was too easy," he muttered.

There before him was the real Queen of Suncrest. The one above him disintegrated and turned to ashes.

"Beaumont, what an unpleasant sight to befall my eyes!" she said scathingly. "Should I call the guards, or will you leave this palace on your own volition?" she asked, not batting an eye.

"I will not leave until I have what I came for!"

"Enlighten me on what that might be?"

"You!" His lips twisted into a sneer. He coiled his hands and wove another incantation, but the queen was too fast for him.

Muttering words under her breath, she conjured a blast wave of air which blew him off his feet. She flicked her fingers and suspended him, mid-air, over the ledge. She toyed with him, allowing the air to bounce him, then she flicked her wrist outward, elegantly. Marquis flew across the room and down to the ground floor of the chamber, shattering a small collection of chairs. As he brushed off the debris, a Half-Orc Woman and a young but stern looking Witch approached him

"Thrasa, Sama!" The queen called out to her personal guard. "Seize this man at once!" she bellowed from above and then leapt over the balcony ledge, floating, until her shoes gracefully landed onto the stairs. Her silk gown billowed around her as she descended coming to a stop at the bottom landing.

The Orc woman, Thrasa, lifted Marquis off the ground and bound his hands behind his back. "You ain't going nowhere, bucko!" she exclaimed, her tusks brandished and her hot breath blowing on his face. With his arms bound behind his back, he knew he wasn't entirely powerless. He just had to bide his time.

The queen approached Marquis with slow deliberation, ensuring to maintain some distance between them.

"You are a fool for coming here tonight, Marquis." She spoke loudly, gliding towards him. "I will throw you somewhere, where you will never see the grace of the sun ever again!"

Marquis laughed maniacally.

"What is so funny?" she asked, pushing his face to the side with her barefoot.

"You, you pathetic bitch. If I wanted to, I could have killed you lunars ago. I have been stalking you and watching your every move. You thought those shadows in the corner of your eye were just a flickering of the light, but no, they were me," he said calmly, her toes inching towards his eyes. She did not look impressed. "No, I need you alive. I may as well take your little friends here, too, good puppets for me to use!"

Marquis slunk down like a snake, his body becoming liquid. As he melted and changed to a gaseous form, his body now a shadowy fog, formed and built slowly around them. As it rose from their feet, it got thicker and grasped at them like a child trying to get their mother's attention. Slinking back into the darkness, he watched from afar as they struggled under the weight of the fog, choking on it as it covered their faces.

"What is this?" the queen asked, trying to cover her nose, but the coughing persisted as she struggled to breathe.

"I don't know my Queen, but don't breathe it in!" the younger Witch coughed, writhing under the fog, her frail frame too weak to combat it. The Orc was the first to fall. Then the Witch. The queen was the last to remain standing.

"Marquis!" she spluttered. "You will not get away with this!" She began to cough and sputter as Marquis's smog invaded her lungs.

As he looked over her passed out body, he smiled. "You will become my greatest legacy!"

In a final flash of light, Marquis, the Queen of Suncrest, and her personal guard disappeared from view.

***

With all three subjects in their pods, Marquis closed their coverings. As soon as he activated the machines, beams of light took samples from each of them and illuminated the room with an eerie purple glow. The first phase of his plan was now enacted.

CHAPTER ONE
BEHEMOTH BITES

An uncomfortable bead of sweat trickled down Brent's back as he rushed through the SorcerySure office from the elevator. He was late, but hoped nobody would notice.

"Late again, hey Brent?" The voice of Paxton, his best friend, followed him as he dashed past their desks and slumped into his chair.

Brent replied through the dreary grey cubicle partition. "Oh, shut it, Pax! I'm only a minute over!"

"Try ten!" Paxton held up ten thick, green fingers, almost knocking the desk with his massive Half-Orc arms.

"Well, Victoria needed to be dropped off." He heard the lie in his own voice as he adjusted his seat. Realising he had sat down on his bag; he stood back up and hung it up along with his coat.

Grabbing his headset, he tried to ignore Pax, who poked at him in his usual way. "She's seventeen. She's old enough to go to school on her own."

Brent traced the cover of the brochures someone had left on his desk.

Trust SorcerySure for all your Magic Insurance needs! Wiccan Woes? Carriage Carnage? Minotaurs barging through your home? SorcerySure, under the authority of the Mage's Union, keeps the city of Spellford safe so that Arcanum can run the way it should.

He knew Pax was right, though he'd never admit it. His daughter was seventeen years old, and he needed to stop controlling every aspect of her life.

Mage's Union: Keeping Spellford a safe place to work, live and magic. For any grievances, contact us through the SorcerySure App.

Brent glared at the second brochure before tossing both in the floating wastebasket beside his desk.

"You sure you didn't want to drop her so you could stay around and see him?" Pax said slyly.

"Him" being one of the other dads Brent had a crush on. Part of being friends for so long meant Pax knew what made Brent tick, and vice versa. The two of them had become especially close after conducting a mind-link experiment back in their academy days, which they had never bothered to reverse. It had proven useful plenty of times, but it could also be annoying...

Like right now. Brent adjusted his headset. "He's taken, and besides, we are both ex-adventurers. It would be way too much trauma in one room."

"No more trauma than what you live with already."

Pax was joking, but Brent didn't respond. Instead, he waved a hand nonchalantly in front of him. A lexicon materialised from thin air in a flurry of blue sparkling lights.

As he stroked the illuminated holographic keys, Brent sighed internally as he keyed in his password and opened his required applications to undertake his job.

Brent let out an extended groan. "Fifty in the queue already!"

"They won't disappear with us chatting! Talk in an hour?" Pax cheerfully replied and Brent got to work queuing up calls.

As Brent took calls, his mind cast back to his first day on the job. Fresh faced and eager to work hard to put food on the table. As time went on, expenses inflated, and he couldn't make do on a single salary anymore. Pax finally landed a job with SorcerySure, and it gave Brent some ease of mind. Pax had been his live-in babysitter, and he owed him a lot.

As he scrolled to the next caller, he looked at the date. Today marked seventeen years exactly since he started. He never intended to remain at this job, but here he was, with only his back-to-back sales employee of the lunar for four years running awards to show for it. Being an insurance salesman wasn't even exciting for him anymore. He looked out the window and pined for the days when he and Pax would go on quest hunts.

He finished up a call and queued the next. Scanning his eyes around to the corner of his desk, he noticed a cobweb had formed amongst a thick layer of dust on top of a few photo frames.

He scanned across them all. In the front was a picture of Paxton holding baby Victoria. Visible fingerprints parted the sea of dust across the glass. He gave it a gentle blow, particles wafted up into the air. Pax's golden eyes and the white of his tusks popped through the dust. It was also around that time he started to lose his long hair.

Brent placed it back in front of another one that was obscured by even more dust. It was of a small group he and Pax had gone on one adventure with.

As the phone call connected, Brent piped up. "Welcome to SorcerySure, where you can be sure your sorcery is insured. Can I please start with your name?" Brent started his rounds of calls with the same repetitive lines he used for every call. The monotony of the job was only bearable because of regular breaks and the decent pay.

The phone call continued and Brent swivelled in his chair. Head back, he looked up at the ceiling and listened to the customer explain their issue. His eyes wandered around his desk until they fell on a framed photo that had fallen behind the rest. He reached forward and picked it up, a thick layer of dust obscured it. Still on the call, he blew on the photo and the dust shifted.

It was a photo of a beautiful man with glistening skin, dark hair, pointed ears, and piercing silver-blue eyes. His hands shook as he clutched the photo. Brent swallowed; his mouth suddenly felt like he had walked through a desert with no water.

How long had it been since he put this photo of Elwin out of his mind?

"Hello, are you there?"

The customer's voice cut through Brent's wandering mind, and he sprung back to life, dropping the photo frame. It made a slight clanging noise against the desk, and he began apologising to the customer. Reaching over, he placed it behind the rest of the photos once again, where it would return to the dusty corner, to be put out of his mind once more. Taking his hand back, he noticed the withered skin around his left ring finger. Elwin and Brent were engaged, but only one of them had lived on.

Brent continued with the customer, trying to force the memory of Elwin from his thoughts. He kept darting his eyes between where the photo sat and his lexicon. "I can offer a competitive discount on our *Accidental Cauldron Explosions and Damages Plan*, but it, unfortunately, will not take effect until three full lunar cycles." Brent waited until he received an answer from the customer over the phone. "Amazing! Thank you for agreeing to sign up for the *Supreme Witch Plan*. I can see here most of it will come into effect from today, your healthcare plan will begin in four lunar cycles and—"

It continued like this until he wrapped up the call. Another successful sale would put him in the running for top insurance salesperson for this Lunar cycle. He couldn't help but feel empty inside. Something was missing. There was no thrill, and everything was stagnant. Too easy. Brent wasn't being challenged. He took off his headset, stretched his arms above his head and moved his neck from side to side. Brent stood up and could see that Pax was still on a call, so he went to fill up his water bottle. All that talking gave him a dry mouth.

As he entered the kitchen, he could hear the whispers of others nearby, but it was the shout-whisper where everyone in the office could hear. As it echoed out into the office, Brent shook his head. He always abided by office etiquette and found others who didn't insufferable.

"Did you hear the Suncrest's Queen is missing?"

"Queen Emilia?" the other person replied, trying to remain quiet. "How are they governing everything?"

"I don't know, but rumour has it—" Brent kept walking back to his desk and tuned them out. Politics rarely interested him.

"Another successful call I gather?" Paxton smiled at him and Brent flashed one in return before he sat back down. He murmured a yes, not even attempting to hide the clear disdain for his job. Pax stood and continued talking. "Mine was an Ogre. I had to tell him, 'Unfortunately, our plans do not cover your Acts of Ogression.'" Pax waited for a laugh, but Brent didn't respond.

"What is wrong with you? That was hilarious!" Pax continued to laugh as a Witch with a pointy hat bobbed past him.

"I thought it was funny, Pax!" said Estelle, one of their co-workers in their pod of desks. Brent saw the tip of her hat above the partition when she stopped by the edge of Pax's desk.

Estelle was, once upon a time, a swamp Witch who lured children into her house. She prided herself on the fact she did not want to eat them. She had always wanted to be a mother, and the desperation of her loneliness drove her to kidnap them. Brent had reminded her countless times it was still kidnapping, no matter how she phrased it.

"Last night's Dragonfire was epic!" Estelle's excitement poured onto Pax, who turned around so fast he banged his desk by accident, shaking Brent's. Estelle and Pax's entire relationship comprised recaps of their favourite vision orb shows.

"It was brilliant! Kiera is truly determined to win the whole thing," Brent replied, and the other two went silent.

"I didn't take you for a Dragonhead." Estelle sounded shocked.

Brent knew Pax was rolling his eyes even without watching him. "He isn't." Pax whispered. "Victoria loves the show, and he has merely adopted it as his own," Pax trailed off and continued his conversation with Estelle.

"We should hang out after work sometime and watch it together?"

Pax mumbled a polite dismissal to her proposal and a moment later Brent saw her pointy hat bob away.

"Uh!" Pax laughed nervously as he watched her walk away. "Is she for real?" he whispered through the divider.

"Well, have you told her you're not interested?" Brent asked back, monitoring her return. "Or gay?"

"No, but I would have thought being a Half-Orc would scare her away."

"Nah, I can see it. The tusks, the hulking muscles, broad shoulders, greenish skin, pig-like nose, you're a catch!" Brent chuckled to himself. Brent thought himself funny, even when others didn't.

Pax made to kick him from under the desks, only to kick the partition with a violent shake, knocking over everything on both their desks.

"You are a lot shorter for a usual Half-Orc though," Brent said. He returned his desk back to normal. "Maybe she likes short, bald Orcs who're built like brick houses?"

"I'm not bald!" Pax raised his voice. He stood up and looked down on Brent, who was not short for a human by any means. He walked around and entered Brent's cubicle. Brent looked up from his seat.

"I'm balding." He pointed to the thinning hair at the back of his head, revealing strands of hair across a pale green scalp.

"My eyes!" Brent pretended like he was being blinded. "It burns, the reflecting light is too strong!"

"Maybe now that you're blind, you can rely on your other senses, like your nose. You'll make a great Orc yet with your new sense of smell!" Pax imitated, sniffing around like a pig, even throwing in a few snorts close to Brent's ear.

"I don't need my nose to be enhanced, Pax." Pushing him off as he sniffed around his neck and head. "I can smell you from my bedroom every morning." Brent held his nose and pretended to wave air around.

"Do you ever tire of being a sassy little bitch?" Pax asked as he walked away to sit back down at his own desk.

"No, actually, I don't!" Brent laughed and then pulled up his Rune-Phone, it was close to midday. "Want to grab an early lunch?"

"Not if you are getting Goblin, Goblin, Goblin again," Pax said.

"Was thinking about it why?" Brent responded sheepishly.

"The food there is gross, undercooked, and always riddled with many random ailments."

"Yeah, but it's cheap." Brent stood up, and the two wandered over to the elevator foyer together.

"Remember the time you got Harpy's Screech and couldn't return to work for two weeks because all you did was squawk in a shrill piercing voice," Paxton said as he picked up his Rune-Phone from his desk and made his way to the elevator. "Although if you ask me, it was an improvement to your normal voice."

"Oh, bugger off!" Brent poked him in his belly, which Pax chuckled at.

"Victoria was so embarrassed she made me drop her off the entire time." Paxton's boisterous laugh echoed through the foyer

Brent pressed the elevator button and waited for it to arrive, expressing his surprise that Pax fit in his old carriage. He was even more surprised that Pax could drive it.

Brent and Pax stood in silence, the only sound being the faint humming of the elevator as it slowly descended to the ground floor. Every person in the building had the identical idea, evidenced by the multiple stops made to pick up more passengers. The unmistakable expression on Pax's face, coupled with the flaring of his snout-like nose, revealed his undeniable craving for a visit to Chrono-Fried Chicken.

"Alright," Brent said, "you go to Chrono's, and I'll grab something from BB's."

"Why don't you trust the Time Wizards?" Pax looked at him. "They always know your order before you even put a foot in the door!"

"The staff of Time Wizards are barely graduates from the academy." Brent shrugged. "Pax, we shouldn't deep fry chicken in milliseconds. And besides," Brent leaned into Pax's ear and whispered, "are we even sure it is real chicken? It could be cockatrice for all we know."

"Cockatrices are extinct," Pax replied in a hushed whisper, ignoring everyone else in the elevator.

"Yeah, because of your people!" Brent threw back and they laughed together, ignorant of the disgruntled looks they received. The majority of citizens in Spellford were fine with Orcs, although there were the occasional citizens who still held onto old ideals. But Brent was sure their looks were about his and Pax's disregard to an extinct creature. "How about Five Knights?"

"Human stomachs confuse me so much, just pick something!" Pax grew impatient with Brent, and he pushed his glasses up his nose.

"Yours is Half-Human, though, could be Troll with what you consume," Brent said sarcastically, bumping his shoulder into Pax's arm.

They arrived at street level and clambered out of the elevator, through the foyer, and outside towards the food court across the road. A crowd of various workers all on their lunch break weaved around them, the fresh air hit their faces and gave a much-needed reprieve from being stuck in the office.

"Ugh! Been craving the Chronos all day," Pax said, waiting to cross.

"Didn't you only have it for dinner last night?" Brent asked, watching the traffic go past. Magic Carpets, witches on brooms, and an assortment of floating and grounded carriages pulled by Rune-Tech constructs or actual horses, all rushed by them in a blinding flurry.

"No, it was Red-Mage Rooster," Pax said defensively. "It was good, but Chrono's always hits the spot."

"Oh, sorry, didn't know there was a difference." Brent held his hands up in mock defence. "I was never a fan of them, although those Elk Cheesy nuggets looked nice." Brent's mouth salivated at the memory of them.

"They were! Devoured so fast." Pax now rubbed his belly and chittered his tusks. He was in an oddly good mood and Brent dared not ask why. "So, you decided?"

"Yeah, the Behemoth Bites one hundred percent." Brent continued to watch the traffic go by. The soft breeze ran across his skin, attempting to ruffle Brent's perfectly styled hair, and he could as easily not return to the boring humdrum of his job. He wondered briefly what would happen if he kept walking.

"I'm glad they confirmed there isn't any real Behemoth in their food." Pax made a gesture like he was about to vomit. "Cockatrice is one thing, but Behemoth looks like it would be too tough." Brent didn't respond as they continued to wait.

"Aren't you on a diet though? Victoria won't be pleased." Pax poked Brent in his no-longer-flat stomach.

"Victoria doesn't need to find out." Brent poked Pax right back. They play fought for a moment while they waited for the lights to change so they could cross. Other citizens around them gave weird looks as if they were misbehaving children, but it didn't deter the two friends. When they hung out, the world around them didn't exist.

As they crossed, a stranger bumped into Brent's shoulder. He turned back to apologise, but all he saw was a wisp of purple haze and the person had disappeared through the crowd. He shrugged it off and turned around to chase after Pax, who was already ahead of him, as he beelined it to the food court. Brent made a mad dash across the road and almost made it before a carriage honked at him.

Brent waved his hands, apologising, and shuffled off across the rest of the street. He burst through the sliding doors of the bustling food court.

Brent got his order from BB's fast and went to find a seat. He looked over at Chrono's, as a tower of boxes with broad, rounded shoulders approached the seat opposite of Brent. Paxton carried enough food to feed three families in his arms, carefully lowering his tower of food that dominated the table before he sat down. However, he always opted for the Pep-Up Max Elixir, avoiding the extra sugar.

"What? An adventurer needs to keep his strength up," Paxton quipped at the smug look on Brent's face looking at all the food.

"We're not adventurers anymore Pax, what are you keeping your strength up for?"

"Myshelf," Paxton spat a mouthful of fried chicken at him. Brent inspected Paxton, who began to devour not one, but four feasts just himself.

Most Orcs would choose hunger over being seen eating deep-fried food, let alone working a nine-to-five at SorcerySure. Brent's appearance hinted at the passage of time since his last quest, with a slightly receding hairline and a slight roundness to his stomach after over seventeen years. Brent liked to refer to it as the Adventurers' Dad Bod. Pax was still as muscular as ever. There might be a minimal layer of fat, but Orcs rarely gained weight the same way humans did. Even Half-Orcs.

As he picked up his Behemoth Bites, Brent felt a soft tremor rush through the ground underneath them. His eyes flickered to Pax, who remained fixated on his food, unaware of the faint quiver of the earth beneath them. He attempted to take another bite. Another tremor rattled through the food court, causing everyone to stop and look around. The unexpected movement of the hanging lights above caught the attention of the captivated lunchtime crowd. Some even rose from their chairs, their eyes darting around in confusion as they tried to decipher the source of the tremors.

"Pax, did you feel that?" Brent asked, but Pax mumbled something unintelligible with his mouth full.

Brent anxiously shovelled one mouthful of his burger after another, as if expecting an imminent earthquake or some other catastrophe. As he ate, a sudden thud shook the building, followed by the sight of a giant, thick-fur-covered purple tail swinging through the food court, creating a hole in the building's side. Debris and shattered ceiling fragments flew, crashing down and causing a section of the building to collapse, leaving it vulnerable and open to the outside world. Panic spread through the food court like wildfire. In every direction, civilians were screaming and frantically running, desperate to find safety.

Without hesitation, Brent and Paxton instinctively took cover under the table. Pax hadn't finished eating his chicken burgers yet. Swiftly, he reached for his bottle of Pep-Up and took a sip, Brent observed the chaotic scene of the remaining citizens fleeing in panic, pushing and shoving in search of safety. He spotted the enormous purple tail with a yellow fur tip as he glanced out of the food court.

"A Behemoth!" Brent confirmed to Pax, who was busy chewing on his food.

"Here? In downtown Spellford?" Brent's deduction failed to convince Paxton, made clear from his sceptical tone. "No way!"

"Yes, come on!" With excitement in his voice, Brent emerged from underneath the table and headed towards the exit. "Let's follow it!" he exclaimed.

"We are too old for this," Pax groaned, feeling the stiffness in his joints as he got up from the cold, hard floor and hastily shoved a half-eaten chicken burger into his pocket, before begrudgingly following him.

Brent sprinted off, his Adventurer Dad-Bod didn't allow him to move as quickly as he wanted, leaving Pax's words unheard as he pursued the beast. He turned his head back when he heard the distinct sound of Pax's teeth crunching into the last chicken burger. Brent shook his head and continued forward.

The adrenaline surged through Brent's veins, causing his heart to race. This was the excitement he had been yearning for, the rush he had longed to feel. Continuing beyond the food court, chaos filled the streets of Spellford. Incredibly large and tough claws gouged buildings, turned over vehicles, and lined the streets with rubble. The sight of people frantically fleeing sparked his curiosity, so he followed the commotion.

"Brent!" Pax's shout startled a woman who ran past them. "We need to go back to work. Let the Mage's Union handle this!"

"Half the city will be destroyed! The Mage's Union will arrive too late," Brent shouted back, as he paddled his way through the sea of people running away. Pax rushed after him as the crowd parted. Pax's gigantic frame allowed him the space to casually stride towards Brent.

It wasn't long before Brent came to a halt and looked out at the carnage that had unfolded. Despite the chaos, he could still see the Behemoth wreaking havoc with each step it took. The Behemoth, standing at over twenty feet tall, was an intimidating force that radiated a sense of primal strength. The windowpanes in nearby buildings trembled at the ferocious growls and roars that emanated from its snarling mouth. It continued, revelling in its own carnage. With its massive size and powerful muscles, the beast struck fear into the hearts of all who encountered it.

While waiting for Pax to catch up, he couldn't help but notice the live reporters on brooms hovering in the sky, capturing the chaos below. Brent scoffed, his eyes scanned the crowd of people absorbed in their Rune-Phones, desperate to catch every gruesome detail. He couldn't believe his eyes as he exclaimed, "What is wrong with these people!" Nobody seemed to be troubled by the chaos or bothered to reach out to the Mage's Union.

"So, what's the game plan?" Pax uttered through heavy panting once he caught up to Brent.

"Not sure yet." Brent's eyes scanned the surroundings, as he tried to assess the situation. "We can't handle this alone, but time is running out," Brent muttered discontentedly to himself, while Paxton nonchalantly savoured the one burger he had brought. With a shake of his head directed at Pax, Brent swiftly assessed the situation, on the lookout for anyone who might intervene to end the rampage. The silence was deafening as he stood there, realising that no one was coming.

"What is taking the Union so long?" Tiny bits of food shot out from his tusks as Paxton spoke.

"They're not usually this sluggish," Brent observed. Out of nowhere, a blood-curdling scream pierced the air, startling Brent.

Looking down into the ruined square, he saw a young child sobbing uncontrollably. Paralysed with fear, they were alone, with no one to offer salvation. As the Behemoth ruthlessly tore vehicles apart, the cry echoed across its tumultuous surroundings. The child's screams pierced the air and captured the attention of the monstrous beast. It swiftly turned towards the source of the deafening noise. With each thunderous landing of the Behemoth's colossal paws, the ground trembled beneath them.

Realising the child was in danger, Brent sprang into action. Sprinting as fast as his out-of-shape body would allow, he took each adrenaline-filled stride as quickly as possible, the wooden heels of his shoes digging in and dodging debris and rubble on the road. The Behemoth closed in, and Brent panicked. He heard Pax call out to the monster and looked back to see him throw chunks of wreckage toward it to get its attention. The Behemoth, now enraged by the child's screams of terror, disregarded Pax's attempts and kept charging forward. Pax darted around, looking for something else to assist. With no innate magic abilities like Brent, he needed to rely on his pure strength and ran over to a torn-up carriage, lifting it above his head.

"Looks like someone needs a nap!" Pax shouted out as he leaped across the road in front of the Behemoth. "Let's see how you handle this!" With a loud grunt, Pax catapulted the carriage into the air.

Brent slowed down enough to watch the vehicle fly and land directly into the side of the Behemoth. The massive creature was blown back, thrown off its feet sideways and crashed into the surrounding rubble. The cheers of the crowd filled the air, though it was soon clear that they had spoken too soon. Undeterred by the wreckage, the monster ploughed through the torn metal and debris, its charge towards the child unyielding. Pax's quick manoeuvre created a window of opportunity for Brent to reach the frightened child.

"Hey there, I got you," he reassured, his voice filled with tenderness as he cradled the child. The moment he made to turn away, a low, guttural snarl sent a shiver down his spine. Another scream escaped the child's mouth, and in response, the Behemoth unleashed a deafening roar.

Brent's fatherly and adventuring instincts kicked in, and he swiftly lifted the child onto his hip. With precision, he unleashed a blazing fireball, its intense heat engulfed the creature's gaping mouth. The Behemoth stumbled backward, disoriented, and let out a cough after it swallowed the fiery projectile. As the smoke escaped its lips, it scorched the creature's oesophagus.

Brent took off, the child bouncing on his hip, and ran back towards the crowd. As he let the child down, she let out a sniffle and said a weak thank you.

"You stay right here; I'll take care of the big scary monster, okay?" Brent gave the child a warm smile and handed her the napkin from his pocket. The child wiped away her tears, smiled back, and nodded. A person nearby took hold of the child, and Brent turned back to the Behemoth.

Pax continued to defend himself against the beast, using the translucent shields he had conjured from his Rune-Phone. The Behemoth easily overpowered the Modern App-Magic, but they offered Pax a temporary respite until Brent could make his way back. With each shield the Behemoth consumed, there was a cacophony of munching and shattering, yet Pax skillfully recreated them in rapid succession.

Brent started to jog back to the battle, but paused, gasping for air, his heart pounding in his chest. His Adventurer Dad-Bod, really feeling the twinge of pain in his sides now.

He watched as Pax braced himself, ducking down to protect his body from the Behemoth propelling towards him. Despite the distance, Brent could still see Pax's tusks trembling with fear, anticipating an imminent attack.

"Oh, no you don't!" Brent shouted and sprinted towards them.

He stood in the destroyed street, surrounded by rubble and debris. The towering presence of the massive creature overwhelmed him and Pax, reminding them of their insignificance in comparison, while its ear-splitting roar filled the entire city with echoes.

The citizens of Spellford gathered in a hushed silence, their breath held in anticipation as they watched the battle unfold. Brent extended his hand, his fingers trembled with anticipation as he channelled his magic energy for his upcoming spell. Though he had eaten, his energy waned. Casting instinctive magic always drained him more than deliberate magic, and his skills were quite rusty.

In the centre of his palm, a spark flickered to life, gradually expanding until it resembled a medicine ball. Brent confidently took a step forward, the fiery ball in his palm crackled and cast an intense glow. Pax's gaze shifted to Brent, who reciprocated with a nod. It was a familiar gesture, signifying their shared knowledge of a move they had used to defeat countless beasts before.

"Oi! Brutus!" Brent shouted, gaining the attention of the Behemoth.

Running at full speed, Pax caught up to the Behemoth and grabbed onto its powerful tail. With a mighty swing, the Behemoth's tail lashed through the air, causing the ground to tremble. Pax's eyes widened in surprise as he felt himself being yanked upwards, his body defying gravity.

Brent lined up his shot and then hurled the ball of flame at the Behemoth. The streak of flames followed the ball's line through the air and as the monster bellowed again, it was hit directly in the mouth once more. With a snap of its sword-like fangs, the Behemoth swallowed the ball of fire, and it appeared to go out in a snuff of smoke. The crowd made a gasp, followed by an instant groan of disappointment.

The Behemoth took a step forward and then stopped. A whine and roar of pain from its burnt oesophagus followed, as it clawed at its throat. Its body writhed as the flames burned throughout its body. Paxton let go of the tail and landed on both feet, rushing off to the side to get out of the way of the monster. The crowd cheered and Brent lowered his guard, unable to contain a smile of relief until the monster let out a wail of pain.

His smile disappeared. He almost felt sorry for it, could the Behemoth be held at fault behaving as a monstrous beast would? A glistening between tufts of the yellowy-mustard hair at the base of its neck caught Brent's eye. Light reflected off something embedded in its fur, and he wanted to get a better view.

"Pax, I think it's hurt!" Brent called out.

"Yeah, duh! It swallowed your fireball!" Pax cheered, raising a fist into the air.

"No, look at its neck!" he called out again, pointing at the tuft of fur. "The blinking purple light."

"Where?" Paxton asked, and he finally noticed it as well. "Oh! What is that?" he sniffed at the air but couldn't deduce it.

Brent could not deduce what it was from this angle, either, and then it came to him exactly how he could get the Behemoth to sit still. He rushed over to Pax and inspected the Behemoth to ensure it wouldnt launch another attack.

"Got any of that burger left?" Brent asked, darting his eyes towards the beast.

"It isn't exactly time for a meal now," Pax wiped his brow as he responded.

"If I can reverse the Time Magic on it, I might restrain the beast."

"With Time Magic? I've got like a bite left. What would it give you a few seconds, a minute tops?"

"More than enough time!" Brent smirked. Paxton handed over the burger. Brent weighed it in his hand, feeling the faint remnant of Time Magic.

It was a school of magic he was not all too familiar with, but he could bluff his way through, reversing the enchantment placed on it. He held the tiny piece of fried chicken in his hands and extracted the magic. He held his breath and concentrated on undoing the spell used to cook the burger. Beads of sweat formed on his brow as his hands glowed yellow. He had done it. He abandoned Pax and ran over to the beast.

The Behemoth was still writhing in agony, its roars loud and piercing. As he was mere steps away, Brent aimed the small piece of burger into the beast's mouth, which fell short. He was never a good throw.

Brent's heart sank and his hand flung down to his side. He noticed that the Behemoth's head and upper torso stopped moving, but its legs and lower half of its body were still flinging around. He looked up in disbelief. It worked! Somewhat.

Now was his chance. He rushed over to its neck and dug around its tuft of long, yellow hair. Its purple flesh was tough, but its muscles were tougher. He could not afford now to slip up. He found the source of the light. Embedded into its neck, a rune encrusted object kept blinking, as it received a signal. He tugged as hard as he could, but it would not budge.

He knew there was not much time before the time spell wore off. Brent created a small lasso of magic light and tied it around the rune. As he stood looking around to see if the Behemoth had returned to normal, he wrapped the rope to his arm and could feel the time spell wearing off. With lightning speed, he sprinted in the opposite direction, leaping off the Behemoth, as it rose to its feet. Brent felt a sudden jolt and the force threw him into the ground. As he skidded across the street, his face scraped against the rough surface, leaving behind trails of blood. Brent quickly rolled onto his back, desperately trying to regain his footing.

The Behemoth rushed towards him and stood over him snarling. As a wad of saliva dropped onto the ground next to Brent, he squinted, his heart racing. He knew this was the end, the beasts jaw and sharp fangs were the last thing Brent was going to see. Suddenly, he felt a giant tongue lick him across his body and face. The slobber saturated him from head to toe, followed by something Brent did not expect.

The Behemoth turned and trotted off toward the southern part of the city, which led to the outskirts of the city into the mountains. As Brent sat up, he watched it disappear out of view. He had successfully freed the beast and saved the city. He stood up and dusted off his pants. A thunderous eruption of roars and cheers filled the air. The crowd of onlookers was applauding him.

"You did it!" Pax yelled from across the pit. He quickly rushed over and congratulated Brent, who was in disbelief. They both hugged each other in celebration, cheering and jumping on the spot. Despite being covered in Behemoth drool, Brent and Pax paid no attention to their messy appearance. They had saved the city, and the praise of gratitude echoed through the streets.

Before they could catch their breath, a swarm of Story Breakers and Media Mages surrounded them. Their Cam-Meras whirred and flashed, recording photos and footage. With a deep breath, Brent took a step back, trying to regain his composure.

A Cam-Mera moved forward and began recording Brent and Pax. Brent's unease was instantaneous, as it made eye contact with him. Its body appeared ordinary, but its distinct feature was its extensive set of four bright yellow eyes, resembling those of a wild beast. Devoid of flesh, the creature's body showcased its intricate machinery; gears and hydraulics worked together, creating a mesmerizing display of motion. Its talons, glinting in the sunlight, looked as sharp as razors, capable of piercing through skin effortlessly. To no shock of anyone around them, they remained serene and followed the Media Mages' orders without question.

Its two mechanical heads resembled a typical lion with a giant mane, but its fur was darkish grey. Its jaws were open wide, and they both brandished large fangs that could crunch you in half. More exposed mechanical parts shaped the Cam-Meras giant eyes. Two long curved horns on either head protruded out and backwards and over its head, a giant tail extended, with the tip being a microphone to speak into. To Brent, the creature had always haunted him with pure nightmares, yet he couldn't help but marvel at the rune-technological wonder before him.

Pax wrapped his arms over his shoulders and held up his thumbs at the Cam-Mera's face. On screens all around the city, the Cam-Mera technology instantaneously broadcast the interview and Brent glimpsed himself on the screens in the distance. Brent adjusted himself and gave off a sheepish smile. He was not one for praise, but he did what he knew was the right thing to do and continued to be polite, waved and smiled.

As they took their interviews, he answered truthfully what it was like in the battle with the Behemoth, and even got in a few choice words about the Mage's Union's apparent disdain for helping the citizens. A giant swooshing noise nearby caught their attention, causing them to turn around.

"And here is the Mage's Union now," one of the media mages commented, them all turning their attention to them. They finished up the interview and the Mage's Union members came over to Brent and Pax, the stern looks on their faces said it all. A couple of civilians had outclassed them. As they approached, their cloaks billowed in the wind, and Brent gulped, he was in trouble.

On giant billboard screens all around the city, the Cam-Mera technology continued to stream a mash up of Brent and Pax celebrating their victory, inter-cut with the carnage of the Behemoth, along with the highlights of the battle and their small interview with the Story Breakers. The same five words sprawled across the bottom of the screens all over the city.

"Spellford Saved by Hero Dad"

Brent offered his account to the Mage's Union investigators and then Pax. Once they had finished up, they were free to go. Brent reflected on the questions, but one stuck out at him the most.

Why did he feel the need to step in and help?
He couldn't answer.

CHAPTER TWO
THE FIVE PRINCIPLES

Victoria sat in class, barely paying attention as she looked out into the courtyard, ignoring her afternoon Rune-Tech studies. While she was gifted and understood the importance of study, she also did not care enough today to learn about the advancements in magic and technology integration. Everything she ever needed in life was in the palm of her hands on her Rune-Phone. From watching content on WicTok, posting glimmers on Wizstagram, and even ordering food from Witches Wagon. What else could she need?

She was not the only one, either. In her age group, everyone seemed to share the same thoughts and behaviours. The faux apathy of her generation spread through them like a contagious cold, yet everyone yearned to blend in. Which meant you could not stand out. However, Victoria had a secret that she kept hidden from everyone, including how she used magic.

Victoria brushed her hair behind her one human-shaped ear, keeping her other pointed-ear hidden. That wasn't her secret, though it was a cause of much school yard bullying back when they were all in earlier class levels.

She was Aphonic. Aphonics did not need to utter incantations or rely on a catalyst to use magic such as a Rune-Phone. They lived in tune with the Augmenti Leyline and could draw from it naturally. They could, within the reasonable limits that their body allowed, think of what they wanted to perform with their magic and just do it. Victoria, however, blended in with everyone around her to not drive suspicion.

She turned to the front of the class again and feigned interest, hoping the lesson would pass faster. Her teacher, Professor Nia Beaumont, had an olive complexion, with striking jade green eyes that stood out in stark contrast. They always seemed to sparkle with enthusiasm when she delved into the topic of ethics by combining magic with technology. She tied back her velour-black hair in a neat bun that accentuated her delicate face. Having a natural glow, she only applied a small amount of blush and lip gloss. Victoria, who often struggled to focus in class, was drawn to her professor's natural beauty, finding solace in observing her while still absorbing the material.

Though she was young compared to the other professors at Spellford Academy, her knowledge of magic and technology was well beyond her age group, which made her a highly sought-after professor at the college. Victoria was an Adept Mage, which meant she had two more years before graduation, and even if she didn't show it overtly, she looked up to Professor Nia as an example of what she would want to achieve.

"Victoria," Professor Nia said, her soft yet firm voice gliding through the air as she walked across the front of the room and making the entire class spring to attention. "Can you tell me some responsibilities which come from such a powerful combination of magic and technology?"

Victoria adjusted herself in her chair and opened her mouth to speak. "There are many schools of thought, but the most obvious answers fall down to The Arcanthus Five Principles of Responsible use of magic and tech—" Victoria started with a smile but also sounded incredibly bored "—the first being always consider the potential consequences of combining the two."

"And why is this important?" Nia asked back instantly.

"As we strive to live in a society of peace, we should prohibit the creation of unstable abominations or volatile weapons."

"Excellent, Victoria," Professor Nia said. "Who is next? Hmm, Hector, can you list the next principle?"

The boy in the front row stood up sharply and bumped his chair into her desk. Victoria resisted the urge to push it back.

"Never use the combination to cause harm or infringe upon others' rights." He spoke firm and sure of himself. His knowledge of the answer caught Victoria off guard. She still didn't like him much.

"Excellent." Nia winked at Hector and turned to the board to write the remaining principles.

"We must always respect the balance of Magic and Tech and understand their limits," she took a pause and continued. "Our use needs to be ethical while also respecting the surrounding environment to avoid harm to the ecosystem." Victoria knew this one as well.

"It is crucial to preserve our privacy and ensure that our private information does not get compromised. Any use of this information is to be used for the benefit of society rather than serving the interests of a single person." Nia finished scribbling, then faced the class

With a wave of her hands, Nia had sent the notes to all the students' emails as she always did. "Class, you will have received today's notes, if you have questions, please let me know." She walked to her desk as everyone's Rune-Phone vibrated. Nia glanced at her lexicon, swiping through her curriculum, and then shifted her gaze back to the class. "Please read chapters three through five of the Arcanthus Handbook before our next class—" but her sentence was cut short by a sudden outburst from a female student in the back.

"Oh, the Tutelary! Spellford is under attack!" The student cried out and it echoed around the classroom, causing everyone to stop and turn their attention to the student who was looking at their Rune-Phone.

"Rune-Phones away, please. This is a place of education, not mindless scrolling." Professor Nia raised her voice to quiet down the class. They had all crowded around the one student. Victoria did not move from her seat, nor did Hector.

"A Behemoth has attacked Spellford! Look!" The student pinched the video with two fingers and then, as if she was flinging her hands dry from water, flicked her hand toward the board behind Nia. Footage of the attack played.

Victoria's heart started pounding as she saw a sweeping video of the attack. Debris everywhere. Multiple wreckages of tipped over carriages and other vehicles torn apart. The footage then became hectic as the Cam-Meras struggled to get a clear view of events. Civilians pushed past and screamed, as they escaped and ran for their lives.

Suddenly, the footage cut to a different scene. Two men were fighting the beast. She sunk in her chair as she recognised Pax and her father. She watched in silent horror while the rest of the class cheered them on. No one could believe what they were seeing. Even Professor Nia gave up trying to silence her students and joined in watching the battle unfold.

"Wait, Tor!" A male student behind her called out to Victoria. "Isn't that your dad?" Victoria shifted lower in her seat.

"Oh, it is!" another student replied. "I saw him drop her off this morning!" She taunted, poking Victoria from behind her.

"I did not know your dad worked for the Mage's Union!" The student beside her exclaimed, his tone tinged with awe. Victoria's embarrassment intensified as the realisation of her oversight sank in.

"He doesn't—" she tried to speak above them all, but they were too rowdy for her to cut through.

The student on the other side of her held out his hand. Lirien, her best friend, was a Sun-Elf with parents who had become overnight sensations after their start-up went viral. He joked now and called himself heir to the Elaria Elixir's fortune.

Victoria always claimed that his parents got lucky that they were the first on the market with authentic Elven elixirs and that her father knew an Elf who had this idea nearly a decade ago.

Lirien's glowing skin beamed a warmth from his hands towards Victoria as he tried to help her remain calm. Lirien was always in tune with his friends, and she really appreciated him in these times where she felt over-whelmed. Victoria shuffled back up in her chair and smiled at Lirien. His golden eyes met hers and she had to turn away. He was way too beautiful for a boy.

She briefly let her mind wander about them married with kids...she shook her head to wake herself from her daydream. It wouldn't ever hap-pen. She was not his type. Hector was. She shot Hector a piercing glare, as if daggers shot out of her eyes. She and Lirien would have been soulmates, destined to be together, if she had been born a boy. She knew it.

Victoria shifted focus back to the screen and continued watching her dad fight for his life. She knew about his past as an adventurer, but he had never displayed abilities to her that would prove he could handle a beast like a Behemoth.

"Who is the green skin with him? What is he doing?"

"He looks Half-Orc," one student replied. "Oh, he is lifting the car...he's stronger than he looks!"

"Most Orcs are all brawn and no brain," another one laughed.

"Shut up!" Victoria snapped back. She was incredibly protective of Paxton, who she considered her family and affectionately called Uncle Pax. Pax always was the butt of the joke in life. She wouldn't tolerate it here, too.

The students all watched as Brent shot the fireball directly into the Behemoth's mouth and watched it writhe in pain. The classroom cheered. Victoria's heart raced. She wanted her dad to win, but she also didn't want him to hurt the beast.

Brent's action of throwing a piece of burger left the students mesmerised as they watched it render the giant creature's head and torso motionless.

As if in a trance, they could not take their eyes off him as he diligently dug through the fur, in search of an unknown device tucked away around the creature's neck. As the Behemoth stood above her dad, it lunged at his face. Victoria let out a stifled scream and covered her eyes. She expected to hear gasps, but cheers went up in the classroom. When she peered through her fingers, she saw the Behemoth lick her father and run away. As the class celebrated, the Media Mages rushed towards Brent and Paxton for an interview.

Victoria released a smile, and the room buzzed with the chatter of her peers over what they had witnessed. Professor Nia quickly shut off the board. The classroom fell silent.

"This," she started, "is a perfect example of why we shouldn't always mix magic and technology," Nia stated, "and proves twenty-four-hour access to news is not always the best thing."

"Professor, what did the guy pull from the beast's neck?" Lirien asked, letting go of Victoria's hand.

"A control rune?" Hector turned around and offered Victoria a smile, but she looked away sharply.

"Good eyes, Hector." Nia patted his shoulder as she glided back towards her desk.

Seated, she placed her hands under her chin, never one to let an opportunity pass to teach her students. "This form of magic is highly illegal. It was a blatant disregard for Arcanthus's principles and responsible use of magic. It is highly unethical to take control of a beast for mass destruction."

Victoria nodded along with the rest of the class and understood the weight of the situation. Was it not for her father, who knew how long the rampage would have gone on or what other damage could have occurred?

Nia predicted these events would continue to be in the news, but considering the rapid pace of news cycles, it was never a guarantee. "But you know how these things go. We'll be onto something new by tomorrow." Professor Nia went to end the class but was distracted when her RuneWatch beeped.

She paused to read the message. "Class you are to go into the auditorium immediately as we await further instructions. Gather your things and follow me." The class all darted around, exchanging nervous looks. Professor Nia rushed over to the door, held it open, and hurried the class out. "Come on!" she demanded.

Victoria and the other students all stood and followed Professor Nia towards the auditorium with a mix of uncertainty and concern about what had just happened in their once safe city. The Behemoth had run off. Surely, they were fine? They filed in and took their seats in the row designated by Professor Nia.

Victoria looked around as the auditorium filled up with the rest of the student bodies and faculty. Chatter and commotion filled the auditorium as everyone talked about what had happened. Victoria sat between students she did not get along with and poked her head down the row to see Lirien sat near their other best friend, Luminia. Victoria shifted back, angry at herself for not paying attention when she entered.

The double doors behind them opened, and the Chancellor walked through the doors with two unknown guests towards the podium at the front. They were both Mage's Union employees, which Victoria recognised by the "M" and "U" symbol lapel on their chest.

"Students, faculty," the chancellor announced, his voice booming through the auditorium. "We are here today to discuss a matter of utmost importance." He cleared his throat and turned to the two unknown people who stood to the side. "I'm happy to welcome two High Sages from the Mage's Union today who will now take the floor to discuss the events that transpired."

Victoria, like everyone else in the room, already knew what had transpired.

Dressed in a pristine uniform of dark robes with golden accents and embroidery, their status as powerful practitioners of magic were clear. The male Sage sat still with one leg crossed and kept his line of sight directly out at the students as if he was inspecting them for something: looking for someone even.

The female Sage approached the podium and placed her hands down firmly. Victoria studied her face as she looked out into the sea of students. She was a much older woman, older than the male Sage, with silver hair and sparkling green eyes. She gave off an aura of ageless wisdom and tranquillity.

"Thank you, Chancellor Eldridge." The woman turned to the Chancellor, who nodded. "I am Elder Evergreen."

Victoria recognised the last name. It was her creature studies professor's last name and she wondered if they were of any relation. On her belt,

Victoria noticed the glint of a metallic object that caught the light but couldn't quite make it out from where she sat.

"As the mid-day sun shone down on Spellford, a massive Behemoth, rumoured to have broken free from a neighbouring research facility, launched an unexpected attack on the city." The students offered no reaction, and Victoria joined them, her gaze devoid of emotion.

Judging from the presence of the Mage's Union, Victoria concluded the Behemoth was still on the run.

"According to the Media Mages, two brave citizens apprehended the Behemoth before the Mage's Union could respond."

One of the students stood up and took the attention. "We know this already!" they shouted. Eyes darted between the student and Elder Evergreen. A professor came up behind him and told him to sit down, which he reluctantly agreed to.

Victoria felt a rush of adrenaline course through her.

"I know there are a lot of concerns, and we don't profess to have all the answers as an investigation is still underway." The male Mage stood up, his voice booming and bouncing off the walls. The clear definition of his sharp jawline enhanced his strong appearance, even under his beard. Despite the hood he kept up, his blue eyes and thin but large nose were impossible to miss.

"The Union has had to sequester off most of the city, as major repairs are already underway. We are here today to warn students to be vigilant on their travels home," he continued.

"So, basically, good luck if we meet the beast?" The same student called out again, who now had the hands of their teacher on their shoulders in an attempt to make them sit. He shrugged them off and sat down with visible reluctance.

"There is no need to be alarmed, as the Mage's Union will work around the clock to bring peace and order back to Spellford. Your parents have all been called and you are to return home for now. Spellford CBD is on lockdown. It's expected to be lifted by tomorrow morning."

The students grew upset and distressed.

"Lockdown?" one shouted. "For a distressed animal! This is a joke!"

The male Sage raised his voice, to get through to the crowd of students. "I understand this is a shock, and no proper answer has come about, but we will provide more information once the investigation is complete," he trailed off amongst the noise of the restless students. "The Mage's Union has dispatched multiple Mage recruits across the city and surrounding suburbs to ensure the safety of our citizens as the lockdowns take place." He turned and sat down.

The chancellor stood up and the students fell silent instantly when he held up his hands.

"Those who live in ArcTech Heights, Enchanted Circuit, Rune Meadows, and Arcane Hills will need to remain behind as we work out alternative transport arrangements, as the trains will not be running." The Chancellor looked out at the audience and concluded the assembly. The chancellor thanked the representatives before they departed. Victoria inspected the male Sage closer. There was something about his face she couldn't quite pinpoint. She felt like she had seen it before, somewhere long ago.

The room erupted into a buzz of chaos as the students discussed what happened amongst themselves. Fellow classmates all began to whisper and talked under their breath, some even pointed in Victoria's direction. Somehow, word had gotten out that the "Hero of Spellford" was her father. She didn't want this much publicity.

"Hey, we both need to stay behind," Luminia, said, coming up from behind Victoria and giving her a hug around her shoulders. "Do you want to come to my place?" Lumina's opalescent skin shimmered as she swished her silvery-blue hair.

Victoria turned and smiled at her. "No Lumi, it will be better if I go home given my dad was involved."

Luminia had Pixie lineage, a fact made obvious by her pure black eyes and glistening skin. She also had wings she kept hidden under her school uniform. Similar to those of a butterfly, they would flutter gently when she would use them to hover, emitting a faint, melodious hum. Victoria couldn't even begin to work out the logistics of a Pixie and a human mating. She tried not to think about it.

"True, you must be proud of him," Lumi replied. Victoria detected some sarcasm in her tone.

"What do you mean?" she asked back.

"What a hero saving the city!"

"I guess, but it isn't all about him," She sighed and dropped the mention that another person was there assisting.

"Your dad's friend?" Lumi asked.

"Yeah, Pax," Victoria replied with admiration for Paxton in her voice.

"Your father's magic was a choice, though."

"Oh yeah, the fireballs. He enjoys the classics." Victoria shrugged.

"Sounds more like Dad Magic!" Luminia scoffed. Victoria gave her a light slap on the shoulder before both girls broke into giggles.

Outwardly, no one could tell Victoria secretly wanted the day to end. She was a master at hiding her inner emotions when she needed to, something she used to her advantage when dealing with her father. She was furious at him for doing this.

"Victoria, Luminia!" Professor Nia called out and made a motion with her hands for them to come to forth. The girls trudged through the row of chairs, to where she stood. Victoria jut out her hip, putting her weight on one leg in an annoyed stance. "Do you have safe passage home?"

"My father is coming to pick me up," Luminia said. "I offered to take Victoria home but she—"

"Ah, that's okay, I am to escort you home. We got through to your father—" Nia said.

"Is he okay?" Victoria cut her off. Though she was furious she was glad to hear he was alright.

Nia nodded, easing Victoria's mind, and explained, "Yes, they have taken him to the local Cleric temple for assessment, but he is fine. He wanted someone to escort you home, and I offered."

Victoria bid farewell to her friend and waited while Professor Nia checked on the remainder of students before they departed.

Victoria and Nia approached her heap of junk floating carriage, which looked like it barely hovered off the ground. Victoria was apprehensive about entering the vehicle but knew Professor Nia would be safe. No one could be as bad a driver as Paxton.

"Ignore the state of the carriage. I can't afford to conjure a new one yet," Nia said, as she clambered inside. Victoria thought it was an odd choice of words but was still yet to understand the truth of adult life.

"That's okay, I gather the teacher's salary isn't as glamorous as it appears to be?" Victoria asked.

"I don't do this for the pay cheque." She flicked her finger at the ignition. "I do it to mould young minds to become great Mages with an understanding of the ethics of technology and magic co-existing."

"You are still young yourself," Victoria pointed out. She gathered she would only be five or six years her senior.

"Thank you." Nia adjusted her mirrors and looked around as she reversed, placing her arm behind Victoria's to get a better view. "It is embarrassing being the youngest teacher and having the oldest car, but facts of life, hey?"

"I should have my licence already, but my father he—"

"Doesn't trust you, but pretends to pose it as he doesn't trust those on the road?" Nia commiserated as she crunched the gears back to drive and exited the carpark. "Sorry, deep-seated trauma with my father issues," she laughed it off and Victoria chuckled. She had not seen this side of Nia and quite enjoyed it.

"By the way, don't let the students push you around about this thing your father has done," Nia said, taking a corner a little too sharply.

"What do you mean?" Victoria asked, holding on to the door handle, trying to push herself off and not get squashed against the window. Maybe Pax was a better driver than her...

"I remember my peers were the same for my father," Nia expressed, and turned the next corner a little too sharply as well, causing Victoria to brace herself on the door handle.

"Oh, Beaumont! You're the daughter of the celebrated Sage, Marquis Beaumont!"

"Yep, that Marquis Beaumont." She could see Nia tried not to show any emotional response. She kept swerving and turning until they had reached the suburbs of Spellford. With the city now placed under watch, there were recruit Mages stationed at exits on patrol.

"What was it like growing up with such a renowned father?" Victoria asked as they meandered through the suburbs.

"Well, let's say I had a lot to live up to."

Victoria let out a sigh. "I feel that!" she replied and gazed out the window at the world around her. "My father may only work in Magic Insurance, but the stories he tells me of his journeys as an adventurer before he adopted me, are something I could only dream of doing myself."

"So, you want to go exploring after you graduate?" Nia asked as they paused, waiting to cross an intersection.

"No, I always wanted to join the Dragoon Corp, but my father isn't exactly too keen."

"I will let you in on a little knowledge, which took me a while to learn and digest. What street do you live on?"

"Starfall Drive, two over." Victoria pointed out as they entered Enchanted Circuit's purple, pink and white floral and tree-lined streets. The name really gave a full description of her street. Amongst the technological advancements, the flora and fauna burst with magic.

Usually, the streets would buzz with people walking around, exercising their pets or sitting amongst the parks and having a good, peaceful time. But with the city on watch, everyone was inside. As they passed Rune Road and turned down Starfall Drive, Nia parked and turned off the car outside Victoria's house. Nia looked Victoria deep in her eyes and Victoria could see her own reflection in Nia's jade-coloured eyes.

"You get to carve your path, stay true to who you are and want to be, and ignore the pressure of your father's legacy or his wants and dreams for you." She offered a strong smile.

Nia waved her hand, and the door opened with a creak. Victoria gathered her things and unbuckled her seatbelt before climbing out of the carriage.

She bent down to look back inside and smiled. "Thank you for taking me home."

"Stay safe! Study and say hello to your dad for me," Nia exclaimed as she took off. Victoria waved at her as she drove away.

She swung her bag over her shoulder and walked up to the path to the front door. As she turned the keys, her father's carriage pulled up in the driveway. Victoria's frustration was instant and could not be put it to words. She entered the house, not waiting for her father or Pax to exit their vehicle and slammed the door behind her. She quickly rushed inside and shut herself in her room.

As she dropped her bag on the floor in her purple room, she knew it was stupid, but she was embarrassed by her father for pulling the hero act. She should be proud, but she couldn't allow herself to be.

CHAPTER THREE
SPELLFORD'S CHAMPION

Two weeks passed before the city had returned to normal. There was a sense of unease mixed with peace amongst Spellford as the Mage's Union continued its investigation on how the Behemoth entered the city. Mage recruits patrolled the streets the first week, with students being escorted to the academy from the station, much to Victoria's inward protest.

As SorcerySure handled all the insurance matters for the damage caused by the Behemoth attack, both Brent and Pax found themselves overwhelmed with work, with Brent being particularly swamped. Brent had a busy day filled with recognition for his service to Spellford, overwhelmed by the multiple interviews lined up and the scheduled ceremony.

Everywhere he walked, Brent could not escape his good deed. People flocked to get a selfie with him much to his dismay as he was terribly uncomfortable with this level of recognition.

Brent sighed as he sat down. "This is the last time I—" Just as Brent spoke, Pax interjected.

"That you what? Help people in need, yeah you said that every day this week," Pax said exasperated, feasting on yet another Chrono burger.

"I'm just saying, I am not cut out to be famous."

"Famous!" Pax laughed so hard he spat food across the table. Particles landed on Brent's arm. Brent glared at him and brushed them off. "You saved the city with sheer dumb luck!" Pax pointed out.

"Shush!" Brent slapped Pax's hand. "Don't let it loose that I don't know what I'm doing!"

"Do you...know...what you are doing?" Pax asked in a genuine in tone. "Like ever?"

"Yes, I studied much more magic than you back in the day. You can barely cast a single true spell and resort to using that." Brent pointed to Pax's Rune-Phone, that was face down on the table. "Come on, we can bicker like a married couple later, we need to go back to work." Brent looked at his own phone and could see countless messages popping through from media outlets wanting his time.

> Mr Abernathy! Please we will offer compensation for your time.

> Sir Brent! Our Hero! Please come on the Late-Night Show with Konan the Bardman, Tell your story!

Brent swiped them all away and paid them no mind. He was tired of the constant attention this week and was sorely regretting stepping in.

"Have you given it any more thought?" Pax asked, grabbing his tray with a mountain of empty food boxes.

"I already agreed to it," Brent said, and Pax scoffed. "What? It would be wrong not to."

"Well, enjoy your moment of newfound fame. Don't forget us little guys," Pax said, standing up. He was anything but little.

Brent looked him up and down slowly, in an obvious, mocking way. "No one could ever forget you, Pax."

Walking back into SorcerySure, Brent's nerves were at an all-time high as they clambered into the elevator. As the day drew to a close, the anticipation over the ceremony built. He could feel the infallible high build again as they came closer to their floor. Exiting into the foyer, the sounds of their shoes echoed against the tiles.

Brent reached out and opened the door, letting Paxton stroll past. They walked to their desks and continued working on claims throughout the afternoon until it was close to the end of the day.

"Gentlemen," the Executive Director's assistant approached them, "Ike, he would like to speak to you," she said, and Brent tried to mask his audible gulp. "Both of you." The assistant then looked over to Pax and motioned with her hand to follow.

With each step toward the Executive Director's office, Brent could feel his previous elation overshadowed by a deep sense of unease.

The assistant led them into Ike's office, the scent of freshly brewed coffee lingered in the air. With a shrug, Brent turned his attention to Paxton, who appeared dejected as he kept his head down. As Paxton sat down in the same room, he had interviewed in all those years ago, he couldn't help but shake his head in disbelief. The positive feeling that had once been present now vanished as their director barged through the door.

"Hello, gents!" Ike took his seat, looking dishevelled. "You can imagine the weeks I've been having because of you two," He stopped himself then, only after realising what he had said, slowly exhaled and scratched his head. "Sorry, because of the Behemoth." He adjusted himself in his chair before he looked to his two employees.

Brent made to apologise but Ike interrupted.

"I don't need another apology, Abernathy. The Mage's Union is full of them, now on to the topic of you two."

His speech was frantic. Both Brent and Pax sat nervously, awaiting their reprimand. Brent would be fine, but he was worried about Pax. No one would hire him now, no matter how heroic their deeds were.

"What you both achieved is not short of outstanding," Ike started. Brent could sense the hesitation in the air, and a wave of impending termination washed over him. "But as a member of the SorcerySure staff, we can't—" he began, but his words were cut short as the door swung open with a sudden, magical force.

In the doorway stood Spellford's Arch Mage. Startled, Brent and Pax exchanged a glance before they focused their attention on the man in the doorway. Ike's eyes widened in shock at the unexpected intrusion.

"Can I assist you?" Ike swallowed loud when he realised who it was. "Arch Mage, my forgiveness for not seeing you there, for what do we owe the pleasure?" Ike stood and offered a humble bow.

"I wonder..." the Arch Mage's voice resonated around the room, breaking the awkward silence "...if I could have a word with these two heroic men?" he sauntered over, his cloak billowing on its own, and placed his hands on Brent and Pax's shoulders. The two friends gulped in unison. The Arch Mage rarely showed his face in public, but both Pax and Brent knew of him.

Director Ike looked surprised. He knew his position and was out ranked here. Ike stood up and gave a weak smile, bordering ominous. Ike's smile only bode misfortune for Brent. With another bow towards the Arch Mage, Ike departed from the room with a final glance at them both.

Brent and Pax exchanged a confused look as the Arch Mage entered through, closing the door on Ike with a swish of his hand behind him. He took his time walking through. The air in the room became tense, almost suffocating. Brent swallowed hard, watching him take his time unfastening his cloak. Flurrying it over the chair before he pulled it out with another swish of his hand, then took a seat. He had not yet made eye contact, instead he looked down in disgust at Director Ike's disorganised table. He flicked his hands. Loose papers and stationery swirled in the air until all found their place in neat, organised piles.

"Now, gentleman," the Arch Made started, finally looking them in the eye. "I am Arch Mage Steiner Magnar." The Arch Mage was a tall and imposing man with sharp features. He held himself with confidence and authority, even when seated. His piercing blue eyes constantly analysing and observing his surroundings. His well-groomed silver hair was neatly tied back in a ponytail, which only accentuated his distinguished appearance.

"First, I would like to extend gratitude from the Mage's Union and all of Spellford for the way you handled the Behemoth that rampaged the city." His voice softened while his gaze fixated on Brent, ignoring Paxton. "Whatever discussion was to take place today, disciplinary or not, the city owes you both a great debt." He now looked at Pax.

Brent and Pax turned to each other and while maintaining face, communicated their thoughts with no need for words. During their academy days, they had conducted a mind-link experiment, which they never reversed. When in such proximity, they could sense what was on the other's mind. The two friends were in disbelief. Expecting to be disciplined instead of praised, they returned their attention to the Arch Mage.

"I also wanted to discuss a matter of utmost importance with you." Magnar's voice switched to a more serious tone. "Before you accept the award for saving the city this evening," he contemplated his words before he continued. "I have to say I am utterly ashamed of how easily you have embarrassed the Mage's Union's reputation by single-handedly taking on the Behemoth." Magnar's voice raised slightly.

Brent gulped, and Pax's tusks twitched. He fidgeted, bouncing his legs out of nervousness. Brent wanted to stop him but remained still.

"As a token of my gratitude, I would like to extend an opportunity to both of you." Magnar paused and looked between them both. "To join the Mage's Union, the Tutelary knows we could use the resources," Magnar finished, with a flash of his perfectly aligned and whiter than white teeth.

Brent and Pax's eyes widened as they realised the weight of the offer. The Mage's Union was Spellford's most prestigious organisation. A governing body of the city. To be offered a chance to join was an opportunity not to sniff at. Brent and Pax both motioned to speak, but Magnar interrupted them as if he knew what they were about to say.

"That way, I can keep a closer eye on you both," Magnar added and sat back in the chair. He dangled this opportunity like a treat over a hungry animal.

The two friends sat in silent contemplation. Brent knew he hadn't asked them to join just for saving the city, although the feat was a great one. There had to be some other ulterior motive by Magnar. This man's reputation didn't escape Brent, known as the man who mistrusted the public so much Magnar seldom showed his face. His casual coercion impressed Brent.

"Can we have some time to think about it?" Brent asked, knowing it was a long shot. He looked at Pax, who adjusted his immediate excited smile to a look of sternness. Brent knew Pax wanted to say yes. Ever since their academy excursion, the Mage's Union and its mysterious allure had captivated Pax.

Magnar looked surprised and shifted forward, resting his arms on the desk. "Why of course, a wise Mage never rushes a decision." His beard twitched as he smirked. "I will give you until the end of the ceremony to think it over and someone will message you all you need to know."

"Thank you for allowing this, albeit small, moment to contemplate, Sir," Brent said snidely, already aware that it wasn't an offer after all, but an order. He didn't care about inadvertently offending Magnar in this moment. He needed Brent and Pax more than they did him.

Magnar's demeanour shifted, and he smiled kindly. "Now, I believe you have a daughter to get home to, so you two better finish up and get to this ceremony."

Brent's heart raced. "How do you know of Victoria?"

"Mr. Abernathy, I am the Arch Mage," he said plainly. His long sleeves ruffled with a flourish of his hands. "It is my job to know about every capable Mage in Spellford." He stood sharply; the chair rolled back. Pax and Brent rose as well, pushing the chairs out from beneath them. Magnar swished the door open and held out a hand. "Come, I must now discuss with Director Ike the good news. I will see you at the ceremony."

Magnar allowed for Pax to walk past but stopped Brent by the shoulder and spoke closer to his ear. "Let's keep the publicity to a minimum from now on, shall we?"

Brent knew he was referring to the moment in one of his interviews with the Media Mages, he claimed the Mage's Union was not doing enough to protect the city, and that if he had a job there, he would bring about the much-needed change.

"Let's see if your words stack up," Magnar finished and then let go of Brent's shoulder, patting him on the back. "Good lad, look forward to working with you, Director Ike." He called out, "Do you have a second?"

Brent and Pax did as directed and walked towards the elevators. Before they left, they took one look back and Magnar smiled at them as he chatted with Director Ike.

As the lift doors shut on them, Pax let out a gigantic sigh. "Oh my! I thought we were done for."

"Same!" A sigh escaped Brent's lips, accompanied by the sensation of perspiration that made its way down his neck. "That offer makes me wary, but like what else have we got going on?" Brent asked nonchalantly.

"Well, Victoria?" Pax reminded Brent.

"She is due to graduate soon. This is as good a time as ever, and besides..." Brent said as the elevator doors opened and reached the bottom floor. "We don't have a choice." He shrugged and took off out of the building, leaving Pax to follow behind him. As he exited the building, a black hovering carriage pulled up in the parking bay.

"Mr. Grimtusk?" The driver tipped his hat out of the window. "Mr. Abernathy?"

They both nodded, and the doors opened. A single set of gold stairs flung out and extended, allowing for them to enter with ease. "This way please, Arch Mage Magnar has arranged this carriage for your journey to the convention centre."

Paxton smiled and rushed towards it to clamber inside. He smacked his legs twice in glee and laughed. "Come on Brent! It's glorious in here."

Pax was enjoying this lush life more than Brent. He sighed, then followed Paxton into the carriage. He didn't appear outwardly excited, yet he was looking forward to the ceremony. Also, Brent just wanted the night to end.

CHAPTER FOUR
DRAGON RIDERS

Victoria lifted her head above the living room couch when she heard the latch of the front door open. Her father and Pax burst through the door. Pax was laughing and raved about how good the food at the ceremony was, whereas Brent was silent, as usual. Pax proudly wore his medal, but Brent's was nowhere to be seen.

Victoria turned back to her phone and continued to scroll on WicTok, chuckling to herself at all the different videos of people dancing with magical enhancement and the occasional tutorial on how to apply your makeup using incantations. Victoria felt one arm of her father lean over the couch to give her a hug.

"Hi Dad," she said without raising her face from her phone. "What's for dinner?"

"Oh?" he pulled his arm back and Victoria looked up at him with a wide smile. "Witches Wagon?"

"Take out again?" she groaned. "But that's the fourth time this week."

"I know, Tori, with the ceremony and all, I just—" Brent started.

"Yeah, Spellford's champion didn't have time to do groceries," Pax interjected from his room across from the living room. His door was ajar, and Brent shot him a disgruntled look.

"You could also help; you can drive now, remember?" Brent added and Pax poked out his tongue.

"Leave him alone, Dad," Victoria defended Pax.

"Yeah, leave me alone, Dad," Pax taunted. He'd changed into track pants and a raggedy shirt he loved, with an ogre on the front.

She moved her legs as her father threw himself down onto the couch, still in the same clothes he wore at the ceremony. She looked at her father, who took his glasses off and rubbed his eyes, then handed her his phone.

"Pick something. Price is no object."

Paxton poured himself a glass of Pep-Up Elixir before he joined them. He pointed the remote to activate the vision orb that projected a screen on the wall.

"You better put something decent on Pax," Brent warned, still rubbing his eyes.

Pax scrolled through the channels until he came to the news. Brent quickly glanced up and the title of the news story caught his attention.

Swamp Witch Accused of Kidnapping Children, Sentenced to Prison

"Wait, what was that?" Brent asked, trying to get Pax to return to the channel.

"Dragonfire is almost on. Let's order some pizza and watch it together" Victoria suggested, always the mediator between her father and Pax. Brent dropped it and put the story to the back of his mind.

Brent didn't particularly enjoy Dragonfire at first, but it had become a weekly reality show they watched. Each contestant would take a dragon from a hatchling to a full-grown dragon and raise it themselves over the course of a few lunars to become Arcanum's next Dragon Rider Superstar.

"Okay, one Mystic Meat Lovers for you dad, two Dragon Breaths for Pax, their signature Vampire Warding Garlic Bread, an Enchanted Garden pizza for me, anything else?" Victoria asked.

Paxton made sad puppy dog eyes at Brent. A clever tactic he always employed when he wanted to get his way with a food order. Brent pretended to not play along, but he always gave in to his friend.

"Okay, and a dessert," Brent said, rolling his eyes.

"Lava Golem Cake, all ordered." She handed her father's phone back to him. "And it's already on its way. That's fast!"

"That's magic!" Brent and Pax said in unison, running their hands in the shape of an arch and wiggling them. Victoria groaned. They always, always did this. Together, they were like children. It was weird that she was more mature than two grown men.

It was only a short while, but the Witches' Wagon delivery arrived with their order. Paxton leaped from the couch after the first knock. The floor gave the usual rumble from his lack of rising slowly.

Victoria snatched the remote and turned on Dragonfire as they all ate their individual pizzas. Victoria watched, half impressed, and half unaffected because Pax never wasted time getting stuck into his meals. Between the loud slurping of stringy cheese and drinks and a wall shaking burp from Brent, the epic intro music began with the reel of contestants rolling through. The show started, and Victoria made an excited squeal with a mouthful of pizza.

Swallowing her pizza fast, Victoria spoke almost out of breath. "Oh! Kiera is on shhh!" she hushed.

Brent smiled back at her and then winked at Pax as they all turned their attention to the screen. Kiera hatched her Emberflare, named Garnet, in the Ashen Wastelands of Cinderscape, across the border in Valtoria. When Garnet was excited and happy, its shimmering scales glowed like a candle flame dancing in the dark. Garnet was only a few weeks old and had already grown to half its predicted size.

The narrator of the show read out the disclaimer about each dragon as they appeared. Born with an excess of internal energy, Garnet's breed of Emberflare dragons had a shorter life span compared to others. Unlike other dragon breeds, this adaptation rapidly depleted their life force. As a result, they lived a fraction of the time that other dragon breeds could. However, during their brief lives, they were extremely powerful and fast-growing, making them highly sought after by dragon poachers and were a protected species under the Dragoon Corps.

"Garnet is such a beautiful creature!" Victoria's eyes glistened with admiration. "I've always dreamed of having an Emberflare as a pet dragon."

"We haven't been to the Dragon Sanctuary in a while. Did you want to go this weekend, Victoria?" Pax asked.

"Uh, don't you have an excursion soon?" Brent's urgent voice broke the silence as he asked, but Victoria silenced him with a tight grip on his arm. Brent shook his head at Pax, his lips curled into a smirking grin.

"Kiera is on, shush!" she turned back to the show.

They watched the rest of the show in a silent awe, periodically interrupted by Victoria's bursts of excitement or the sporadic commentary from Brent and Pax. During some scenes where the overconfident contestants bragged, Victoria would groan.

"I hate Oren. He is such an—"

"Awful contestant," Pax called out from the front door, while Brent and Victoria cleaned up. "People out there walking their pets, getting exercise, and there is me with my pizza boxes and belly full to the brim!" Pax said proudly, patting his stomach. Despite his cuddly appearance, Pax possessed a hidden strength beneath all that pudge.

"You exercised Pax; you moved your arm to your mouth when you almost inhaled your entire meal," Brent laughed to himself, placing the dishes in the washing cauldron.

"Oh, stop it, Dad. Orcs need their nourishment," Victoria feigned being upset and then flashed a smile. In the background, the vision orb displayed the news and the interview with Brent flashed across the screen.

"I'm glad everything is back to normal." Victoria commented.

"Well, almost, but not quite." Brent closed the lid on the dishwashing cauldron, the clinking of the metal echoed through the kitchen. "Let's grab a seat. There's an important matter we need to discuss."

Victoria noticed her father's posture change.

"Oh, is this about you being the town's hero again?" Victoria said calmly. "I've seen the interview so many times, actually getting quite sick of it now."

"Well, no, yes, but no," Brent stammered and took a seat. He waited for Victoria to sit and could see Pax standing off to the side, keeping his distance, but clearly wanting to still be involved in the conversation. Brent resisted the urge to scold him through their mind-link.

"So, this afternoon, Arch Mage Magnar visited Pax and I at Sorcery-Sure." Victoria raised her eyebrow and Brent shook his hand. "Before you ask, no one has fired us," Brent assured her, a mischievous glint in his eyes. He took a moment to savour the refreshing burst of Pep-Up, the fizz dancing on his tongue. "Oddly enough, he offered us a job within the Mage's Union."

"What kind of job?" she asked, rubbing her eyes.

"It was less of an offer and more. You will do this," Pax returned from his bedroom and leaned against the doorframe between the lounge and kitchen.

"Yeah, he was really...what's the word?" Brent scratched the back of his head sheepishly.

"A bit of a dickhead," Pax replied, and Victoria smirked. "But you don't ask the Arch Mage questions, you just go along with what he requests."

"Why? He is like anyone else in this city." Victoria stated.

"You are right." Brent placed a hand on hers assuredly. "But unfortunately, it is what it is." Brent shrugged.

There was a buzzing on the countertop behind him from Brent's phone. Pax pulled his own phone out of his pocket as it also vibrated in his hands. Brent returned and read the message aloud.

> Welcome to the Mage's Union, Mr. Brenton Abernathy.

He read out loud slowly and scrolled down. Victoria watched with eagerness and stifled a giggle at her father's full name being used.

> We have assigned your orientation. Please follow the prompts to open your first assigned task - Marquis Beaumont Disappearance,

He continued to scroll.

"Beaumont? Professor Nia's father?" Victoria's eyes widened with surprise.

"I didn't know he was missing?" Brent's question wasn't met with a reply.

"Another message has come through," Pax said.

Victoria rushed to stand beside her father and read the message.

> Thank you for confirming that you will attend tomorrow at Mage's Union Sanctum. We will welcome you at 0800 hours for your orientation. Uniforms provided.

"But you didn't accept it?" she asked.

"Yeah, it's like I said. We didn't have a choice." Brent lifted his arm to place it over Victoria's shoulder and kissed her on the cheek. He gave her a hug, sniffing the top of her head. No matter how old she got, she was still his baby, and he would always protect her. Sniffing her head gave him that comfort. It was security.

Brent pulled her back and looked at her, followed by a gentle stroke of her cheek. Victoria's eyes were a shade of blue he had only seen once before. "Run along and finish your homework. I want to discuss something with Pax," Brent said, and Victoria agreed, leaving them both to their discussion.

She could hear them chatting over the anticipation for the next day as she entered her room. It was a colourful collage of posters featuring her favourite bands and characters from Dragonfire. The Brimstones were easily recognizable as the prominent ones. They were an all women led grunge rock band that Victoria adored. Her phone lit up with a notification just as she sat down to finish her homework. It was from Luminia.

> Hey, Tor, have you chosen your career goals yet?

> Not yet. We have a while yet, no?

She closed her books. The sound of the pages slapping together echoed in the quiet room.

> Due next, lunar, any clue what you want to be?

As she made to write a reply to Luminia, her heart sank. Victoria was in the second to last year of her education path in the academy. She did not know what she really wanted to do, but she always dreamed of working with dragons in some capacity. The Dragoon Corp was always looking for new recruits and if she received top marks in her exams, she would be a shoe in for an early placement next year and could skip her final year all together.

> Maybe apply to the Dragoon Corp?

> Someone with your grades could aim higher.

This response instantly disgruntled Victoria and she furiously tapped back a response .

> Well, someone with your grades could aim a little lower!

> Bitch!

Victoria placed her phone on the moon lamp to let it charge overnight. Landing back onto her bed, she laid her head down and stared at the ceiling. She needed to summon the courage to discuss with her dad the future, but her apprehension was already there, knowing he would not allow it.

Maybe she could forge his signature so that she could submit the form and get the ball rolling early. It wouldn't be the first time she did something without his explicit consent. She pondered on it a few moments more and then shifted the idea out of her mind.

Much to her dismay, she would need to discuss it with him before it was due. She rolled over in bed and with a flick of her hand; the lights went out. Her mind wandered, almost drifting into a sleepy state, until the thought of the upcoming excursion jolted her awake. Rolling back out of bed, she reached into her bag and pulled out the permission slip, its crumpled edges still waiting for her dads signature.

Victoria bolted out of the room and ran into the kitchen to see Brent sat alone at the table going over his phone.

"Uh, Dad?"

She watched as Brent lifted his face up from his phone. "Yes, my Love?"

"I need this permission slip signed for the excursion to the Dragon Sanctuary." she waved the paper and Brent tapped the table.

"I'll look at it soon. Leave it here, please," he mumbled, clearly distracted, before he returned to his phone.

Victoria wondered if now the right time might be to bring up her plans. "There is another thing." She drew out her words in a serene sing-song tone that she knew her father couldn't resist.

"Yes, what is it?" he asked and put his phone down.

"Well, as you know, in the next two lunars, I have to submit my career path ideas."

"Yes, have you figured out what you want to be?" he asked sweetly, with genuine interest and an immediate change in his tone.

With a sinking feeling in her stomach, Victoria did everything in her power to steer clear of this dreaded conversation, the same one she had gone over countless times while standing under the hot water of her shower. But here it was. Now or never.

She began to stammer and murmur. She gulped. Hard. And then grimaced, "IwanttojointheDragoonCorp!" Her nervous words came out jumbled.

"Come again?" Brent asked her.

"I want to join Dragoon Corp," she repeated, clearer this time. And she could see the instant change in his expression. Holding her hands up in defence, she smiled, hoping it would warm him up. "I know what you are going to say and hear me out."

"I don't think there is anything you can say that will sway my mind, but go on," Brent replied coldly.

It was like a knife to the chest, and he twisted it. "Fine, whatever Dad, if you will not listen, I won't bother." She made to leave, but Brent called her back.

"I'll listen, go ahead."

"I don't feel like it now. I'm going to bed. Just sign the stupid form." She ended the conversation there and went back to her room. She resisted the urge to slam her door. Even being seventeen, she would get told off.

Victoria shut the door and jumped into her bed, covering her body. There was a soft knock at the door. "What?"

"Can I come in?" her father asked.

"It's your house," she snapped back, and the door opened. She felt the weight of her father when he sat on the edge of the bed and tugged gently at the blanket.

"Yes?" she asked sternly, as their faces met.

"What's got you all—"

"All what?" She pushed back.

"This, so combative."

She shifted in the bed to sit against the bedhead. "The problem isn't me. Dad, you're not listening to me."

"Victoria, I'm listening. Tell me," he breathed, and it struck Victoria that she hadn't once factored in how he felt about her decisions.

"You always told me to follow my dreams. Working with dragons is mine," she said with firm resolve.

"I know you love them. They are fearsome and wondrous creatures..." Brent replied to her and held out his hand, but she refused. "Perhaps we can do the excursion first and then decide?"

"I don't think the excursion will change my mind," She repeated his own words back to him with conviction. "The Corp offers security and stability, innovative Magic-Tech research opportunities and making a positive impact on dragon populations."

"Sounds like you've been studying the brochure," Brent started. "You raise many good points, but I am sticking to my original statement."

"This is not fair!" Her voice filled with frustration. "You never allow me to do anything!" She turned on the bed, dragging the quilt over her head. "Just leave!"

The air grew tense. Brent stood up sharply. "Your excursion is before the cutoff date. We will talk about it after then," he put an end to the discussion. When he went to leave, he shut the door behind him with a little more force than necessary.

Victoria's regret was instant. She felt bad and wanted to chase after him, but also knew he had to hear what she said. She would apologise later. Too angry to think about anything else, she rolled over and closed her eyes, praying for sleep.

CHAPTER FIVE
THE MAGE'S UNION

Brent awoke with the blaring sun pointing directly in his eyes. He had forgotten to close the shades on his bedroom window last night in the fury of his argument with Victoria. He fumbled in his blind morning stupor for his phone and accidentally knocked the lamp onto the carpeted floor.

"Ugh…" He groaned in frustration, his eyes still heavy with sleep, as he dragged himself out of bed. He tapped his phone and read the time. His alarm was due in ten minutes, but he got up anyway.

He shuffled over to the door and wrapped himself in the robe that hung on the back before exiting. The morning was always cool in Enchanted Circuit, and you could feel it through the floorboards. As he turned the corner, the kitchen was already in use by Pax, who appeared to be making breakfast.

"Morning," Brent slurred over the sound of sizzling sausages and eggs. "When did you wake?"

"I didn't sleep." Pax turned around with a wired look, but obvious tiredness in his eyes. "Too buzzed for today," he said, almost bouncing on the spot.

"I wish I shared your enthusiasm." Brent sat down at the table with a loud yawn. "Is there fresh coffee or will we grab some along the way?" Brent stretched his arms above his head with another deep yawn. A ring at the doorbell halted all movement in the kitchen.

"Expecting someone?" Brent asked, and Pax shook his head. With a grunt, he pushed himself from the table, but not before the door opened and closed.

"Dad!" Victoria shouted; unaware Brent was right behind her. "Package for you both," she said softly, and placed it in the lounge room. "It's come from an A. Callahan at the Mage's Union, whoever that is?" Victoria walked over to the kitchen to set the table.

Pax dropped the spatula in his excitement. Oil splashed across the countertop and rushed over to the package sitting on the floor. Brent sighed and continued to finish breakfast.

"Oh, it is our uniform?" Pax smiled widely, holding up his own. "Looks a little snug, ah! It expands"

"Is there a note?" Brent called out.

"No, oh wait, here it is," Pax said and the sound of an envelope ripping open carried across the room.

Dear Mr. Grimtusk and Mr. Abernathy,
Thank you for accepting the role as Magical Strategy Consultants. To help you feel the part, please wear the provided uniforms, which are enchanted and will adapt to any size, even for Orcs. Looking forward to your starting today!
Director Arden Callahan

"Well, that was a pleasant surprise," Victoria remarked. It was a relief to know what her father's new job title was. She poked Brent in the side with the fork handle and he made an "ooft" sound.

Brent remained quiet. The title was meaningless to him. It explained nothing, so he forced a smile and served up their breakfast. "Put those down, Pax. We will look at it later. First, we need to eat." The two would need to get their energy and motivation up to start this new job.

"Ooh food! I'm there!" Pax dropped his uniform and rushed over to the table to sit opposite Victoria, who eagerly awaited food herself.

"It is like living with two teenagers, sometimes with you two." Brent handed them both a plate, then returned to the bench for his own. "But I wouldn't have it any other way." He leaned down and kissed the top of Victoria's head.

"And where's my kiss?" Pax playfully insisted.

"I draw the line at your greasy bald spot," Brent quipped back. "I don't want to be cursed with Orcish features."

Victoria snorted a laugh and couldn't stop. Pax joined in her laughter as well for a mere moment before he dove right back into his feast of a breakfast.

"So, what will your job be exactly?" Victoria looked at Pax and Brent, then took another bite while she waited for their answer.

"Honestly, the description was very vague." Brent swiftly pulled out his phone, typing in the words of the department into the 'Ask the Elders' search engine. Anticipation built as he waited for a result. "It says here we will assist the Mage's Union in development and implementation of strategic plans and solutions related to the use and regulation of magic."

Brent paused and looked at it again. It didn't seem the right fit for either of them, but then again, Magnar made it clear he meant to keep a watchful eye on them both. Maybe this was his way of demotivating the friends further from taking public attacks into their own hands.

"Sounds like just another tedious nine-to-five desk job." Victoria stood and placed her plate in the dishwashing cauldron. "I'm going to get ready."

Brent heard the bathroom door shut and then the sound of the shower turning on followed by Victoria playing her favourite shower time music.

"Good, we have time." Brent looked at Pax quickly and turned in his seat, scooting closer to him.

"Watsh ups?" Pax slurred his words around a mouth full of food, bits of food sprayed through his tusks.

Brent looked him dead in the eyes. "Pax, I forbid you from telling her anything we do, and we have to maintain all it is, is a desk job, you got it?" Brent felt his warning was clear, but he knew Paxton and his limitations to understanding subtlety. He had to be told directly.

"Uh, sure, but why?" he asked with another mouthful.

Brent looked around and then at the box. He did not trust it. Brent pointed his hand at the box and cast a silencing bubble around it. There was a flicker of light as the translucent bubble formed around it. "I don't trust the Mage's Union in the slightest. There is something else at play here. I fear they are after Victoria."

"Victoria, why?" Pax swallowed and put his cutlery down. "The only other person who knows about how we got her at Erimosia is gone."

"I can't quite pinpoint it, but the way Magnar mentioned Victoria gives me an uneasy feeling," Brent exhaled; the sound escaped his lips like a deflating balloon. "Let's be careful okay, consider this an adventure and our quest is to be a double agent."

"You mean triple agent, we are lying to Victoria, lying to Mage's Union and keeping our true desires hidden," Pax corrected Brent, and smiled with a big piece of egg poking through near his tusks. "It's been seventeen years. Surely before now they would have approached us."

"Just please watch what you say," Brent stood up and placed his own dishes in the dishwashing-cauldron.

"Have I ever once spilled the truth of her origins?" Pax asked, joining him.

"No, but you forget when you are around me that others exist. Use the mind-link if you need to talk in private."

"Yeah, good luck getting any now, being Union workers."

"Well, nothing like being forced into a role, hey?" Brent walked off towards the box and removed the spell. He was wary of it and gave it a gentle kick. It appeared to be a normal cardboard box, but his paranoia never failed to get the better of him.

He reached into the box and pulled out his own uniform. "Blergh! Brown and black, really?" He hung it against his body and cringed. "Couldn't they have some better colours?"

"Since when are you such a fashionista?" Pax came over to grab his own. "Oh, I didn't see this." He stroked the stitching on the breast. "They have our names embroidered. This is nice," he added, then walked off to his room, standing tall and full of pride.

Brent heard the shower turn off and Victoria exit into her room. He took this as his opportunity to get ready. A quick shower and then back into his room. He sat on the left side of the bed and glanced over at the right bedside table as he put on his boots. Layers of dust had accumulated, untouched for what seemed like an eternity. Brent could not bring himself to clean up Elwin's bedside table. He picked up the photo frame. It was the twin to the one Brent had in the office that now sat in a box in the room's corner.

It was of Elwin and himself, looking deep into each other's eyes. This moment left a lasting impression in his memory. The beautiful Mirewood forest was on full display in the middle of autumn, vibrant hues of crimson, orange, and gold painted the landscape.

As Brent blinked and pulled himself out of the moment, he smiled at the photo in his hands. If Elwin were alive today, he would still bear an uncanny resemblance to the person captured in this photo. With a heavy heart, Brent let out a sigh that echoed through the room. Back then, he exuded a vibrant energy and exuberance that made him seem much younger. With no worries to weigh him down, he looked forward to a future full of potential. When he looked at his reflection in the silver frame, he could see the deep lines etched on his face, evidence of the time that had passed.

"Where did that Brent go?" The weight of last night's conversation with Victoria lingered in his thoughts.

He knew he ought to be more lenient on her. After all, she was only seventeen, still navigating her way through adolescence. He could not help being the protective father that he was. Brent smiled weakly, then kissed the frame where Elwin was. There was a quiet knock at the door. He placed the picture down and turned around as the door opened.

"You ready, Brent?" Pax asked at his door.

Brent collected himself and wiped away the tear that formed. "Yeah, let's get going."

As they left the house, Brent and Pax noticed the carriage from last night parked outside their driveway. The two moved towards it and recognised the driver from last night.

"Oh? A Mage's Union carriage. I don't know, maybe I'll just take the train." Victoria hesitated at the door and chose not to join Pax in the carriage, who was clearly enjoying himself as much as he had the previous night.

Brent looked back at his daughter, who could not hide how she felt.

"What's wrong?" Brent wished his tone hadn't sounded so firm; he didn't want to repeat last night's anger. He reached up to her hair and pushed it back over her pointed ear.

"Nothing!" She rolled her eyes in exasperation and shook her hair back to cover her ears. "Okay, look...you saving the town is one thing, but if I arrive at school in a Union carriage, imagine the gossip that will spread." She paused and in a mocking voice added. "Her father's a fame whore, and so is she."

"So? Let people talk." Brent spoke gently, rubbing her shoulder to comfort her. "What have I always said?"

"Their words are nothing but a reflection of their own insecurities of themselves," she repeated in a droning voice. "That's fine, dad, but I am the one that will have to deal with it. Can we skip the lecture for today? I'll see you later tonight, okay?"

She didn't wait for Brent to respond.

His shoulders sagged. He didn't want to create any more issues for his daughter but didn't feel safe leaving her alone. "Wait a sec, hand me your phone," he called out to her.

"What? Why?" She stopped and dug out her phone from her pocket to hand back to him.

"Don't worry, I'm not snooping. I prefer your location to be shared with me at all times, just in case." Brent conjured a tracking rune and affixed it to the back. It melted into the phone with a bright blue flicker of light, then disappeared. "You also can not remove it. I made sure of that."

"Won't that chew up the incantation data?" Pax stuck his head from the carriage and smirked at Victoria, who stuck her tongue out.

"I'll get her more if that's the case. Now, I promise you I won't snoop. It is just a precaution, okay?"

"Right, whatever." She scoffed with a roll of her eyes. She snatched her phone back from Brent's hands. Brent waited and watched her leave. She crossed the street and made her way towards the train station, stuffing her phone in her pocket.

"Love you!" Brent called out, but she didn't stop to reply. When she was out of sight, he entered the carriage.

"Ready, Mr. Abernathy?" the driver asked Brent. He nodded as he buckled in. "Alright, I didn't get to tell you this yesterday, but this baby is the Sorcerati Mach-4 model."

"You're kidding! Oh boy!" Pax looked incredibly chuffed. "I knew it!" he slammed a fist down on his knee out of excitement and bumped Brent's shoulder with his own. Brent was distracted and barely glanced up from his phone., He had done the exact thing he said he wouldn't do and kept an eye on where she was going.

"Oh, sorry...what, what's up?" he shook his head. "Sorry, I am worried about her." Brent put his phone behind the armour plate across his chest where a pocket for it existed. The carriage weaved in and out of traffic like it was in the middle of a high-speed car chase.

"She will be fine," Pax said with reassurance. "She is incredibly resilient, and her App-Magic is top-notch." He smiled, and the tips of his tusks aligned with his nostrils as they always did. "If she gets into trouble, she will manage herself until we arrive."

"I know, it's fatherly things you wouldn't under—" Brent cut himself short and looked up at Pax.

"I care about her, too. We practically raised her together," he reminded Brent and Brent went to apologise but Pax had one last thing to add. "I know you meant nothing to it. Just don't be such a vicious Vessarian."

Brent shook his head and still mouthed an apology. He inspected the driver as the carriage continued to be driven forward and noticed two glistening objects in the driver's temples.

The Sorcerati Mach-4, with its innovative magical technology, was a standout in Spellford's advancements in vehicular magic. Every time the advert came on, it captivated Pax. The driver of the Sorcerati Mach-4 used psychically linked runes attached to their temples to communicate with the carriage and control its movements based on their thoughts and intentions. The runes also connected to the driver's own magical energy, enabling them to tap into the carriage's capabilities and navigate through the world with ease.

"Riding with magic at the speed of thought!" Pax imitated what Brent assumed was a tagline from a commercial.

"That is pretty cool," Brent acknowledged, looking to the driver who had swivelled around to face them but was still "driving" the carriage.

"I have set it to auto-drive," they said with a warm smile, the runes on their forehead a blinking array of lights at different speeds as they weaved in and out of traffic.

"We never had these kinds of things as kids. The advancements we are achieving is next level!" Pax could not remove the look of fascination from his face.

It was apparent to Brent how ecstatic Pax was to be inside the Sorcerati. Sounds of elation and joy from his Half-Orc friend followed every button he pressed.

"It also has levitation capabilities, allowing it to fly and avoid traffic." Pax pointed to a specific button on the dashboard. "Could we?" he begged.

"I thought you'd never ask!" The driver turned back around and pressed the button. The vehicle veered to the left and picked up speed. As it reached top speed on the ground, a subtle vibration built up on the carriage floor.

The sound of rushing air grew louder and there was a strange feeling around Brent's head and ears, as if he was being pushed downwards. He felt the force of gravity take him, pulling him backwards into his seat. He noticed Pax did not move an inch and, for the first time, was jealous of his bulky frame.

After a few seconds, he adjusted and looked out the window. They had lifted off the ground, hovering quite a few feet above the streets. He felt a thud under the carriage as the wheels retracted and folded into the body while the entire carriage started to elongate and shift, transforming into an aerodynamic shape with streamlined wings and a more pointed nose.

The windows darkened and a faint blue glow emanated from the body as the magical enchantments activated, creating a force field around the carriage. With a sudden burst of speed, the carriage rocketed across the city skyline, leaving a trail of blue flames behind it.

***

As the Sorcerati Mach-4 descended through the air, both Brent and Pax looked out the window in awe. The clouds parted as they approached their destination, revealing the sprawling cityscape of the Mage's Union Sanctum.

"Welcome, Gentleman, to the Mage's Union headquarters," the driver said, pressing a few buttons and putting a call through to seek permission to land.

In the distance, Brent could see the grand spires of the Mage's Union rising high above the other buildings. As they drew closer, he could make out the intricate carvings and runes etched into the stone archways that glinted in the sunlight.

"We are so high up; everyone looks so tiny from here," Pax commented, and Brent agreed with a short mutter.

The carriage slowed down as they approached the main entrance. It hovered in mid-air as they waited for clearance to land. Brent was finally feeling that rush of excitement and anticipation, knowing that this was the beginning of a new chapter in both of their lives.

The driver received clearance and guided the carriage to descend. That same rush around Brent's head came on, and he leaned back in his chair. As the carriage touched down on the landing pad, he felt a sense of relief as the engines powered down.

The doors opened, and Brent stepped out. Cool air washed over him along with the sounds of Sanctum. It was a grand structure, and he couldn't help but feel a little intimidated. A testament to the magical prowess and hub for the Arcane elite in Spellford, it was its own bustling metropolis within the centre of Spellford. The colossal structure commanded attention with its imposing height, shimmering façade and seamless blending of magic and architecture.

Towering statues of celebrated Mages throughout history adorned each corner of Sanctum, and Brent recognised a few of them. He had driven past many times but never had a reason to enter. Enchanted archways marked the ground entrance to Sanctum, each inscribed with protective runes and symbols that glistened even in the morning light. As he took it all in, the shimmering of the façade felt like an ever-changing tapestry of magical patterns and symbols, symbolising the union's rich heritage of magic.

Other Mages, both young and old, entered Sanctum on foot and in carriages. He could not help but feel a sense of kinship. A belonging. He took a deep breath and steeled himself for the experiences that lay ahead. This was the beginning of a new journey, and he was ready for whatever lay in store.

"Welcome, Gentleman, to the Mage's Union. I am Cyrus, and I will be your guide here at Sanctum."

Brent and Pax turned around and a young Mage in a white and blue cloak with short buzzed blonde hair approached them.

"Sanctum?" Brent asked, adjusting his clothing from being seated.

The young man pointed to the Mage's Union's headquarters building. He appeared visibly nervous and offered Brent a clammy handshake.

"I am Cyrus, your guide," he chuckled. His voice betrayed a hint of nervousness. "Oops, I already covered that."

"Take all the time you need, it's alright," Brent reassured politely.

"Thank you." He gestured towards the landing courtyard. "This is where many visitors arrive, greeted by the sound of bustling footsteps and excited chatter."

It was a large open courtyard, boasting many grass patches, small gardens, and trees. They were all immaculately tended to, with winding pathways leading up to the main building. The sun was shining down brightly, making the entire scene feel almost surreal in its beauty and vibrancy. Brent and Pax couldn't help their sense of excitement and wonder continue as they looked around at their new surroundings.

Both had adventured in the past with a party of various members seeing many castles and wondrous landscapes, but they had never encountered such an intricate building complex such as this up close. Most people would never have entered the Mage's Union unless invited, regardless of how much time they lived in Spellford.

Cyrus escorted them through to the closest building on the left and stopped just short of the small staircase leading up.

"This is the main administrative building." He appeared less nervous now, but still periodically checked notes on his clipboard to ensure he was right. "You both need to check in and out until you are issued with security passes. But you are lucky, you can avoid the daily fortune check with our resident Tarot reader.”

“How long does that take?” Pax piped up quickly, ignoring Cyrus’s mention of the Tarot cards.

“You’ll need to take a photo first.” Cyrus looked down at his notes and muttered what sounded like “hand the guest passes to them now” under his breath.

“These are your guest passes.” Cyrus nonchalantly flung back two passes which hovered in front of both Brent and Pax and then he turned. “They will grant you access to amenities and other locations around the Union.”

“Is there a Food court?” Pax almost leapt out of his skin.

“Why yes,” Cyrus stated plainly. “We have it all here. We are basically a self-sufficient small city in its own right. All amenities are available for those who live on site.”

“Well, we won’t be needing that,” Brent answered. “I have a seven-teen-year-old at home.”

Cyrus acknowledged, “It must have been difficult to raise Victoria all on your own for such a long time.”

Brent stopped in his tracks.

“How did you know my daughter’s name?” he asked, a mix of surprise and suspicion in his voice.

“Mr. Abernathy, the Mage’s Union, prides itself on conducting the most extensive background checks in all of Arcanum, ensuring the highest level of security.” Cyrus turned to him, a mischievous smile spread across his face that sent a chill down Brent’s spine. “Nothing escapes our watchful gaze.”

Instantly turned off by this new discovery, Brent replied with disdain. “If you were to ask me, it’s quite clear that this is an invasion of privacy.”

Ignoring Brent’s remarks, Cyrus pressed on towards the food court, drawn in by the mouth-watering scent that wafted through the air. As they made their way down the corridor, Cyrus abruptly pivoted and turned to face them, catching them off guard.

“Inside here is the food court and general hub area for everyone to relax and unwind. Although a lot of the superior Mages don’t hang about too long.” He held out his hand and pointed to the stairs on the left. “Let’s proceed to the Magic Strategic Department, where you will meet with your Director.” He made to walk and then halted, causing Brent to stop abruptly and Pax to knock into Brent.

Brent stumbled and had to gain his balance against the wall. "What's up?" He glared at Pax, who mouthed sorry and slapped him on the back.

"Before you mentioned something about privacy?" Cyrus stood firm, and he looked the least nervous he had the entire guided tour. His voice also sounded off. It was an incredibly odd shift in behaviour, and Brent inspected him briefly before he answered.

"Yes, why?" Brent asked and looked Cyrus dead in the eyes.

Cyrus took a step back and cleared his throat with a loud grunt. "I understand your concern, Mr. Abernathy. But please understand that the Mage's Union has a responsibility to protect all citizens of Arcanum. Knowledge is power, and it is our duty to be aware of any potential threats or dangers. Our monitoring of citizens is done with discretion and only where we believe there may be a cause for concern."

He paused for a moment before continuing. "As for your daughter, Victoria, her origins indeed fascinate us. It is our duty to monitor individuals with such unique backgrounds. We mean her no harm, only to ensure her safety and well-being, passively of course." This was not the same nervous Mage that they had met earlier. An air of confidence and assertiveness filled him.

Cyrus looked at Brent, followed by a rapid flutter of his eyes. His head dropped and when he raised it again, it was with a smile.

"Sorry Mr. Abernathy, Mr. Grimtusk. I must have dozed off there for a second." Cyrus spoke in his normal voice "I do that sometimes," he laughed it off. "Come follow me to your office."

Brent and Pax hung back, before they followed him. Brent held his hand on Pax's shoulder and muttered a quick incantation to link their minds without touching. He took them on a straightforward path and into an elevator up onto the fourth floor.

As they walked through the halls of the Mage's Union, Pax turned to Brent and spoke to him telepathically. "So, you were right."

Brent nodded. "Yeah, I knew something was up."

"Definitely," Pax agreed back "Well, that confirms your suspicions. Now to prove them."

Brent nodded again, pretending to listen to Cyrus. "I think we watch it play out more."

Pax nodded in agreement. "Let's continue to keep up our guard."

At the end of the path, Cyrus came to an abrupt halt in front of them, spinning around in a whirl of motion. They arrived at the Magic Strategic

Department, where a single mahogany door with a gold nameplate bearing the department's name stood as a barrier between them and their old life.

Upon entering through the door, a brightly illuminated room greeted their eyes with towering ceilings and panoramic glass windows that framed a breathtaking view of the surrounding Sanctum. Multiple desks filled the room, each adorned with a lexicon and an assortment of magical equipment. At the front of the room, there were desks arranged in a semicircle, facing the large projection screen at the front.

The map of the city, projected onto the screen, revealed a mesmerizing display of magical hotspots and mysterious anomalies. Brent's excitement was obvious as he looked at Pax with a smile that resembled a kid in a candy store. This was Pax's dream as well, made more apparent by the sparkle of excitement in his eyes, to work in a place where he felt like he could make a difference. As they walked past the desks towards the director's office, they got the vibe their department was one of the most important ones.

The sleek and modern space impressed Brent, as it looked both efficient and sophisticated, a reflection of the Mage's Union's commitment to staying at the forefront of magical research and development.

"Gentlemen, it has been a pleasure. I must, however, leave you here in the hands of—"

"Ah, Cyrus!" A man dressed in a two-piece suit walked out of the office at the back of the room. Brent turned and was rendered speechless as he took in the man's figure. He swore he had seen him before.

"And who are these strong young men joining my team?" The man extended his hand to shake Brent's. Brent's gaze faltered as it landed on him. When he blinked, for the briefest moment, he convinced himself that the man in front of him was his late fiancé, back from the grave. They looked so alike it was as if they were mirror images of each other.

"Elwin?" Brent whispered, feeling like he was about to faint.

"Mr. Abernathy, Mr. Grimtusk, this is the newly appointed Director Arden Callahan." Cyrus smiled and stepped to the side. Arden stood, tall and slender, his face adorned with sharp, chiselled features. His deep-set, piercing blue eyes seemed to hold a world of secrets, while his strong jawline, accentuated by a thin, well-groomed beard, added a touch of ruggedness to his appearance. With his impeccably tailored suit and commanding presence, he carried himself with confidence and authority.

Brent realised that beads of sweat were forming on his forehead as the heat flushed his face. He brushed his hands on the back of his pants, and blinked furiously as his eyesight grew worse. Brent made to shake Arden's hand. He felt like the room was spinning. Before he even could touch fingertips, everything went black as he fell backwards towards the ground.

CHAPTER SIX
LESSONS ON AUGMENTI

After Victoria placed her things down on her desk, she let out a loud yawn and stretched her arms high above her head. Victoria and the other students eagerly awaited Professor Aurora's tardy arrival to Enchantment class, allowing them with extra time for animated discussions before the official start of the school day.

"Got little sleep?" Lirien asked.

Victoria looked through the gap of her arms to her friend, who sat down beside her. She lowered her arms and continued to speak through a yawn. "Yeah, it was a late night." She smiled weakly. "Had a fight with my dad about wanting to join the Dragoon Corp."

"Ah!" Lirien let out a sigh. "Let me guess, he won't allow it."

"Nope. Not while under his roof at least and by the time I move out it will be too late," She sighed and continued to look around the room, hoping Professor Aurora wouldn't come in mid-conversation. "He said we would discuss it after the Dragon Sanctuary excursion," Victoria added.

"Well, that is something, at least. Just don't bring it up again with him until after that then," Lirien suggested, almost dismissively, and changed the subject when Victoria's mournful look didn't change. "So, did you finish the assignment from last week?"

Victoria shook her head, an ashamed expression on her face. "Not yet. I've been so busy with other classes, and...well, last few weeks with dad have been, well, you know?"

Lirien nodded sympathetically. "Yeah, I get it." He smiled. "I'm sure you'll get it done in time."

Victoria gave Lirien a grateful smile. "Thanks, Lirien. You always know how to make me feel better."

Just as the door swung open, the Enchantments Professor entered, her footsteps echoed throughout the classroom and the books on her desk created a loud thud as she placed them down. She clapped her hands twice like she always did to get the attention of her students, signalling the start of class.

"Good morning, students," Aurora sang as she steadied the books on the desk. "Today I thought we would turn our attention to the Ancient Mage civilisations and Augmenti," she said with an inflection on the word.

She waited for the room to react, but no one did. Not even Victoria. Even though she knew of the word, she wasn't one hundred percent sure of its origins. Victoria looked around and noticed the heavy bags under people's eyes, suggesting that everyone had a rough night.

"Is Professor Nia issuing you all too much homework?" Professor Aurora attempted a joke and still received no response from her class. "Education of our students is vital," she said, pausing her steps, a smile played on her lips. "So!" She exclaimed, clapping her hands loudly. "Let's change the energy in the room."

Victoria and Lirien naturally paired up without hesitation. They knew they were expected to perform a faux battle with enchantments from their Rune-Phones. Tired and a little nervous, Victoria worried that performing in front of everyone would reveal her secret. With a flick of her wrists, the desks and chairs in Professor Aurora's class rearranged themselves, creating a new configuration in the room. When Victoria looked at Lirien across from her, he playfully stuck out his tongue. Victoria couldn't contain her burst of laughter. No matter what happened, he remained unfazed, and she couldn't help but feel a twinge of envy.

She chuckled while shrugging her shoulders, feeling instant defeat from knowing that Lirien would be unfazed as he always was in the mock battles. She watched all the students effortlessly take out their Rune-Phones from the depths of their cloak pockets - this being one of the rare instances where Professor Aurora permitted using them in class. All the students obediently followed the instructions to place their enchantments in the lowest settings, ensuring that no one would be at risk of actual injury. Victoria, although aware that she wouldn't be using her phone for the performance, also complied with the directive.

The room fell silent as Aurora declared, "On the count of three, you may begin." Anticipation filled the air. She counted down from three and the class started around them.

Lirien took the initiative and was the first to act, summoning a spell that resulted in creating a small, radiant orb of light. Without hesitation, Victoria cast a spell that resulted in a delicate flower forming out of ice. The flower floated gracefully in the air. In response, Lirien conjured a powerful gust of wind, causing the flower to disintegrate into tiny particles. With a swift motion, Victoria raised her arm and summoned a shield of energy that effectively blocked the small shards of ice, ensuring they could not harm her.

She readjusted herself and glanced around to observe her classmates. There were a pair of students who experimented with light spells. Mesmerizing displays of vibrant colours and intricate patterns that elegantly danced throughout the entire room. Another pair worked on sound spells, trying to create soothing melodies and calming rhythms. A third pair worked with fire spells, creating small flames that danced and flickered in the air.

Each pair were engaged in a meticulous process of testing the boundaries of their spells, attempting to determine the extent to which they could harness their magic, causing no actual damage. Despite the competitive atmosphere, the duels all felt friendly and experimental. Each student sought to learn from their partner's approach and technique.

The duel between Victoria and Lirien carried on for several minutes, during which both continued to cast counter spells. Despite the appearance of being an even match, she placed her confidence in her enchantment prowess, knowing that her skills far surpassed those of Lirien. She had practised with Pax many times when her father was out, and she felt confident in her abilities.

Victoria flicked her wrists and conjured a winding vine above Lirien, that transformed into a snake made of gems. It hissed at him and lunged. Lirien dodged to the right and in a puff of smoke it turned into butterflies. Victoria received applause and cheers from her classmates from her display of magic.

Professor Aurora clapped twice. Everyone in the class came to a halt. As she waved her hands, the desks materialised out of thin air, and the students hurriedly resumed their seats. "Abernathy has been practising her enchantments!" The acknowledgment caused Victoria to blush.

"Everyone wide awake now?" She looked directly at Victoria with a warm smile. "If I'm not mistaken, all of you are studying Erimosia in history." There were a few nods, and even Victoria agreed. "Good. Well, from a purely Enchantment point of view, the city has a rich ancient history of the most advanced enchantments for its age before it fell."

In her history classes, Victoria learned of the incredibly beautiful multicultural society and dreamed of seeing it at its peak.

"Erimosia heavily enchanted its infrastructure, and some believe it was the birthplace of Magi-Tech." Aurora glided around the class, giving her lecture and appeared to hover above the floor, with her long robes forming a train behind her.

Victoria learned how they imbued the walls with protective spells, lit the streets with glowing magic orbs for easy navigation at night, and purified the water supply with ancient enchantments to eliminate imperfections.

"Some speculated there were defence mechanisms for natural disasters such as earthquakes and hurricanes." Professor Aurora made her way to the board and wrote the word:

Augmenti.

She turned and paused, looking at her students. "Does anyone know what Augmenti is?"

"Isn't it just magic?" Lirien asked after a brief pause.

"Good answer," she started. "You are correct, it is magic, but it is also much more than that." She paused, the students hinged on her every word. "It is the substance of everything and nothing all at once." The looks on the student's faces portrayed their confusion. "Augmenti exists in a constant state of flux being both tangible and intangible."

"So, it exists and doesn't?" a student at the back asked.

"I wouldn't say that." Aurora walked to the side of the board. "Its properties are so unique that it has earned a reputation as the very foundation of magic itself."

Victoria wondered to herself what Augmenti would look and feel like and as she closed her eyes to imagine it, her fingertips tingled. She felt a crackle of fiery sparks from her fingertips. Victoria opened her eyes. Professor Aurora's stare was fixed on her. She shook her hand and pretended to listen.

"According to legend, the ancient Mages of Erimosia were the only ones who truly understood Augmenti." Aurora walked down from her desk and through aisles of desks. "They spent centuries studying and harnessing its power to create extraordinary magical wonders. They could weave spells without incantations, they could bend reality itself, and the very fabric of time and space, all of creation, was at their fingertips." Professor Aurora, with an air of confidence, rolled and flexed her fingertips, causing bolts of lightning to crackle and dance between them.

Murmurs filled the room. Everyone was enthralled and showed noticeable excitement at the prospect of its power.

Amid their conversation, Lirien raised an intriguing point regarding the limited research efforts, expressing his belief in the potential to achieve a utopian society by harnessing such research. Observing this exchange, Aurora responded with a smile, signifying her appreciation for his insight.

"The Mage's Union built Sanctum atop of Spellford's reserves of Augmenti, hoping one day we could replicate its unlimited power." She glanced around the room before she returned to her desk. "The Mage's Union manages the Leyline that flows from the Augmenti reserves, fuelling the entire city. Only those truly attuned to magic can feel its essence, but that wouldn't be any of your generation, sadly." She looked at her students with a warm smile. "The invention of App-Magic came to be because that ability died out years ago."

Professor Aurora paused, eyes fixed on Victoria, examining her. Victoria maintained eye contact and didn't blink throughout the awkward exchange. The lesson would soon be over, and while Victoria had a million questions about Augmenti that would help her on her paper about Erimosia; they would have to wait for another time.

"Ok class, I think you have deserved an early minute, as an apology for me being late and for you all being such wonderful listeners," Aurora said, the students clear happiness visible.

As they packed up their bags and headed on their way to leave, Aurora called Victoria aside. Victoria asked Lirien to wait for her in the courtyard.

"Yes, Professor?" Victoria asked, slinging her bag over one shoulder.

"How is everything?"

"What do you mean, Professor?" Victoria asked back.

"The recent events with your father's newfound fame as Spellford's champion must be weighing on you. Do you need to speak to anyone or?"

"I am absolutely fine," she stated confidently, but deep down, she concealed the truth. "I'm just exhausted with homework." She hoped her lie would be enough to convince her teacher.

"Okay." She offered a wide smile. "There is one more thing. Can you show me your hands?"

The question took Victoria aback. "What do you mean?"

"Your hands please," Aurora demanded.

With reluctance Victoria gave a quick show of both sides of her hands. "Are we done?"

Aurora grabbed hold of them and inspected her fingertips. "As I suspected, you didn't use your apps, did you?" Aurora had caught her out.

"Well, no," she admitted. She could try to lie, but it seemed her teacher already knew the truth. She swallowed her reservations and spoke the truth. "I don't need to, I've always been able to cast magic without incantations or catalysts like a Rune-Phone." Victoria pulled her hands back and crossed them under her arms for comfort. "I can connect to the phone and simulate magic if I wish, but my actual skills are much more natural."

"Fascinating. There aren't many non-verbal Mages like yourself left."

"Aphonics, Professor." She let her hands drop to a more natural position.

"Yes, that's the term. My apologies." Aurora offered an apologetic smile.

Followed by an awkward silence between them before Aurora spoke again. "So, you pretend to use the Rune-Phone to what? Fit in?"

"Basically." She felt awkward by the interaction with her professor, even though Aurora wasn't being offensive. Victoria turned to look at the other students who walked past, then back at Aurora.

Aurora sat down and pulled out a drawer, she couldn't help but express her astonishment that the discovery Victoria was Aphonic came so close to Victoria's final year. "The Academy Board would be interested to know that you learned to feign use of the phone and imitate your peers, setting magic spells in the app. Perhaps even suggest one-on-one tutoring,"

"My father isn't aware of my abilities, either," she admitted.

"Well, who is your home group teacher? Is it Professor Nia?" she asked, and Victoria nodded.

"I will arrange for your father and her to meet to discuss options going forward. In the meantime, keep it under wraps. We wouldn't want this to get out."

Victoria was unsure what to say or do. She politely thanked her professor before leaving to room. As soon as she walked out of sight, she made a breakneck pace to the courtyard where Lirien waited under a large tree.

"Girl! What took you so long?" He called out from the middle of the courtyard.

"Aurora held me back," she said, a little puffed out. "She wanted to discuss, well, tutoring."

"Tutoring, are you that far behind? Doesn't seem like you," Lirien asked.

"Victoria! Lirien! There you are!" Luminia called out from across the courtyard and rushed over. She stopped to catch her breath, then sat down on the ground in front of the bench where her two friends sat. "Ritual 101 was a bloody snooze fest. It is the one class I wish I never took."

"But don't you need it if you are to become a healer?" Victoria asked.

"Oh, right. Yeah, guess I'll keep slugging with it, could always go into alternative healing afterwards." Luminia shrugged, her hair gleamed in the sunlight.

"Please don't become some swamp Witch, waving a crooked muddy stick at us and trying to steal our essences." Lirien imitated a hunchback, he pointed his fingers out to represent a claw and snatched at the air.

"You've been watching too much vision orb, pointy ears!" Luminia smacked him over the head gently.

"You are probably right, dust fairy!" Lirien replied, and they laughed together, the friends were close enough they weren't offended by each other's slightly racial taunts.

Victoria stretched her arms behind her and sat back, enjoying the break before their next class.

"So, what is this tutoring for, then?" Lirien asked, disrupting Victoria's peace.

"Tutoring? You?" Luminia sounded gobsmacked.

"Yeah, that's what he said." Victoria pointed to Lirien and smiled. "It is nothing like what you think, I'm just..." She paused. She swore to Aurora that she wouldn't spread it around, but Victoria could trust her friends. "I'm Aphonic," she whispered.

After a brief pause of confusion written on his face, Lirien spoke in a whisper. "Aphonic, what's that?"

"It means she can use incantations without words dummy," Luminia slapped him on the shoulder. "I don't know why you would want to waste your own energy, though. Not when we have everything for free from our fingertips." Luminia made a show of shaking the phone in her hands.

"Well, you must have unlimited incantwation data from mummy and daddy, because mine sure isn't free." Victoria smirked and received a playful slap from Luminia, too.

"I guess having an affinity for natural magic means you would have less reliance on external tools. Easier when you don't have your phone on you and stuff like that." Lirien paused and looked to Victoria and her phone.

"Wait a second, I saw you pick your enchantments in class!" He stood and turned to point at her phone.

"Yes, uhhh..." She smiled widely, "I merely pretended." Victoria shrugged. "So what? I am sure there are many other Aphonics around."

"Not these days, your father's era were one of the last generations who had to learn magic from the ground up, and even they have to utter incantations they spent all their time learning. Magic was much different back then, my parents aren't using their own as much, either."

"I see you've been paying attention in history class, Lumi!" Victoria spat at her.

"Can you show us something?" Luminia asked, intrigue flashing across her face.

"You know I can't. It's against the rules."

"Is the little town hero's daughter scared of a little punishment?" Lirien sung in a teasing voice.

Victoria's body jolted with a visceral reaction., She jumped to her feet followed by an abrupt rush of blood that flooded her head and momentarily distorted her vision. Shaking her head, she pushed her dark brown hair behind her shoulders, keeping her pointed ear hidden and felt the soft strands glide against her fingertips. "Fine! I'll do it!"

"I have a request!" Lirien piped up and Victoria looked down at him. "Levitate that statue over there!" Victoria followed the direction to where Lirien pointed.

In the left corner of the courtyard stood a tall statue of a beast with the head of a lion, wings of an eagle, and a serpent's tail. A fabled Chimera but nothing like the beasts that record footage for Media Mages. Even from this distance, the details were immaculate, each feather, scale, and hair etched with precision visible in its marble structure.

"Wait, that's—"

"So, you are all talk then," Lirien instigated. "Guess there is no doubt if you're adopted then."

"Stop being a jerk, Lirien!" Luminia jumped to Victoria's defence.

"You don't have to show us. I was just curious, that's all." Lirien backtracked.

"You're on!" Victoria kicked him in the leg as she rushed past to the statue.

Determined not to fail, she wanted to prove, not only to herself but also to the entire student body, that she was capable. If there was anyone who could match or even exceed her father, it was her. As she took each step, the sun's rays bounced off the statue, creating a luminous and sparkling effect on the surface. With a deep breath, Victoria extended her hand forward, focusing her magic to lift the statue off the ground. As the magical energy built, the veins in her hand raised. She held her breath and closed her eyes.

Without Victoria saying a word the magic unleashed with immense power, A shimmering magenta aura formed around her as the statue shook, catching the attention of all the students in the courtyard.

The statue rose off the ground in a sudden burst of energy. Its weight defied gravity as she held her hand out, steadying it. With her eyes still closed, she concentrated and channelled the magic within her, causing the muscles in her arms to twitch from the effort. The statue wobbled, it appeared to be on the verge of tipping, but Victoria's firm grip and powerful magic prevented disaster. The other students around her watched in amazement, their mouths agape at this show of power. She tuned out the noise and let her magical energy flow.

Finally, Victoria brought the statue back down to the ground, lowering it gently. The magenta aura faded away. She opened her eyes, feeling a bit drained but triumphant. With a satisfied smile on her face, she turned to be congratulated by her peers, but the high instantly faded.

"Abernathy!" Victoria gulped as a stern-looking Professor O'Sullivan, the Magical Ethics instructor, stood behind her, arms crossed. His face looked as if it could melt the flesh off of hers. "What do you think you're doing?" She attempted an explanation, but the professor cut her off. "You know the rules. No unsanctioned use of magic on school grounds. To class all of you!" His shout echoed through the courtyard. "Abernathy, follow me."

Victoria hung her head down in shame, some of the more uptight students sneered and taunted as she passed.

Students scurried off to their classes as O'Sullivan approached them. One student almost tumbled onto the ground as they tried to rush away. Professor O'Sullivan was strict and always in a foul mood, which he took out on the student body.

Reluctantly, Victoria followed Professor O'Sullivan into his classroom, feeling deflated and utterly embarrassed. She knew she'd be in trouble, and a sense of dread settled in her stomach. Picking up her bag, she shot Lirien and Luminia a disapproving glance before trailing behind her professor.

CHAPTER SEVEN
MARQUIS' DISAPPEARANCE

Pax rushed over to Brent's side, catching him before he fell to the ground. Lowering him slowly, Pax called his name, and tried to revive him with a few lights taps to his face. Arden with visible concern, knelt beside them to see if Brent was okay.

After a few moments, Brent regained consciousness and sat up, rubbing his eyes. Brent looked between Pax and Arden with a mix of shock and confusion, unable to believe what had happened.

"Are you okay?" Arden asked, placing a hand on Brent's shoulder. Brent looked down as if in slow motion at the hand on his shoulder and the man in front of him. The man he thought he saw was not his Elwin, but a much older doppelgänger. Sort of. This man did not appear to be one of the Alasïr, like Elwin was.

Brent stared at him for a moment longer and took a deep breath in an effort to compose himself. As he regained his sight and blinked a few times, he couldn't help but notice that the man who stood before him bore no real resemblance to Elwin.

"I'm sorry, I just...I think I'm overwhelmed, new day and all." Brent's voice was shaky. He lied not only to himself, but to everyone around him.

Arden nodded sympathetically. "I understand. It's not the first time someone fainted at the sight of me." Arden chuckled and Brent awkwardly laughed with him.

Pax helped Brent to his feet, and they both took a moment to collect themselves.

"Gentlemen, I was going to have a brief meeting in my office before we begin work, but perhaps Pax you would take Brent here to the infirmary—"

"I'm fine, Sir, just need some water," Brent interrupted.

"Cyrus, if you would be so kind to bring some water in. This way then." Arden turned and showed them to his office.

Brent swallowed hard and took in a deep breath. His first step was a little unsteady, but determined to walk on his own, he managed to weight bare himself with each step after. Brent and Pax walked into the room taking seats opposite of Arden who sat at his desk.

Cyrus walked in shortly after providing a glass of water for them all. He placed them on the desk, and Arden shooed him away.

"Gentlemen, firstly thank you both for agreeing to join this team so quickly. I didn't expect it, actually." Arden swivelled forward in his chair and placed a glass in front of each of their spots.

"Well, to be honest, Sir, we didn't exactly have a choice." Brent pulled up his phone and showed him the email.

"Oh, I know." Arden sat back, disregarding the email and pondered. "If the experience dissatisfies you after today, you are free to leave."

Brent put his phone face down on the desk. "Oh. It's not that I am ungrateful for this chance—"

Arden interrupted. "And you, big boy?" Arden asked Paxton, who nodded. "Settled then."

"Isn't it a little unethical, and by a little, I mean a lot?" Pax asked, taking his glass that looked entirely too small in his large greenish hands.

If Arden was taken aback, he was an expert at hiding it. He momentarily stared at Pax, considering his question. "Consider it...a transfer of position. I sorted the paperwork with SorcerySure." Arden smiled, sitting forward. "You are here and that is what we are focusing on." He looked to Brent and gave a quick wink.

Brent gulped his water and accidentally spat. He attempted to catch it with the cup but missed, the water landed on the table in a puddle.

Arden pulled out a handful of tissues, then reached over and dabbed at the small mess. "Did you hit your head when you passed out?" Arden joked.

Brent leaned forward and tried to assist, but only made it worse. With a little back and forth, Brent relented, letting Arden finish. Arden rested his hand on his shoulder again and Brent made a beeline to his hand with his eyes. What was with this man wanting to touch him?

"You sure you're, okay?" Brent looked up, tracing Arden's hands all the way up his arms to his round shoulders, then his perfectly manicured beard and finally landing on his blue eyes. A similar set of eyes that had once melted him. But these did not have the same light in them as Elwin's did.

Swallowing hard, he attempted to clear his throat "Ah...uh...yes," Brent said in a jumble of words, he felt a boiling warmth in the face and hoped it wasn't showing. "Can we please continue?"

Arden smiled back at Brent and gave his shoulder a gentle squeeze.

"Alright." Arden released Brent's shoulder, and it felt like his heart was about to pound through his chest. "Your first quest is a doozy but perhaps we can narrow down the facts."

"On the whereabouts of Marquis Beaumont?" Paxton cut in, drawing Brent and Arden's attention back to him. Pax sat there with an accusatory smirk as he looked between a flustered Brent and Arden, who was very obviously flirting with his new employee.

"His apartment has been abandoned for weeks now; we were first notified by Suncrest Health Centre of his disappearance." Arden clicked at his keyboard and projected a screen on the desk in front of them showing the map of the city. "His wife is in their care for treatment. The Clerics expected for him to show up, but never did." Arden allowed paise for questions, but none came.

Brent and Pax were not used to this kind of casualness from a boss.

"We are here." Arden proceeded, turning his attention back to the image. He pointed and made a circular motion with his index finger to the general location of Sanctum. "His apartment is in downtown Spellford, ironically one of the few buildings that was not attacked by the Behemoth, suspicious, right?"

"Why is this all-important, Sir?" Brent sat forward and spoke clearly, his nerves finally dissipating.

"Glad you asked." He gave a stern look. "The day the Behemoth attacked was also the anniversary of their marriage."

Brent didn't respond, he didn't see the connection.

"Wait, a second." Paxton spoke up and both Brent and Arden turned to him. "Isn't this a strategic department? Why are we doing a manhunt for a missing person?"

"Well," Arden made finger quotes, "Your 'official' job is to manage strategy and policies here at Mage's Union. Your unofficial job is more of an investigative function, operating in secret." Brent and Pax sat in silent acceptance.

Arden smiled and swiped the map away. "We will continue with this later. Let me show you to your desks."

Brent followed Arden and Pax out of his office and towards two of the desks in the open space and then Arden wandered off allowing them some solace from prying eyes.

It was a few moments, and they did not see him return yet, so Brent took his chance to talk to Pax about what happened.

"Man, could he flirt with me anymore?"

"Him?" Pax exclaimed in a whisper. "That whole fainting schtick, mate?" Pax asked, simulating the way Brent fainted, flopping backwards into Brent's arms. "Pretty sure he was putty in your hands after that," he said, looking up at him.

"I genuinely fainted, you dick" Brent pushed Pax off of him and sat back in his seat and adjusted the items on his desk "He looked a bit like..." Brent couldn't bring himself to say the name.

"Elwin?" Pax said after a long enough pause. "I thought so too, but Elwin was one of the Alasïr, they don't age the same as we do. This man has greys in his hair."

"True, their names are so close it is very odd, but god he is hot!" Brent laughed and Pax joined in.

"Well, it is official. You have a type, the unobtainable god-like men" Pax couldn't contain his laughter and let it out loud, and Brent smile watching his friend enjoying himself.

"You bitch" and he stopped, eyes widened as he noticed that Arden had walked behind them.

"Thank you for the compliments," Arden said with another stern look. Pax froze on the spot. The two friends gulped hard and looked back at their new boss.

"Now if the two of you are done messing around, let's go over what is required in your roles. I find the best way is to get into the thick of it, but first, shall I show you around Sanctum?" Arden turned swiftly and headed towards the elevator. Pax and Brent followed close by. It was their first day and it had been going terribly. Brent felt entirely responsible.

As they stood, Brent took in their office. Was it him, or was it severely under resourced for a team that is an investigative arm?

***

The two men ventured through the network of corridors of Sanctum, closely tailing Arden, who hurried along as he led Brent and Pax. The walls were sleek and clean of any markings. In fact, the interiors would be cold and sterile by normal standards.

"Here." Arden stopped and turned on the spot. Pax, not paying attention, bumped into Brent, pushing him forward. Brent held up his hands in front of him and managed to stop before he bashed into Arden. Arden looked at them and shook his head.

Arden gestured, opening a door into a vast chamber with high vaulted ceilings. "This is the Hall of Chronomancy, where the Union studies time-related magic and temporal artifacts."

A wondrous display awaited Brent and Pax as they poked their heads through the open doors. Inside the Hall, orbs of light danced around a central platform, emanating a soft glow that illuminated the intricate diagrams on the walls. Floating hourglasses and suspended clocks, each marking different eras, adorned the room. A singular Mage stood at the platform and smiled at them.

Arden hurried them on and waved at the Chrono-Mage inside. They passed through another set of doors, leading into a room adorned with glowing symbols and pulsating runes. "This is the Archives," Arden explained. "It houses ancient scripts, grimoires, and runestones collected over centuries. Only authorised Mages may access these powerful artifacts."

"So obviously not us?" Pax it was more a statement than a question that Arden didn't bother to remark on.

"No. Pax," Brent sighed. "I don't think this is what we will be doing."

They continued the tour, wandering through a series of grand halls and laboratories showcasing various magical disciplines. Brent, impressed with some of the App-Magic developments shown to them, wanted to stay and observe more, but Arden rushed them on. As they went down one last corridor, Arden paused before a door bearing the inscription: *DMW*.

"This is a specialised facility for Mages dealing with psychological challenges or emotional distress," Arden informed them. "They offer a unique form of therapy tailored to address magical afflictions, trauma from anomalies, or any mental strain caused by extensive spellcasting."

"Do they offer other normal sessions?" Brent asked, intrigued by what a magical mind therapist could do.

"If you would like I could set up an appointment with Dr. Ashton Frost for you, you can discuss anything you require with him. We are very open about the need for good mental health and wellbeing. I would not want to put you or any of my employees in a situation where they feel they aren't okay to work."

"No, I am fine, was just curious, that's all," Brent responded.

"Curiosity often leads us to understanding." A voice came from inside the magical mind therapy office and out stepped a man dressed in a shimmering blue and green cloak. His voice was soothing and gentle but also firm and masculine. "Ah! Callahan, I see your new recruits have joined you. Are they as fascinating as Steiner says?" He leaned against the door frame and crossed his arms. His forearms bulged in his tight sleeves. Brent looked at him and wagered if he flexed hard enough, he could rip his tight clothing.

This man was on a first name basis with the Arch Mage, but instantly used Arden's last name as opposed to his first. Brent sensed the power difference between the two and knew not to step out of line with this man. "Hello, I'm—"

"Brent Abernathy, yes, I know who you are. All of Spellford does, the champion who saved us from the Behemoth." The man chuckled.

Brent felt the strength in the man's hands when he grasped Brent's hand in both of his. The man looked to Brent with a warm, comforting smile, showing the soft creases around his eyes. Brent gathered he was only a few years older than himself.

"Very fine use of time magic reverse engineering." A striking figure, his presence was very commanding. His well-groomed beard caught the light when he flung his slightly greying, tousled hair away from his face. Brent wondered if every man in this place was attractive, which he wouldn't be too upset over. However, it would cause much distraction from him focusing on the job.

"And Paxton! Who can forget the beefy Half-Orc who was behind it all? If it weren't for your piece of leftover burger, neither of you would be the heroes you are today."

"Not heroes, just two citizens doing the right thing." Brent could not tell if he was being facetious, but Pax lapped up the attention.

The man smiled and let go of Pax's hand. "Right, of course. I am Dr. Ashton Frost, welcome to Sanctum's Department for Magical Wellbeing. Would you care to take a visit?" He gestured to the open door. Brent ducked a tad and looked inside. The room gave an instant sense of calm serenity. With a soft glowing ambience and a gentle luminescence, he knew it would be a place of tranquillity, but also safety.

"No, Frost, we're on an orientation tour of Sanctum," Arden pipped up and Brent could see from the look on Dr. Frost's face he was not pleased. "Your department is, however, crucial in the support of all our staff. Thank you."

Dr. Frost inclined his head gracefully. "Indeed. Magic can leave deep imprints on the mind, and understanding these effects is of utmost importance. If you ever need guidance or help to navigate this, my door is open." He waved them goodbye and re-entered his office. Brent lingered as he watched Frost depart. Frost turned and winked. It gave Brent a little jolt. He sprung back, then rushed forward to catch up to Arden and Pax.

The three men departed down the corridor, and Brent looked back once more. Ashton still stood in the hall. There was something about him Brent couldn't quite place, but he shook his head and continued with the tour. Ashton seemed familiar, but Brent was certain they had never met.

Not long after Arden led them to the food court within Sanctum and shouted them all a drink. Brent preferred his coffee. Pax opted for another can of Pep-Up Elixir, while Arden also had a coffee. Now seated, and not distracted with work, Brent inspected Arden closer. There was an uncanny resemblance to Elwin minus the hair colour and human shaped ears. But Elwin could not grow a beard and would always drink water regardless of what was offered.

"Men!" Arden said suddenly.

It caught Pax by surprise and caused him to choke on a sip of his drink.

"This mission is very important; Marquis is a well-respected Mage, and I believe you two are the best chance we have of finding him."

"When do we start the investigation for this mission?" Brent asked, not thrilled to be a desk guy again he was keen to get to work.

"Not today, goodness it is your first day. We have to get your passes sorted, fill out forms, you know all the usual orientation bull-crap." Arden took a sip and gulped after he glanced at his RuneWatch. "Speaking of, we are late. Come on."

The three of them pressed on and Brent wondered what else the day would bring. He hoped for something a little more exciting than just admin work. Time flew past throughout the day and to Brent's demise, he had indeed spent the day doing admin work.

"Okay, Gentleman, now that you are both settled in, before you go home for the day, I would like to take a day one photo," Arden said, sticking his head out of the office.

This man was far from the greatest boss. Everything about the day was chaotic, but Brent appreciated Arden's willingness to relate to them on a more casual level.

CHAPTER EIGHT
APHONIC MAGIC

Victoria sat quietly in her ethics class taught by Professor O'Sullivan, the no-nonsense professor that had scolded her in front of most of the student body for using unsanctioned magic on school grounds. The tall, grey-haired man entered the room and welcomed his class with a stern tone.

"Take out your notebooks. Today we will discuss the ethical considerations of using magic in a medical setting." His presence zapped the energy out of the room. It was the dullest class of them all, but Victoria needed this class for her future prospects.

Victoria sat forward and listened. However, her anger with Lirien and Luminia for not warning her made it difficult to focus. She wanted to relish in the uniqueness of her abilities of being Aphonic but had been deprived of that.

O'Sullivan began the lecture, explaining various ethical issues that arose when using magic to heal, including issues of consent, patient autonomy, and the potential for abuse. As the class dragged on, half the students appeared asleep, but Victoria remained alert hoping it would keep her out of any further trouble.

When the lesson ended, everyone finished their notes and departed the classroom. Professor O'Sullivan pulled Victoria aside. Held back yet again, Victoria tried to stifle her groan.

"Victoria, I need to talk to you about your use of magic in the courtyards."

Victoria remained stoic and looked him dead in the eyes. She felt a defiance build in her and refused to feel guilty for something that was natural. "I didn't intend to break any rules, Professor."

"I did not know you were Aphonic. Why is this the first time I am witnessing this?" he asked.

She took a moment to let what he said sink in. "Uh yeah, for magic, I cannot wrap my tongue around incantations, and using a phone always felt stupid to me. But when I think of something, I can perform it."

"It is a very rare gift to have at your age, Victoria. I haven't met many like you. Does it run in the family?"

"I'm adopted," Victoria said with pride. "So even if it was, I wouldn't have inherited it from my father."

"Ah! Yes, well...Sorry I didn't know you were adopted, you look so like your father" O'Sullivan shifted on the spot, clearly awkward.

Victoria let out her own awkward chuckle and smiled, hoping it would comfort her professor. "Professor Aurora noticed it earlier, which is why I showed it to Lirien and Luminia. They didn't believe me because I faked using my phone in the mock battle during class."

"Oh, I see, so you even taught yourself to pretend to use magic?" he asked. "You are an enigma child."

"I wanted to be like everyone else," she said, her cheeks flushing pink.

O'Sullivan continued to listen attentively and offer his support, suggesting strategies on how to cope with feeling different from the other students. He encouraged Victoria to be patient with herself.

"There was a time where being Aphonic was more commonplace in our student body, but with the wave of technological advances the old ways of magic are being lost faster every year." He smiled, and Victoria finally saw the kinder side of her professor. "Do not hide who you are. You are special and that ought to be celebrated."

"Thank you, Professor. I truly thought I would get a detention or something."

"Oh, do not get me wrong, your actions did warrant one, but you explained yourself sufficiently to me, I will talk your home group professor later and discuss with her what we talked about here." He smiled again. "Oh, and I almost forgot." He leaned over his desk and grabbed a note. Victoria smiled and took it in her hand. "Professor Beaumont wishes to see you before you leave for the day."

***

Victoria approached the hallway toward Nia's office, she made a sharp turn right and bumped into another student holding a box of loose paper.

On impact the other student fell over backwards, the papers fluttered through the air to the ground. Victoria apologised profusely and, in a rush, crouched down to help.

"It's okay." The student waved it off with a smile, her auburn hair falling beside her face, and hurriedly picked up the remainder of paper. A gust of wind caught one, Victoria's eyes darted to see if anyone else was watching before she used a summoning incantation. The paper flew back to her with impressive speed. Victoria quickly grabbed it and placed it in the box.

"Wow! That's impressive," the girl commented on Victoria's magic. "I'm Emily Coleman, by the way, Professor Nia's research assistant."

Victoria couldn't help but notice how kind and genuine Emily's smile was, not to mention cute. Victoria felt the heat rise in her face.

"I've seen you about. I always thought you had amazing dress sense!"

Victoria felt a flutter in her chest at the compliment.

As they stooped to pick up the box, their hands brushed against each other. Victoria felt a jolt of electricity shoot up her arm and quickly pulled her hand away, hoping Emily hadn't noticed.

"Are you okay?" Victoria asked, their eyes met for the first time. "I hope you didn't hit your head." Victoria's heart pounded in her chest, and she suddenly realised how dry her mouth was.

"Yeah, I'm fine," Emily shuffled her hand back and took the box. "Thanks for helping."

Victoria couldn't help but notice how pretty Emily was, with hazel eyes, an adorable, freckled nose and full lips. She felt another warmth form in her cheeks and hoped it wasn't noticeable.

"I'm Victoria Abernathy, by the way." Victoria smiled. She held out her hand. "I can help you carry that."

"It's alright, I got it."

"Where are you headed?" Victoria asked.

"I'm delivering these to Professor Nia." Emily pointed to the door at the end of the hallway. "Are you in your final year?"

"Yeah, uh no, second to final," Victoria said, falling into step beside Emily. "I study the basics, not picked a focus yet, but Nia's classes are my favourite."

"Isn't she the best?" Emily smiled wide. "It is a shame she doesn't teach final year; I'm doing my final thesis on Arcanthus' Legacy."

"One of my favourite topics!" Victoria returned her smile, her heart filled with joy at the prospect of someone else knowing her favourite subject.

Victoria felt a sense of comfort and ease chatting with Emily as they walked to Nia's office. She couldn't help but feel a flutter of excitement in her chest. Victoria inspected Emily from her side peripherals and took everything in.

Emily's long auburn hair pulled back into a messy bun, a few stray strands escaped and framed her face. Her hazel eyes, shimmering with warmth and curiosity, drew you in. A gentle warmth spread across her face as her inviting lips formed a sincere smile. She wore a comfy sweater and jeans, hugging her shapely figure, making her look casual, yet stylish at the same time.

Professor Nia stuck her head out when she heard the girls approach her office.

"Ah, Emily, I wondered where you got to. Oh, and Victoria, you are here too, excellent. Both of you come in."

The two entered the office behind Nia. It was neat and organised; a large wooden desk dominated the space. Nia took a seat behind her desk and resumed writing notes.

"The box can go over there." She pointed to an empty desk, not looking up. "And then you can go, Emily. I won't be needing your services this afternoon."

"Thank you, Professor," Emily placed the box down. Before she left, she gripped Victoria's arm and winked. "See you around?"

Victoria nodded and watched Emily glide out of the office, her perfume trailed behind her, filling Victoria's nostrils and captivating her instantly.

"I see you have met my research assistant; she is attempting to get extra credit on her Arcanthus Thesis, since I don't teach the final cohorts, so this is the next best thing." She paused what she was doing and turned. "Now, how can I help you, Victoria?"

"Umm, I have this note you wanted to see me." Victoria dug out the piece of paper and showed Nia.

"Oh right! Sorry," she rose to her feet. "It has been a hectic day. I have word from a...Cyrus at Mage's Union that your father is—"

"Here, right on time!" Brent's voice came from behind as the door swung open. Victoria's eyes lit up. He was never on time. Maybe this new job would be a good thing. "Front office said you would be here." He smiled at Nia and then Victoria, who stood up and swung her bag over her shoulder.

"You have one bright daughter, Mr Abernathy." Professor Nia looked between them. "I was wondering, would now be a good time?" She raised her eyebrows and then looked at Victoria.

"Oh, I will go wait in the car," Victoria said, holding out her hands for the keys.

"Pax is waiting for you." Brent smiled and waited until she left the room before he returned to look at Nia. "What is it?" he asked concerned, his tone shifting immediately. "What has she done?"

"Professor O'Sullivan told me Victoria used magic today."

"So?" Brent didn't understand what was wrong with the use of magic in a magic academy. "This is a magic school, isn't it?"

"Yes, it is." She gave a single chuckle, but didn't shift her composure. "Students may not perform magic on the school grounds, but Professor O'Sullivan informed me it was not just App-Magic she was using, rather something else entirely."

"Is my daughter in some kind of trouble?" Brent tried to gauge what she was getting at.

"Of course not, it is that she used her own magic, something uncommon for her generation."

Brent couldn't help but feel a mix of pride and concern. Victoria's magical prowess was not a surprise, but that she displayed abilities beyond the ordinary for her age raised questions.

"Is she in trouble?" Brent repeated. His tone was more concerned than confrontational this time.

"It's not about trouble, Mr. Abernathy," Professor Nia explained, her voice adopted a more reassuring tone. "It's about understanding her potential as an Aphonic Mage. Victoria has exhibited talents that go beyond what we typically see at her age. We want to ensure she gets the proper guidance and support."

Brent's expression softened. He understood the importance of guidance, especially considering the power his daughter might possess. "I've always encouraged her to explore her abilities, but I didn't realise she was Aphonic as well."

Professor Nia nodded. "Victoria is exceptional, but sometimes that comes with its own set of challenges. We want to make sure she's equipped to handle them."

"I appreciate your concern," Brent said with gratitude. "I'll speak with her about it. Is there anything specific you suggest?"

"Encouragement and mentorship," Professor Nia replied. "Perhaps guiding her towards a better understanding of her abilities. It might also be beneficial for her to have someone she trusts, a mentor perhaps?"

Brent nodded thoughtfully. "I'll talk to her. Thank you for letting me know." Brent made to turn but got stopped by Nia, who rushed towards him.

"I offer one-on-one tutoring. My father Marquis Beaumont was once a great mentor to you, if I remember correctly?"

"That is correct. Hells, I can't believe you remember. You were so young then."

"My father always spoke highly of the gifted students he taught. I feel it is my duty to repay the favour forward with my own. Think it over and I will be in touch." She smiled and it was clear the conversation was over. She sat back in her seat and looked up at Brent when he hadn't made a move to leave.

"Is there something else, Mr Abernathy?"

"How is your father?" He hoped to gleam some information on his whereabouts.

"I have not heard from him since he departed to Suncrest last lunar," she responded in a dismissive tone. It was just as Arden said. "I already informed the Union, so if you want any more information, I suggest you ask them. Certainly, one of their own is privier to this information than I?" she raised an eyebrow and smiled. She paused only briefly, then returned to marking papers.

As he left the room, Brent's mind raced. He knew the open conversation with Victoria about her magical abilities had to take place soon, but the confirmation of Marquis' potential whereabouts had him excited. He quickly jotted down what he learned and flicked a message to Arden about them later.

> Mr Callahan, this is what I discovered… As suspected. Nia has no idea where Marquis is….

As he entered the carriage, Pax was regaling Victoria about their day at the Mage's Union. Brent barely got into the driver's seat before Victoria leaned forward, gripped the headrest and talked in his ear. Brent smiled as she used to do this a lot as a young child.

"What did Professor Beaumont have to say?" Victoria didn't even wait for the door to shut.

Brent turned his head toward Victoria, meeting her inquisitive gaze through the rearview mirror. He could see a mixture of curiosity and anticipation in her eyes.

"Apparently, Professor O'Sullivan noticed something unusual about your magical activity today," Brent said, keeping his tone casual, yet intrigued.

Victoria's eyes widened with curiosity, and she shifted in her seat. "Oh? What did Nia say?"

"She mentioned you were using more than App-Magic," Brent replied, gauging her reaction.

Victoria blinked, a puzzled expression momentarily clouding her features. "Really? I mean, yeah, I used some spells, but nothing beyond what we've learned."

Brent listened intently, nodding to encourage her to continue.

"I guess I was just experimenting a little," Victoria explained, her voice tinged with excitement. "It's nothing major, Dad. A simple levitation spell."

Brent's smile widened at her enthusiasm. "I'm proud of you for exploring, Tori. But they seemed a bit concerned. They think there's something unique about your magic."

Victoria leaned back, a mix of surprise and curiosity painted across her face. "They said that?"

"Yeah," Brent affirmed. "They think you might have some extraordinary abilities."

Victoria's expression transformed into a mix of amazement and uncertainty. "Like what?"

"I'm not sure," Brent reassured her. "But it seems like you're quite gifted. Maybe it's time we explore this a bit more?"

Victoria's eyes lit up, excitement dancing within them. "Okay."

As they drove back home, excited conversation filled the car over Victoria being offered mentoring by a Beaumont, just like Brent had when he was younger. Brent glanced back into the rearview mirror and smiled as Victoria shuffled back in her seat, grinning ear to ear.

The rest of the evening past rather uneventful. They all had dinner and regaled about their days. Brent sat in silence while Pax was telling Victoria all about the Mage's Union.

"They even have a Chronos in there!" Pax exclaimed, mentioning how Sanctum was like its own small city.

"That's nuts! You both seemed to have had a good day," Victoria replied as she stood up to take the dishes.

Brent's phone vibrated, and he pulled it out. It was a reply message from Arden.

> Thanks, Abernathy. This solidifies the suspected whereabouts of our target. Discuss more tomorrow.

Brent joined Victoria and stashed his phone in his pocket with a smile.

"What's that face?" she asked.

"What face?" He tried to hide the biggest grin but the more he fought it, the more it showed.

"That one!" Victoria flicked her hand and soap inadvertently sprayed Brent in his face. Victoria gulped and then laughed as Brent stood still with his eyes closed in shock.

"Wouldn't be the first time he has taken something to the face," Pax quipped, bringing his own dishes over.

"Ew, Pax!" Victoria exclaimed. "I do not want to know about my dad's sex life!" She handed Brent a dish towel, and he wiped his face clean.

"Believe me, my darling, there isn't much of that living with you two," he said, and they all laughed. Brent wasn't sure if it was at him or his joke, but he was thankful for the two of them and proud of how far they had all come as a unit. "If you must know the message was from my boss, and I was right about something so that face was one of pride."

"Looked like a face of infatuation to me," Pax said, placing his dishes in the sink. "I'm going to go shower." He walked off, leaving the two alone to finish up.

"So, what is your new boss like?"

"Here, we stupidly took a group photo for day one." Brent pulled out as his phone and swiped it open to the photo. He held it in front of Victoria's face while she washed dishes.

Instantly, she let out a laugh. "Pax pulling that face, as usual!"

"I thought I looked distinguished!" Pax called from the hallway as he made his way to the shower.

"In your dreams," Brent muttered. "So, yeah, this is my new team. Myself, Pax and..."

Victoria interrupted by grabbing the phone.

Brent snatched it back. "Hey what did I say about water and Rune-Phones!"

"Oh, it's the iRune XVI it will be fine," Victoria said, dismissing her father's concerns, her hands dripping with soap. "I know this man. He came to our school to discuss the Behemoth attack."

Brent dried the phone off with a towel. "Arden Callahan, Director of the Magical Strategic Department."

"Strategic Magic, but what you told me, it is investigations?" Victoria asked.

"Yeah, I don't know," he admitted and shrugged. "Adult jobs are never as they advertise, but I am discovering it as I go along."

"You can still come to the excursion, right?" she asked with concern in her voice.

"Of course. When is it?"

"I told you already, end of the lunar." Victoria finished the dishes and placed them to dry on the rack. Though Brent fitted the kitchen with a self-cleaning washing cauldron he wanted Victoria to know how to do things by hand should she move out on her own one day.

"The permission slip is still on the fridge." she called out heading to her room "Unsigned!" she sang, followed by a slight slamming of her door.

"Turn the handle." Brent flinched at the slammed door. He looked at the fridge and made a mental note to sign the slip.

CHAPTER NINE
THAUMATURGIC PANOPTICON

Flintday came around faster than they all would like. While Victoria adjusted to after-school tutoring with Professor Nia, Pax and Brent had already got themselves accustomed to commuting to and from work every day. Pax remained in the office while Brent and Arden headed to the Cafe within Sanctum grounds, something that had become habitual.

"I've got it," Brent said to Arden, thrusting his Rune-Phone in front of him to pay. Arden patted him on the back and went to get a seat.

"Ah! Abernathy! What will you have today?" the barista called out to him as he made the coffees. The Café, named Enchanters' Goblet, was a cozy little nook in Sanctum. Brent felt he could stay here all day if he wished. Yellow and orange walls with brown stripes added to the warm and cozy environment. A gentle guitar song played in the background as Brent approached the counter.

"Hey Nimbs, Two *Wizards Wakeups'* please. Extra strength," Brent said, already on a nickname basis with the barista. He waved his Rune-Phone to pay for the drinks. Nimbs full name was Nimbus Starblend, she came from an extensive line of magical baristas.

"Busy day ahead?" Nimbs asked while getting stuck into the orders. Brent watched as she infused citrus and herbal notes into the coffee. This had quickly become a favourite of Brent's.

"Sadly so." Brent rolled his eyes then smiled gently at Nimbs.

"Well, the extra shots are on the house." Nimbs smiled back, taking out a cup tray and readying the drinks.

It was not long before Brent and Arden had walked back. Brent had quickly learned his way around Sanctum on these little walks with Arden, and they, too, had become increasingly acquainted.

"How is Victoria?" Arden asked. Something he always asked in the morning and then never brought up again. Brent was wary to divulge too much but also knew it would be pointless to hide anything now that he was in the Mage's Union. The scrutinising eyes would keep an even closer watch on him.

"She is good, started her tutoring yesterday and has another session today," he said, trying to gulp the mouthful of coffee before he spoke.

"Tutoring? I thought you said she was doing well in school?"

"She is," Brent said proudly "She is actually quite gifted, Aphonic sort of like myself, but unlike me can generate multiple forms of magic based on what her mind wants, whereas I can only really use the ol' fireball." Brent imitated casting a fireball and a little puff of crackling fire accidentally fell to the table. Arden quickly snuffed it out with clapped hands.

"No magic in the halls," a passerby Mage said to Brent sternly, as Brent apologised and shook his hand.

"What is this, high school?" he asked Arden. They both giggled, and Arden bumped his shoulder into Brent's, sending a jolt through his heart.

"So, they just want to build on her skills?" Arden prodded and then took a sip of his coffee.

"Basically, they feel she is highly gifted and want to nurture it."

"That's good to hear," he said, slightly dismissive. Brent raised an eyebrow at him, but it went unnoticed.

They continued forward until they made it to their office, where Arden quickly rushed off into his own and shut the door behind him.

"So much for an open-door policy, huh?" Brent motioned his head towards Arden's door and Pax just shrugged as he pulled out his seat and sat down next to Pax.

"Finally!" Pax said, standing up abruptly. "I didn't want the alerts to go off with no one here." He turned to make a sprinting beeline toward the bathroom.

"You know we get the notifications on the app, right?" Brent shouted after him, but Pax did not hear him. Brent shook his head and set his coffee down. Waving his hand across his lexicon, he logged in and checked his emails.

There was nothing new. Just an article about cursed graffiti pulling people into a wormhole. The victims were now in the Cleric wards still being treated for Realm Hopping Pox. A violent disease, if not treated within the first week that could spread to the entire body and cause limbs to disappear.

Brent remembered seeing a glimmer at the Wonder Theatre where a man's arm got lost through a wormhole and came back to kill him. He shuddered at the thought as he dragged the email to the trash. He picked up his cup and took another sip of his coffee, the ginger notes hitting the back of his throat.

He opened the report he was working on last evening and gave it a quick read through. Arden had made some changes, which were superfluous, but overall, it was satisfactory. He accepted the changes, trusting that Arden knew what he was talking about, and sent the report off. As he pulled his coffee back in for another rejuvenating sip, Pax came rushing back.

"I finished the final edit of our report of the monitoring task we performed yesterday and sent it through," Brent said to him.

"Perfect," Pax said with a relieved sigh and sat in his chair, which gave a strained squeak from his large frame settling in. "Nothing new?" He stretched his arms behind his head and looked at Brent, his amber eyes gleaming through his glasses.

"Not today," Brent replied.

Pax sat forward and whispered, "I meant between you and Arden." He pointed his head sideways at Arden's office.

Brent took another sip, then spoke, "Yeah, no. Um nothing of note, I wish he would—"

The alarm sounded and two purple lights flashed, interrupting Brent.

Brent and Pax turned their heads, unsure what it meant. The main screen lit up, spanning from floor to ceiling. Brent and Pax stood up and watched as runes ran across the screen.

Arden's door swung open with a bag into the wall. "About fucking time!" he exclaimed as he nearly flew out of the room with an excitement. Brent had not yet seen this face; it made his heart flutter. He wondered what face Arden made in bed.

"This is what we have been waiting for boys, come on over." Arden gave a gigantic wave of his arm, his grin positively beaming and infectious as he ushered Brent and Pax towards the giant screen that dominated the west wall of their office.

Brent, Pax, and Arden stood side by side with Arden in the middle. He spoke with excitement in his voice. "This is the Thaumaturgic Panopticon, or Opticon, for short. It allows us to navigate the entirety of Spellford from this office and pick up any magic anomalies. It also taps into the Cam-Mera system and gives us live feedback."

In a vast radiant display, akin to an electronic textile woven fabric with luminescent threads, it was a Magic-Tech marvel. Towering above them, it pulsated, capturing the essence of the city's layout in a magical fluctuation.

"Ah, so this is how the Mage's Union tracks down its criminals," Pax was clearly impressed. Arden nodded, pressed a few buttons and waited for the screen to react.

"And before you ask, I would have shown you earlier, but I find a more hands on approach works wonders for your information retention with this job," Arden commented to them both with his back turned, attention focused on the screen.

Brent shot Pax a raised eyebrow, and he just shrugged.

Multiple lights on the screens flashed read and alert icons displayed in one location east from Sanctum.

"It looks like reports are coming in fast," Arden commented as lights flickered erratically across the Opticon in one location.

Sigils lit up on the eastern side of Spellford, responding to magical frequencies fluctuating. "The Augmenti Leyline around the city allows for intricate pinpointing." Arden pointed at the thicker lines showing up and stroked a few more keys. Then, with a twist of his wrist held his forefinger and thumb out. The screen zoomed in to a specific street and Arden stepped back.

Brent inspected keenly at the notifications flowing in. "That is no natural surge," he remarked, pointing at the anomaly that formed and continued to grow. "Is it an attack?"

"Hard to say from here," Arden replied in a serious tone. "But it is definitely something we need to investigate." Arden swished around on the spot and Brent made to follow. "Grimtusk."

Pax stopped on the spot

"I will ask that you remain behind and communicate from here, I will send someone to come and assist with utilising the Opticon," Brent added.

"Already here, sir!" Cyrus bellowed from the hall and glided toward where Paxton stood. "Good luck out there." Cyrus patted Brent on the shoulder.

Brent felt bad for leaving Pax behind but if there was a true magical disturbance, Pax did not possess the magical capabilities that Brent or Arden did, and App-Magic would not suffice in this instance.

"I'll see you soon Pax," Brent said as he brushed past him, and Pax gave a dismissive grunt that let Brent know he was upset, but it would have to be dealt with later.

***

Arden and Brent emerged onto the bustling streets of Spellford. It was mid-morning, and people were either at work or out tending to their daily lives. As they traversed the city's winding paths, the magical disturbance became increasingly clear. In the distance, only a few blocks away, the sky crackled with energy as sporadic flickers of uncontrolled magical surges shot into the air. Arden maintained his focus while Brent felt his heart rate increase. The thrill of the unknown and the potential to save the day once again, he couldnt help but feel the addictiveness flow through him.

They both traced the disturbance to a bustling district and paused as they saw crowds gathered around across from a warehouse that had its roof blown off. Whispers of concern spread amongst the citizens, and Arden sprang into action.

"Okay, everyone, the Mage's Union will handle this. Please stay back while we investigate what has happened."

Arden drew a long line across the street and conjured a vast golden barrier between the civilians and the sight of the anomaly. Arden nodded to Brent, who guided civilians through the barrier, and then both turned toward the warehouse.

A brilliant burst of energy blasted through the roof again and purple sparks crackled. "Okay, let's do this," Arden said firmly.

Brent followed behind Arden, who had slightly jogged toward the warehouse doors. As he touched the door, the disturbance from within pulsated once again and grew stronger. The air charged with a blast of invisible fluctuation, almost knocking them both off their feet.

"Keep your wits about you, Abernathy," Arden warned.

Brent nodded and after a few seconds, they slid open the warehouse doors. Sending shivers down their spines, a thick mist obscured their vision, making it challenging to discern the source of the disturbance. "Guess we are going in?"

"Correct!" Arden shouted with an excited glint in his eyes and stepped forward first. Holding up a single finger, he conjured a flaming ball that followed him, illuminating his surroundings.

Whispers of arcane energy danced around them as they entered the fog. The only light besides Arden's, filtered through the hole in the ceiling. The sound became distorted by the ambiance carrying with it faint echoes of foreign incantations and mystical chants. Brent treaded carefully behind Arden, who waded his way through the thick fog.

They came to the centre of the warehouse and could see strange glyphs etched into the ground pulsating in tandem with one another as the magical energy around it fluctuated from a rift on the ground. A lilac hue flashed multiple times as the rift pulsated, growing larger with each flash.

"Here it is," Arden said, his eyes scanned the area, observing the glyphs surrounding the rift.

Brent walked up beside him with caution as he noticed that arcane relics of an unknown origin lay strewn about. They also held the same unnerving purple glow. He could not make out what their purpose was but could see it was contributing to the swirling disturbance. As he gazed around, the hairs on the back of his neck stood up. Someone or something stood behind them.

Without hesitation, the being launched a magical attack of dark energy at them both, but Arden was too quick for it. Pushing Brent behind him, he conjured the same golden barrier, but this time as a shield, and reflected the beam of dark energy back at the assailant.

"You are too late. The Code Weaver's plan has already begun!" The voice was feminine and young. No older than Victoria would be.

"By order of the Mage's Union, reveal yourself!" Arden called, but his order went unnoticed as the assailant stood there momentarily and then lifted its head slightly. Under the hood, Brent could see a smirk and then the person faded away in a purple flash.

A surge of intense energy blasted outward behind them as the assailant disappeared, almost knocking them off feet once again. The rift crackled and flickered like a candle in the wind, its energy teetered on the brink of chaotic instability.

"What now?" Brent asked, and they exchanged a worried glance, but Arden shook his head.

"Know any protective wards?" he asked, looking down into the hole, now fully forming and spurting out large blasts of purple energy.

"Only one, but I am not sure it is strong enough," Brent admitted, not shifting his gaze.

"Okay, well, let's do this together then." Arden grabbed Brent's wrist and smiled. Brent smiled back. He felt the heat rise in his face and a flutter in his stomach, but he shook it off and shook his head to return to focus. Arden pulled Brent to a spot. "Stand here, I'll go to the other side."

Brent adjusted his foot, so he was comfortable, and waited for Arden to get into his vantage point. The rift grew at an alarming rate and seemed to swallow everything in its path.

"On my count!" Arden exclaimed over the rift and Brent maintained contact with his boss.

"One!"

Brent's heart was racing so fast he felt it would pop through his chest.

"Two!" Arden exclaimed and Brent whispered along with him, looking down into the rift and then back to Arden, who winked at him. His heartbeat even faster as a unique feeling swirled inside of him. One he hadn't felt in a very long time

"Three!"

Brent and Arden both conjured a protective ward, their magic channelled together to slowly form a barrier around the rift, stabilizing the growing anomaly. The clashing energies surged against each other. Sparks flew past their heads into the warehouse walls and around the entire room. Brent could feel the burning in his hands as the conjuring took its toll. He was out of practice for radiance magic, but he was not weak.

Slowly, their efforts took effect as the chaotic energy swirling underneath their wards was quelled. In a last burst of energy, it sent a spark into the ward, which was deflected backwards from which it came. The rift gradually diminished in intensity as the swirling energies from within subsided. The once turbulent magical disturbance faded into a now calm and, most importantly, an inactive hole in the ground.

Arden let out a cheer and ran over to Brent, pulling him close and almost lifting him up. "Abernathy, we did it!" Arden cheered.

Arden let Brent down, realising what he did and returned to his normal composure. "Uhh..." he stammered. "Sorry about that, I got a little carried away." He then turned back and stuck his head over the closing rift.

"It's fine," Brent said, because it was. He imagined Arden to lift him up again and again and drifted to that place of newly formed infatuation. Shaking his head, Brent refocused himself. "You think it's finished?"

"Yup." Arden held his phone over the once active rift and scanned it for signs of activity. "I'm just sending some data back to Sanctum for Pax and Cyrus to analyse." He took a few photos then walked back to Brent. He raised an eyebrow. "Want to commemorate this moment?"

"With another photo?" Brent asked with uncertainty.

"No, with a kiss," he said sarcastically, but Brent wasn't sure if he really meant it. He squinted his eyes and thought, *well if he is offering.*

"Of course I meant with a photo." Arden sounded slightly hurt. "Never mind, moods dead." Another flippant comment that Brent ignored.

Brent needed to maintain his distance between his boss and working relationship and any desires he may or may not have for this man. Brent looked at Arden, who was busy on his phone.

Exhausted but relieved, Brent and Arden stood outside the warehouse, now tranquil and silent. Their collective magic had quelled a raging tempest. However, an ominous sense lingered in the air. On the way back, they both continued the topic, to Brent's relief, about the unknown assailant and who or what were the Code Weavers. He avoided any mention of Arden's proposed kiss.

When they returned to the office, Pax and Cyrus both cheered. Arden and Brent, both exhausted, slumped into chairs and felt nothing but pride at their hard work.

"Callahan, I have sent out a clean-up crew, and we received the data and images. It was crazy as you entered the warehouse, we could not track you on the Opticon, we thought we lost you," Cyrus said then fluttered away after Arden whispered a thank you.

"Thank you all." He then looked at Brent with gleaming gratitude in his eyes. "I expect a preliminary report on my desk before we head out to the next mission this afternoon," Arden said calmly, looking back at him a little too long.

Brent shifted, feeling that same uncomfortable infatuation. One thing was certain, Arden made Brent feel exactly how he once felt about Elwin, and he couldn't help but let those feelings flood his mind. He had only hoped that he could maintain his feelings professionally. But what if Arden came on to him?

***

By the time the afternoon hit, Brent, Pax, and Arden were off to their next assignment. As they departed the elevator and headed to the courtyard, a cool breeze blew across them all. They walked towards the carriage stands and Arden hailed down a driver.

"Oh, I was hoping to ride the Sorcerati again." Pax whined, commenting on the age of the carriage before them.

Arden chortled a laugh and went back to his stern look. "Yeah, no, that would have been too flashy for a quick ride."

"But we—" Pax started, and Brent waved his hand, dismissing him.

Brent clambered inside the aged carriage, first followed by Pax and Arden. Arden signalled to the driver that they were ready to fly off. As the driver snapped the reins, two holographic horses materialised in front of the carriage. Sprinting with a few gallops, they headed towards the cliff edge of Sanctum. Arden and Pax sat perfectly still, but Brent flung upright into his seat. The carriage vibrated against the ground as the horses were on uneven ground. Brent looked out the window and could hear their hooves clopping against the cobblestone path. As they neared the platform's edge, the horses gathered enough speed that they became airborne.

After what felt like mere minutes, the carriage began its descent. As it gently touched down, they landed on a platform attached to a sky-rise apartment. Brent stepped out first, taking in the towering structures from this high up. They were in the citys heart. Wind whipped around, his usually well-kept hair now in a swirling tornado, and Brent adjusted the collar of his arcane cloak, shielding himself against the wind. Brent leaned over cautiously and looked down toward the ground. The city below sprawled out like a patchwork of ants going about their day.

As he waited for the other two to climb out, he looked back towards Sanctum in the afternoon sun and then to his left and could see the academy where Victoria was. Taking in the sights of Spellford, humbled in this moment of how insignificantly small he was, compared to the vastness of the city.

"Wait, I know where we are," Pax announced as he climbed out in his own cloak. "This is Marquis Beaumont's apartment."

"Correct you are, Grimtusk," Arden replied, climbing out himself, dressed in his own cloak. "This is our mission today, to investigate his abode and see if we can find any signs or new information."

"He has been missing over a lunar. Why have the Mage's Union not sent somebody yet?" Brent shouted over the wind. The carriage behind Arden turned its engine off and the horses disappeared.

"Good question. I will explain everything inside." Arden walked forward and opened the doors with a wave of his hand.

Brent watched as Pax vigilantly kept a watchful eye on their surroundings. They entered a foyer that was quite plain. A few large pot plants, an elevator and a door into the corridor. Brent expected a little more for a building of that status.

"Marquis had the penthouse apartment, from this floor up was his entire home. We can access it through that door, but I must inform you first," Arden started, and Brent and Pax stood firm. "In answer to your question, the Union sent two investigators out here last lunar, but they regrettably did not return from assignment."

Brent was stunned that he chose now to tell them as they were about to enter the location where two investigators had gone missing, along with their once cherished professor.

"Why did you wait so long to return?" Pax asked.

"We didn't," Arden said. "I am the last of my team. The previous director had to send two rounds of investigators under pressure by Magnar."

"So, why did you bring us? I have a daughter I can't—" Brent started and walked towards Arden, but Pax pulled him back.

"Relax, please, Abernathy. Every Mage I sent had neither one of our abilities, and what you showed me today, you and I are perfect for this because we don't need to utter incantations or rely on App-Magic."

"But what about Pax? He has no magic capability," Brent replied, the unease in his voice echoed in the empty foyer. The wind continued to howl outside, bashing and brandishing against the windowpanes.

"Precisely. I have been monitoring the energy source here in this building for quite some time, and it matches with the anomaly we closed earlier today."

"You could have said this on the way, you know," Brent said, bringing his heart rate down.

"What, and ruin the chance of seeing you get all worked up?" Arden winked, and Brent wanted to smack the look off his face or kiss him. He hadn't quite decided. "Now if you are both done complaining, shall we?" Arden made a motion with his arms to move inside. They both nodded and Arden walked towards the door.

"Let's keep our guards up," Brent commented, and Arden agreed.

As they entered through the plain door, the apartment exuded an eclectic blend of modern Magi-Tech marvels and cultural richness. The spacious living area featured holographic displays showcasing intricate spell diagrams and schematics that Marquis had won awards for in the past as a Magi-Tech Professor. Vibrant tapestries and artwork reflected his Aravilian heritage west of Arcanum, in the lands of Ilathier. Masks and sculptures of artists from his homeland sprawled neatly, and mixed with an assortment of paintings, traditional, and some more modern. All his possessions mirrored Marquis' dual expertise of innovation in modern magical advancements while keeping his traditions alive.

In the centre, a fireplace adorned with many photographs stood still to time and was now covered in a layer of dust. Brent could make out photos of Marquis with his daughter, Professor Nia. Both beaming wide smiles in the pictures at Nia's graduation and then one of him and another woman who Brent knew was his wife, Niamh. Marquis, a much younger Nia by his side and Niamh were all in this photo together. In her arms, Niamh held a baby. He assumed it was Nascien, Marquis' son. But by the age of the photo, he could not be certain.

"As you can see, no one has touched anything, and there is no sign of the investigators, but also—"

Pax interrupted Arden. "No cleaners either." Pax wiped his finger through a thick layer of dust that had settled on a small altar, showcasing enchanted artifacts and family heirlooms. "But there is a scent to the air. Can you smell it?"

"No?" Brent and Arden said in unison.

"It is definitely here," Pax said, flaring his nostrils and sniffing around like a puppy for a treat. His tusks would move up and down as he tracked the smell. "It is almost...incense like... it's coming from down below." Pax sniffed in multiple directions, moving toward the staircase door and the two men followed.

"Grimtusk, wait, we need to assess the situation," Arden demanded, chasing him down the stairs.

"Once he has his nose set on something, there is nothing stopping him," Brent added, following and taking three to four steps at a time. "You should see him on the weekend markets, beelines directly for the doughnut stands."

As they headed down, the scent flooded Brent's nostrils. There was a sweet, alluring fragrance reminiscent of blooming night flowers. He felt a tranquil sensation from the smell and shook his head. His eyesight began to obscure as if in a haze and he stopped midway through to lean against the wall.

"You feel it too?" Arden asked, slurring his words. He stood against the wall further down the steps, breathing deeply. Brent caught up and waved his hands to conjure a small burst of air around him and Arden's faces, clearing their airways.

"What is that smell? It's so intoxicating." Arden said, regaining some oxygen to his brain.

"It's Nightshade Bloom," Pax called out only a floor below them. "I'd recognise it anywhere." It was a scent commonly used in the old Valtorian war and frowned upon by modern day states. The scent, while benign to most races, did have a significant effect on humans. But those with keen senses, like Orcs, could pick it up and were immune to its more sinister notes. "I studied it in botany classes when I wanted to go into potion making," Pax said, side eyeing Arden.

"Why didn't you?" Arden asked, still trying to regulate his breathing with the air wrap around his face that supplied him with clean air.

"Why didn't I what?" Pax asked back.

"Go into Potion making." Arden stood tall.

"Would you trust an Orc with your liquids?" He turned away and kept going down further into the Nightshade heavy aroma.

"I mean I would, but I don't have a problem with Orcs," Arden replied.

"Yeah, you might not, but a lot of others still do harbour ill toward an Orc. He has had a harder life than someone with a kind heart like his should. Best to be mindful," Brent said sternly and followed behind Pax.

"Would you two come on? The scent is coming from in here," Pax called out slowly, shoving a barricaded door open.

Brent caught up to Pax and poked his head into the room, followed by Arden. A colossal hole yawned wide, reaching down through multiple floors of the building. Its edges were jagged, as if something powerful had erupted from below.

Arden, his expression severe, took a step into the room with caution. The floorboards under him creaked but held strong as he approached the hole.

Pax followed; his nostrils flared as he examined the hole. "Oh, it is strong even for me, thankfully I am immune."

Brent knelt down and took a sample of the dust and dirt and rubbed it between his finger and thumb. Brent connected the dots. "Whatever made this hole has to be connected to the Nightshade Bloom." As he sprinkled the dust, it twinkled in gold flecks.

A rumbling groan came from below. Brent leapt to his feet. The trio exchanged glances. From behind them they heard a crunching of debris in the doorway. As all three turned, a man in a black cloak with his face concealed stood strong. Before they could react, the man raised a staff. Magenta light shone out of the tip and the magic spell cast around both Arden and Brent's faces faded away. Instantly, they began choke on the Nightshade Bloom and fell to the ground, clutching at their chests.

Pax rushed over to help them out of instinct, but he was too slow to act. As Pax ran towards Brent and Arden, the man in the cloak held out his hand and froze him on the spot. Pax struggled and let out a loud groan, struggling against the man's magical binds. With a simple flick of his wrist, Pax flung across the room, flying through debris and a glass door before he landed out on the balcony. Pax rolled across the ground and then fell into a heap on the ground and was immobile.

"You all should not have come here!"

Brent made to shout out to Pax to see if he was alright, but he was choking on the thick poisonous air. The cloaked man approached him and knelt down to inspect Brent. He waved his hands, and the air became clean around them. He turned Brent over to his back and he peered up at the cloaked man's face but could only make out a purple glint.

"I see the Guardian survived after all." A distorted voice spoke, and he ran his hand over Brent's face as if he was analysing him.

The man's voice was heavy and robotic, the same distorted sound followed with every inhale and exhale as if he was wearing a face mask.

Brent's lungs were heavy with the lingering toxin of the Nightshade Bloom, making it difficult for him to breathe, while his vision remained blurred from its potent effects.

"Who are you?" Brent croaked as he coughed.

Brent could not summon the strength to move. The toxin had damaged his ability to react. His eyesight was blurred, his awareness of his surroundings impacted. As he waited for the cloaked man to respond, he heard scurrying from behind him. Wind howled, forcefully pushing the cloaked man in the opposite direction. Arden's face met his as he inspected Brent for signs of life. His damaged hearing strained to catch some of the muffled words.

"Get up...come on!" Arden screamed as he dragged Brent up to his feet. Awkwardly, Arden propped Brent up with his arm flung over his shoulder. He felt Arden madly darting around the room, looking for Pax. Brent weakly pointed to him outside on the balcony. The man in the cloak made to stand up. Arden didn't hesitate, Brent heard a muffled incantation. Glowing barbed bindings formed around the man, rendering him immobile.

Arden dragged Brent out onto the balcony through the shattered glass, that crunched under their feet. The city air hit them in the face and Brent allowed it to fill his lungs. Arden dragged Brent towards Pax's collapsed body and placed him down gently. He pulled out his phone and attempted to call the carriage driver when a bolt of magenta magic flew past their heads, narrowly dodging Arden.

"Hand over the Guardian!" The distorted voice called out. Brent turned his head and could see the cloaked man pulling the barbed bindings from his body. Once he had freed himself, he charged towards them.

Arden ducked down and grabbed both Pax and Brent by the scruff of their collars, and then it felt like he was being sucked through a straw as the surroundings of the apartment building became less and less until it was the size of a pinhole.

Brent wasn't sure if it was the Nightshade Bloom or the swirling blueness, but his stomach churned. He was close to vomiting up his stomach contents when Sanctum came into view.

As they exited the portal, all three landed inside Arden's office. Brent collapsed on his back, his head spinning. Pax was still out cold. He saw Arden rush out of the office and down the corridor. Brent moved to sit up and an overwhelming feeling of saliva rushed into his mouth. He scuttled across the floor, diving headfirst into the pot plant and let out a burst of vomit. It was a few more minutes of vomiting before the feeling subsided. Even as he lay on his back again the room continued to spin.

"They're in here."

Brent heard Arden's voice call out through the office. Two Clerics dressed in white robes fashioned with blue crosses on their lapel walked in. They quickly assessed the two friends and conjured stretchers for Pax and Brent. Brent refused.

"Abernathy, we insist. You need to get treated for Nightshade Bloom poisoning. Either you come willingly, or we force you," the Cleric twirled their hands conjuring restraints.

"What kind of Clerics are these?" Brent asked Arden, who stood beside his stretcher.

"The best in Spellford. Just lay still until we are sure you are fine," Arden replied, forcing him down with all the weight on his shoulder.

"What about you?" Brent asked. "You took in as much of the toxins as I did," Brent asked, but the Cleric wheeled out the stretcher before he could get a response.

"I will tell you once the assessment is done," he called out to Brent, who watched him disappear from view as he and Pax were taken to the medical ward.

As he got wheeled away, Brent pulled out his phone and saw a message from Victoria about her permission slip underneath his cracked screen. He attempted to unlock the phone, but the shattering of the glass made it inoperable. He laid back and felt his phone vibrate again.

> Hey Dad, I am staying at Lumi's tonight.

He spoke the message into the receive and it replied to her.

> Ok, Kiddo, be safe and have a good night.

He sighed a relief knowing she would be safe with Luminia. He laid back and promised to make it up to her as soon as possible.

CHAPTER TEN

CAULDRON

Victoria pulled out her phone and saw no message from her dad about picking her up. It was odd for him not to have told her he would be late or that she would need to get her own way home, but she accepted it. "I guess, can you drive me home again?" she said to Professor Nia once they had finished their latest tutoring session.

"Back-to-back trips home with your favourite teacher." She smiled wide and Victoria laughed in agreement.

"Thank you, Professor."

Nia swung her bag on her shoulder and smiled. "Shall we?"

Victoria leapt to her feet. As they walked out of the office, Victoria felt grateful for Nia and the connection she was building with her professor over the past few days.

Parked outside Victoria's home, Professor Nia gave her a warm smile. Victoria barely spoke along the way home. She didn't want to leave school and come home to an empty house. Now that they were here it sunk in even further that her father's new job was busier than she'd expected.

"Still no word from him?" Nia asked, leaning her arm on the door with the window down.

Victoria turned toward her teacher. "No, but I will be fine. Dad's been on business trips before this job, usually Pax is here, but I know how to take care of myself."

"Okay, well, you have my number and don't be afraid to call me if you need anything," Nia said as Victoria climbed from the vehicle.

"Thanks for today's session. I look forward to our next!" Victoria called out as she swung around, her backpack flinging with her before she skipped to the door.

Victoria went inside and waved one last time as Nia drove off. She was thankful for her professor's help, but didn't want to become accustomed to relying on anyone. She locked the door as she shut it behind here and headed to her room. Greeted with the familiar lavender interior walls and hardwood floor covered with a fluffy, white rug in the centre. She threw her bag onto her unmade, queen-sized bed, undressed and went straight to the shower to wash the day off.

Victoria slipped into her favourite lumpy sweatshirt and looked into the mirror with a weak smile. The sweatshirt had the words "Dragon Queen" embellished with fire behind it and a picture of her favourite kind of dragon–the Emberflare dragon like the one Kiera would ride on *Dragonfire*. Unfortunately, she would need to wait until next week for the latest episode. Her hopes of meeting her idol were slowly crushing within her. Her dad had still not signed the slip, with the field trip being only a week away, she was getting anxious. Everyone else had theirs and tomorrow was the last day she could get it signed and returned.

> Dad, I need you to sign the permission slip as soon as you come home. It's for the field trip in a WEEK!

She typed out a text and set her phone down on her nightstand. A message came through with a fierce vibration. She leapt, hoping that it was from her dad, but it was from some else.

> Hey Victoria! A few of us are heading out tonight to Cauldron to hangout, meet us there?

The message was from Emily. She and Victoria recently exchanged numbers after they'd bumped into one another a few times.

Victoria had never been out in the city at night without her father, let alone hung out with friends after school except at their houses for sleep overs and even those were far and few between as she got older. She was aware of her father's trust issues but considered them unfounded. With no sign of him returning this evening, she figured why not sneak out for a little as long as she returned before curfew.

Victoria sent another message to her dad that she'd be at staying she would stay at Luminia's home working on an assignment.

> Hey Lumi, if anyone asks, I am at yours tonight

> Sure Babes!

The two friends did it often, but usually it was together. The culmination of the latest events in her life, with her father's heroics, her abilities being scrutinised by everyone, and the tutoring after school had all culminated and made her want to do something out of her norm. She felt confined between these four walls and could use a night out. Plus, the prospect of meeting some more mature people and spending more time with Emily made her heart pulsate.

Hey Emily, I'll see you there!

Butterflies filled her belly, that instant rush of excitement. Her night was looking to be not as boring as she initially thought. Before she started to get ready she walked out to the lounge room and turned on the vision orb to catch the last of the evening news playing out.

They were running a news story about the recent attack on a warehouse in the city's east district. As the newscaster presented the story, the screen displayed

"Mysterious Warehouse Attack Shakes Spellford."

"The recent attack on an abandoned set of warehouses in Spellford's East district, which led to chaos and carnage in its wake, has raised security concerns laid out by the Mage's Union. A representative from the MU has commented about the security of Spellford's people. We go live now to Arch Mage Magnar." Victoria raised an eyebrow. He had been showing his face in public much more as of late. Enough for her to notice.

The show switched focus to the Arch Mage, who promised that this was a random event and there was no cause for concern. The screen started to flicker; static took over the screen. Victoria groaned and hit the remote, trying to get it to work but with no luck. Annoyed she walked over to turn the vision orb off when the screen flickered to another image.

A hidden figure with a slender frame appeared amongst the static. Cloaked in a flowing dark robe, a featureless mask hid their face. As they spoke, sound waves materialised over where the person's mouth should be, distorting their voice and hiding their identity. Victoria stood still as she watched on.

"Citizens of Spellford." They lifted their hands and flourished their fingers causing purple magic to crackle with them through the air. "We are the Code Weavers. We stand in opposition to the constraints imposed on magic by the Union. Stifling of its true potential, your fear of its untamed power clouds you and blinds you to the possibilities it holds."

Victoria couldn't move from her spot. Whoever this was, their courage to hijack the airwaves grabbed her attention.

"United in our mission to liberate magic, to unravel the shackles that it's been bound with. No longer the few shall control its intricate threads. It belongs to all. Augmenti's essence exists within us all," the figure paused for a moment. "The tide of change is upon you. We are united. We are liberation. We will rise."

The video stopped, and the screen went black. The newscaster appeared again, issuing an apology for the technical difficulty.

Victoria let out a laugh. "Tide of change, sure thing pal!" She turned off the vision orb, completely apathetic to what she had just seen. She walked to the kitchen, shaking her head at what she had heard.

She ate a quick bite and then got ready as fast as she could. Struggling to figure out what to wear, she settled on black jeans, boots, and a shirt with her favourite band, The Brimstones, displayed on it. She realised she looked her age and found a black leather jacket to wear over the top. Attempting to age herself even more, she applied some eyeliner and dark eyeshadow with a burgundy lip. Smacking her lips in the mirror, she tussled her hair a few times and grabbed her belongings to leave, ensuring she had her keys, phone, and any cash she had saved. She locked the door behind her and ordered herself a Witches Wagon ride into the city.

The driver was a friendly Half-Elf woman who only chatted a few times here and there along the trip. As they winded their way through the streets, Victoria's stomach filled with butterflies. Banked up traffic lined the streets, and Victoria grew impatient out of anticipation. They were only a few streets away from Cauldron, so she asked the driver to pull over and let her out.

"Are you sure, dear? You look a little young. I don't want to leave you just anywhere," she said. That comment annoyed Victoria after going to the effort of applying makeup to look older.

"No, it is fine. I do it all the time!" Victoria dismissed, trying to act cool and mature. She thanked the driver as she pulled over and inadvertently slammed the door of the carriage a little too hard in her excitement, but the driver took off before she could apologise.

The sounds of the city buzzed in her ears as the cool evening air wrapped itself around her. A street musician using magic to control instruments caught her attention and nearby a group of friends huddled around a Behemoth Bites vendor, laughing and chatting. Victoria checked her Rune-Phone and made sure of her way to Cauldron. She began her path towards it through a narrow street and took in the ambience of the colourful storefronts and busy restaurants. She could hear snippets of conversations and laughter from the patrons inside, only adding to her enthusiasm of a night out.

One street from Cauldron her eyes locked on a graffiti message on the wall. I was as if the letters had come alive, she gravitated towards the words as they pulsed with a strange energy that made them shimmer and glisten. She couldn't help but feel drawn to it, like it called out to her to touch it.

The message seemed to writhe and twist; the letters blurring and reforming into new shapes. Victoria squinted, trying to make out the words, but they kept shifting and changing, as if they were trying to hide their meaning from her. The words extended themselves, resembling hands clawing for the sides of a pool, as if desperately trying to grab onto something.

A chill ran down her spine.

"Victoria!" Emily's voice came from behind her. Victoria whipped around so fast she almost tumbled. She blinked furiously and shook her head. The graffiti returned to normal.

"What the hell?" Victoria murmured to herself.

Emily came rushing up and caught on to her arm, preventing her from falling. "Careful girl, you don't want your first night out to land you in a different realm," Emily said, pointing at the graffiti. "Although this one looks pretty standard."

Behind her, two other female students Emily's age walked up. Victoria recognised them from around the academy but had never interacted with either of them. All three girls dressed up differently than they did at school and Victoria was glad she'd put in the extra effort.

"I'm so glad you came!" Emily exclaimed and pulled Victoria in for a hug.

The sweet aroma of Emily's perfume surrounded her. She took in a deep breath and let the scent sit in her nostrils for a little longer. It was a fusion of sweet jasmine and hints of citrus entwined with a subtle scent that reminded Victoria of blooming gardens after a summer rain. "This is Thrash and Sam, my partners in crime." Emily introduced the two other girls behind her. "Thrash is the brawn, and Sam here is the beauty, I'm the brains." The three girls laughed together. Victoria felt Emily was selling herself short as just the brains.

"Nice to meet ya," Thrash said. Thrash was Half-Orc, but unlike Pax, her tusks were much more delicate. She fashioned her black hair in a faux hawk with a braid running along it on both sides. A towering figure standing six-foot-four with broad shoulders and bulging muscles, she had much greyer tones to her skin compared to many other Half-Orcs and her yellow eyes seemed to pierce their surroundings. Despite her intimidating appearance, she gave Victoria a warm smile and gave a hearty laugh at a joke Victoria made comparing her to Pax.

"Oh! Am I'm glad you aren't some Orc hating bitch. I would have had to flatten you here and now," she teased, and Victoria gulped nervously.

"Oh no, I couldn't hurt a fly." Victoria could feel that Thrash was trying to reassure her, but she was still nervous.

"Okay, Thrash, let's not scare off the poor girl." Sam spoke, pushing forward. She had a tall athletic build with curly blonde hair which was down and styled. She wore a leather jacket over a black tank top and ripped jeans with a pair of combat boots. "Come on, let's line up." She headed toward Cauldron with Thrash following her, leaving Emily and Victoria alone to walk behind them.

As they made small steps towards the front of the line, the Bouncer Wizard was taking his time slowly inspecting all their IDs. Emily turned to Victoria and smiled. The cool wind rushed by them, and Victoria shivered a little.

"Once we are in, you'll warm up."

"You guys go out often?" Victoria was a complete virgin to the nightlife. She had so many questions but also didn't want to seem uncool.

"All the time, we love to go out dancing, have a few bevvies, let our hair down, you know? You got your ID, yeah?" Emily asked, looking forward as they edged closer. Victoria nodded, patting her bag. "Hand it over." Emily held her hand out.

"What? Why?" She felt stumped and asked loud enough to make Thrash turn around.

"Don't worry, Em's an expert at illusionary magic. She has confounded the entire strip!"

Victoria rummaged around in her bag for her purse and pulled out her ID card.

Emily snapped it out of her hands and held a cloak over her face like a smoker lighting a cigarette in the wind. There was a bright sparkle of lights from the App-Magic she cast and then she revealed her face once again.

"Done!" Emily chirped. Thrash snatched it before Victoria could even look.

"Best work yet! You are getting too good, Em!" Trash handed it back to Victoria, who vetted it. Everything looked the same except for her birthdate. It was two years prior to her own, making her nineteen.

Victoria was impressed, but fearful that it wouldn't work. They came to the front of the line. The Bouncer Wizard wasn't a big burly man who could lift you with one hand, instead he looked like he could perceive if you were about to pull a fast one and would use magic to push you out of the line. Perhaps even send you to a different dimension to serve out your punishment.

"Oh, this will be good," the bouncer said, smirking, when it was Victoria's turn. She started to sweat and looked at Emily, who urged her forward with a reassured smile. "No, seriously, let me look at your ID miss. I'm sure whoever you stole it from looks nothing like you."

When Victoria handed the ID card over, the bouncer's smug face disappeared in a flash, and he handed it back. "In you go!" he said with such defeat in his tone.

Victoria stuffed it back into her purse. Her heart raced as she descended the steps to the entrance of Cauldron. The thumping bass and blaring music reverberated through the concrete. Victoria's heart skipped a beat, causing her lips to curl into a joyful smile. As she entered the dimly lit hallway, she was surrounded by a sea of people of various shapes and sizes, all dancing energetically to the beat of the music.

As Victoria took Emily's extended hand, she felt a sense of relief wash over her. She was glad to be with someone in the crowded club. The thumping music and flashing lights created a dizzying atmosphere, and she was overwhelmed.

Emily led her through the crowd, expertly weaving her way through the throngs of people, and Victoria followed closely behind. Her heart raced with excitement and nerves. This was her first time being out like this, but she was determined to enjoy herself. She couldn't wait to rub it in Lirien and Luminia's faces.

Victoria took in the surrounding scene. People filled the club, wearing a wild array of outfits. Some wore elaborate costumes, while others dressed in outfits that couldn't even be considered undergarments. The sweet smell of hookah, alcohol and sweat permeated the air. Victoria followed Emily through the thick smog. She was thrilled to be amongst it, even if it was chaotic. Emily turned to Victoria with a grin when they reached the bar.

"What'll it be?" she shouted over the music.

Victoria looked down at the menu on the bar and could not make sense of the strange cocktail names. She settled on something that sounded fruity and colourful. As the two girls waited a wave of unease swept through Victoria. The strange graffiti she saw on the wall outside was still on her mind, and she couldn't shake the feeling that something bad was about to happen.

"Come on, Thrash and Sam are over at the back." Emily handed Victoria her drink and took hold of her free hand. Victoria's heart skipped a beat as she was pulled through the sea of people once again.

As they made their way to the back of the club, Victoria glimpsed some interesting characters. A group of Drow elves chatted animatedly, while a group of dwarven women were downing tankards of ale.

Finally, they arrived at the back of the club, where Thrash and Sam waited. Thrash looked up and grinned, revealing a set of sharp teeth. Sam waved them over and Emily let go of Victoria's hand, joining her friends.

Victoria took a seat next to Emily and noticed the drinks had a strange purple tint to them but thought little of it. Victoria sat and sipped at her drink, soaking in the atmosphere as the three friends engaged in conversation.

This wasn't Victoria's first alcoholic drink, but it was the first one this strong. She pulled it up at eye level and inspected the purple tint It looked so magical and shimmered like the graffiti she'd seen earlier. Swirling around like water being drained out of a bathtub, Victoria was transfixed.

Victoria blinked, her eyes adjusting to the sudden sound of Emily's voice asking her a question. As she lowered her drink, she blinked a few times, momentarily overwhelmed by the bright lights of the bustling bar.

Victoria didn't hear Emily, distracted by everything. "I'm sorry, what did you ask?" Victoria looked back at her drink, which was perfectly still, and the purple tint had disappeared. Thrash and Sam had gone to get more drinks, leaving her and Emily alone.

"Are you okay? Do you want to leave?"

Before she could even think about a response, the drink took control of her. "No!" Victoria jumped out of her seat. "Let's go dance!" She pulled Emily with her toward the dance floor.

In the dimly lit club, the pulsating rhythm of the music echoed through the air and thumped through the floor, enveloping Victoria and Emily as they moved in sync with the hypnotic beats. Victoria, her movements fluid and graceful, swayed gently, her eyes sparkling in the ambient lights. Emily was also captivated by the rhythm, leading her to gracefully twirl and dance. Together, they crafted a spellbinding dance while she showered Victoria with compliments. While swirling, Victoria found herself unable to resist manipulating the lights around her. The soft glow of the ambient lights created a mesmerizing display, with a cone of light enveloping them.

"Woah nice!" Emily commented on the spotlight on them and then continued to dance. Their sweat and heat combining.

The music made its gradual crescendo, elevating the energy in the club. Victoria was lost in the cheering and shouting. Surrendering to the moment, she shut her eyes, but her tranquillity abruptly shattered when a person rushed past and forcefully pushed her to the side. Victoria stumbled slightly but Emily caught her.

"Hey, dickhead! Watch where you're going!" Emily pulled Victoria in closer and inspected her face. Emily pushed Victoria's hair back behind her ears. Both of them. Victoria gulped, feeling a pit form in her stomach, but she let it happen.

Emily's face gleamed with a mix of sweat and elation. "You alright?" She noticed Victoria's unease at her hair being pushed behind her pointed ear.

Before Victoria could respond, the music stopped abruptly, plunging the room into an eerie silence. The two girls spun around, looking to see what was going on. Both felt a momentary surprise and turned to each other with curiosity and confusion written on their faces. As did the majority of the crowd.

"Play the music!" someone shouted, and others joined in, chanting the same words over and over.

Amidst the sudden stillness, up against the far brick wall of the club, a dark cloaked figure emerged from behind a group of people and shoved onlookers aside. Victoria remained oblivious as the mysterious figure in a cloak approached. Emily on the other hand instantly spotted them and pulled Victoria around and pointed them out. Victoria's heart stopped as she felt a chill run down her spine, her gazed fixed on this mysterious person.

Glowing purple eyes pierced through the shadows of the hood, casting an unsettling hue that illuminated the entire figure except for their face.

As the figure approached, the lights went out, plunging the room into darkness except for its eyes. Victoria heard panicked screams and shouts. Emily's hand gripped hers tightly. Thrash and Sam's shouts rang out in the dark as they searched for them.

"What's going on?" Victoria's heart pounded as she was pulled from the dance floor.

"I don't know," Emily replied, her voice trembling. "But we need to get out of here."

"There you two are!" Thrash ran up, she sounded winded.

A shriek rang over the club floor, causing people to scream and hold their ears. Victoria and Emily froze.

"What the fuck was that?" Thrash shouted as Emily found them in the dark.

"No time to find out, we need to find an exit. Where is Sam?" Emily's panicked voice rang out.

"We split up trying to find you. She was going to look for another way out of here, help people get out if she could." Thrash explained in a rush then grabbed both Emily and Victoria's hands and pulled them along.

"We are looking for Subject V," the figure whispered, encasing the room in its eerie, demonic voice. The cloaked figure forced the entire club to look as if under some spell. Emily looked at Victoria, her fear building. "Hand them over and you will all be set free."

"Why would we listen to some freak in a cloak, anyway! Go have another drink and leave us all alone!" a random guy shouted out. The hooded figure turned and held out their palm. In a quick burst of purple fire, the hooded figure set the person alight. The flames flickered and illuminated the darkness as their wails filled the room.

It happened as if in slow motion. Victoria was horrified to witness the guy getting burned. The smell of burning flesh filled the nostrils of everyone across the dance floor. The fire sprinklers activated, dousing the club in heavy rain. But the crowd didn't move.

"Follow me." Thrash lead the way through the still crowd and up the stairs to the employee lounge in search of a way to sneak out. Crouched down, the three kept an eye on the cloaked person. She just witnessed a murder in the middle of a public. Victoria couldn't help but wonder why everyone around them seemed frozen in place. Had the cloaked person put them into some sort of trance?

The door was locked, but Thrash wasn't taking no for an answer and instructed the other two to step back. The cloaked figure had not moved a muscle, still inspecting each of the members of the crowd one-by-one, searching for someone. Thrash kicked in the door and the cloaked figure looked to where the noise came from. Their position was compromised.

"Run!" Victoria screamed and the club all turned to face them like controlled puppets. Thrash and Emily pulled Victoria in front of them. Clambering over the kicked in door, the employee lounge was empty besides boxes of drinks for the club. Darting around, Victoria found a door that led to the roof access. She could hear wails of pain and outcries from people in the club below and could only fathom what torture they were under. Thrash barricaded the door the best she could with boxes as Victoria and Emily ran down the narrow corridor.

They came to a dark ladder illuminated by a green emergency exit sign that led to the roof. Emily rushed Victoria up and waited for Thrash to come down the corridor. Bashes against the door to the hallway could be heard as the figure tried to get in.

"Why are you two still here?" Thrash exclaimed, running down the corridor. "Go!"

Victoria made it almost to the top of the ladder before she heard the barricade smashing. The figure had breached through and was headed their way. She rushed to the top and came to the hatch of the roof. Bursting through, Victoria scrambled up onto the roof, gasping for air, followed closely by Emily and Thrash.

She stood straight and looked around. They were surrounded by nothing else but towering buildings and the only way down safely was through the ladder she had just climbed.

"Is there any way down?" Emily asked, closing the hatch fast and joining the other two.

"I can't see any fire exit!" Thrash exclaimed, punching the side of the building roof with her fist.

The door burst open like a hurricane blew it off and the figure clambered through. All three froze in terror, unsure of what to do next.

The cloaked figure, now clearly visible, was a tall man with a hood covering his face. Pulling the hood down, his face appeared pale, and hair was slicked back. An intricate black mask covered his mouth and illuminated a flickering light wave across it as he breathed. His eyes emitted the same purple glow, but now more intense as they met Victoria's. Her heart raced, her palms slick with sweat, as he gradually shifted his gaze toward them.

"Who are you?" Emily shouted, backing away, her voice shaking with fear.

The masked man didn't answer but moved towards them. Victoria saw the fear in Emily's eyes and knew she needed to act fast. Her eyes darted to a toolbox by Thrash, Emily nodded her chin toward it when she caught Thrash's attention. Thrash lifted it up and hurled it through the air. The man lifted a singular hand up and without looking, froze it mid-air then propelled it back towards Thrash. She attempted to dodge it, but she was not fast enough. It hit her square in the back of the head and threw her forward onto the ground. Knocking her out cold.

The man lunged forward, hand extended, making to take hold of Emily. Victoria's insides felt is if they would burst from within as she saw Emily about to be attacked.

Victoria let out a wail that sang across the rooftops of the city as a surge of power coursed through her veins. Magenta flames engulfed her, and she closed her eyes, feeling the heat of the flames radiate around her. The man and Emily turned and watched on as her body changed, shifting and contorting in a way that was both terrifying and awe-inspiring. Their faces were covered in a pinkish glow from the flames.

The flames continued to lick the air as Victoria's body shifted and contorted. Emerging from her skin, delicate stems held iridescent dark purple flowers, creating a stunning ethereal effect. Extending themselves above her, they eagerly sought the moonlight, their leaves greedily drinking in its energy. As the flowers grew larger, their petals unfurled, revealing vibrant hues. Slowly, they detached from the stem and temporarily hung in mid-air, surrounded by the stillness of their surroundings, then evaporating into nothing.

When she opened her eyes, she was no longer within the same body. Her skin had turned a dark shade of purple, and her eyes glowed with an otherworldly pink light. Her hair had grown longer and was now white and crackled with a violet energy. Victoria's instincts took over; she let out a primal scream. Lunging towards the figure, her new form gave her incredible strength and agility. With a flick of her wrist, she sent a blast of purple energy sending him flying across the roof. She flew after him and picked him up in one hand, looking him dead in the eyes.

"You are magnificent," the masked man said a muffled an awe-stricken praise of Victoria, his own purple eyes glistening. Victoria let out another primal scream, the sound reverberated off the rooftops. She did not hesitate, she threw him off the edge of building, allowing him to hover in midair for a moment before he fell.

Victoria turned to face Emily, who appeared to be in shock. Looking between Emily and the passed-out Thrash, Victoria leapt towards them and took hold of them both in either arm. Emily struggled in her distraught state, but Victoria maintained her hold. Victoria bent down and then used all her strength to launch herself into the air and off the building, down into the streets. She jolted side to side, making sure the coast was clear, and took off toward the city outskirts, in the direction of home. She had no plan to wait around for the Mage's Union to find them.

They were halfway out of the city when Victoria's new form began to fade, flickering between this one and her normal self. Victoria let out one last scream, which slowly transitioned into her natural voice. The unknown power dissipating, Victoria collapsed, landing face first. She skid across the sodden grass, both friends thrown from her arms, all three passing out on impact.

Victoria rolled to her side, looking through blurry eyes, she attempted to get up from her crash landing. All she saw was a figure in blinding light lean down and look over her. The light became too much for her eyes to handle and she once again passed out from exhaustion.

CHAPTER ELEVEN
UNDERGROUND REBELS

In the medic ward, Pax finally awoke. The Clerics had cleared Brent only an hour ago. Brent sat with his legs outstretched, resting them on the end of Pax's bed. Pax was immune to the effects of Nightshade Bloom, but he'd need time to recover from being launched through debris and glass. Cuts and bruises covered his body causing him to wince when he moved in certain directions.

"What the hell was that mission?" Pax asked, taking a sip of water.

"We were completely unprepared, hey?" Brent replied.

"I figured Arden had some idea of what he was doing. You know, being a director and all?" Pax looked around the room. "This Cleric ward is nice. We would never have seen the inside of it otherwise."

Brent looked at Pax, and chuckled. "You are an idiot, you know that."

"Proudly!" Pax replied with a grin on his tusks, chittering. "You hear from Victoria?" Pax changed the subject.

"She is staying with Luminia so us being here all night won't be a problem," Brent replied. "Shall we see what's on the news?" He pointed to the vision orb hanging from the ceiling above his bed.

"Nah, I have seen enough bullshit for one day." Pax took another gulp of water. "I should be discharged soon, so then we can go."

The doors to Pax's room burst open.

"Sir, he needs rest!" a Cleric nurse called out from the ward corridor.

"Don't worry, I won't be long." It was Arch Mage Magnar. Brent instantly jumped out of his seat and stood before the Arch Mage walked past the curtain. With a screech, the curtain was pulled back and there he stood.

"My boys." He looked between them both and smiled, his piercing blue eyes analysing them. "Well, you made it back. That says much more about your abilities than the others we sent." His words were cold and devoid of any remorse.

"To be fair, sir, Director Arden saved us from—" Brent was interrupted when Arden walked into the room.

"They aren't lying, sir. If I wasn't there, it would have been another casualty." Arden stepped in from behind the curtain. Pax noticed Brent's immediate shift in posture.

"Well, I am glad these boys had you then," Magnar responded. "I expect a full report on my desk tomorrow morning. Give these boys a few days off, will you?" Magnar swished around and left as quickly as he had arrived.

There was a silent exchange between the three of them before Arden walked over to Brent and pulled him in for a hug.

"I am sorry I dragged you into this." He shuffled over to Pax still holding Brent and grabbed hold of Pax's giant left hand. "You too Pax, I was foolish, I thought after how well we performed at the warehouse we could do this."

"Umm..." Brent felt a certain unease creep in, not because Arden was hugging him so close that their thighs touched, but because of the revelation that his own boss was unprepared. "It's okay," Brent responded, not sure what else to say.

"It most certainly isn't okay. I was injured on the job," Pax growled.

"You will be compensated and allotted time off to recover," Arden said, not letting go of Brent just yet.

"I'll think about it," Pax brooded. An awkward silence permeated the air all around them.

Brent cleared his throat after the silence became too much and Arden let go of him. "Oh sorry, Abernathy," he muttered as a Cleric nurse came in.

"Okay, Mr. Grimtusk, time for your last check. I ask all visitors to leave momentarily."

"Alright, Pax, I'll see you out front?" Brent asked, and Pax nodded as the nurses gave their final examination.

Brent and Arden wandered out of Sanctum's medical ward toward the front entrance.

"Umm, Brent..." It was the first time Arden had used his first name. "Do you have a moment? I thought we could have a little chat?"

"Sure."

Brent followed when Arden changed direction and headed toward his office.

***

"Well, you managed yourself with confidence from what I could see and remember. The Nightshade Bloom toxin was pretty strong." Brent took a seat inside Arden's office once again.

Arden's expression was stern. Brent's stomach dropped, and he didn't know exactly why. He didn't think he could be in trouble, but somehow, he felt like he was. It only proved he had never fully dealt with the trauma that led to the adult anxiety of being micromanaged time and time again.

Arden opened his mouth to speak, and Brent's heart rate skyrocketed. He wanted to shout an apology at his boss but refrained.

"Earlier this evening, when you and Grimtusk were in the ward, the Opticon received a strange energy reading." Arden typed on his keyboard, searching for something.

Brent's heart rate settled. "Okay," he said plainly.

"I am not sure if you know of it, but a little club by the name of Cauldron had an incident tonight."

"I mean, I know of it, but have never been," Brent answered truthfully.

Arden pulled back from his keyboard and inspected Brent. "Well, your daughter has." Arden turned the screen around and there displayed plain as day was a screen capture of a recording of Victoria and another girl on the dancefloor.

Brent stood up and grabbed hold of the screen. "It can't be!" He was more hurt that she lied to him than her being out at the club.

"So, you say that isn't Victoria?"

"No, it is her, but I can't believe she would lie to me about where she was tonight."

"I will keep that for you to handle in your own time. My intention isn't to snitch on her whereabouts," Arden said, and Brent sat back down. "The energy reading, and other reports came in, along with video evidence on the club floor of something strange. Hold on." Arden turned the screen to find what he needed to show Brent.

Turning the screen back around, he pressed play on the Cam-Mera footage. "Tell me if you recognise someone else."

The footage played out and Brent could see Victoria dancing with a ginger-haired girl of a similar age along with other patrons. It was a friend he'd never met. Perhaps it was a secret girlfriend. Victoria never told him about anyone she liked in that way, so he couldn't be certain. Even though his head was now clear of the toxin, he felt the swirling building up again. The footage moved on, and the music stopped. In the background, a man in a cloak similar to the one they encountered at Marquis' apartment stood. The vibrant, purple glint in the cowl of their hood stood out against the washed out, faded colour of the footage.

"That's..." Brent's words died off in disbelief.

"It seems our assailant has a taste for you Abernathy's." Arden pointed out as Victoria went upstairs and the cloaked man followed her and her friends "The footage ends here as we have nothing else to show," Arden finished, and Brent stood up sharply. "Where are you going?"

"I need to get home and ensure Victoria is safe," he replied.

"She is fine. Don't stress it was the first thing I checked. The Opticon has picked up her signal at your home." Arden ushered Brent back to his seat. "There is more I want to discuss about the girl she was with."

"I've never seen her in my life," Brent instantly responded.

"Brent, please stop acting like I am interrogating you. I am not." Arden smiled at him warmly. He stood up taking his tablet with him and sat next to Brent. "There is another thing that occurred this evening while we were busy."

Arden relayed that the news broadcast was interrupted by a video message to the City of Spellford. He showed Brent the second log of footage. He sat back and awaited Brent's reaction.

A stirring sense of unease and curiosity washed over him. Despite being a seasoned Mage, Brent had only recently become a newly appointed member of the Mage's Union. Brent was never one to truly challenge the way things were, falling mostly in line with the government decisions of his time. He stood up for what was right, and of course voted, but in an era of peace he resigned no issue with what magic had become. He understood the need to maintain safety and order while preventing the misuse of magic. But he also recognised the validity of the person's argument for freedom and exploration of magic's full potential.

Torn between his two thoughts, he let out a sigh.

"I can see you are contemplating something heavy. Don't worry, I had the same thoughts." Arden crossed his leg over one knee. He clasped his hands with two fingers poised on his lips.

"And that is?"

"That the Code Weavers are basically right. We have too much control over, well, pretty much everything. Now I wouldn't admit this if I did not think you felt the same." Arden leaned forward, placing his hand on Brent's shoulder.

"Well, yeah, but—" Brent looked down at the hand on his shoulder and followed it to Arden's face. "These Code Weavers are going about this the wrong way."

"That's my man." Arden grasped his shoulder tighter. "I knew picking you for this job was the right decision."

"What are we to do about this warning and of that cloaked guy? Do you think there is a connection between them?"

"There is no doubt in my mind that there is," Arden said.

"And you think Victoria is involved in it?" he asked.

"Correct again." Arden smiled. "But not directly, no. I think your daughter is an innocent bystander, just in the wrong place at the wrong time."

"What if they are hunting her?" Brent asked.

"Why would they? She is just a teenager?" Arden pulled his hand back. "Now granted, she is Aphonic, but I think there is more to it than that."

"I am Aphonic too. Why not target me?"

"Now you are asking the right questions." Arden stood up straight, getting excited. "The Code Weavers are mostly, from what I have been able to gather, delinquent teens and homeless youths."

Brent forgot often that few have had Victoria's opportunities for life that he awarded her. That even in a city such as Spellford, with magic at people's fingertips, without the means to afford it, they would be barred from participating in society completely.

"The person on screen with the warning, in the cloak at the club, and at Marquis's apartment was no teenager," Brent said suddenly.

"You are correct. The person at the club, apartment and who gave the warning appear to be three separate people, however." Arden elaborated on how their voices sounded different even when distorted and also a variance in body shape. "One of them is the leader of the group and for ease we will call them, Weaver."

"And the other two?"

"Marquis one and Marquis two."

"You think he is behind this?" Brent asked.

"It has crossed my mind, whether willingly or implicitly I'm not sure. But we cannot rule it out." Arden sat back further in his chair before adding. "We cannot rule out the possibility of the girl Victoria was seen with, either."

"That is a lot of suspects, all with unclear motives."

"Indeed, but somehow, they all lead back to you and or Victoria."

Brent raised his eyebrows. "What do you mean?"

"Similar assailants show up at both the apartment and club once you were there. It can't be a mere coincidence," Arden commented.

Brent sat back and thought for a moment. A million questions flooded his mind all at once. The ones he could make sense of pushed forward. Was this the right time to tell him about how he found Victoria in the Orb? Would there be any link to her origins and this moment?

"There isn't anything you are hiding from me, is there?" Arden asked, as if he was reading Brent's mind.

"You tell me. The Mage's Union has tracked my entire life," Brent replied.

"Well, no, I have only undertaken background checks as per employment history to see if you were suitable," Arden said firmly, then stood up and went back to his desk. "I have a request." He placed his tablet back and changed topics.

As the air in the room changed, Brent adjusted himself. "Yes...sir?"

"Please, when we are together, call me Arden."

"Okay, si— Arden," Brent replied catching himself. "Is that it?"

"No, I want you to track the girl Victoria is with. See what you can find out."

"I am not even sure if she and Victoria talk or if it was a one-night thing," Brent answered truthfully.

"Well, maybe you should get home and find out as there were two signals when I checked at your premises. They matched with your daughter and the girl she was with at the club."

Pax's knock at the door interrupted their conversation. "Here you are! I was wandering out front looking for you. I almost went home when I thought, let me check the office first." Pax's hulking frame squeezed between the door frames.

"Grimtusk, I am glad to see you up and about!" Arden clasped his hands and stood. "Abernathy and I are done here, so how about I make your journey home smoother?" Picking Brent's interest, Arden smirked, sending heat to Brent's face. "Would you be interested in portal magic?"

"Isn't that not permitted for general use?" Pax asked, walking inside the office.

"Only for Civs," Arden replied. "But there are some allowances for the Strategic Department and as Director, I am making it a requirement of your role." Arden dug under the papers he had on his desk and handed them each a card with a QRune Code on it. "Scan and redeem this through your Rune-Phones to download the app!"

"Generating a portal through an app. Are you serious?" Brent asked.

"That's fucking cool," Pax exclaimed, and instantly whipped out his phone to scan the code.

Brent followed suit and pulled out his phone, recalling that the encounter had damaged it.

"Ah! Give it here," Arden said, and Brent handed it over. Arden placed it on the desk. Hovering his hands over it, they glowed golden. The phone repaired itself as if it was moving backwards in time. The cracks all disappeared, and Arden handed him the phone once again. "Like new!"

Brent scanned the code, and the app appeared for download. He accepted its terms and conditions and let it download.

With that, Arden turned to Brent and Pax with a warm smile. "Thank you for investigating this matter with me., I apologise again, for my oversights and hope you both wish to stay on as result of any damages to your person." Arden walked to his desk and then sat down.

"Seeing today is Flintday. Have the weekend. I'll write the report up." Arden smirked. "Oh, and payment will be deposited shortly. Rest up boys, we have a busy week coming ahead," Arden replied with a smile, and a quick wink at Brent. "Open the app, enter your desired location, and a portal will open. You step through and you're there," he finished.

Pax and Brent clearly knew that was their cue to leave. Brent opened the app and typed his address, as did Pax. "Alright, see you later then." Brent said, pressing the open portal button. Two swirling archways of blue and black energy materialised in the room in front of Pax and Brent. Pax smiled and Brent winked back before they each leapt through their own portals.

CHAPTER TWELVE
ACADEMY DORMS

V ictoria slowly opened her eyes, wincing at the bright light shining through the open window. The white curtains moved in the warm breeze. A wave of calmness washed over her. A sharp pain shot through her head and across her body when she tried to sit up. She groaned from the pain and placed her palm to her back, hoping to ease the pressure building. She fell back down onto the pillow with a soft thud.

Confusion overtook the pain as she looked around the unfamiliar room. Beams of sunlight streamed through the window, highlighting the posters and pictures on the walls. She was alone and unsure whose bedroom it was. Her body ached all over and she winced from the pain as she tried to move. The last memory she could recall was when she entered the club. Everything after that was a blur, and she couldn't recall how she ended up here.

She managed to sit up. She shuffled over to the vanity mirror. Her eyes widened with shock at her dishevelled appearance. Her hair was wild, like a bush caught in the wind, her face smudged with dirt and grime. Concern built in her like a toddler haphazardly playing with building blocks, and they had tumbled everywhere.

She sat there inspecting herself and wondered what had happened. There were scars in the shape of flowers on shoulders, in addition to the soreness she felt all over. Her jacket hung over the chair, but the rest of her clothing was on, albeit slightly torn. Did someone attack her? Had someone taken advantage of her? She hung her head and tried to remember anything, but no memories came.

Victoria sat back down on the bed when she heard voices from the hall, they grew louder as footsteps approached the room. As the door handle moved, she shuffled from the bed and with one hand, readied to cast a spell at whoever it was entering the room.

Her heart felt like it was about to leave her chest and just when she was about to manifest her energy to push the entrants back, she realised who it was. Behind a small pile of clothes, Emily's warm, inviting smile faced her. The other person wasn't Thrash or Sam, but Professor Nia.

"Oh, Victoria, thank goodness you're awake!" Nia said, her face relieved.

"How long was I out for?" she asked. "And why are my clothes all torn—" she looked between the clothes in Emily's hands and her own.

"Let me give you these and we will come back in and explain when you are ready," Emily said, placing the clothing on the desk by the door, then the two left the room.

Victoria waited until it was clear and changed out of her torn clothing. She sat back down on the edge of the bed, then let them know to come back in.

Professor Nia glided through the door, Emily followed behind her, looking as perfect in Victoria's eyes as she always had, minus the noticeable scab forming by her forehead and smudged makeup around her eyes. They both looked worse for wear and Victoria wanted answers.

Nia waved her hand forward. A chair followed her and sat in front of Victoria. She sat down and inspected her from afar. Emily stood beside her and smiled. The light bounced off her face and illuminated the skin between her freckles and revealed a previously unnoticed bruise on the left side of her face.

"Now, hold still, I'm going to perform an Augmenti reading." Nia said and didn't hesitate, holding her hands up in front of Victoria's face. Her hands glowed a faint yellowy-white aura around them, and Victoria felt the warmth off of them. She closed her eyes and let Nia undertake her examination.

Nia ran her hands above her face and across her torso, stopping momentarily at her heart and then to her stomach. Victoria felt a gurgling as Nia ran her fingertips gently across her stomach and, as they did, the pit in her stomach grew.

"Okay, you may relax now," Nia said, sitting back in her chair.

"What did you do?" Victoria asked.

"I was searching for any anomalies, also checking your energy reserves."

"What did you find?" Victoria couldn't hide her curiosity.

"Well, nothing to be concerned about," Nia started, and her face changed to serious, "But the transformation exhausted your magic reserves. They need replenishing."

Victoria looked confused, and then Emily smiled. "You are hungry, dingus!"

"Yeah, I got that part," Victoria laughed. "But transformation?" she asked, taking in the concerned looks on both Nia and Emily's faces. "What do you mean?"

"You don't remember?" Emily asked, and Victoria shook her head softly. "Here, let me show you." Emily held out her hand and Victoria hesitated. "Not only am I great at forgeries," she looked sheepishly at Nia, who rolled her eyes. "I also am skilled in thought transference, amongst other talents."

Victoria took hold of her hand and closed her eyes, the events that brought her here flurried past her eyes in a rush.

She witnessed the night from Emily's perspective and could feel all of Emily's emotions. Seeing her own face brought her joy and a new perspective on how others saw her. She felt the heat between them while dancing and was glad Emily felt the same.

The night moved on. Victoria could feel Emily's anxiety and panic. The vision turned into a hectic runaway as the hooded figure chased them up to the roof. The memory ended as she witnessed herself transform into a strange and wondrous ethereal form. Flowers bloomed from Victoria's body and detached as her skin turned a dark purple.

She wanted to watch that memory over and over and inspect every fine detail of her transformation. From how her skin changed to a dark shade of purple to her eyes glowing with an otherworldly light. She was awestruck by her hair, flickering like a candle with violet energy.

Emily pulled back and let go of Victoria's hand.

"That was me?" Victoria asked.

"Yes, you were..." Emily paused, in search of the right word. Victoria looked from Emily to Nia. "Pretty fucking cool!" Emily said in such an impressed tone and sat on the bed beside Victoria giving her a hug.

The two girls began to laugh but stopped when Nia cleared her throat, a stern look on her face. "What you became is something we cannot share with anyone. Do you understand?"

"What about my—" Victoria started, but Nia quickly interrupted her.

"Nobody, not even your father," she stated firmly.

"I was going to say Luminia, as I assumed my father was alright," she responded.

"He currently holds a position at the Mage's Union."

"What am I supposed to do now that I know?"

"Expect to hear from me soon. I hope to return with some answers by the end of the lunar until then..." Nia looked between them. "Don't tell anyone."

Nia tried to give a comforting smile, but the air in the room was still tense. She stood to leave, pausing at the door, she added. "Emily, I trust you will escort Victoria home?" She shut the door behind her, not waiting for an answer.

"Yeah, maybe in an hour!" Emily laughed and laid back down on the bed, resting her arms under her head.

Victoria sat still. This was the first time she had ever been in a dorm room before; let alone with someone she was developing feelings for. The thought transference really messed with her brain, and she could not get the way Emily felt out of her mind.

"Why don't you lay back down with me? We can hang out a bit before you leave."

An almighty roar sounded from Victoria's belly as it rumbled, screaming out for food like an alarm being activated, declaring war.

"Ah, sorry about that," Victoria said nervously. She didn't know why she was apologising for a normal function of her body, but she felt like she needed to fill the air with the noise of her voice to shield herself from the embarrassment building in her.

Emily shuffled forward and then brushed Victoria's hair behind her pointed ear. Victoria's heart raced. She let no one touch that ear, not even her father as much anymore. She didn't know why, but she felt embarrassed to show it.

"Don't apologise, should we go get something to eat?" she asked. Victoria now immediately aware of how close she was to her face. Victoria could see every distinct tiny little pore and freckle, how Emily's blue eyes took her in. She felt each deep breath as her chest rose and fell. Victoria looked down at Emily's lips and they met her own.

Before she could register what was happening, she was deep in the throes of kissing Emily, her first proper kiss. Pulling Victoria down with her, Emily rolled her on top as they continued making out. Emily's hands ran all over her body, her fingertips traced down her torso and Victoria twitched. She opened her eyes momentarily to see Emily's own closed as she was in the heat of passion. Victoria closed her eyes once more and made to further the kiss when her stomach groaned once again.

They both opened their eyes at the same time unable to contain their laughter. The two girls laughed until their cheek bones stiffened. Victoria didn't know why it was so funny, but she couldn't stop. It had been very long time since she had laughed like this and truly meant it.

"Let's get you some food." Emily stood and pulled Victoria with her.

Victoria took hold of Emily's hand and together they rushed out of the dorm towards the elevator. Victoria had never felt this feeling before, like a ball of light inside of her growing. It was warm and fluttering and filled her with happiness.

***

Victoria felt much better and her energy returning after they finished a meal. Emily sat across from Victoria and smiled at her.

"What?" Victoria asked a little too strongly.

"Oh, it's nothing...you are just incredibly cute, that's all. The way you ate a burger like it was your last meal."

"I blame Pax for how I eat. He practically raised me. My father was around, but he had to work to support us both until Pax got a job at SorcerySure as well."

"Pax a messy eater?"

"No, he is just Half-Orc," Victoria said, and Emily adjusted herself in her seat. "He is so gentle, nothing like his Orcish brethren." Victoria tried to justify Pax's existence and didn't know why. Thrash was Emily's friend, after all.

"It's okay, Tori,"

Victoria's heart fluttered when Emily happened to use the nickname that only her father and Pax did.

"It isn't all too uncommon to see Orc or even Half-Orc in Spellford, but I am not one of those bigoted assholes. I mean, duh, Thrash is my best friend, I would love to meet both your father and Pax one day," Emily continued.

"Brent," Victoria said, taking a sip of her Sparkling Pep-Up Elixir.

"Ah! yes, the 'Hero of Spellford' with the *Dad Magic*." Emily said jokingly also taking a sip of her own drink. "He was—"

"Lucky?" Victoria offered a response and could see Emily shake her head and held a finger to her lips, her mouth full of drink. "No you can say it,"

Victoria replied seeing Emily try to adjust what she was going to say. "He was extremely lucky he wasn't eaten by that beast and that his reversing time magic trick actually worked."

"I was going to say he is incredibly skilled." She smiled widely with a chuckle.

"I'll pass that on to him when I see him next."

"His generation mostly were, though, right? As time went on, and magic changed, we transitioned to App-Magic. A lot of that knowledge has died."

"He wouldn't have passed anything on to me,' Victoria said glumly. "He isn't my actual father. I'm adopted."

There was a long pause between them. "But you are both Aphonic?"

"What are the odds?" Victoria said with a shrug.

"Does your dad transform, too?"

Victoria shook her head. She took another sip until the noise of sucking air met her ears. "Well, I am feeling better. Shall we get going?"

Emily nodded and stood up with Victoria. They discarded their rubbish in the bins and headed towards the exit and out to the street. Victoria could see the academy in the distance and the path towards her train carriage.

"Well, home's this way," Victoria said, pointing to the train overpass down the street.

"I'll message you later." Emily said and pulled her in for a hug. "But I want to make sure you get home safe, so..." Emily said, extending the 'o'. "Why don't I just walk you home?"

"That works for me." Victoria's reply was muffled by Emily's shoulder.

CHAPTER THIRTEEN
TRUANT TEEN

Brent's skin was being tugged from the muscle and bone, twirling around in a nausea inducing whirlpool of colours and sounds. Then, in a blink of an eye, he appeared in front of his house at the same moment as Pax.

"Thank fuck we are home!" Pax let out a groan and slunk to the door, hunched over.

"Let's not let on to Victoria that we almost died, okay?"

Pax nodded. Brent made a mental note to talk to Pax later about the task given to him by Arden when the sickness subsided. Arden was a fool to place his complete trust in Brent. Pax and he shared everything. As night had fallen, Brent expected the lights to be on and Victoria to be home. He pulled Paxton back from the patio and walked closer, inspecting the area.

"Something is off," Brent said to Pax, whose face was confused. "The lights aren't on."

"Victoria's probably asleep," Pax suggested.

Brent shook off his naïvety and placed his hand against the door and used his other to put a finger to his lips, signalling to Pax to stay silent.

The door was unlocked and left open slightly. He pushed the door with his foot until it hit the wall behind it with a loud creak. Complete darkness blanketed the house. Usually, he would hear music coming from Victoria's room or the vision orb playing, but the house was deadly silent. He checked his phone and there were still no messages from Victoria. *Where could she be?*

"Anyone home?" Brent called out. He heard a rustling and smashing sound coming from Victoria's room in the back.

"Intruder?" Pax asked, and Brent shrugged.

Brent slowly crept through his house and signalled Pax to clear the other rooms. As he approached down the hall, he could hear something of a muffled whisper and more rustling.

"All clear." Pax crept up behind Brent and whispered in his ear, almost making Brent leap from his skin.

"Fucking hell, Pax!" he whispered, grabbing his chest, trying to regain his composure. He held a finger to his lips and grabbed Pax's shoulder to transmit his plans telepathically.

Brent crept to the door and opened it slowly. His eyes adjusted to the dark, he could barely see the blanket covering the bed moving around in the darkness. Muffled noises and a low moan came from the bed. Brent turned on the lamp on the desk. A warm light engulfed the room, illuminating everything around him.

"Victoria? You, okay?"

There was a loud gasp and Victoria's head popped out from under the covers, as did another girl with her. They were clearly in a position that Brent did not need to see.

"DAD! GET OUT!" Victoria shrieked.

Brent spun around to leave but bashed his face against the door frame in his haste. Stopping momentarily to gain his bearings, he made to grab the door and muttered an apology that sounded like "I saw nothing, sorry!" before he closed shut the door.

Brent heard Victoria mumble "Fuck I'm sorry" from the hall.

His forehead bleeding slightly, he held his hand to the cut. "They're umm..." Brent started. His face went a deep red when he looked at Pax. "Let's go to the kitchen and decide on dinner, they aren't ready." Brent dragged Pax with his free arm toward the kitchen overwhelmed to have walked in on his daughter being intimate with someone.

***

Brent barely ate a bite, his heart heavy with the embarrassment he caused his daughter. Victoria and Brent looked toward Pax, who shovelled in food like it was his last meal. Victoria had sent Emily home quickly after Brent had walked in on them.

Brent nervously cleared his throat, searching for the right words to bridge the uneasy waters he created between his daughter and him.

"Victoria," he started, "I...I'm sorry." He laid down his knife and fork next to his untouched dinner. Remorse filled his voice. "I never intended to intrude on your privacy. I was worried something was wrong or there was an intruder." He lifted one hand to his forehead where Pax had fixed a small bandage to the cut.

She remained silent.

"I understand you are angry with me right now," Brent continued, his sincerity clear in his voice. "But please know that I love you and I would do nothing to embarrass you." He paused, hoping for a response.

Victoria sighed and dropped her cutlery. "I'm not angry, or embarrassed." She rolled her eyes. "Just knock next time I have someone over please," Victoria groaned. "Emily laughed it off, so it's fine, I guess."

Brent nodded. They ate the rest of their dinner in less uncomfortable silence but the air around them was still off. Having no energy to address it now, he let Victoria go to her room while he and Pax cleaned up.

Later that evening, Brent and Pax sat in the living room, their eyes fixed on the vision orb. Preoccupied with the recent events in Marquis' apartment and the video footage, Brent's attention continued to drift from the show in the background. The glow of the screen cast a soft light across the room, illuminating his sombre expression.

Pax broke the silence, his voice laced with concern when he saw the look on Brent's face. "What's up?"

Brent sighed heavily and ran a hand through his hair, pushing it back. "Annoyed that I walked in on her and Emily. Can I just turn back time and knock?"

"There are always the Time Magicians on 34th Street?" Pax suggested.

"Messing with time for personal gain is highly unethical, and as a Mage's Union member, you should know better," Brent replied, trying not to laugh in his fake scolding.

The Time Mage shop was not a legitimate business, but a joke store for kids to have fun with harmless time magic, like growing plants or quick or hair tonics that work in mere seconds, but also wore off just as fast.

"She is clearly okay about it, though. At least you saw nothing," Pax said, and Brent returned a small but grateful smile to Pax and thanked him for his support.

They both turned their attention back to the vision orb. Pax had turned on his favourite show, *Ghosthunters*, where spirits of the departed are called back by the hosts and together they hunt down their past grievances to right any wrongs. Pax liked the really weird stuff that few did, and occasionally it hooked Brent, too. As the night pressed on, Brent still could not shift his thoughts away from the task Arden assigned him and took himself to bed, leaving Pax alone to watch his shows.

***

Morning came as quick as he hit his head on the pillow. Brent awoke more drained than he had been. Back-to-back nightmares haunted by the cloaked man, followed by an endless dream cycle of Elwin falling down into the chasm. One he hadn't had for a long time, many years in fact. Was being around Arden awakening these thoughts again, he wondered as he rolled in his bed.

Reaching over, he looked at his phone under the moon lamp Through one open eye he noticed it was barely past nine and laid back down, ignoring the notifications. He was supposed to take the weekend to rest. He assumed Victoria had taken herself to school as she had a mentoring session booked in and pulled the sheet further up over his bare torso.

The buzz of his phone drew his attention, he rolled over to see it was a call from Victoria's school. Brent answered the call.

"Hello?" Nia's voice came through clearly. "Brent?"

"Uh, yes, Nia. What is wrong?"

"I have been trying to contact you for an hour now." He pulled his phone back and blinked, opening both eyes now. Sure enough, he had countless unanswered calls notifications. "I apologise for that. I was asleep."

"That is okay."

"What is this about? Is Victoria, okay?"

"I was expecting her today. Is she unwell?"

Brent pulled the sheets off his body and rushed through the house towards her bedroom, holding the phone close to his ear. Cracking the door, she was not in the room and Brent made up a lie on the spot, trying to not have his voice shake. "Ah yeah, my apologies. I should have called. She is quite unwell today." Brent figured it was better to lie than alert her teacher of her not being home. They ended the call, and he put his phone in his pocket.

"Pax! Victoria is missing!" he shouted, swinging Pax's bedroom door wide open. Pax startled awake, threw off the blanket and tumbled off his bed in the confusion. Brent rushed to his own room to change. "I am going to go to work and try to track her from there—" Coming down the hallway in a rush he saw Victoria's legs hanging over the couch.

"No need, I'm in here," Victoria said lightly, laying on the couch in the dark. Brent stood there dumbfounded, and Pax came rushing through, hopping on his one foot as he tried to change into his clothes.

"What's the holdup?" Pax glanced around the room as he pulled the other leg of his pants. "Oh!" he breathed in and out, then mumbled quietly on his way to his room. "I'm going back to bed."

Brent waited until Pax shut his door. He came to stand at the back of the couch, eyeing his daughter who stared at the ceiling past him.

"Why didn't you go to your mentoring session today?"

"Not feeling well," she said simply, twiddling her thumbs on her stomach, still avoiding eye contact.

"Okay," Brent said with a drawn-out expression, "and why didn't you come tell me so I could have informed Nia?"

"You were asleep." She kept the same tone and composure while she continued to twiddle her thumbs.

"Please stop that." One of Brent's biggest annoyances was when people fidgeted while he talked to them.

Victoria stopped and looked at him. "What do you want me to say? I am not happy about yesterday and don't feel like going in to today. Emily will be there, and I will have to deal with all that embarrassing shit."

"She surely understands I didn't mean to—"

"This isn't about you, or when you barged in."

Brent hung his head. He walked around the couch and lifted her legs up to sit. She extended her legs over his lap so he could massage her calves and feet to comfort her, like he did when she was a child.

"What is going on? Tell me." Brent looked at her with concern.

There was a long pause, and Victoria appeared to be struggling to find the right words. She found them and took a quick breath to speak.

"Am I really adopted?"

"What?" Brent asked, stunned.

"We have the same hair colour and eye colour. I look like your daughter besides this ear." She swished her hair back to reveal to her pointed ear. "We both are Aphonic."

Brent was speechless. He didn't know what to say. He had not given this as much thought as she had, and clearly her line of questioning had only begun.

"Did you ever wonder why other kids aren't like me? How is it I can still perform Aphonic magic, but no one in my age group or school can besides some professors?" Victoria sought answers to her birth and who she was. Brent unprepared and stumped for words, offered nothing of comfort to her. He couldn't even confirm most of his own past yet, let alone her own origins. It was all hearsay from a man whose intention was not yet clear.

Victoria continued. "The professors are all shocked at my skills, especially O'Sullivan."

"What did he do?"

"Not give me detention. I used magic in the courtyard showing Luminia a simple levitating spell. As you know the school put up an anti-App-Magic field to prevent inappropriate use. He was furious at how I performed it, but once I showed him how I use magic and how I blend in with others he didn't issue a detention," she explained the full story.

"To tell you the truth and thinking on it, I was probably a little too naïve and focused on work, ensuring you had the best life, that I never questioned why the world is vastly different to my era of magic learning. Or how it happened so fast," Brent responded to Victoria's earlier question.

"Did you know children in Ilathier are showing signs of magic wielding, like me?"

"I've heard things around," he lied. He'd been so preoccupied he wasn't on top of the news how he should be.

"Emily told me all about how magic used to be for the people and free to use and experiment with," she started, and this was exactly what Brent needed to hear to wake him up to the conversation he had last night with Arden.

"Tori, can I ask you something?" he asked after a bit to break the silence, and she nodded. "When did you meet Emily?"

"The day you discussed my mentoring with Nia, why?"

"Seems fast to be having sex already, doesn't it?"

"I guess so," she said sheepishly. Victoria pulled her legs to her chest then rolled around facing the back of the couch. "Though we weren't having sex, just kissing," she admitted with sadness in her voice.

"I just don't want her to be taking advantage of you."

"She isn't like that, Dad." Victoria turned and sounded offended.

"I'm not saying she is." He tried to calm her. "I am saying sometimes we don't really know people even after many years." Brent could not help but let some of his own doom and gloom out.

"What do you mean?" She was curious, and Brent needed to tell her the truth, but the words stayed hidden.

"I want you to take things slow, with whoever you choose to end up with," Brent started. "Get to know them and don't rush things."

"I will." Victoria smiled at him.

***

"So, you both have the weekend off?" Victoria asked between bites of her lunch.

"No new assignment yet," Pax said, laying spread out on the floor and scrolling through his phone. "We can't act like we did as kids, we are Mage's Union employees now, we need to act, accordingly," he added, mocking how Brent spoke, and Victoria giggled.

"So, until then we are on break, which means," Brent pulled the permission slip he hadn't signed yet from the fridge, "your class excursion is next week, and the slip is due today." He waved the paper in front of her face.

"So, I can still go?"

"Yes, on the condition Pax and I will chaperone."

"We will?" Pax shuffled upward with a cheerful grin.

"You will?" Victoria expressed the same sentiment.

"I know it isn't ideal but with everything happening at the moment I'd rather err on the side of over cautious, and besides," Brent smiled wide, "don't your friends want to meet the 'Hero of Spellford'?" Brent stood up and flexed what muscles he had while sucking in his gut, which didnt move no matter how much he inhaled.

"Ew! Tickets!" Victoria exclaimed, standing up and headed toward her room. "Whatever, you both can come, but don't embarrass me like you did with Emily."

"I promise." Brent made a cross on his heart and breathed deeply, sitting back down.

Brent signed the permission slip, and it disappeared into thin air. A notification pinged on his phone.

It was from Arden and contained a single sentence.

Can I see you?

Pax finished making himself a third lunch for the day and returned to the couch, turning on the vision orb then noticed Brent staring at his phone.

"You got to touch it to activate it, mate."

"Yeah, I got that much, no it's this message," Brent said, and Pax slunk down into the couch. "From Arden," he added. Pax sprung forward, grabbing the phone out of Brent's hands, and dashed to the kitchen, his lunch balanced in one hand as he inspected the phone.

"Excuse me!" Brent attempted to snatch the phone back immediately.

"Can I see you?" Pax drew the words out slowly "Well at least he isn't demanding, oh another message has come through."

Brent walked over to Pax with a stern look, holding his hand. "My phone please."

Pax dropped the phone into Brent's hands and shrugged, then walked off to the couch once again. "I wonder what he wants. Surely it isn't about work."

How about dinner at Elysian Echoes?

"He just wants to have dinner."

"Haha sure, sure, just don't put out on the first date, mister. Unless he pays, then you might have to," Pax laughed while stuffing his face.

"Paxton!" Brent's neck grew warm, not knowing what to say.

"He isn't wrong dad!" Victoria called out.

"Excuse me," Brent responded. "Both of you are as bad as the other." The three of them laughed together.

"Let me just..." Brent trailed off, beginning a message to Arden.

"What he say?" Pax asked after Brent had walked off into the kitchen to reply in peace.

"I'm having dinner with him tonight." Brent looked up from the phone. "Pax, can we talk about something?"

"It hasn't been that long, has it?" Pax asked, inferring something about sex on a first date, which Brent would be the first to admit was long overdue, but it wasn't what he wanted to discuss.

"No, not that." He looked down the hallway. Victoria was listening to music in her room, so this was his chance. "When you were being assessed, Arden and I discussed something."

"Did he show you his big, thick wand?" Pax giggled and Brent couldn't help but chuckle along with him.

"Get your mind out the..." he stopped himself. "Wait, what do Orcs have for gutters?"

"Troughs? How would I know? I was raised with a human parent."

"It is about the underground Tech-Mages causing the Union all sorts of trouble. It involves Emily, the girl Victoria was umm...kissing, and that cloaked guy we encountered."

Brent walked over to the lounge room and laid his hand on Pax's shoulder to ensure they could have privacy. Talking telepathically was something he would do often when raising Victoria.

Brent explained everything about the Code Weavers and Emily's connection to them. The task he was assigned to watch over and how he was to investigate how this had to do with Victoria and what their interest was in her.

"So, he was flirting with you non-stop the entire conversation?"

"Did you hear anything else?" Brent asked, exasperated by Pax's obviously over the top excitement today about him having something going on with Arden.

"Oh, yeah, well, I mean I can't do anything can I?" he stated softly. "The task is yours, not mine, but I will watch Victoria tonight while you are out. I wonder what the Code Weavers really want with Victoria?"

"My guess is that her Aphonic Magic is a good asset for them, she doesn't have to speak or use a catalyst like a phone. Anyway, don't let her leave this house tonight, got it?" Brent warned Pax and he nodded. "I will have my phone on me, shall we go play some games to kill the time?"

"Nah, I'm going to go paint some of my model kits."

"Ah, okay," Brent said as Pax walked off to his room. He felt completely out of sorts. This was the first weekend off from work he had in a long time since he had started at SorcerySure. He had been working overtime to afford all their expenses and saving his leave to use on a holiday surprise. He wanted to take Victoria and Pax to Iron Helm, but that would now be put on the back burner due to his new job with the Mage's Union. Brent checked his phone and saw it was barely midday.

"Um, Dad?"

"Yes, my darling?" Brent responded to Victoria, who popped her head out of her room.

"Can Emily come over for dinner tonight? She wants to meet you properly."

"Oh, um, tonight? I, uh, um..." Brent wasn't sure how he should say it.

"He can't tonight. He has a date with his boss," Pax called out through the house.

"It's not a date!" Brent called back.

"Sure, it isn't!" he replied.

Brent was about to go shout at Pax when Victoria stopped him.

"So, yeah, um... I can't meet her tonight, but she is welcome to come over, Pax is here."

"Oh, well, okay then. You'll meet eventually," she replied not as glumly as he thought she would. "So, a date?"

"It's not a date, just dinner out."

"Sounds very close to a date."

"Fine, it is a date," he conceded, and smiled to himself at the thought. He was going on a date with someone, and he didn't make the first move for once. It had been longer than a decade of flaky men who were scared he had a child.

A whistle came from Pax's room, and Brent shook his head.

"Here's some cash, go get some snacks or whatever you want for tonight," Brent said.

Victoria's eyes beamed. She walked closer to him and looked up with a big grin.

"What's up?"

"I am so happy you are getting out there again," Victoria pulled in with her arms around his torso.

It had been forever since she wanted to hug him of her own free will, and he didn't let the moment go by. He hugged her tightly. "Love you," he whispered into her ear.

"You too, Dad,"

"Doesn't matter how, you are my daughter."

She gripped onto him even tighter before letting go. Brent smiled as he watched her leave and heard a sniffle as the door shut.

CHAPTER FOURTEEN
FIGURINES AND FABLES

Pax insisted he and Victoria go to the shops to give Brent some time alone before he went out on his date. Pax haphazardly drove Brent's carriage to the local mall, where magic tradition and modernity coexisted. Victoria held on to the handle, praying they wouldn't crash. It wasn't because he was a careless driver, it was because he was too big for the carriage, and it made for some unexpected turns. Especially in the rain.

"You got an idea of what you want to get?" Pax asked, pushing the cart while Victoria walked beside him.

"I am not even sure what Emily eats," Victoria admitted and shoved her hands in her hoodie front pocket.

"You can never go wrong with Pixie Popcorn, or Ember Nuts," Pax picked up both and placed them in the cart. "Oh, and no movie night would be complete without chocolate, there are so many kinds. What's your favourite, Tori?" Pax's excitement level was becoming a little too much for Victoria.

"Uhhh..." she stammered and remained still. "I honestly don't have a preference."

"Yes, you do," Pax insisted. "I've seen you devour candy and lollies."

"Pax, would you stop!" Victoria raised her voice, and he looked taken aback. "If I knew you were going to be like dad, I wouldn't have—" she stopped herself from saying something she would regret.

"I'm sorry, Victoria," Pax said and meant it. "I get a bit too much, especially when food is involved, I know."

"No, it's me," Victoria said almost instantly. "I haven't been the same since I was at the club with Emily."

Pax could see she needed to have a long conversation and out of other shoppers' earshot. He placed the items into the cart and pulled Victoria closer, bending down to her eye level.

"Listen, I will do a quick run around. Would you like to go get us both a drink at Eye of Newt's, and we can chat more there?" Pax asked with a warm smile. warmly. She nodded, and Pax pulled her in for a hug.

Pax watched her as she drifted away and smiled. He couldn't help but feel partly responsible for her upbringing, even though Brent was her father, he had contributed just as much. He knew little else of a life before her, the same as Brent. They discussed it at length one evening and even joked they should get married. Well, Pax suggested it. Brent thought it was a joke. Pax was only looking out for Victoria's best interest and having someone at home to look after her. It must not have been easy to grow up how she had.

Pax was quick about collecting the snacks and drinks. He pushed the cart towards where Victoria had grabbed a seat with their drinks in front of her.

"That was quick," Victoria said cheerfully. "Sorry about before."

"No, don't be." Pax pulled the cart closer to them and sat in the chair. It released a distressed creak, but it held. "Tell me what is going on?"

"Well, before I do, you need to promise you won't say anything to Dad," Victoria prefaced.

"I promise, and besides, you are almost an adult. Whatever you do is not really a concern of mine anymore," Pax said, a little saddened to hear himself say it.

"Alright, then." Victoria took in a breath and shook her hands at her side accompanied by a full body shudder. "I don't know why I am nervous. I looked everywhere online, and it said to discuss this openly with trusted people."

"Victoria, who you choose to sleep with, or love, is always going to be accepted by your father and I, as long as they are good people."

"What?" Victoria asked, confused what Pax was trying to say. "I'm not coming out," she laughed, and now Pax held a look of confusion. "Although I thought it was obvious, I am Bisexual."

"I thought it was odd you were making a point of coming out to me, but wait..." Pax paused, taking a sip. "If you weren't coming out, what were you trying to say?"

"I guess it is still coming out, I err..." she stammered and struggled to find the words. Looking at Pax's gaze through his glasses, his tusks twitching, she formed the words, and they escaped past her lips. "I transformed!"

"Transformed?" Pax asked. "What do you mean?"

"Damn, I wish Emily was here. She can transfer thoughts and show you."

"Well, she is coming tonight, yeah?" Pax asked. "Why don't you have her show me then?"

"Oh right! Okay, let's park this for now."

"Good, because I have my eyes on the Dragon Hoard Emporium." Pax stood up in a rush. Victoria shook her head with a playful roll of her eyes.

She should have known better the reason for his insisting on coming with her. She appreciated the help and small chat, regardless. "Okay, let's go."

A few shops down from the groceries, one could easily see the whimsical dragon themed exterior of The Dragon Hoard Emporium. Pax appeared to levitate towards it, taking the cart with him as they approached.

"Sorry, buddy, no room for carts," the shopkeeper said, waving his hands up from behind the counter as Pax turned to take the cart inside with him.

He turned to Victoria and began to plead for her to take it.

"Alright!" She had to roll her eyes again, but truthfully, he knew she would do anything for him. "Just don't take forever like last time!"

"I won't!" He yelled from inside and, despite his hulking frame, he became lost among the mounds of toys, figures, and other collectables.

Victoria scoffed and pulled out her phone to scroll WicTok. She lifted her head up and saw Pax asking the shopkeeper to take down two specific figurines, even though he already had others in his arms.

"Why, Ms. Abernathy, I didn't know you were a Dragon Hoarder." A familiar voice exclaimed in front of her. Victoria slowly turned her head. It was her Creature Studies professor Silas Evergreen. Clad in earth-toned robes, his long and heavy attire couldnt hide his imposing frame. His dark-ginger hair contrasted with his emerald, green eyes that seemed to hold a world of knowledge and curiosity. He trimmed his beard to a short stubble.

"Oh, Professor Evergreen, I didn't see you there," she started. "I'm not, I'm waiting for—"

"Victoria, who is this?" Paxton walked out with two bags full of figurines and placed them into the cart.

"Ah! You must be her father. It is wonderful to finally meet the 'Hero of Spellford' in the flesh!"

"He's not my dad," Victoria said.

"I'm not her father," Pax's reply almost overlapped Victoria's. Pax introduced himself and gave a brief explanation of the relationship. Silas was quick to apologise for the mistake.

"Well, Mr. Grimtusk," Silas held out his leather gloved hand, "it is a pleasure to meet a gentleman with such fine taste in collectables."

Pax almost blushed, but for an Orc, his cheeks only turned a darker shade of green. He gripped Silas' hand with his own. Silas' grip was firm, and it felt like he was challenging Pax to a squeezing match. Pax made eye contact with Silas as they shook hands and grinned, his tusks extending into his cheeks.

"You are a Dragon Hoarder as well?" Pax asked, completely ignoring Victoria was there.

"Use to." Silas rubbed the back of his head. "Too busy now tending to real life creatures." Silas gave a playful reply.

"Ah! That's too bad," Pax replied with disappointment in his voice. "Would have been nice to chat Hoard."

Silas must have noticed as he pointed at one in the cart. "Maybe you can show me your collection sometime?"

"I would love that. What's your number?" Pax and Silas exchanged numbers and shared a certain smile that lingered a little too long. Pax's tusks twitched, and he went a few shades darker again.

"I appreciate a good...collection," Silas said with a warm smile. He raised a hand onto Pax's bicep and gave a light squeeze. "Well, you two, I must be off. I am making dinner for my grandmother tonight." He smiled at them both before he walked away.

Pax stood silent for a moment, admiring the man walking away and dreaming of a life he could have with him. You know, the normal lonely geeky Half-Orc thing to do.

"See you at school Professor," Victoria finally said.

"Shit!" Pax jumped. "Victoria, you scared me!" Pax clutched at his chest.

"I've been here the entire time while you two flirted like teenagers!" She scolded him with a slight slap to his forearm. "Is everyone in my life hard up for some?"

"Well, not like you can say any different?" Pax snickered to himself.

"What do you mean?"

"Sneaking out to go clubbing with a girl you just met?" Pax pushed the cart towards the carriage park. Victoria looked on dumbstruck.

"We were with her friends, too!" Victoria defended as she chased after him.

Pax loaded the items into the back of the carriage, the rain threatening to fall from the sky once again and buckled his figurines in the backseats to protect them. Once Pax was satisfied that the items wouldn't get damaged, he hopped into the front seat.

"You know, I could have just carried them," Victoria said.

"It's not that I don't trust you," Pax replied, reversing the carriage and heading toward the exit. "I am like this with your dad, too."

"What made you collect them?" she asked as Pax navigated out the mall carriage park and back onto the busy streets.

"Ah, it's a bit of a sombre reason, but before your father and I lived together, he lived with another...uh, friend."

"That was Elwin, right?"

"Yeah, well before he died as a sort of olive branch between us, he bought me my first Dragon Rider figurine and I have been buying them ever since," he admitted, taking his hand off the wheel briefly to wipe his eye.

"Oh, sorry I didn't mean to..." Victoria rubbed his arm and handed him a tissue.

"Don't be." He sniffled and turned a corner, taking the tissue. "He meant a lot to Brent and me," he added with a tender smile.

"How did he die?" Victoria asked, and Pax looked to her. He couldn't believe she didn't know, but clearly Brent was keeping some secrets from her.

"That is not my position to say," Pax admitted truthfully. "If your dad doesn't want to tell you, it wouldn't be right of me to say, we all grieve differently, your dad through silence and I in buying toys."

"Fair enough." Her reply came off a little snooty even though that wasn't her intention.

"What is up with you two at the moment anyway?" Pax asked as they closed in to their street.

"We're fine."

"Doesn't seem it."

"He just...he's a little overbearing and untrusting of me. He's also not willing to budge on my wishes."

"Your wish was to join the Dragoon Corp, Tori. I don't think he would be a good father if he didn't fear for your safety. You are his entire life. It would devastate Brent if you got injured, or worse. Died."

Victoria sat still. She hadn't thought of that. Her focus was on him trying to control her. She failed to see how he might feel.

"Still, why can't he say that to me?" she demanded, and they turned into their street.

"Brent is a man who hides his true feelings," Pax sighed. "It is something I wished he would have grown out of by now, if I am being honest."

"What do you mean?"

"He says and does all the right things, as a father, as a friend," Pax replied, "But deep down he is aching inside and has been ever since Elwin passed. And it is preventing him from being a complete version of himself."

"Elwin was much more than a friend, wasn't he?" Victoria asked.

"Yes, they were engaged," Pax confessed with a nervous gulp. "I was not meant to say that. Forget I mentioned it."

"Ah," Victoria sat in silence until they pulled up into the drive.

The front door opened, and Brent walked outside. Pax turned the carriage off and grabbed her hand. "Secret Keeper?" he asked, and she repeated the words back to him. It was their code from when she was a child, especially when he babysat her, that any foods he got her he was not meant to, would remain their little secret away from Brent. This conversation was one of those moments.

Brent opened Victoria's door and stood there beaming. "Was wondering where you two got to."

"Pax dragged me to his toy store." She rolled her eyes.

"Ah, well, a man has to have some hobbies," he replied with a pep in his voice. "Come on, let's get the shopping in and watch him unbox it."

CHAPTER FIFTEEN
ELYSIAN ECHOES

B rent stepped out from his Witches Wagon in downtown Spellford. The night air was cool as it hit his face. He exhaled air from his nose, taking it all in. He was nervous. This was his first date in a long while. He had been on some—you-could-call-them dates—over the years, but since Elwin's passing, Brent truly had given up on finding another "the one". His focus had been providing for his family; for Victoria.

He wandered down the street towards his destination. Brent wore his blue suit with a white button-up shirt and no tie. He paired it with brown boots, which were entirely too uncomfortable, and dug into his heels, but they were the only ones that matched his outfit. Droves of people on dates and groups of friends walked past him. Brent even caught the eye of a very handsome Mage who was entirely too young for him, probably in his early twenties, but Brent received a wink, and the Mage flashed him a smile.

The wink sent a flutter through his body, and it boosted his confidence. He adjusted his shoulders and pressed on, standing tall.

Brent paused when he saw the sign for the restaurant poke from around the corner. Arden had booked a table at Elysian Echoes, a stylish restaurant with a fusion of contemporary cuisine and classic décor. The golden glow from inside streamed out into the streets and basked the pathway in its warmth. Brent entered and was hit with an ambiance that was cozy yet sophisticated. Soft jazz melodies lingered in the air, complementing the intimate atmosphere.

"Name?" Brent turned and could see that the hostess was behind a small desk inside the vestibule, she looked up at Brent and he noticed she was a Succubus. She had a round magenta face and black eyes that looked like endless pools in the night sky. Her hair was brown and pulled back in a tight bun, with two strands down on either side of her face. She did not remove her frown when Brent smiled at her and pulled the pencil out of her mouth. "You deaf? What's the booking name?"

"I believe it is a table for two under Callahan or Arden," Brent replied, taken aback by her attitude.

When Brent responded, she let out a 'tsk' sound like she was sucking her teeth and scrolled down the booking list. "Ah! Yes, there it is," she said with no enthusiasm and hopped off her stall. She was short, much shorter than the Succubi Brent had encountered in his life but was clearly a firecracker and not one to mess with. "I am Dresen, keep up!" She spun away in a flash towards the restaurant floor. He followed and kept a good pace as he inspected every detail of the restaurant.

The restaurant's walls were adorned with elegant art pieces that sat above the plush booths that ran along the wall. By the long window side near the entrance to the deck, candle lit tables were interspersed. The centrepiece was a grand piano on a small stage with room for a singer.

Weaving through tables they approached the one where Arden waited. Arden stood when he had spotted Brent.

"I see your date noticed you, so off you go!" she said, sucking her teeth again when Brent thanked her.

"What is with the hostess?" Brent asked when she was out of earshot. Arden was dressed in a dark maroon suit, crafted with luxurious fabric. Brent checked out how his suit was tailored to perfection, complimenting his tall, lithe frame. The suit jacket fit snugly, accentuating his broad shoulders, and the pants were just as tailored. His white dress shirt was crisp with a black silk tie, and to complete the ensemble was a polished black leather shoe that could blind someone should the light reflect just right.

"Don't even get me started, devil hostess from Hell," Arden joked, and Brent offered him a chuckle even though it was slightly insensitive toward Succubi.

They stood there taking one another in. It was like two dogs sniffing each other out. Arden was smiling, wider than he had yet ever shown Brent in such a short time getting to know him. Brent could not help but swallow down his nerves. Though he dressed up, he still felt out of place. He was used to getting takeout at midnight, not dinner by candlelight.

"Eh, shall we?" Brent grunted gently and then pointed to the table. Arden nodded, and they both sat down in the soft chairs.

"I've taken the liberty to order us some wine for when you arrived. Ah and here it is, you drink red?" he asked Brent as he took the bottle from the waiter and the glasses and placed them down.

Brent nodded and couldn't remember the last time he even had a drink. Elwin wasn't much of a drinker and by proxy, nor was Brent. Arden poured them both a glass and put the bottle down. He held out his glass for a toast and Brent quickly followed.

"Congratulations on surviving our first mission together." Arden smiled, his eyes radiant.

"Couldn't have done it without you," Brent volleyed back.

"I appreciate that." Arden took in a sip of his wine before he placed it on the table. Brent joined him. "I am very glad to have sourced you, who knew that Spellford's champion would be this handsome in person."

Brent smiled and they both took another sip of wine. That was definitely flirting. There was no mistake about it. "Well, I am just glad to be out of magic insurance and in a job where I am making a difference," Brent offered his most diplomatic response, still wary of Arden's intentions tonight.

"SorcerySure wasn't it?" he asked back handing Brent a menu.

"That's the one." He hoped his snide remark didn't show his resentment for his old job. He gazed down at the menu, as did Arden. "Everything on this menu sounds so delectable, much more high quality than Chrono's or Pizza Pyres."

Arden pulled his face out of the menu and smiled. "Everything here is like a work of art, from the bursts of flavour to the way they are presented. They have the finest Cuisine Magus' across Arcanum working here."

Brent could feel Arden's excitement from across the table in the animated way that the spoke of the restaurant and menu.

"You were here before?" Brent buried himself back into the menu but was not looking at any meal in particular.

"A few times," Arden said, his tone shifted but wasn't quite dismissive. "Alright, I'm going with the Phoenix Poultry, don't worry it's not real Phoenix," Arden laughed at the expression that Brent pulled. "What about you?"

"I had a big lunch, so was thinking maybe the salad?"

"Might I suggest getting the Whispering Forest, then? It comes with an elixir-based dressing made from radiant dewdrops harvested at dawn."

"Sounds good," Brent said, and Arden waved down a waiter.

Arden and Brent continued their chatter while they waited for their meals. The wine was already going to Brent's head. He needed to get some food in him before he was too far gone.

"Keep offering me these drinks and I'll be yours," Brent said to Arden, without even realising it, who was pouring Brent another glass.

"Oh, is that so?" Arden asked in a flirtatious tone. "Why, Mr. Abernathy? I think you are drunk."

"A tad, I'll be fine though, once the meal comes out."

"I know, lets split our meals, get something more than a salad in that belly of yours." Arden took another sip. Brent had not seen someone hold their alcohol quite like it, or he was severely a lightweight.

Brent agreed and when the meals arrived, they did just that, enjoying half of each other's meals. The Phoenix Poultry was a fowl imbued with phoenix feather dust, giving it an extraordinary tenderness as well as rejuvenating properties. Something Brent needed right now. The ember sauce dressing gave a kick of warmth and zest that ignited his numbed tastebuds.

"Oh, this is great," Brent said with a mouthful, not taking notice of his messy eating. As he shovelled in a few bites all at once, he looked up at Arden, who was smiling widely at him.

"I see Grimtusk's eating habits have rubbed off on you after all these years," Arden replied, taking in a small bite and savouring it.

"Sorry, it's just...this is fucking good," Brent replied, taking in another bite. Arden let out a good-natured chuckle and Brent couldn't hide his smirk that turned into a laugh.

The night progressed and Brent was lit like a Rune display at Yulefire. Enough that if Arden suggested taking him home, he would be completely uninhibited and oblige. He would have stone cold sober, anyway. Arden paid for them both and Brent surprised himself by letting him. He was really enjoying being the centre of attention from someone else for a change. He loved Victoria and his life, but this was well overdue.

"All paid," Arden said as he exited the restaurant and met Brent who was chilling outside, with his hands tucked in his pockets. "Shall we continue?"

"Where to?" Brent asked, enjoying being out in the night air once again.

"What about dessert?" Arden suggested. "And then maybe go back to my—" Arden stopped and pulled out his buzzing Rune-Phone. "Scratch that. There is an alert on the Opticon."

Brent stopped on the spot, the concern on his face struggled to take shape because of the alcohol. Arden was stoic as he stood next to him. The alert popped up on Brent's phone next, breaking the silence.

"I know you are on break, but would you mind escorting me back to Sanctum and we can sort this out?" Arden asked.

The excitement to join Arden again, solo on a mission, took over and Brent agreed.

***

The Opticon's alert siren blared through the Strategic Department office as Arden and Brent burst through the door. Urgency filled the air, but Arden and Brent's movements were hindered by the lingering effects of the night's revelry. Both men stumbled over to the central desk, fumbling with the keys to access the Opticon.

Brent, though feeling the remnants of the evening, moved with a bit more steadiness. He glanced at Arden. A mix of concern and determination in his eyes. "Come on Arden we need to focus," he hiccupped. "What's happening?"

Arden managed the key in the commands, his fingers moved much slower than usual. "It's coming from underneath Sanctum." Arden hit a key and then the screen shifted, showing a new map of the underground of Sanctum.

The Opticon's swirling patterns intensified as it struggled to pinpoint exactly where the disturbance was. Multiple flashing lights emanated from below the dungeons and sewerage system.

"It looks like it is coming from the—" Brent started but was interrupted by Arden turning from the Opticon's screen.

"Wait here. I will communicate with you from there."

"Arden, wait! We should call for—" but Arden had already taken off "—Back up," Brent finished.

Brent turned back to the screen, not knowing exactly how to use the Opticon, but assumed it would be easy enough. Brent's phone rang. He picked it up and placed it on speaker.

"Abernathy, can you hear me?" It was Arden, and it appeared he was back in work mode.

"Yes, Ar...sir, loud and clear," Brent replied.

"It looks like whatever it is, it's headed for the Augmenti reserves," Arden breathed heavily as he rushed through Sanctum. "I am almost at the elevator; it will take me directly there. To stop it being accessed, I will need to turn off the flow of Augmenti into the Leyline."

"But that will shut down the entire city, and all communications, too, won't it?"

"No, just Sanctums. Everything else has enough pumping through it will remain protected."

"Alright, hurry!" Brent demanded.

He felt useless up in the office. He could be down there helping Arden. The thrill of joining him on another mission drained from him. He realised this was how Pax must have felt when Arden and Brent checked out the factory.

Brent listened and tracked Arden on the cameras that were active in Sanctum's under croft. He watched as Arden swayed on the spot slightly, but with a look of determination. It was not long before he had arrived at his destination.

Brent waited until he heard the elevator doors open. "You in?"

"Yes, now I will go find the emergency shut down button, but from where you are, you can control when the flow is off to raise a shield around this chamber, I will remain inside and wait for whatever tried to penetrate it."

"You sure this is a wise idea? Shouldn't we call for security or something?" Brent asked, now sobered up enough to question their decisions.

"It would take too long and by the time they arrive, the Augmenti could be compromised or syphoned," Arden replied sharply.

"Okay, no, you're right. Tell me when you are ready."

"Just watch the screen. It should prompt when I shut it down."

Brent watched Arden on the camera as he walked up to the door of the Augmenti Chamber.

"Alright, when you do this, Sanctum will still be powered, but it will use the emergency reserves, I will get you to re-flow that to the Opticon before you proceed." Arden walked Brent through what to do and then waited for his signal.

Brent kept his focus on the screen as Arden entered the chamber. Brent pulled the camera up to a larger view.

***

Arden stood before the door of the Augmenti Chamber. Placing his hand on the scanner, he was granted access. An ethereal pink, yellow and blue glowing force field shimmered in the doorframe. It looked exactly like a bubble and that with one prod of your finger, it would pop, bursting everywhere. But when Arden stepped a cautious foot through, it granted him access.

Inside the cavernous chamber, the space was bathed in the same ethereal glow as the force field. In the centre, an enormous orb almost the size of the room was filed with a swirling mass of what appeared to be pink shimmering liquid. The air was thick with arcane energy as Arden walked under the orb with hesitation in each step. Shimmering Leylines crisscrossed the chamber, converging to a single focal point. Arden followed his line of sight down to directly under the orb.

A large ornate pedestal stood at the heart of the room, adorned with intricate runes that flowed with a soft, pulsating light. These runes were ancient compared to those he was used to seeing. He narrowed his eyes as he observed the magical currents from above. The normally stable and harmonious Augmenti seemed to be agitated.

"I've never seen it behave like this," Arden said.

"What is wrong?" Brent's voice came from the speaker of Arden's Rune-Phone.

"It shouldn't be acting this way, unless—" Arden muttered, his voice like a hushed reverie. Arden looked over the pedestal but could not access it.

The entire chamber quivered, and the Leylines surged with an unpredictable energy. The glow of the Augmenti intensified around him, casting an eerie radiance that danced across the room like shadows flickering from a flame.

"Arden, you need to get out of there!" Brent urged.

"Give me a moment, if I can just—" Arden began mashing the lexicon on the pedestal, but it was unresponsive.

"I'm coming," Brent said.

"No, Brent, stay there!" It was too late. Brent had hung up the call. "Fuck!" Arden exclaimed, slamming his fist down on the lexicon.

A burst of green magic energy rippled through the chamber, causing the Leylines to flicker in response. The glow from the Augmenti's swirling currents intensified briefly and then if in response to the impact, arcane symbols materialised in the air above the pedestal.

It lit up the room, and words formed from the symbols. Shimmering with a soft, ethereal light. Arden focused on the mystical script that formed before him.

The symbols coalesced into a message that he could not translate.

ᛗᚱᛁᛗᛟᛇᛟᛏ ᚠᚱᛗ ᛗᛟᛏᚠᚱᚲᚺ ᚲᚺᛁᛚᛟᚱᛗᛏ

Arden stared at it. "Well, that's helpful," he said out loud, scratching the back of his head.

"What's the problem? Can't translate Ancient Erimosian?" a voice that was familiar spoke from behind.

Arden turned slow on his heels. He had heard this voice before back in Marquis' Apartment only days prior. He turned and there stood the same cloaked man.

"It's you!" Arden said. "What are you doing here?" Arden eyed him with heavy suspicion.

"You have access to something I desire." The man spoke, his voice distorted.

"And what is that?" Arden asked and maintained his distance.

The mask on his face had mechanics that displayed a wavering line as he spoke.

"Abernathy's child, her powers are...beyond measure, and a marvel to witness in person."

A purple glint came from under the darkened hood, and it was clear this was the same person who attacked the club.

"What powers?" Arden asked, "What do you want with her?"

The man stepped forward and pulled his hood from his face. There in the light shimmering from the Augmenti Orb, Marquis Beaumont stood. He was not like how Arden had remembered from photos in all the published journals and in his apartment. His once neatly tied-back curls were now greying and unkempt. He was gaunt, his skin had become pale and washed out. Across his mouth, he wore a mechanical mask like a breathing apparatus. When Marquis took in a breath, the mask lit up and a sound wave would flicker.

He looked at Arden with darkened irises surrounded by bright scarlet and bloodshot from his sclera. His eyelids looked pulled back as if surgically removed.

"Marquis?" Arden asked. "What in the world happened to you?"

"This is what the power of a Monarch looks like." Marquis raised a fist, and magenta sparks ignited around it as he flexed his magical prowess. "Some sacrifices had to be made, but I think you will find they were worth it," Marquis laughed. His voice distorted by the mechanical mask.

Arden did not know what to say. He stood there, unsure if he needed to prepare for a battle.

"Why did you come here?"

"I had to separate you from Abernathy, he will cause me too much trouble." Marquis raised another hand, this time purple lightning sparked. "I will make this simple, bring me his child, and you will have my word that everyone in this pathetic city will remain unharmed." Marquis warned and even though there was no colour in his eyes Arden knew it was a serious threat.

"If you have the power of a Monarch, why do you need Victoria?" Arden asked, stalling for time. If Brent was on his way, he wouldn't be too far off.

"Power is finite, but not hers, her is limitless." He raised his voice and moved from his spot causing Arden to change his stance. "She inherited it from her father's when she was created." Marquis stated "When Brent and Elwin placed their hands in The Cradle, it didn't just take their genetic information but copied and blended their powers as well. It created a child, that child is Victoria."

"Brent never said—"

"Well, no, why would he?" Marquis surmised. "The nature of her origins he wouldn't know himself, but in his grief of losing Elwin that day, he let slip to me how he pulled her from safety." Marquis moved again now standing directly in line with Arden. "Before the ground underneath them broke, in his desperation to save himself and the child, Brent could not save Elwin, too."

Arden did not know what to say. He had only started to get to know Brent, and they hadn't touched on his past.

"Why now the sudden interest in her?"

"It hasn't been sudden. I have been travelling Arcanum, searching for information about the Monarch Children that were born from The Cradle. The same kind that also birthed Victoria, but she is the only one of her kind, born from the Ancient Erimosian Cradle."

"So, that is what you discovered?" Arden demanded.

"No, she wasn't the only one born from The Cradle." Marquis spoke, and it looked like he was smirking, but Arden could only make it out from his eyes.

"I don't believe you," Arden said, "and I won't be a part of this plan."

"You see I have been able to breach through Sanctum's defensive walls. Nothing will stop me from what I want, but I will cut you a deal, bring her to me and I will grant you far-reaching power beyond your imagination. You would be considered a God!" Marquis' tone shifted to something more triumphant as he waved his hand in front of him, his fingertips crackling with magic.

Arden stood there, contemplating what he had said. It was all too far-fetched. And he wasn't about to jeopardise what he had started with Brent for an unknown power.

The chamber door flew open with a swoosh. Brent stepped in to the outer cloister of the chamber. Marquis snapped around on the spot and, without blinking, conjured a swirling, black portal. He fell backwards and disappeared into it like he was tugged from behind.

Arden looked on as Brent stopped dead in his tracks. He looked straight at the man he once considered a father figure, now dressed in the person's cloak who attacked him only days prior.

"Arden!" Brent shouted, locked out from entering the room. Brent felt as if the air was taken from his lungs. That man had looked like Marquis, *but it couldn't be?*

Arden darted around to see if Marquis was still around them, but there was no sign of him, not a trace of him could be detected. Arden left the chamber as fast as he could and ran into the outer cloister where Brent stood.

"What the hell is going on Arden?" Brent demanded. His eyes wide from seeing Marquis. "Was that, really?"

"Come, let's get going. I will explain everything." Arden grabbed Brent by the hand and guided him out of the Augmenti Chamber. As the doors to the elevator opened, Brent pulled Arden in with him.

***

In Arden's office, Brent's mind was swirling. Maquis had reappeared after being confirmed missing for lunars. Arden confirmed he was the assailant in his apartment who attacked them all.

"This is not how I pictured tonight going." Arden took a seat and stared into his glass, consuming another drink to calm his nerves. "I was planning to invite you back to my place."

Brent grinned and raised an eyebrow. "Oh, you think I am that easy, do you?"

"I mean, let's not beat around the bush." Arden smirked. "Well, actually I don't know if you trim or not."

Arden broke the tension in the air with a playful comment, his voice laced with the effects of the alcohol.

"So, the man in the chamber, that really was Marquis?" Brent walked aimlessly around the office still dumbfounded by the encounter.

"Yes." Arden nodded.

"I haven't seen him in, god almost seventeen years," Brent replied, sitting down next to Arden. "He looks like shit." Both men shared a laugh over Brent's comment.

"You are not wrong, a far cry from the man in those photos we saw," Arden said. "But Brent, there's more."

"How so?"

"He asked me to do something for him," Arden replied, looking up from his drink.

"What?" Brent looked to Arden, who was reluctant with his answer.

"He wants Victoria."

"Excuse me?" Brent shot upright in his chair.

"He had an interest in her powers and how she was born. I don't know. It was all very confusing and a lot to take in."

Brent stood and looked down at Arden. "Well, try to make sense of it. What exactly did he say?" his voice shook, his distress more than evident.

"That she was a Monarch Child."

"A Monarch what?"

"Child." Arden finished his whisky. The ice cubes clanked around the empty glass as he set it on the desk with a shaky hand. "Believe me, I am as confused as you."

"Did he say anything else?" Brent turned away.

"Something about an Elwin and you putting your hands into this Cradle to create her." Arden stared at Brent's back as his shoulders tense. Brent turned to face him and hoped Arden didn't notice the change in his posture.

"Well, that's preposterous. I adopted Victoria when she was a baby." He stared down into Arden's blue eyes.

"So, what Marquis said wasn't true?" Arden prodded.

Brent swallowed, knowing that he needed to lie to protect her. "I have the orphanage papers and all documentation at home."

"Alright, I believe you, still seems odd he would mention it. There isn't anything else you are hiding from me, is there? A long-lost lover?"

"No, just that he and I were working on a project together when I graduated from the academy, and we had a falling out. I'd rather not relive that time." Brent was short with his reply, eager to dismiss the topic. He took in a swig of his drink to distract from his inner turmoil, not about to admit to Arden the real reason they had parted ways. Brent wasn't ready to trust anyone else with the truth.

Arden walked over to Brent and took the glass out of Brent's hands and placed it on the desk.

Brent's gaze shifted from Arden's eyes to his lips, he couldnt resist any longer. The desire to kiss them had consumed him throughout the entire night. Arden's lips met his, soft and warm. Their beards intertwined like a thicket, the sensation reminiscent of wading through tall wheat in the summer. He immersed himself in the ocean of their passion fuelled kisses, diving deeper with each moment, until he finally surfaced for a breath. Their tongues met in a furious angsty dance of lust. With his eyes closed, Brent felt the familiar sensation of being with Elwin. Ardent. Fiery. Turbulent.

Arden pushed Brent toward the desk. Their beards tangled together; the crinkling of their hair echoed with each kiss. Slowly they undressed each other, the scent of their sweat filled the room. Brent loosened Arden's tie before freeing his lips. He pulled it off, followed by his jacket. Arden pushed Brent's jacket from his shoulders in return. They stood apart, chests visibly rising and falling as they watched each other unbutton their own shirts. Arden's lips were on Brent's neck, his fingers traced the contours of Arden's physique, lingering near his crotch. Arden's hands caressed the muscles of Brent's back finding their way to his rear. Lips locked in a fervent kiss; Brent couldn't fight off the shiver of delight that radiated through him.

Their skin ignited in a thousand sparks of electricity as the two men explored the other with ravenous curiosity. Arden's skin glistened like it was lit from within, so incredibly warm to the touch. Brent's heart raced, he was rock hard, an ache that needed to be tended to.

Arden traced his tongue from Brent's ear down his neck and to his chest. He sucked on each nipple gently. A moan of pleasure was forced from Brent's throat. Arden continued his descent, running his tongue down Brent's stomach towards his naval. In a greedy display he pulled Brent's pants down to his ankles with a quick yank and dropped to his knees. Arden wrapped his lips around Brent's tip, he coated his cock inch by inch as he took him completely in his mouth.

Brent let out a gasping moan. With each stroke of Arden's wet and warm mouth, Brent got closer to an explosion that felt as if it had been built up for over a decade. And then he succumbed, a guttural cry that could be heard from the ground floor. Ropes flew past Arden's face. He dodged with a precision unlike any Brent had seen, the cum landing all across the floor. Arden smirked while Brent tried to stifle a chuckle.

"Sorry it's been a while." Brent blushed.

Arden stood and gripped Brent's cock once more, sliding his hand down his shaft, pulling his foreskin back and forth. "You're still hard." Brent was raw from shooting his load, but his arousal continued to pump blood through to his throbbing cock.

"You're hard, too," Brent commented, stroking Arden's dick through his pants. It flexed as he stroked with his palm, rubbing up and down.

"You going to just rub one out of me through my pants or you going to whip it out?" Arden pulled Brent forward to run his tongue down his neck and along his jawline. Their lips met once more, Arden thrust his tongue deep into Brent's mouth, only for Brent to reciprocate as he took control and lowered Arden's zipper.

Brent made a move to lower himself to his knees, but Arden gripped him by the arms and whipped Brent around, forcing him up against the desk.

"Do you have any lube?" Arden whispered into Brent's ear, pulling his own pants down.

"No, and it's been too long for spit to do the job," Brent laughed.

"Never fear." Brent heard Arden say followed by a whooshing noise as he conjured something. Before he could react, Brent felt his cheeks spread apart, not by Arden's hand but some form of magic. The familiar, yet cold sensation of lube glided across his hole.

"Did you just…"

"Conjure lube directly onto your asshole?" Arden asked, and Brent nodded. "Yes, I did."

Brent's initial response was to remind Arden magic should not be used in such a way, but his words were lost when he felt the mounting pressure as Arden slid his cock between his ass cheeks.

"Last chance to say no," Arden warned with a lustful groan in Brent's ear.

"I want you to," Brent released the soft words on a sigh.

"Want me to what?" Arden tugged on Brent's hair slightly and he grunted in response.

"I want you to fuck me," he said through heavy breathing.

Arden's cock teased as he slid up and down between Brent's cheeks. The delicious sensation had Brent growing restless. Eagerly, boarding desperate, he pushed his ass against Arden, hungry for more. Arden took that as consent and thrust in with no hesitation, the lube allowed him to enter with some ease. Brent let out a gasp of air, he wanted to bite down on something. It had been way too long.

"Fuckkkk!" Brent cried out and Arden groaned as his cock burst inside of Brent, expanding inside and sitting comfortably. Then again, maybe it had been just long enough.

Arden pulled out just far enough to thrust in again with a slow and steady stoke. He took his time between thrusts, Brent's moans and cries of pleasure echoed in his office as he built up the tension. Each time he slid in and out, Brent felt his skin goosebump with pleasure as a shiver went up his spine. He couldn't remember the last time someone fucked him this way. His entire body tingled. Arden's cock got harder with each thrust. Arden continued to grunt his satisfaction. Brent pushed back, not wanting it to end.

As the ecstasy of the moment took over, Brent felt himself enter a new state of mind. Arden increased his pace, he was close. With a passion riddled moan, Arden thrust himself into Brent, he reached his cock as far into him as he could, his release overpowering and intense. The sensation of Brent's dick flexing was matched by the feeling of being filled as streams of cum from Arden's cock shot inside him, bringing him to a new level of ecstasy. Brent shot a second load all over Arden's desk, covering the mahogany in silvery-white puddles.

Arden collapsed onto Brent, their bodies slick with sweat and radiating heat, both gasping for breath from sheer exhaustion.

"Well, as first dates go, this isn't the worst I've had," Brent laughed moments later. Arden returned a chuckle as they disentangled to get cleaned up.

"You could say that again," Arden quipped. "Dinner, danger..."

"...and the best dick I've had in a long time," Brent added with a smirk, causing them both to burst into comfortable laughter that echoed through the room.

"Come here, you got a bit of..." Brent grabbed a tissue and wiped Arden's face. "I hate to do this, but I must be getting home. I am a father, after all." Brent scurried to redress.

"How is Victoria doing?" Arden asked as he scooped up their shoes from the office floor.

"She is fantastic, tutoring is going well." Brent took his boots from Arden and slipped them on. "But you are wondering about that other part, well, she was seeing Emily tonight, actually."

Arden raised an eyebrow in clear interest.

"Look, I don't know what else there is to say. I haven't found out anything except the fact that they are hooking up after only knowing each other for a few days."

"She told you that?"

"No, I walked in on them," Brent laughed at the look of surprise on Arden's face.

"What? No way!"

"Yes, it was very messy." Arden stopped short and gave Brent a certain look. "Oh my, not the kissing, me walking in. Oh god!" Brent hid his face. "I'm believing I don't have that much Dad Magic. Parenting a teenager is very hard work and, in some cases, Pax is no help."

"When it comes to Emily, do you think of her as just a girlfriend, or is there any association with the Code Weavers?" Arden questioned.

"I honestly couldn't tell you yet. I've met her that one time and it was brief. Perhaps you can come to my house now? She is hanging out with Victoria tonight." Brent smiled. "Drop your date off?"

"Alright, let's scope it out." He gave a cheeky smile. "I also want to see what kind of place you have."

Victoria was the most important part of his life for so long, but soon she would move out and begin her own life. Tonight, even with its dangers, was exactly what he needed. Dread flooded Brent. How could he explain who Arden was? Was he just his boss? His boyfriend? It would be weird to ask, he didn't think one date and sex constituted for him to ask, no matter how spectacular the sex was.

And how could he forget Marquis showing up? Brent desperately wished to talk to Pax about it. All of it. Hook-up included.

Arden took Brent's hand and pulled him closer. "Let's take it slow Brent," he said, as if he read his mind. "And for now," Brent felt his breath against his face and his heart pounded in his ears, "let's keep the Marquis discussion for at work."

Brent gave a simple nod, and Arden's lips met his own once more.

CHAPTER SIXTEEN
MAGIC DAMAGE CLAIMS

"So, what you are telling me is, your dad and you are basically the same?" Emily asked Victoria. The two girls sat at the kitchen table with Paxton, who was playing host, as they all devoured their favourites from Mystic Pizza that had been delivered by Witches Wagon.

"My dad and I are nothing alike," Victoria said with a mouthful. She wiped her face clean of the greasy cheese residue left around her lips with a napkin. "Not a single bit."

"That's not true. Brent is a lot less stubborn," Pax said. He had tried to remain unbiased all night and not let on to Victoria the knowledge he possessed.

"Pax!" Victoria cried out in defiance, "If I am stubborn, it's because you helped raised me." She scrunched up her nose and stuck out her tongue.

Pax chuckled into his Pep Up Elixir. "Brent worked a lot in those early days, his claims work demanded a lot of him before he got the SorcerySure desk job."

"Oh, what did he do back then?" Emily asked before taking a sip of her drink.

"Well, when I was between jobs, happened a lot being such the Orcish hunk that I am, my workplaces couldn't handle how hot I was," Pax said with an air of obvious flippancy to it, and brandished his tusks while flexing slightly.

Victoria rolled her eyes, but he got a laugh from Emily.

"Brent worked for a division of SorcerySure's Magic Damage Claims Unit as an inspector. A role he ended up despising, and one claim job I remember in particular made him take a few steps back and decide it'd be better to have a less intensive sales desk job."

"Let me guess, almost butchered by Trolls?" Emily asked, intrigued by the story she was told. She leaned forward in her seat, placing her arms on the table, keen to hear more.

"Nothing that simple I'm afraid," Pax said. "This well-known and re-spected collector reported theft of several rare and powerful artifacts from his secured vault," Pax started to tell the story.

Five Years prior to current day

The Collector claimed that the theft occurred under unknown circum-stances as Video Cam-Mera footage did not show any break-ins, magical disturbances or forced entry. Video Cam-Mera's could detect most magic energy wavelengths, so to bypass their security systems, was impressive, to say the least. Brent took Pax along with him as they planned to go out afterward to see the newest Swordsman of the Witch film starring his favourite actor, Henrich Carvally. Pax followed inside the collector's home, determined not to fidget while Brent did his work.

Brent looked around and made some mental notes of the collector's foyer. A door opened on the landing above them and a frail but agile man bounded down the stairs. The collector stopped short in front of Brent and Pax.

"Gregor Solley, I am Brent Abernathy, the SorcerySure's Claims Inspec-tor. We spoke on the phone earlier." Brent held out a hand and Gregor offered a reluctant shake.

"Didn't know they hired Green skins," Gregor said to Brent, pointing his head at Pax. "I thought this was a solo inspection. I am very private, you see, and I don't like unwanted guests, especially those who—"

Brent cut him off. "Paxton is a long-time friend and will not interfere with the inspection in anyway, Sir Solley. Will his ethnicity be a problem?" Brent asked, half closing his lexicon pad. "Because if it is, I will arrange for someone else to—"

"Not at all, Abernathy. Your track record speaks for itself. I have many Orc friends, just a very private person. With the past war in Valtoria, allegiance to Spellford is paramount. You can't be too careful."

"Yes, well, Pax was born and raised in Arcanum of Half-Human heritage if that gives you any consolation of his allegiance?" Brent stood firm. "Shall we continue, or will I have to report your archaic views to the Union?" Brent snapped his lexicon shut.

"Brent, it's fine, I'll wait outside." Pax's tired sigh screamed *I'm used to it.* Pax turned to leave. Gregor looked at Brent with panic in his eyes. Brent remained determined in his stance, his lexicon now tucked under his arm.

"Uhhh...Mr Paxton, wait!" Gregor started, his voice shaky "I am not myself currently, what with the break in, please forgive my rudeness on account of my stressed state. Please take a seat in the kitchen, my staff will give you anything you need, food, drink..." Gregor snapped his fingers. One of his servants quickly scuttled to Pax's side and dragged him to the kitchen.

Brent watched the servant and Pax leave, his eyes on them until they had left the room. He rotated fast on his feet in Gregor's direction. Panic still covered his face. "An Incubus?"

"Let's both agree to not judge each other's company?" Gregor stated, wiping sweat off his brow. "I apologised for getting off on the wrong foot. I am incredibly str—"

"Stressed, yeah...yeah I got it," Brent said, waving his hand and opening his lexicon with deserved disdain.

Back in Modern Day

"I didn't hear too much after that as I had a small feast in the kitchen, but what Brent told me was that it was an artefact, The Collector, Gregor Solley stole from the Mage's Union that drained the person of their soul."

"You forgot to mention that I was bound and gagged for over an hour while Gregor attempted to use that Soul Stone device on me," Brent said, leaning on the kitchen archway. He and Arden had slipped in without the three taking notice. The two men walked into the room to join them at the table.

"We didn't hear you come in," Pax said with a nervous laugh.

A quick introduction was exchanged between Arden and the girls, and Brent was able to get a formal introduction himself with Emily.

"So, Dad, Pax was telling us about the last job that made you quit claims work," Victoria said, clearly intrigued.

"Yes, well, he was definitely a collector, and it was all a ruse to collect me, so to speak," Brent replied with a shrug. "What was weird to me is, I wasn't famous."

"It all made sense in the end why he was distrustful of Orcs, we are impervious to a soul stone device. So, when I came bounding through the room and knocked the lights out of him, I could remove Brent before the transference was complete," Pax said imitating with his hands crashing into something.

"Sometimes I wonder if I got all of my soul out of that stone now that I think about it," Brent said, then looked at Emily, who was smiling at the exchange. "So, have you all been having fun? I hope Pax hasn't made you watch his re-runs of Dragon Rangers."

"Nah, we just got pizza. Been talking about school. He was a very good babysitter," Victoria responded.

"Good to hear Grimtusk!" Arden spoke up, drawing himself a glass of Pep-up elixir.

"What did you two get up to?" Pax asked. Brent and Arden's eyes darted to the others, followed be a secretive smirk before they looked away.

"Nothing much," the men said in unison, and tried to hide their child-like grins. Pax eyed Brent, who gave him a look that said I'll tell you later.

"Emily, I hear you study under Professor Nia also," Brent was quick to change the subject.

Emily swallowed her drink and smiled wide. "Yes, she is the best. Tor thinks so as well, and Professor Nia thinks the world of Tor, but then again who wouldn't?" she nudged Victoria, who gave a light slap on Emily's arm in return.

"Well, she is my world, my everything." Brent's smile was warm as he looked between the two girls. It was a serene moment, but he could not help letting his fatherly instincts take over. "How was Cauldron a few nights ago?"

Victoria stopped short with her glass to her mouth and Emily looked to her at a loss for what to say.

"I am not overly impressed that my underage daughter is going out to clubs, but I am glad she had a friend looking out for her while I was away." Brent's tone held a little too much sarcasm.

He was still furious with Victoria for not telling him the truth about what went down.

"Dad, can we not?" Victoria pleaded.

"Yeah, Brent, let it go. She is alive and well." Arden laid a hand on Brent's gently; it helped calm his anger. He looked to Emily.

"Sorry, Emily. I get very protective of my daughter."

"More like overbearing," Victoria groaned.

"No, Victoria, I think it is good to have a father this protective." Emily gripped her hand and smiled.

A silence grew between them until Arden spoke again.

"So, Emily, what is your major?"

"The Arcanthus Legacy on Ethics and Magic and Technology," she said proudly.

"Victoria loves Magic Ethics," Brent said.

"What's your views on Magic resources, like Augmenti, being controlled by the Mage's Union say versus a free will of use for all?" Arden asked, and Brent knew where he was going. He had to maintain face. Arden was, after all, still his boss, even if he went down on him only an hour ago.

"I think there should be some regulatory body," she said. "But is the Mage's Union the right one? That's what I am exploring in my paper," Emily offered a diplomatic response.

"I would love to see your paper once it is complete," Arden said.

"What do you do at the Mage's Union?" she asked him point blank.

"I am the Director of the Magical Strategic Department."

"What does that entail?" she asked almost as soon as Arden finished.

"A bit of this and that, nothing a few students of the academy need to be concerned with." Arden faked a laugh, trying to divert from divulging too much.

"Well, Victoria told me that Brent had been working on the disappearance case of Marquis Beaumont? So, I assumed he was in some sort of investigative field?" she pressed.

"Ah, that is classified information," Arden interrupted, shooting eyes at Brent, who looked away, taking a sip of his drink.

"She must have overheard Pax and I," Brent said into his cup.

"I take that as a yes, then?" Emily looked smug. There was something about her that Brent couldn't quite put his finger on, she almost looked familiar.

Anyone looking down into the kitchen could feel the tension being cut with a knife. Arden and Emily were locked in a standoff and only Brent knew the underlying reason. Victoria nudged Emily under the table. Brent looked from the girls to Arden, who was taking his time answering. Pax stood up and cleaned the table in an attempt to diffuse the tension.

"Brent, would you like to tell Emily what you discovered?" Arden asked.

"I don't think it is of the business of academy students, whether they are close to Professor Nia or not," Brent responded.

"Spoken like a true Mage's Union loyalist," Emily retorted, and Victoria nudged her again.

"It's okay, Victoria. Unfortunately, we have no conclusion yet as to the whereabouts of his location."

"Well, it is getting late, Arden. I should let you get home?" Brent stood and Arden followed his lead.

"I probably should go, too. Thrash and Sam are expecting me back at the dorms." Emily rose to her feet.

"I'll walk you out," Brent and Victoria said at the same time.

"Not like your father, hey?" Emily winked at Victoria.

"What's that about?" Brent asked, but no one responded.

Brent and Arden hung back to let Emily and Victoria say their goodbyes. When the door shut, Victoria said a brief goodnight and went into her room.

Pax walked up to both Brent and Arden, standing in the living room.

"So, boss, see you Runeday?" Pax asked.

"Yeah, come bright and early. We got some projects to work on that I would like the three of us to tackle."

"Will you be more prepared than last time?" Brent tried to be professional.

"Maybe," Arden joked and the two chuckled together.

Pax, unaware he was overstaying his welcome in the conversation, stood there smiling.

"Okay, Pax, I'll see you Runeday then?" Arden said awkwardly. Pax stood there with a wide grin. Brent squinted at him hoping he would get the hint to bugger off. They all stood in awkward silence until Pax finally walked away.

"Let me walk you out," Brent said, and Arden followed Brent to the front door.

All Brent wanted to do was kiss him again. That was a lie. He wanted to jump his bones. Arden was still looking stupidly fuckable. But he couldn't just yet in front of everyone.

"Enjoy tomorrow. Come Runeday, we got a lot to do." Arden smiled.

"Oh, that reminds me," Brent said, with an exasperated tone. "Pax and I are chaperones to Victoria's excursion to the Dragon Sanctuary this coming week. It is for one of her subjects, and she has a *fascination* with dragons," Brent emphasised.

"Well, let's refrain from putting you both into the wards again." Arden smiled, and Brent homed in on his lips. "Okay, see you Runeday?"

Brent glanced around to ensure they were alone and then didn't waste time, taking his opportunity to give Arden a brief kiss. The kiss wasn't brief, though, and their tongues began to fight for dominance. Brent let his defences down, his dick twitched as he started to give in. He either had to take Arden to his room or stop before this went any further.

Pulling apart from one another, Brent opened the door.

"Goodnight," Arden said, before he left the house. Brent could see him adjust his own pants as he took the stairs down from the door. Brent waved once more then lifted his fingers to his lips.

"Good kiss?" Pax crept up behind him as the door shut. Brent almost leapt from his skin.

"Fucking hell, Pax! You were watching?"

"Only briefly," Pax cried out in defence as Brent chased him. "Can't blame a Half-Orc for admiring two hot men kissing, but ah, cover that!" Pax pointed down at Brent's crotch.

Brent untucked his shirt and let it hang over but realised that only made it more obvious.

"I have to tell you something," Brent started.

"About?"

Brent paused contemplating what he wanted to say, but in his still drunken stupor he smiled and then burped slightly. "You know what, I'm too drunk and going to bed, it can wait. Brent announced with a slight kick in his step. He wanted to tell him about everything from the night, but he needed to take care of his situation more. Well, no, he wanted Arden to help, but the memories of that night would have to do for tonight. "Goodnight," Brent said with a smile.

"Sleep well," Pax chuckled to himself before heading back to his room.

CHAPTER SEVENTEEN
WEAVED CODE

Runasday came around quicker than both Pax and Brent would have liked. Now that Victoria was taking herself to school, Brent could arrive early for work. Still tending to a headache from the weekend's frivolity, Brent had picked up an old Orcish remedy Pax swore by. Brent swirled the brown and mustard frothing liquid and then chugged down the Bat-Ghoul Gut Tonic, a foul—acidic-smelling liquid made from fermented stomach contents of Bat-Ghouls and Pep-Up Elixir. It settled his stomach and eased his headache, as well as the nausea.

"Whatever you are drinking Abernathy, I will have one too." Arden looked down at the fizzing mucus coloured drink, slightly off kilter.

"When a hangover strikes, Pax confidently sprang into action and mixed whatever ingredients he could source at the local authentic Orcary, an Orcish run market. The taste was never pleasant for humans and other races, but Pax swears by their effectiveness in banishing the effects of a night of revelry," Brent explained.

Arden took a sniff of it and pulled his nose away. "You swear this works?" Arden held his nose and looked down at Pax with one eye covered by his left arm, holding the drink to his mouth.

"Yup," Pax said with assuredness. "Drink up!" He stood and lifted Arden's arm tilting the concoction down his throat.

Upon the first drop of the liquid, Arden almost gagged. He looked at Pax once again, rolled his eyes and finished the entire drink in one gulp. With a gasp for air, Arden held out his tongue to show he downed it.

"I'm sure you've swallowed worse," Pax giggled and walked off.

Arden paused and walked over to Brent's desk while Pax took the glasses to the kitchenette.

"You told him about us?" Arden whispered, looking at Brent, who waved his hand signalling him to shut up.

"Told me what?" Pax asked, coming up from behind Arden.

"Nothing," Arden said, but he wasn't a talented liar. Pax eyed the two, but let it go. The three men sat together, Arden continued to nurse his headache, rubbing his temples waiting for the remedy to take effect.

"I won't drink ever again if it means I never have to drink that. What did you call it?"

"Bat-Ghoul Gut Tonic," Brent and Pax said at the same time.

"Yeah, that. They really don't warn you that when you get older hangovers last all weekend." Arden shook his head and tried to collect himself.

"We didn't really have that much, did we?" Brent asked.

"Alright boys, our next assignment is—" Arden stood and ignored Brent's question. He was back to business mode.

"What about Marquis?" Pax asked. Brent and Arden exchanged a quick glance before they looked away.

"What about him?" Arden replied too quickly.

"We have found no evidence of his whereabouts," Pax elaborated, and noticed the look Brent and Arden shared once more. "Alright, what is going on?"

Brent made to speak, but Arden beat him to it. "We found Marquis, well, rather he found us."

"What do you mean?" Pax asked.

"Arden, are you certain you want—"

"He has a right to know. He will sooner rather than later, anyway."

"Okay," Brent swallowed his own objections. He wasn't certain how he felt about what happened with Marquis' reappearance and his demands regarding Victoria, her powers and The Cradle. Then there was the matter of these Monarch Children. But one thing was unanswered. What was Marquis' angle in this? Was it revenge against Brent for not joining him? A fierce desire to go hunt Marquis down and find out overtook him, but Brent couldn't deny his best bet in finding Marquis was his job with The Mage's Union. As if by fate, he had the ability to monitor the entire city at his fingertips with the Opticon.

Arden gave Pax a very brief, but well put together version of the events that unfolded when they arrived here on Shroudasday after their date.

"One thing remains unclear. If he can just waltz in here, what is stopping him from going to the academy now and taking Victoria?"

"Well, the academy holds significance to him. That and he is in hiding," Arden replied. "Not to mention the security measures, but as you said, he broke through Sanctum's."

"He was there at the club the night Victoria was, so clearly he can find her if he wants to." Brent looked at the evidence they had laid out. "I ought to take her out of school and somewhere far away."

"Where would you go?" Arden asked.

"Suncrest?" Pax knew all too well that it was a place he desired to visit with Victoria.

"Running away won't solve the problem. He will hunt you down, and outside of Spellford you have even less protection."

"I know," Brent replied after a brief pause. "I think there are a combination of many factors preventing him from any drastic measure, and possibly even ones we haven't considered."

"Marquis is a celebrated Tech-Mage. He can't exactly go unnoticed." An elderly woman's voice sounded from behind them.

"Ah, Elder Evergreen, thank you for coming." Arden sprung up and went to the office entrance to help her inside.

Seraphina Evergreen was one of Arcanum's most renowned Sages, known for her wisdom and vast knowledge of ancient magic. Her gentle nature and quick wit matched her commanding presence. As one of the oldest and well-respected members of the Mage's Union, she served under the Arch Mage, representing the body corporate across Spellford. She was often sought after for her counsel in matters of great importance.

"I don't need your help, Callahan," Seraphina muttered as she shuffled along through the room. Arden's rejected hand hung limp.

"Ah! Mr Abernathy, I presume?" Her voice was laced with the gravelly sound of a pack a day smoker. Brent stood to take her hand. "It is a pleasure to meet the 'Hero of Spellford' at last," Seraphina added with emphasis.

"Elder Evergreen," Brent beamed. "The pleasure is all mine, truly!" Brent bowed his head, which was customary in the Mage's Union to those of Elder status. Seraphina slapped him on the shoulder.

"No need to bow to me, boy!" she teased. "Callahan isn't working you over too hard, is he?"

"There's nothing Arden can do to work me too hard, ma'am." Brent chuckled to himself, knowing too well that all he wanted was Arden to test that limit later.

"Glad to hear it." She turned to Paxton. "And who might this strapping young lad be?"

"Paxton Grimtusk, ma'am," Pax made to bow, and he was rewarded with a slap on the upper arm, too.

"I will not accept an Orc bowing to me. You are placed into positions of persecution enough," she said gruffly, walking towards their desks. Arden hurried to get her a chair.

Brent had yet to see him this way around his superiors, and he had to admit it was a little fun to watch.

Seraphina was dressed in blue and grey robes and had a mahogany walking stick. Attached to her hip on a thin golden weaved belt, an ECC, Essence Cloud Caster, hung. It was a handheld vaporising device that allowed its users to emit aromatic and magical clouds, each imbued with unique essences or incantations.

"So, Marquis is alive after all?" she asked, taking her chair. The three men joined her.

"It appears so and claims to have gained the powers of a True Monarch."

"Preposterous!" Seraphina spat.

"Elder?" Arden turned to her, but Seraphina didn't shift her gaze from the Opticon.

"The Monarch Program was shut down over forty-five years ago. Arch Mage Steiner saw to that. That's how he rose the ranks so fast."

"Why have I not been able to find any record of this?" Arden asked.

"You don't know where to look," Seraphina replied with a haughty lilt in her voice. "The young are always so blind to what's right in front of them." She gave an annoyed grunt and unhooked her ECC, she took in a puff and a sweet aroma filled the room near her and disappeared as fast as it was generated.

"I read over your report of Marquis' apartment investigation." She placed the ECC on the desk with a thud. "Do you know what that building stands on to this day?"

"No?" Brent asked.

"It was the original Sanctum," Pax replied. The other three turned, but only Arden and Brent wore looks of surprise.

"Correct, you are, Mr. Grimtusk." She smiled. "Probably way before you were all born, but it was the heart and centre for all magic activity within the city, and it was the location of Spellford's Augmenti Well."

"Is that what lays beneath Sanctum now?" Brent looked to Arden for an answer.

"The Orb?" Seraphina asked, referring to the structure Brent saw when Arden and he investigated the breach. "That was what was left of the Augmenti Well when The Monarch Program ended, Magnar decreed its removal to under Sanctum around the same time as he became Arch Mage."

"But Arden—" Brent said, and they all turned to him "That chasm in the apartment."

"What chasm, that wasn't mentioned in the report?" Seraphina spoke up, grabbing her ECC once again.

"I didn't think it was relevant," Arden admitted sheepishly, taking his lexicon and scrolling through the report.

"A giant hole in the ground where the Augmenti Well used to be is pretty fucking relevant. You are lucky my replacement died. No idea how you got this job, boy," Seraphina shook her head and released another puff of sweet-smelling vapours.

"Must you do that in here?" Arden waved his hands around to clear the air. "It can't be good for the Magi-Tech."

"Uh, actually Arden, the vapours are completely harmless to the tech. To her lungs, the debate is still out," Pax interrupted. Brent got a kick out of watching Arden squirm as he was ganged up on. He knew he shouldn't, but it was a little too enjoyable.

"They are herbal, Grimtusk. But also, would you really deny an old lady her one joy?" Seraphina blew another puff.

"No one denies you anything. Just do it outside next time."

"Alright, Callahan, keep your jockstrap on," she retorted with a dismissive chuckle.

Brent turned his head to muffle his snickering into his robe collar, and tried to pretend it was a sneeze. "Okay, so that chasm is linked you think?" he asked, coming up for air.

"Without looking at it myself I wouldn't know," Seraphina said. She looked to Arden with a smile, her teeth were stained from the ECC. "When shall we depart?"

"You read the report, when we last went, we were attacked, not to mention the other investigators we lost."

"Callahan, now that you have registered his energy signal once with the Opticon, you can retrace it, and replicate it for additional searches." Seraphina pointed to the Panopticon and shook her head "Did you not read the guide I spent many devoted, unpaid hours to write up?"

"Wait, we can do that?" Pax stood and rushed over to the main desk.

"You were the Director before Arden?" Brent asked.

"Quite a successful one, too." She had pride in her tone and looked at Brent with a glint in her eye. "I originally passed it on to another man, but he passed. Magnar has kept me on as a consultant of sorts. For moments like this, it seems."

"Alright, you two, enough disparaging my abilities," Arden quipped, disgruntled that he was out of his league. "Grimtusk, can you run that scan now?"

"Already working on it," Pax uttered, typing away. "But replicating an energy signal retroactively will take some time. Perhaps the three of you can go get a coffee?"

Pax was entirely focused on the Opticon. Brent was impressed by his friends' abilities to utilise this technology. While Pax was great for a lot of things, like hauling heavy items around and baby-sitting Victoria, he had never shown Brent much interest in using Magi-Tech except for the basics. Like ordering food off Witches Wagon or watching the vision orb. Brent and Arden rose together, but Seraphina remained seated.

"Coming Evergreen?" Arden asked.

"I'm fine here. I will monitor Grimtusk," Seraphina muttered.

Once the two men were out of earshot on their errand of grabbing coffees, Seraphina hobbled over to the Opticon's main desk to sit beside him.

"I have a grandson around your age," she started clipping her ECC back onto her belt. "He is a professor at the academy, works in Creature Studies."

"Silas Evergreen!" Pax burst out, turning to Seraphina, who motioned to the Opticon. Pax returned his attention to his work with a jolt.

"Yes." Seraphina examined him with a scrupulous eye. "So, you're the handsome Orc he met at the shops I presume." Seraphina leaned back and smiled to herself. "Spellford is a small world and there are only a handful of Orc Men I would call handsome."

"Thanks." Pax blushed but tried to maintain his focus on the screen.

Brent and Arden returned with the coffees and placed them on the table.

"Anything yet?" Arden asked.

"Unfortunately, I am picking up no trace of him anywhere. I am, however, picking up signals that are like the Anomaly you and Brent closed. They're showing up throughout the city and outer suburbs."

"Show me," Arden demanded. Pax brought it up on the big screen. Arden inspected them one by one and then he moved forward, closer to the screen. "These are all connected."

"Converging at the centre of the city," Brent said.

"It looks like a giant web." Seraphina spotted the pattern and pointed it out. "It mimics the entire Leylines that used to exist from the Well."

"Whatever Marquis has planned will be found at the bottom of the chasm," Arden said.

"But you said it yourself. We got attacked," Brent reminded him.

Arden turned and grinned. He was excited, just like when they first entered the apartment building. "We are going to need some additional resources then."

"From where? There's no staff here," Brent replied.

"Uh, yeah, you are right. Well, guess it's us four then," Arden responded, but the glint didn't leave his eyes.

CHAPTER EIGHTEEN
ARCANTHUS GROUP PROJECT

"Ugh! Rune-Tech studies," Victoria sighed.

She sat with Lirien and Luminia during their lunch break. She was so bored it become stifling. Nothing had the same thrill as it did that night at Cauldron. The three sat a garden table, Luminia perched on top. The sun was out, warm and bright. The lingering scent of dew wafted through the courtyard.

"But you are so good at it." Lirien tried to encourage her, but his smile was weak.

"*So?*" she bit back with too much venom in her voice. "Just because I can do things well doesn't mean I enjoy them."

"What is wrong with you today, Victoria? Are you alright?" Luminia looked down at Victoria as she stretched her arms out, soaking up the warm sunlight spreading across the grass in the academy's gardens.

"I'm fine," Victoria's tone was dismissive.

"You aren't your usual—" Luminia started, but paused and gave a slight shrug when she couldn't pinpoint what it was. "What would you call it Lirien?"

"High-functioning depressed Queen Chic?" Lirien asked cheekily. "Or Sombre Chic? What do you prefer?" He struck a pose that was reminiscent of a runway model. Luminia slapped him on the shoulder.

"You've been avoiding us," Luminia poked Victoria in the back with accusation.

"No, I hav...well, yeah...I don't know. I am fine, just been busy you know?" she stuttered through her explanation. Her two friends exchanged a look. "What was *that*?" she glanced between them.

"We have barely talked in the last few weeks, in messages you left us both on read, your socials are all dark and depresso," Lirien interrogated, clearly upset. He pulled up a recent post Victoria made on WicTok. It was an assortment of photos with sad lyrics.

"Do you even want to be our friend anymore?" Luminia jumped up in a sudden burst, staring Victoria down.

This over dramatic attack was stupid. She was so focused on Emily it was affecting her entire demeanour. Wasn't that allowed? The issue was that she hadn't told her friends yet, it felt too early.

"So? I've been moody, it hasn't even been a full lunar cycle. You two are acting ridiculous. I'm fine." she said with a shrug.

Lirien stretched out his hands and urged Victoria take them in hers. She rolled her eyes and handed him her hands. He twisted her palms upwards and inspected them.

"Someone's mood cycle is a filthy brown today." Lirien's voice was soothing, it felt like she was embraced by a soft, white cloud. Weightless and airy as he traced the back of her hand. "But I see a river of positivity if you would tell us what is going on?"

Victoria attempted to snap her hands back, but he held on too tight.

"Look, Tor, we are worried. Are you okay?"

Victoria's pocket buzzed. She ripped her hand from his, almost throwing Lirien off the seat. It was Emily. Lirien leapt over to get peek at her phone.

"Who is Emily?" he questioned. Victoria hid her phone at an angle to reply.

"Emily?" Luminia stood with a curious look and leaned against the table. "That girl you went to Cauldron with?"

"Yeah, the same one. What about it?" Victoria said with exasperation.

"How was it?" Lirien shuffled closer to Victoria. She leaned away and sent a hurried reply to Emily.

"I've always wanted to go clubbin," he added with a swish of his hair. He was about to make this about him. It was one of the traits that she did not like about her best friend.

"Wait a second, you are still underage. How did you get in?" Luminia spoke up when her two friends remained quiet.

"Oh," Victoria pulled herself from her phone. "Uhm, well, Emily adjusted my ID. Here." She rummaged in her pocket and pulled out the ID to show off.

Lirien snatched it from her, turning it over for thorough inspection "The date hasn't reverted yet? That's so cool. How did she learn to do that?"

"Doesn't matter how, it's highly illegal," Luminia said.

"Can it, killjoy!" Lirien quipped, too impressed with the ID's transfiguration to care. "How did she get this past the bouncer wizards?"

"She is a master at illusionary magic, at least that's what Thrash said. I...my memories of that night are so fuzzy."

"You didn't drink, did you?" Luminia scoffed with disapproval when Victoria nodded her head. Victoria let out a sigh, as this conversation went on, she realized maybe she needed to clue in her two closest friends.

"Are you going to be an insufferable ass all day or would you like me to explain?" She stood so her face could be level with Luminia's.

"Can't I be both?" She gave a wide smile.

"No!" Lirien and Victoria chimed together. The three shared a laugh before Victoria went into the details of the other night.

"So, if you don't have your own memories, how do you know what happened?" Luminia asked.

"Emily showed me through thought transference." Victoria flourished her hands to simulate the magic of thought transference. "But I don't possess any of my own memories...something, I think something happened to me."

"What do you mean?"

"Maybe I can show you all?" Before Victoria could explain, Emily's voice broke in from behind. She came to lean against the table where the group sat.

Thrash and Sam stood close behind her, talking amongst themselves. Victoria hadn't seen or even spoken much to Emily since the awkward dinner with Arden.

Victoria walked over to give Emily a hug. "How are you? I've been thinking about you since I last saw you." Victoria's face was buried amongst Emily's ginger hair. She smelled like vanilla and cherries. Victoria couldn't help but inhale the sweet scent.

Victoria's mood shifted from glum to elated in seconds. Emily truly made her happy. The words her father said rang in her mind. Did she really know Emily all that well? Everything had been moving at an incredibly fast pace. She too began to question if she should lean on the brakes a little. It was hard when Emily made her feel this way, though. She leaned into the hug before letting Emily go.

"Em, this is Lirien and Luminia," she introduced Emily to her friends. "These two have been in my life longer than I care to admit."

Lirien slapped Victoria slightly on the arm.

"About that thought transference?" Lirien rose to his feet.

"Oh, yes! Hold out your—" The high-pitched ring of the lunch bell cut her off. "Ah damn, it will have to wait. We have Magic Defence Training."

"Next time then. Have fun in training," Lirien replied. "It was great to meet you, even if brief."

"Pleasure to meet you," Luminia replied coldly, she hadn't moved from her spot.

Victoria eyed her over Emily's shoulder as she gave her one last hug. She waved goodbye to Emily and her two friends. The wave of dread hit when she remembered Rune-Tech studies were next.

Lirien, Luminia and Victoria walked the opposite direction through the academy yards to their classroom, wading through the wafts of students. Victoria had tried to ignore Luminia's standoffish attitude, but as expected Luminia spoke up now that it was just the three of them.

"She seems lovely," Luminia said, but Victoria heard the sarcasm. "We should plan a proper hang out."

"Yeah, that would be nice," Victoria agreed but wasn't fooled by her friend, whose words contradicted her behaviour.

"Oh! I got to go toilet. Wait for me?" Lirien rushed off and left the two in silence.

"What is wrong?" Victoria pressed Luminia. "You can tell me. I won't get mad."

"I think she is bad for you," her reply was instant. Victoria was taken aback by the abrupt opinion her friend had drawn. "I can't pinpoint what, but something feels off." Victoria took a moment to process what she said.

"You always think this, you did with Lirien, and look at us now?"

"Well, I wasn't wrong, there was something off about him." She started to laugh but stopped when Victoria stood there glaring at her.

"Emily isn't bad for me. I hope to prove that to you," Victoria said firmly. Lirien stepped from the toilet at the perfect time. Victoria was relieved, Luminia was much easier to tolerate when he was around.

"What are you two talking about?"

"Emily," Victoria sighed, losing patience. "Luminia doesn't seem to trust her," Victoria said, trailing off ahead of them. It took some time for Victoria to notice her friends hadn't followed. Lirien had an uneasy look on his face.

"I think we should get to know her better, if you let us?" Lirien tried to reassure Victoria. He caught up with Victoria and turned back to Luminia. "You coming?"

"Ah yeah, look," Luminia said tugging at her hair nervously. "Sorry, I just want to make sure you aren't being used."

"If I was, I would handle it. Can you accept and trust that I will be fine?" Victoria defended herself as they headed towards Professor Nia's classroom.

"I will have to take your word for it, I guess," Luminia said with a week smile as they trudged to their next class.

The afternoon passed fast. her Rune-Tech studies weren't as bad as she feared. It was near the end of the day when Victoria received a message from Emily.

Hey, Thrash, Sam and I are going to the Pier after school. Want to come?

There was a pause between messages, three dots moving as Emily continued to type.

...

Your friends are welcome.

Sounds great! I'm in! Will check with others.

Victoria replied saying she was up for it and would check with her friends later before she tucked her phone away. At the front of the class on the board, the five principles had been written up by Professor Nia. Victoria hurriedly took down notes. She figured she would ask Emily for help on the project should she get lost, as Emily was focusing on Arcanthus' Legacy as her final thesis.

"Alright, class, I want you to divide into groups. We are going to work on this project in small groups," she said, looking around the room. Her eyes met Victoria's, and she shook her head. Victoria took that to mean her professor had no more information on what had happened. Victoria tried not to feel too disappointed.

This will be fifty percent of your grade. You all will be graded individually and as a group, so choose wisely."

The entire class groaned at the knowledge that this assignment would be worth more than any of their previous assignments. Victoria looked around and grabbed Lirien.

"Em and her friends are going into the Pier after class. Want to come?" Victoria whispered to Lirien. Victoria wasn't focused on finding a third for their group, as long as it wasn't Hector she could care less who it was.

"Hmm, is Luminia coming?" Lirien asked.

"I haven't asked, I can now." Victoria pulled out her phone and quickly typed a message to Luminia. She looked up to see the one person she didn't want to. It annoyed her that she still found him attractive. "Everyone else is paired up, can I join you two?" Hector asked sheepishly, his tone was almost defeated.

Lirien's mood and tone shifted and welcomed Hector to join them. Hector sat opposite them both and started talking about which principle they would prefer to talk about. Victoria felt her phone buzz. Luminia replied stating she would meet them there.

"Lumi will meet us," Victoria interrupted Hector and Lirien's intense discussion on the second principle.

"What have you got planned?" Hector asked.

"Well, Victoria was going down to the Pier after class," Lirien replied as if Victoria was not even there.

"But you're still coming, right?" Victoria asked and Lirien's face shifted from happy to awkward.

"Do you want me there?" Lirien asked with a pointed tone.

"Of course." Victoria tried her hardest not to sound hurt. "You're my best friend."

"Alright, I'll come." Lirien looked at Hector. "You want to come as well? Lirien asked, and Victoria nudged him in the ribs. He knew how she felt about him.

"The Pier?" he asked, slowly changing his gaze between Lirien and Victoria. "Going to the Amusement Park?"

"Not sure yet, but with Emily and her friends, it is bound to be somewhere fun," she exclaimed.

"Yet to be seen," Lirien replied once again filled with his usual sarcasm. Victoria rolled her eyes with a sigh.

***

Victoria and her friends made a beeline to trains after class. She was looking forward to a good night with her friends and was happy that the two groups were going to mingle. Even with Luminia's sour attitude earlier, Victoria was determined to have fun.

She could see Emily and Thrash in the distance and was surprised Sam was not with them.

"Oh, is Sam not coming?"

"No, something about her father coming down on her hard after the club," Thrash said, brandishing her tusks up in angst. Victoria felt apprehensive herself, knowing her father wouldn't approve of her gallivanting around town once again, but she figured it was still daytime, she survived the first time, and she was with her usual friends, too. It should be fine.

Emily pulled Victoria in tightly. "Who needs her? I have the one I care about the most." She planted a kiss on her lips. Victoria went bright red. She was not expecting to be so public with their displays of affection this early on, but she was also enjoying it immensely.

"Oh, I am hurt, Ems!" Thrash nudged her shoulder.

"Tor, you going to introduce me to your friends?" Thrash asked, pointing to Lirien and Hector who stood there awkwardly as Em finished giving Victoria small kisses on her cheeks.

"This is Hector. He is also in our Rune-Tech class." Victoria couldn't help sounding unenthused. "And this is my dear friend Lirien. Don't let the pointy ears fool you, he is always this jarring."

Lirien held out a hand to Thrash, who swatted it away. "None of that wimpy handshaking shit!" she teased. "Bring it in!" She dragged him in and squeezed him so tight he struggled to breathe. Letting him go, she ruffled up his hair and let out a loud cackle.

Lirien stepped back, his face all red and meticulously fixing his hair. Hector started to help, and Victoria's heart skipped a beat. It felt like jealousy. She turned away, unsure why she felt that way when she had Emily.

"How about we get a carriage to the Pier instead?" Emily turned to them all and smiled. "Arrive in style!"

"The stations right there," Victoria suggested, pointing across the road, and not wanting her to spend money on them all. "And the Pier is one of the last spots."

"If that's what my girl wants," Emily said, putting her phone away. Victoria felt a shift in her energy and tone. She wanted to address it, but not in front of her friends, so, she let it slide. Instead, she took hold of her hand, and they joined the others as they headed down the hill towards the station, their destination, Chrono Pier.

CHAPTER NINETEEN
UNDERNEATH SPELLFORD

Upon their arrival, the group found themselves on the balcony of Marquis' apartment, which was the exact location Arden had used to take them back through the portal last time they were here. Fitted with Warding Runes and other enchanted defensive tools, Brent commented how he felt much more prepared this time.

"You all entered the premises with no defences?" Seraphina asked, taking in a drag of her ECC.

"Okay, Evergreen, we are much more prepared this time," Arden replied with a bit of venom in his voice and brandished the warding runes around his wrist.

"I am just saying," she coughed through the vapours, "if my investigating team went missing, I wouldn't just waltz into the same place..." Seraphina trailed off when Arden walked off waving a dismissive hand in her direction.

"Pax, can you keep her distracted?" Arden patted Pax on the shoulder and Brent could see he was tired of Seraphina. "She seems to respond to you the best."

Pax nodded to Arden and went to talk with Seraphina.

Brent turned to look over the ledge of the balcony. Arden's footsteps came from behind, but Brent didn't turn around. He pulled out his phone and took notice of the time. It was barely midday. Victoria would still be in school, plenty of time to finish the mission.

As he turned, Arden stood in front of him, shoulders back and chest out. Excitement of the unknown was rising in him slowly, but he was trying not to show it.

"We can turn back," Arden said. "I can find other people to undertake this?"

Brent turned to face Arden, whose stood shoulders back and chest out. The excitement of the unknown rose in him slowly, but he tried not to show it. Arden stepped closer, attempting to pull Brent in to combat the cool winds from this high up, but Brent dodged him.

"Let's get this done," Brent responded, moving towards Seraphina and Pax. Brent acknowledged Arden's raised eyebrow and perplexed expression, but he needed to maintain focus.

"Alright, so I am not sure how much you remember of this place you two, but last time we entered the Toxin took over. With the ventilation made by your body being thrown through the glass, I don't think this will be a problem," Arden said, pointing to Pax who scratched the back of his head. "Here are some earpieces, with a touch of a button they can turn into face masks and also allow for us to communicate back to the Opticon."

"We are recording this mission?" Brent asked as he put in the earpiece. "What the hell?" It felt like something stabbed him in the eardrum. Brent made to pull it out, but Arden stopped him, helping him adjust it.

"It's a Bio-Magi-Tech device. The Magi-Tech Department call this the Auricle," Pax said, and Arden nodded "Discreet and blends in with the wearer's anatomy for minimal visibility. Here, check it out. Mine turned green!" he said with much excitement, pointing at his ear hole.

"Since when do you know so much about Magi-Tech?" Brent asked. He shook his head, closed one eye and stretched his jaw as he got used to the sensation of the device in his ear.

"You know the emails I send you?" Arden said, he then leaned over and whispered into his other ear. "Perhaps you should think less of ways we can fuck and have more focus on your actual job throughout the day?" Arden added with a cheeky wink.

Now it was Brent's turn to feel inadequate.

"Noted," Brent said calmly. Arden made to speak but was interrupted by Seraphina.

"I guess this is the entrance?" They all turned as the voice of Seraphina emanated from the device in their ears and throughout their head. It was the oddest feeling, and it tickled Brent's ear as the audio streamed through.

Brent walked to stand beside Seraphina. "We entered further up last time at the penthouse level."

"Well, let's get going," Arden said, moving past Brent, gripping him on the waist as he passed, sending a jolt right through Brent's body. Arden walked toward the hole in the glass panels.

Brent couldn't ignore the odd sense of impending doom. The building looked unchanged. If Marquis was up to something, wouldn't he want to hide it?

"I thought that, too," Pax said out loud, mostly to Brent but forgetting where he was. The Auricle was interfering with the mind-link.

"Thought what?" Arden asked through the auricle, trailing behind Seraphina.

"Didn't Brent...never mind, must have heard something."

"*The Auricle appears to have connected to the mind-link?*" Pax asked Brent in his mind.

"*Seems so. Well, this makes it even easier to talk to you freely,*" Brent said back.

"*Ah good...well, Arden seems open about you guys fucking.*"

"*Not now, Pax,*" Brent replied, trying to shift the disgruntled look from his face to not alert Arden or Seraphina.

The group of four walked through the rubble and entered the room where the three men had been attacked. The hole was still there. Arden and Seraphina approached it with caution. Pax looked around for any sign that someone had been there. Brent hung back near the entrance and watched for any unsuspecting assailants. This part of the building differed completely from the upper penthouses. Brent looked around the room, he could see a shimmering of light flicker across certain parts. He craned his neck sideways, but the flickering stopped. When he tilted his head upright, it returned.

"*It was an illusion,*" Brent said in his mind, forgetting to speak the thought aloud. Before Pax could reply, Seraphina's gruff voice cut in.

"This hole is a fake. This entire room is disillusioned," Seraphina said, unhooking her ECC and the familiar bubbling and crackling of vapours came as she inhaled.

"Wait, are you serious?" Arden asked.

"I'll prove it." She spoke out of the corner of her mouth, careful to not let any vapour out. She let go of her walking stick which remained perfectly still, almost as if it had buried itself into the floor and inhaled a deep gulp of vapours. She appeared to inflate like a balloon as her chest expanded, so did her cheeks. Once she had taken in a sufficient amount of vapour, she blew it out a big gust of wind that covered the floor.

The room shimmered and cracked all around them as the vapours distilled the illusion. Her exhale was impressive, especially for someone her age. Rippling through the air, the arcane illusion that was bending the fabric of reality around them shattered. The scene of destruction and chaos that had once been Marquis Beaumont's apartment shifted into the familiar and undisturbed foyer of this floor.

The vapour swirled and twirled, creating a fleeting dance of ballet that erased the image of rubble and chaos. The cracked walls miraculously repaired themselves, as if time was reversing its course. Every detail of the mystical reconstruction carefully extended throughout the room, creating an enchanting atmosphere. The foyer, with its shattered decorations and displaced furniture, restored to its original state.

The vapours settled, and the room stood renewed. Brent stared on in awe, thoroughly impressed with Seraphina's abilities and control over the vapours to remove the illusions. The artistry of her magic was beautiful to witness.

"Well, as I thought," Seraphina said, arms stretched wide, taking in the room. She wobbled slightly. Brent rushed forward and handed her the walking stick.

"Thank you, Son," she replied and then quickly got flustered "Oh, sorry...Abernathy."

"My pleasure Elder Evergreen."

"Call me Seraphina, please. I am sick of this Elder Council title crap," She quipped and walked forward, her stick echoing in the room.

"It was a trick?" Pax looked perplexed. He leaned over the ledge of the balustrade that hung over a long drop down to ground level.

"Evidently, Marquis did not want anyone coming here, but why here, particularly?" Arden began to inspect the foyer closer.

Brent looked around himself. He remembered this room from fifteen years ago. "I know this place," he said out loud and the other three turned to him. "I took that elevator over there down into the basement." Brent pointed to the elaborate gold encrusted glass elevator.

"This looks like a private elevator?" Seraphina hobbled along, noting how the other sets of lifts around them looked plain.

Arden approached the elevator and pressed the button. As if it had been waiting for them, the chime of the bell echoed through the foyer, and the elaborate glass doors opened.

"Welcome, Sir Beaumont." The voice over sounded as they all clambered into the elevator. "Please select your desired floor from the panel on your left."

A lexicon panel with the list of floors materialised to the left of the door. There were only three. The floor they were on, street level and one that had the letters "MCP" carved into the screen covering the word basement.

"MCP?" Brent said to Arden as it clicked. "Monarch Children Program? That's way too coincidental."

"I am not taking anything as coincidence any longer, not with Marquis," Arden said, placing a finger over the "MCP" button. The doors snapped shut, and the elevator moved downwards.

As the elevator descended, Brent could not shake the feeling that they were delving into something far more complex than an ordinary investigation. Every link tied Marquis and himself together. With the revelation that he was seeking Victoria, he knew he would have to face him...eventually. Brent suspected the truth about Victoria's true lineage, but he knew Marquis had the answers.

Memories of pulling Victoria from the orb, as Brent called it, while the surrounding facility crumbled still haunted him. He would never forget seeing Elwin fall into the void as he called out his name, holding baby Victoria in his arms, her cries matching his own.

"Everything alright, Abernathy?" Seraphina asked from behind him.

Brent shook his head. Victoria couldn't be one of these Monarch Children. The ruined lab was located outside of Spellford.

Brent turned his head and smiled. "Uh yeah, sorry, long few weeks," he said in an attempt to convince himself as much as the others.

"Don't stress, you will get used to it." She reached up and gripped his arm. "Keep focus on the task ahead and you will find time for leisure after."

It wasn't leisure Brent needed. It was answers to questions that had no obvious answers. She was right, though, and Brent shook off the feeling. He needed to maintain focused for what lay ahead. The glass walls offered a fleeting glimpse into the lives of residents on each floor, a silent reminder that the entire city around them were relying on this small group of people to protect them and they had no idea.

Beneath the surface, underneath Spellford, unknown secrets and mysteries awaited. The group descended further underground. The glass only showed concrete walls until the elevator slowed. A dimly lit corridor came into view and the elevator came to a complete stop with a subtle ding. The doors opened wide, and Arden took the lead.

The corridor was long and bathed in a muted magenta glow emanating from the subtle runes etched into the walls. The air felt heavy with

Augmenti, like when Arden and Brent were underneath Sanctum. As if they were whispers from a time long past, the sounds of their footsteps reverberated softly against the cool, polished floor. There was a dip in temperature and Brent was thankful for his coat. Behind him, Pax and Seraphina surveyed the corridor.

As they continued, the light got weaker. Arden clicked his fingers, manifesting an orb of light into his hands. He chucked it upwards, and it floated above him, providing the group with light. Along the walls, faded murals of chalk and paint depicting childlike drawings surrounded a symphony of symbols and scribblings that could not be deciphered easily.

"Children used to play here," Arden touched his hand to the wall, an intense look in his eyes as they spanned its full length. "This is—"

"Let's keep going." Brent pulled Arden away. Whatever happened here wouldn't be answered with the drawings.

They proceeded down the corridor that seemed to extend without end, as if it bent time and space beyond its limits. The air charged with an otherworldly energy the further they went in, clarifying that this place held ancient secrets that were calling to be unravelled.

Finally, they arrived at a pair of aged doors bearing scars of forgotten histories. The four of them approached with caution. Arden held his ear to the door, he stroked it slowly, feeling its cool structure. He pushed on the middle of the door. It was unlocked and opened with ease, a slight screeching as it swung along its tracks to reveal a darkened room. They all paused behind Arden, who did not hesitate. The room illuminated as soon as he stepped one foot inside. The old lights buzzed overhead, nearing their last use. The room that laid out before them filled the air with ghostly whispers of the past.

Brent's eyes adjusted to the lighting. Rows of rooms laid out before them on either side. The chilling realisation settled in. These were not ordinary rooms but holding cells for unwilling test subjects of the Monarch Children Program. One by one, they investigated the rooms in stunned silence. Each one served as a haunting reminder of a darker chapter in Spellford's history. A residue of forgotten dreams and the muted sobs of children who once occupied these cold, sterile confines, were trapped in the echoes of their footsteps.

The atmosphere in the room thickened as they continued. Brent, Arden and Pax exchanged sombre glances, silently acknowledging the weight of the revelation. Seraphina had found a chair to rest on. She took in a few puffs of her ECC and expelled some vapours, checking for any magic anomalies. The silence in the room was a stark reminder that the quest for knowledge sometimes exacted a toll far beyond the understanding of those who sought it.

Brent heard Pax muttering names as he read them off the nameplates next to each room. "Subject *T.A.L, Kohvakka, Valina, Noble, Holliday, Bell, Renee, Layton, Alexander, Sunderland, Oleander, Hightower, Duckett, Bee, Rowe, Winn, Krista, N.Queen, Brea, Lopes, Burton*...there are so many names, so many children..."

Brent's eyes remained transfixed on the last room. Inside, he could see scattered, torn pages with illegible drawings and scribbles across the floor. The bedding, torn to shreds with its frame, turned over. Scorch marks lined the walls and, in the centre, a wooden chair. Scratch marks covered the nameplate, all but for the letters "thy."

Brent was overcome with in intense and deep sense that he had been here before. The walls seemed to close in on him, and a strange sensation tugged at the edges of his memory. He approached the observation window that allowed him to look inside from the main room. He pressed his face up closer and could see perfectly inside.

By the wall, an old, withered desk lay on its side. Brent squinted his eyes and knew he had to get closer, he needed to search it. He tried to open the door; it slid open a fraction with some difficulty but then wouldn't budge when he pushed again. He turned to his side and sucking in his gut managed to squeeze through the crack. Brent hurried to the desk and turned it up onto its legs. A jolt of recognition surged through him.

He traced his fingers over scorch marks and dug out etchings that were scratched out. He could barely make out the word that was carved into the wood. It seemed to spell a name with the letter B and ended in T. He took a steady step back as a memory flashed in his mind. An unknown person stood above a child lecturing him on something he couldn't quite determine. He stood in a daze of confusion, unsure why this room was so familiar.

Sweat trickled down his back, his head began to pound as the air left his lungs. The room swirled around, the floor moving beneath his feet. A strong shoulder on his hand brought him back. Brent looked up from the crouched position he had assumed on the floor to see Arden stood above him.

"What is up Brent, find something?" Arden asked, referring to the desk and room.

Brent wanted to express how he felt but could not correctly frame his mind to articulate the right words. As soon as he looked at Arden, he had forgotten what it was about the room, it looked like any other room. No scorch marks, nothing that felt familiar. "I was just being thorough, checking for anything that may give us answers." Brent hoped his lie sounded convincing.

It was clear this room and underground facility had a significance beyond his understanding. It was a suffocating feeling, and he needed to get out.

"Come on, let's keep exploring. These cells give me the creeps," Arden said with a mournful look to Brent. Arden could see right through Brent, but Brent had to keep his defences up.

Pax poked his head in. "Come on, you two. Seraphina has already walked ahead."

"I told her to stay put," Arden groaned a sigh. Arden looked from Brent to the desk one last time before rushing through the open gap. Brent was not far behind.

Pax pulled him aside and looked at him with the warmth of a concerned friend. "You okay, Brent? You look like you've seen a ghost."

"I'm okay." He shrugged off Pax's hand. "The desk had some carvings, wanted to see what they were."

"Okay." Pax squinted, hurt in his voice, but Brent ignored him and pressed forward. They followed the sounds of Arden's footsteps down the corridor when Pax started to chuckle.

"What's funny?" Brent asked.

"Why do we say seen a ghost? Ghosts get seen daily. Why don't we say you look like you saw a demon from the pits of Hell? Now that, that would take the green out of my face."

They walked in silence, the faint memory from before flashed again, preoccupying Brent's mind. No matter how hard he tried to shake them off, the things he saw in his mind were plaguing him.

The group continued to explore the facility lost to time, traces of ancient experiments lined their path. The blue ambient lighting cast from suspended orbs hanging from the ceiling, carved shadows across the walls that looked like evil spirits breaching into their realm. Etched between each windowpane, intricate rune patterns were scrawled, adding to the sinister atmosphere of this abandoned place.

Brent gazed into the rooms, glimpsing peculiar machinery encased in protective barriers. Each looked inoperable, like relics from a bygone era. A heavy breath heaved from the bosom of the facility's history with each unfolding of new information they discovered.

The flashback played back in his mind once more. An adult in a white coat overlooked a child seated at that desk. The harder Brent tried to brush it off, the stronger it came back. The further he dove into the belly of the beast, the more challenging it became. For Brent, this journey through the facility was no longer just a physical exploration, but it had become a descent into the enigma of his own memories. Perhaps even his own past that even he wasn't ready to face.

Arden and Seraphina stood outside an archway both their eyes fixed on a decaying sign that stood above the doorway.

"Cradle Chamber," Arden said, pointing up to the sign. "I guess Marquis wasn't lying."

"Cradle as in baby?" Pax asked.

"One would think so," Seraphina said sombrely. "Listen, what we are about to walk into will change how you perceive Spellford and even the Mage's Union forever. I hope you are all ready for this."

"You sound like you know something?" Brent stepped forward to Seraphina, who unhooked her ECC again. She blew a wave of vapours into the doorway.

"Well, so much for the security system." She hooked the ECC back on her belt. "It's not even armed."

She went to move ahead, but Arden held her back by placing both hands on her shoulders. "You know something Elder, what aren't you telling us?" Arden asked, not letting her move.

Seraphina looked up at him and sneered, "Even if I do, it doesn't change what you are about to witness in this room." She shrugged off his hands. Arden stepped aside, allowing Seraphina to plunge herself into complete darkness. Then, one by one, the lights turned on above her.

Brent looked up at the sign. Whatever lay ahead would raise more questions than provide answers. The word "Cradle" floated inside his mind as he pondered what they would find. He drew in a deep breath, his first step into the room echoed louder than it should have.

It was a room of cells. Towering pods were lined up on either side of the chamber, each was large enough to encase a person. A few still contained remnants of liquid that Brent imagined suspended whoever was trapped inside. Giant black cords wrapped around the tops, all interconnected, they snaked their way across the ceiling toward the middle of the room.

A glint from a reflective piece on a pedestal in the centre of the room caught Brent's attention. He noticed how the convergence of wires and thick cords resembled the spiralling Leylines that descended in the Augmenti Chamber underneath Sanctum. They could have been twins in their design. Brent walked up the short staircase to the pedestal.

In the limited light filtering down from the dusty, old fixtures above, Brent could discern a decaying, rusted tablet nestled firmly in its grooves atop the pedestal. Brent ran his hand over it, but it was so old, he doubted he'd be able to pull it from its place. He jumped when the tablet's screen suddenly came to life, accompanied by a subdued twinkling noise as it powered up. He did a quick glance around the room, Serephina hadn't moved, and the other two men continued to search for any clues that could lead to much needed answers.

A symbol unfolded on the screen, revealing an unfamiliar design. The tablet completed its boot-up sequence, words materialised on the screen. Initially illegible, Brent squinted his eyes to decipher the text. Slowly, the characters transformed, becoming clear and comprehensible. Four words formed on the screen

Monarch One - Cradle Chamber

A chill ran down Brent's spine, the unease mimicked that of the unsettled moments he had in the cell. It was as if someone had left him a trail of puzzle pieces, each unlocking a piece of hidden knowledge in his mind.

More words materialised on the tablet. With a slight buzzing sound, the rust-covered screen transitioned to a main menu. Among the functions he couldn't fully comprehend, there was an "Access History" log. Intrigued, Brent opened the log, and before him, a chronological record of when the tablet was last accessed unfolded. It revealed someone had accessed the tablet only a week ago. The last date prior was years before Brent had been born.

"What was accessed?" Arden's voice sounded next to him, causing Brent to jump. Both him and Pax had finally made their way to the centre of the room.

"Geez, Arden," Brent jumped, and slapped Arden's arm with a light smack.

"Whoever accessed this went straight to a file called the 'Subject Roster."

"Well, open it," Pax said, as he sat down on the stairs at the lower level of the Pedestal.

"Can you display it?" Arden asked. Brent fumbled around with the settings until he noticed a casting icon.

He clicked and the screen materialised above for all to see. Soft footsteps approached from behind them, as they now had piqued Seraphina's interest.

"What's that?" Arden pointed to the log.

"Looks like whoever accessed this went straight to the last uploaded file," Brent replied.

"It's a video," Pax exclaimed, standing up.

"Play it," Seraphina demanded as she approached.

Brent looked at the title of the video file. "Subject B XX00YZ7."

He placed his hand on Brent's "You, okay?" Arden gave a warm smile.

"I..." Brent stammered, a lump formed in his throat. His hand hung and began to shake over the play button. He was unable to stabilise and then he felt a thick hand rest on his left shoulder. He looked up at Pax feeling the blood drain from his face, again.

"You know what I always loved about you, Brent," Pax said softly, and Brent shook his head. "Your ability to delay all the good details by always making everything about you," Pax joked and he pointed his head at the tablet signalling to play the video. This knocked Brent out of how he was feeling and brought him back out of his head.

"Ha, you're so funny. I would have played it by now had you two not interrupted," Brent deflected. With a heavy sigh he pressed the button.

An image of a woman, adorned with dark black hair and tearful blue eyes, appeared on the screen. She wore a laboratory coat with a tucked-away necklace beneath her dark green turtleneck. Brent pressed play, and the woman spoke.

"Whoever is watching this, please forgive us. We were foolish. All we wanted was to research how the boundaries of magic could be pushed, to discover the unknown. The new Arch Mage and council of Elders have decided we must be shut down. All remaining Augmenti will be moved to a new location." She looked solemnly into the camera once again. "The Monarch Children Program is no more, and with it, all my discoveries about the potential of The Cradle with it. Only one test subject remains now, and I have placed him into hibernation," she said, pulling the camera along as she walked toward one of the pods.

Brent's eyes widened. The group stood in the very room depicted in the recording. He followed the woman's steps, tracing her path to the exact pod as the scene unfolded, craning his neck back to watch as he stood in front of the same pod.

The camera turned back to the woman, a shadow of a boy floating inside the pod behind her. "This boy was much more to me than a mere test subject. We bonded. He had love in his heart and warmth within him. Unlike his many Monarch siblings."

The woman continued her sombre revelation, her voice heavy with regret. "I named him Brent. Yes, the same name as the program's lead scientist, Brent Abernathy. The truth is, he was our son."

Brent's heart thudded in his ears, he tried to catch his breath as the truth was revealed. The woman in the recording was Seraphina and the boy. *Was he...?*

"He carries within him the essence of pure magic, the harmonious convergence of different magical bloodlines. He is the Monarch, a living vessel of immense power. To protect him, I placed him in a state of suspended animation, hoping that one day he would awaken to fulfill his destiny," Seraphina explained, her gaze fixed on the pod containing the young Brent.

"However, I fear that nefarious forces within Spellford have discovered the existence of The Cradle. They seek to exploit its power for their own purposes. I will do my best to shut this place down and protect everyone from harm. Brent, my son, if you have somehow escaped and are watching this, know that you are destined for greatness. Embrace your magic and beware those who would manipulate it for their own gain."

The video played on. The younger Seraphina gestured toward the pods containing the other subjects of the Monarch Childrens Program. "Your fellow siblings shared in this destiny, but the program finished, and there is no record of their status. I was told they had been moved to an undisclosed location. You, however, were spared and placed in a state of hibernation to protect you from those who would exploit your powers."

The holographic Seraphina turned her gaze to the central pedestal. "The Cradle is the source of immense magical energy. It has the power to unlock your latent abilities. But be warned, Brent, as you awaken, others will seek to control or destroy you. This world is not what it seems, and dark forces are at play."

With those ominous words, the recording ended, leaving Brent standing in the dimly lit Cradle Chamber, surrounded by the suspended animation pods that held the remnants of the Monarch Children Program. Pieces of the puzzle fell into place. The Cradle, the Monarch Children Program, and his mysterious connection to it all. He couldn't speak, he could hardly breathe. Brent wiped at the nameplate on the pod with his sleeve. "Subject B" had been crossed out and replaced with "Brent Abernathy" written in marker. Brent repeated his own name on a soft exhalation of breath. The soft footsteps of Seraphina came up from behind him. She looked as sad as her younger self captured in the recording.

"I never expected you to find out this way," she whispered.

Brent could not form words. He backed away. His shoulder blades pressed hard against the pod behind him. He stumbled forward as the loud thud echoed in the room.

"I'm sorry Brent," she said, her voice filled with regret, "but every word is true."

Brent looked from Seraphina. His heart raced faster than he could control, and he felt like he was suffocating. His neck dripped sweat that ran down his back. He needed to get out of there.

Without even thinking, he turned and rushed past Seraphina, not knowing if he had knocked her down or not, and ran back the way they came, searching madly for the exit.

Staggering through the dimly lit passages of Spellford's underground, the weight of what he witnessed pressed upon his mind like an insurmountable rock. His footsteps echoed against the cold metallic walls and floor. Each a reminder of his reality being shattered before him. He hadn't paid attention to which direction he ran. His only instinct was to escape the claustrophobic confines of the underground laboratory.

He wandered for what felt like hours through the twists and turns of the labs halls until he came to a single door at the end of a corridor. Brent rammed it with his shoulder. It gave way and a gust of fresh air hit his face. He had made it outside into the vibrant chaos of Spellford's Streets. He tried to gain his bearings and darted around to figure out where he had emerged from.

He shut the door and placed a hex on the handle, hoping that no one would follow. Brent turned and watched as carriages sped through the streets. He had surfaced in the middle of the botanical park. He proceeded on foot, leaping over a bollard and broke into a sprint across the road, headed directly into the parklands. Even the city's parklands tranquillity seemed to mock his internal turmoil bubbling over in his mind.

For Brent, Spellford no longer felt like the haven it once was. It was now just a realm of shadows concealing secrets he had never fathomed.

His mind replayed the revelations over and over as he tried to make sense of it. Seraphina Evergreen, a member of the Elder Council, was a scientist on the Monarch Children Program who created children and experimented on them to push the boundaries of magic. The worst of it was that Brent was revealed to be Subject B. Seraphina was his mother. She gave her biological material to form a child in The Cradle with someone, that same someone who she named Brent after.

Brent always wanted to know the truth of his past before the orphanage, but he hadn't expected this. He was an experiment, just a puppet on unseen strings. If this had been hidden from him, what else could The Mage's Union be hiding? The path he walked in had transformed into a maze of uncertainty, mirroring the labyrinth of his emotions. As he maneuvered through the bustling streets, memories flashed like elusive spectres.

Everything he had experienced until now weaved together and meshed into a conglomerate of chaos. Moments with Pax in the academy, bonding over being orphans, meeting Elwin and finding true love. Losing that love but finding a new purpose in Victoria and the joy of raising her as his own. The pain of loss, the joy of love, they interwove with the recent revelations.

He took in slow breaths of the cool air, the adrenaline rushing through his body began to subside. Brent settled on a weathered bench in the Spellford Botanic Garden. It offered a brief respite from the onslaught of thoughts in his mind. Beneath the shade of the ancient trees, he heard the gentle rustling of leaves and the distant chirping of birds. Today, amidst the countless moments of joy and sorrow it had seen, the park became a silent observer as Brent Abernathy's identity fell apart.

He stared off into the distance, his phone began to buzz in his pocket, messages from Arden flooded in.

> Brent, please answer my calls. We should talk about this.

Brent turned off his phone. He wasn't ready, he could hardly keep his own thoughts together. The city's enchantments cast hues of magic across the sky, a spectacle that once brought him awe. Now, it was a sign of the duality within Spellford. Dark truths hid in plain sight, and it should have stayed that way. A city with a shadowed history of experimenting on children for the betterment of magic. And Brent was one of them.

Was any of his life real?

Brent closed his eyes, allowing the tranquillity of the surroundings to envelop him. In the stillness, the echoes of Elwin's voice, a melodic cadence that transcended the boundaries of time, whispered through the recesses of Brent's consciousness.

"When shadows entwine and your hope falters, remember, our love is the eternal ember that lights even the darkest of paths."

Elwin's words rang in his mind and memories flashed before him. They painted vivid portraits of moments he shared with Elwin. A dance beneath the moonlit canopy, whispers exchanged in the language of the Aesir. A love that defied the ephemeral nature of mortal existence. Brent remembered Elwin's gaze, his stunning blue eyes, two crystal pools of endless oceans.

That was what he knew was real.

With his hand, Brent reached up to his cheek. The same cheek that Elwin once stroked as they'd look deep into each other's eyes for hours on end. The cool evening air brushed over him. Brent could not hold it in anymore. He released a stream of tears. His face fell into his hands, the endless tears flowed between the cracks of his fingers.

CHAPTER TWENTY
PAST LIVES COLLIDE

Victoria's laughter echoed against the vibrant backdrop of Chrono Pier as she strolled along with her friends. They continued downhill from the station and spotted Luminia waiting in the distance. The sound of the amusement park resonated with sounds of joy and excitement. It was a welcome escape from the recent events plaguing Victoria's life. Her mentoring sessions with Nia, the events that took place at Cauldron paired with everything with her father, she desperately needed to relax.

Victoria stretched her arms up, the tension in her shoulders started to release. A refreshing breeze filled with the scent of salt washed over her. Lirien's silver hair shimmered in the sunlight as he walked alongside Hector, engrossed in a lively debate about the various attractions and rides. Thrash vibrated with excitement as she animatedly chatted with Emily about conquering the Terror Tower.

"There she is!" Victoria exclaimed after they had waded through the crowd at the front of Chrono Pier.

Luminia's face transformed from intense concentration to pure, radiant joy as she looked up. "Tori!" she called out, her voice echoing through the air as she waved with enthusiasm. Luminia extended her wings in a graceful motion and effortlessly glided across the park entrance, leaving a trail of shimmering pixie dust in her wake. People around her were adorned with a delicate sprinkling of pixie dust, some of them gently shook it from their hair. "Oh, sorry!"

After profusely apologising to a disgruntled man, she trotted over to the group, her face flushed with embarrassment. The group of friends gathered in a tight circle. Their voices full of cheerful greetings.

"Oh my, I didn't know Luminia was a Pixie!" Thrash's voice boomed through the space.

"Ha-ha, yeah well, she rarely flies," Victoria muttered.

"You think you could carry me?" Thrash pushed forward past Victoria, bumping her into Emily.

Emily held Victoria and made sure she was okay then tapped Thrash on the shoulder. "Yo! Thrash, apologise for bumping into Victoria," she demanded.

Thrash turned and realised what she had done. "I am so sorry Victoria! I get too excited sometimes."

"It is fine," Victoria stammered, confused at why Emily seemed that upset over an accident. "I am fine, really." She stood up tall and bounced on her feet.

"I've bought us passes, my treat to you all." Luminia ignored the interaction and opened her bag to retrieve the tickets. They soared out of her bag and into her hands.

"Oh, Ace!" Thrash grabbed hold of her ticket. "Wait, these passes don't expire until the end of Emberfell? We are in Bloomveil now, that's three lunars, that must have cost—"

"It doesn't matter," Luminia interrupted. Her effortless smile remained, her eyes glistening with a smooth smothering of glittery eye shadow. "Mums loaded and bought the tickets before I told her to leave."

Victoria shifted on the spot, apprehensive of Luminia flaunting her mother's wealth in their faces.

"Well, send her our regards!" Thrash gave a mini jump and flicked her ticket in her palm. The rest of the group joined in and thanked her.

The ticket inspector waved his scanner over the tickets to scan the rune barcode as they walked through the gates. The tickets glistened and let out a miniature set of fireworks with a single cheer.

The group entered Chrono Pier with buzzing excitement and anticipation. The lively atmosphere of the amusement park filled their senses as they strolled further along. Laughter and screams echoed from the various rides. A sweet and savoury aroma wafted through the air from multiple food stands. Victoria's heart swelled with excitement as she saw the giant Ferris wheel turn slowly at the end of the pier.

Thrash led the way, oblivious that her size and overconfidence parted the crowd around her. She excitedly pointed out the different rides and attractions they could explore.

The two boys wandered off to grab a bite to eat and planned to meet the girls at the end of the pier near the Ferris wheel and the ride Past Lives.

The four girls strolled through the game section. Thrash stopped at a game where you tried your luck knocking down a tower of enchanted bottles.

"What do you think Victoria?" Thrash chucked her a ball. Victoria, not one for sport, caught the ball haphazardly.

"Keen?" Thrash flashed her puppy dog eyes. Victoria might not be an athlete but nor was she one to not give something new a try, and she couldn't refuse that face Thrash gave. "Okay, let's do this." She stood in the designated spot behind the line.

"Alright we have two more challengers!" The stand operator bellowed standing up from where they were leaning against the back of the attraction. "Best out of three wins, no App-Magic allowed, put your phones away." The operator tapped the sign at the back.

"You got this, Tori!" Luminia cheered on her friend.

"Get her Thrash!" Emily called out. Victoria looked at her with surprise. Emily shrugged and then blew her a kiss. "You can do it too!" She winked, and it sent a little flutter through her body.

Victoria picked up a ball and waited for the operator to signal. He clicked a button, and the bottles manifested out of thin air. Suspended in the middle of the tent they floated around and shifted spots in fast repetition.

"Bring it Thrash!" Victoria smirked and watched as the bottles shifted across the tent. Victoria stuck out her tongue, squinted her eyes and attempted to learn the bottles movements. She took in a quick breath and then focused. The operator said no App-Magic, but nothing about Aphonic magic. Giggling to herself, she lined it up and then threw a ball.

The ball went flying with the help of some of her magic and looked as if it was going to make an impact but missed at the last second.

"What the?" Victoria exclaimed and Thrash chortled, throwing her head back, her tusks chittering.

"You've got to do a lot better than that, Abernathy!" she laughed and slapped Victoria on the back. "Let me show you how it's done!" Thrash licked her lips and took a ball in her giant hand. She looked back at Luminia with a wink.

"This one's for you Lumi!"

Thrash lifted her knee like a Spellball Pitcher and cocked her arm. Her muscles bulged when she flung her arm forward. The ball left her hand and went flying. Victoria watched as the clanging of the ball against the bottles resonated, knocking them all to the ground.

A slight heat of jealousy overtook Victoria. She didn't understand how Thrash did it. It was her turn again, she focused and flung another ball, but once again it was a miss.

"Come on, Tori, you can do it!" Luminia encouraged her.

Beaten but not defeated, Victoria stepped back and let Thrash have another turn. She repeated her actions from before, including the wink, it made Luminia blush the slightest bit.

Thrash walked back with the biggest grin after she knocked down the tower a second time. She leaned into Victoria and pattered her on the shoulder. "Let me let you in on a little secret," she whispered and slunk around behind her. "You need to expect where it will move to next. They all follow a pattern." Thrash drew her finger in the pattern of the remaining stacks. "Concentrate on your breathing and you will find your target point."

Thrash skulked back and then gave Victoria a light nudge. Victoria took her last ball and passed it between her hands, watching a stack. It moved from one side of the tent to the other in a flash. This time, she relied on her own instincts and forgot using her magic. Taking a deep breath in, she began to concentrate and remember the pattern of the bottles. With a loud clanging, the bottles fell to the ground. She landed a hit. She jumped on the spot and cheered out loud with ecstatic joy.

"Fuck yeah!" Victoria shouted in triumph. Emily and Luminia cheered her on. Even Thrash looked impressed.

"Shame you won't win. I only need to make one more hit!" Thrash commented, deflating Victoria's mini victory.

"Don't be a bitch, Thrash!" Emily snapped back.

Thrash lifted her arm and ditched a ball at the last bottles. It was a direct hit. The operator blew a whistle, and it was over.

"We have a winner!" Thrash made a motion of fist bumping the air and then flexed. "You have a choice of two prizes."

Victoria walked off and joined Emily and Luminia, while the operator handed Thrash a medium-sized stuffed toy.

"You did amazing, Tori!" Luminia stated.

"Yeah, you'll get her next time." Emily gave her a consolatory hug.

Thrash approached the group with an impressive looking plush Phoenix, its vibrant feathers shimmered with various colours.

"For you," Thrash bent down on one knee and held the plush above her head, offering it to Luminia.

Luminia scooped up the plush after Victoria nodded and urged her on. "Thank you, Thrash." She graciously accepted the plush toy.

"Anything for the prettiest girl in the park," Thrash said, a slight blush took to her cheeks.

Luminia cheeks blushed in return. Not expecting the attention, she stammered an awkward thank you.

Emily leaned over and pulled Thrash up by her arm. "Come on, you big romantic, let's get going!" She dragged her away, leaving Victoria and Luminia alone.

"What do you think that was about?" Luminia asked. "I don't know Lumi, maybe she was just being friendly?" Victoria offered as they walked a little behind Thrash and Emily.

"Well, she is friendly, but I haven't ever considered seeing myself with a woman let alone an Orc. I am part Pixie after all, my family would not approve." The stuck-up attitude from her parents was something Victoria hoped she would have grown out by now. "I'm not saying I wouldn't date her. She is hot, but..."

Victoria realised maybe she was judging Luminia too harshly. Even in a city as liberal as Spellford, certain cultures and ethnicities still felt it was very important that their communities remained within their own community. Brent had raised Victoria to be accepting of everyone's differences and to embrace all cultures, she couldn't necessarily hold it against her friend if she was raised a different way.

Pixie, Fae and Elves were stubborn in their strict cultural upbringing. They were also the reason the Orcish kind have had such a hard time adapting into Spellford. Even though her best friend, Lirien, was a Sun Elf, she held deep resentment for what those three races had done to the Orcish kind. As time passed, the many races came to some form of agreement, but it was years before any of them would ever mix with an Orc. Elves rarely would even marry a human, and those who did were outcasts.

"Luminia, you know you can date who you want to, your family shouldn't dictate how you feel," Victoria started.

"Date?" Luminia scoffed. "She just handed me a plush, don't be so silly Tori," She rolled her eyes and chortled, it was a classic Luminia deflection.

"Okay, but just think about what I said, alright?" she finished as they approached the end of the pier, the giant name "Past Lives" flashing on a sign up ahead.

"Fine!" She sighed and nudged into Victoria letting her know she'd at least think about it.

Hector, Lirien, Thrash, and Emily waited outside the ride.

"Line up, Line up!" The ride operator called out. "Unravel the threads of time! Dive into your past and discover the tapestry of your existence! You must be over sixteen to enter!"

"Are you excited?" Emily asked Victoria as they paired off.

Victoria hardly heard as she focused on Thrash chatting up Luminia.

"Hello, is anyone home?" Emily waved in front of Victoria's face.

"Sorry, Emily, what did you say? Been a long day," she blinked her eyes, returning her vision out from a stare.

"I said, are you excited about this ride?"

"Oh, yeah! This is going to be awesome!"

Victoria stood in line, her anticipation growing as she watched her friends embark on the journey into their past lives one by one. The surrounding atmosphere filled with a mixture of excitement and nervous energy as patrons eagerly approached the ride. The line slowly inched forward, revealing a dazzling array of lights and intricate decorations that adorned the entrance to the Past Lives attraction.

Amidst the rhythmic sound of the rides machinery and the soft hum of magical energy, an otherworldly ambiance resonated. Victoria approached the ride platform. She felt the energy intensifying, sparking her curiosity about what awaited her on the other side of the veil.

It was Emily's turn next. "See you on the other side," she squeaked out a little nervous laugh and then entered through the veil.

Victoria observed the expressions on the faces of those exiting the ride. Some wore looks of wonder, while others seemed deep in thought, as if the experience had stirred profound emotions within them. Victoria couldn't help but feel a mixture of excitement and trepidation.

Finally, it was her turn to step onto the platform. A staff member gestured for her to take a seat in the ride carriage that was adorned with intricate runes and symbols that began to pulsate with magical energy. Victoria settled into her seat, securing herself for the journey that promised to unveil the secrets of her past lives. The runes on the carriage illuminated, and then the attendant approached her.

"If you feel unsafe, say this word." The attendant handed her a piece of paper which Victoria stashed into her pocket.

The ride attendant activated the enchantments, and the platform beneath Victoria's carriage ascended. Ethereal music played softly, creating an immersive atmosphere. The veil between the present and the past seemed to shimmer as the carriage moved forward.

Victoria entered the mysterious realm of Past Lives, and she braced herself for the revelations that awaited her. The enchanting lights, mystical sounds, and the feeling of transcendence surrounded her, transporting her consciousness to the echoes of her own history. The journey had begun, and Victoria was about to delve into the tapestry of her past.

Victoria descended into the endless, ethereal realm. The sensation of falling was both exhilarating and disorienting. The lights that encircled her during the ride were truly enthralling, but as she ventured deeper into the currents of her own mind, they transformed into streaks of vivid colours, producing a mesmerizing and captivating show.

The bottom of the carriage had vanished. Victoria felt weightless, as if her very essence was merging with the magic that permeated the surrounding space. Strange symbols and arcane patterns danced in the void, forming a surreal dreamscape that defied the laws of reality. Amidst the swirling colours and patterns, her awareness expanded, transcending the confines of the ride.

The boundaries between time blurred, and she found herself in a scene that felt both strangely familiar and incredibly distant.

Victoria entered a majestic throne room adorned with regal tapestries, towering pillars, deep blue silk curtains. A grand throne sat atop a high elevated platform.

At the centre of the room, Victoria looked down at a vision of a regal woman dressed in royal garments, wearing a crown that glittered in the filtered sunlight from outside. The air in the throne room hummed with an otherworldly energy as the subjects in attendance bowed respectfully as this woman, The Queen, took her seat on her throne.

Victoria saw her face once she sat. It was her own, but significantly aged. She felt instant confusion. The ride was only meant to show the past, not her future. Intrigue overtook Victoria, and she watched as she floated above. Her heart raced on as she tried to comprehend what she was bearing witness to. A feeling of familiarity hit her as if she had stepped into a destiny that awaited her in a timeline not yet realised.

Scenes unfolded in succession, Victoria saw herself ruling over the realm of Suncrest with wisdom and grace. The subjects revered her, and her

Queendom prospered under her benevolence. She was successful in a war between a neighbouring empire and even though she lost many soldiers, she was still considered a successful queen. The scene changed once again, and, in her arms, she held a child with red hair. A daughter. The past version of her murmured the child's name but Victoria couldn't hear it as she was pulled from the vision. No matter how hard she fought it, she was powerless to stop her return to her present reality.

Victoria ascended back through the swirling colours as reality descended onto her once more. She had to close her eyes as the swirling patterns made her queasy. Suddenly, as if she was pulled up from underneath the surface of a deep lake, she was dredged out of the ethereal realm and back into her carriage, which had not moved. As if time had not even passed, she was back in the present.

She opened her eyes and took in a deep breath. The lights turned on and revealed she sat in a tiny room with a small vent above to allow for a flow of cool air. The door behind her remained closed. Instead, the one to the exit illuminated and opened in front of her. She departed her carriage and ran down the stairs past the rest of the patrons to join her friends once more.

The sun had set over the course of their wait for the ride, and the group agreed it was time to head home. The friends parted ways after Luminia and Thrash exchanged numbers leaving only Emily and Victoria behind. "This was such a good idea," Emily said, standing with her arm next to Victoria, their hands linked.

"Agreed, I had, however, hoped we'd get to ride the Ferris wheel."

"Let's do it next time, besides I can think of something better," Emily replied, turning Victoria's face with a single finger.

"And what's that?" Victoria asked, trying to sound flirtatious.

"Did you want to come back to my dorm before you go home?" she asked. Victoria nodded. Her stomach flipped, and tingles swept across her lower abdomen. "Good, because I was taking you, anyway. At least now it's not an attempted kidnapping," Emily snickered and began to walk ahead. Victoria pulled her back and laid her lips against Emily's for a soft kiss.

Her scented lip balm tasted of cherries, Victoria's favourite. The entire world disappeared around them, Victoria's senses were slipping. She wanted her first time to be special, and the voice of her father kept crawling back in. How well did she truly know Emily? Was it too fast? She pulled away from Emily, who gave a smile that made Victoria's insides melt into a puddle. Raising her hand to her face, she stroked a long strand of her back behind her ear, and she smiled back.

"Come on, let's get going," Emily whispered, and Victoria let her take the lead.

CHAPTER TWENTY-ONE
BOTANIC GARDENS

In the twilight hours, the city embraced the hushed tones of the impending night, Pax traversed the enchanted streets of Spellford. The echoes of his footfalls resonated against the cobblestone pathways, a rhythmic cadence that mirrored the clandestine pulse of the city itself. In his search for Brent, Pax navigated the spellbound alleys and shadowy corners, guided by an instinct honed through years of navigating both the magical and mundane.

Pax had taken it upon himself to locate Brent. He forced Seraphina and Arden to return to Sanctum, as he knew Brent better than anyone else. If there was anyone who could locate Brent, it was him. Pax remembered Brent's love for the parks in Spellford. Pax knew it was half the reason he lived in the Enchanted Circuit, all the parks and trees for him and Victoria to explore.

With ease, Pax made his way to the park and was now wandering along the path, sensing out Brents aura. Though Pax was not traditionally magically skilled, his nose was attuned to the magical signals of his friends and loved ones. He could sniff Brent out.

Across the rise in the park, Pax got a whiff of a man experiencing inner turmoil and knew it was Brent's aura—a mosaic of emotions that shimmered in the magical ambiance. Pax approached with caution, there was a good chance Brent wouldn't be in the headspace to talk. He softened his footsteps into a silent trot amongst the grass. He stopped not far from where Brent sat.

"Pax." Brent lifted his head when he sensed he was no longer alone. "How'd you know I'd be here?" His voice a subdued reflection of the storm within.

"After all these years, you think I don't know who you are? How to find you?" Pax approached the bench, towering over of him. He placed a gentle hand on his shoulder. Brent's eyes were red from crying. "I know this is your crying bench. Remember when Victoria was only a toddler, and you were too overwhelmed?

Brent looked up and saw Pax's golden eyes convey a silent understanding between them.

"So, do you want to talk about it?" Pax asked, shifting around the bench and sitting down.

"When have I ever wanted to talk about it?" Brent laughed, sniffling and wiping his eyes.

"Maybe that is the problem," Pax said. Brent opened his mouth to speak but Pax laid a hand on his leg. "You never open up and tell me what's going on, I have seen you at your worst," Pax began, and Brent listened intently not taking his gaze off his best friend. "From the moment Elwin left our lives, I have been there to pick up all the pieces, and here I am again. But enough is enough. You are your own man, and it is about time you stand up and take control of your life." His nostrils flared and his tusks looked like they could bite through an entire Ox after he laid some tough love on his friend.

Brent sat in silence for a moment, absorbing Pax's words like a soothing balm to his wounded soul. The park, once a witness to the echoes of a love long gone, now became a backdrop for a different connection—a bond between friends that weathered the storms of time.

He was right, and Brent knew it. He also hated to admit how right he was.

"You're right," Brent finally said, his gaze shifting to the intertwining branches above. "I've been carrying this past for so long, keeping it locked away. Maybe it's time I face up to the fact that I'm not okay."

Pax nodded in a silent show of support, as Brent delved into his experience in the underground. He described feeling as though the ground had crumbled beneath him, tugging him downwards, unearthing memories of Elwin. Pax listened attentively, his expression a mix of concern and unwavering support.

It all felt too surreal even saying it out loud but as Brent shared the weight of his revelations; he felt a sense of liberation. "I have been burying the shadows of my past ever since I was left at the orphanage. And now they have caught up to me," Brent confessed. "I need to find out the truth, not just for me, but for Victoria as well. She was created, just like me, in that…" Brent paused, and used the name for the contraption that once held Victoria. "That Cradle…where Elwin fell into the void."

Pax placed a reassuring hand on Brent's. "Then we'll find the truth together. You don't have to carry it all alone."

"You are right, thank you." Brent looked out over the park. He was thankful for Pax, more than he ever had been. "Was Arden pissed?" Brent asked after a while.

"Arden? Yeah, but I told him to shove it. If he has a problem with you running off, he has a problem with me."

"You actually said that?"

"In less friendly words." Pax smirked and the friends shared a laugh. "I told you years ago Brent, men or children, doesn't matter. You have me forever."

In that moment, beneath the ancient trees and the fading light of the day, the bond between Brent and Pax strengthened. A commitment to face the shadows of the past and navigate the uncertain paths ahead, together.

"One thing is bothering me." Pax rose to his feet.

"Yeah, what is that?" Brent followed Pax's lead.

"If you were in hibernation, how did you get set free?"

Brent had no real memory of the laboratory, the little bits he did were all scattered like the missing pages of a torn-up book. "I think we should go visit Seraphina and find out."

"Arden sent her home and wanted us to check in with him. Once I found you, that is." Pax paused to think a minute. "Want to get a bite to eat before we go home?"

"All that crying has made me hungry." Brent gave a sly smirk and allowed himself to laugh freely. "I've been around you for far too long."

Pax ran from behind and hugged Brent, and they laughed together. The cool evening breeze brushed over them and Pax planted a kiss on his lips. His tusks pressed into Brent's beard and caught a few of the tangled hairs as he pulled back from the platonic kiss.

"Never change." He smiled his golden eyes looking to Brent's. "Well, no, please change the things we just discussed, but always stay my friend." Pax said warmly and released him from the embrace. The two continued down the pathway back into the city.

Brent knew as he walked side by side with Pax, that everything would be okay.

"Thanks for cheering me up, Pax."

"Don't worry about it, you can just shout me some Chronos," Pax chortled, running forward and hailing down a cab.

CHAPTER TWENTY-TWO
ENCHANTED NIGHT MARKET

B rent and Pax walked through the serene suburban streets from the station, the sunset casted a soft glow on the neatly lined houses. They approached home and a sense of unease settled in but when Brent and Pax rounded the corner to Enchanted Circuit, there was Arden. He stood outside, leaning against Brent's carriage, arms crossed.

Arden's expression was grim, Brent tried to avoid contact with his eyes as he approached.

"Since you refuse to come back to the office," he said in way of greeting, his expression didn't waiver. "I'll just have to come to you." He flashed a smile, but it didn't have any of his usual warmth behind it.

There was a long silence between them. After a while, Pax muttered something about going inside and moved to the door. "I'm going to go check on…"

Brent didn't hear the last of what Pax said, but assumed he meant Victoria. He sighed and ran a hand through his hair. "What are you doing here?" he asked a little too coldly, still not making full eye contact. Was this the man who fucked him only two nights ago, or was this his boss? Brent started to realize the challenges their potential relationship could pose.

"You tell me?" Arden stepped close to Brent, his voice stern. "You just run off like that?"

"I…" Brent paused as he felt a chill run up his spine. The hairs on the back of his neck rose. Brent snapped around and caught Victoria mid-step as she attempted to creep up behind him on the grass.

"Oh, dammit!" she laughed. "I was trying to scare you!"

"Damn, well you win Victoria!" Arden said behind them.

"Win?" Brent raised his eyebrows. "You're having bets with my daughter?" Arden shrugged in response.

"What? I arrived when she did, and we got to talking. Somehow a bet was made between us on who would scare you the fastest."

"I know you are good at sensing your surroundings, so I tricked Arden into betting that I would scare you, because I knew you would catch me before I could." Victoria cheekily smiled "You should not be a betting man, not against someone like me who knows her dad so well." She ran towards the door "You owe me!" She spun on the spot and waved.

As she walked up the steps, the door swung open. "Victoria's not home!" Pax blurted out in a panic only to see Victoria standing in front of him. "Oh, never mind." His soft laugh dissipated his nerves, and he welcomed her inside.

"Can't believe how easily tricked he was," Victoria said, shutting the door behind her.

Brent looked from the door then back to Arden. "I'd appreciate you not placing bets with my daughter."

"Look, she suggested it. I just joined in when the deal seemed too good to pass up. And besides, as your boss, I need to test your skills from time to time."

"She would bet with my money." Brent raised his voice a little and Arden stopped smiling. "Anyway, as I was saying—"

"Doesn't matter. I have seen that you are home safe. I have scheduled you a psych examination with Dr. Frost. Everyone has already been assessed, except for you."

"I'm fine," Brent snapped back. Immediately regretting his tone, he opened his mouth to speak, but Arden held up a hand.

"Regardless of what you think, it is Mage's Union policy before you can undertake any more field work," Arden exhaled through his nose and crossed his arms. His expression grew more serious. "Brent, you can't keep running from your past. We've unearthed something significant today, and you, more than anyone else, need to confront it. The Monarch Children Program, Subject B, Seraphina being your..." he paused, taking in the sombre look of Brent's eyes, "well, you know. You're entwined in this and ignoring it won't make it go away."

Brent tightened his jaw but remained silent. Arden continued, "The psych examination is just a formality, but it needs to happen. We need to understand the full extent of the connection between you, Seraphina, and the Monarch Children Program. There are questions, and we need answers."

"We...meaning the Mage's Union?" Brent asked.

"We, meaning you and me," Arden replied with a warm smile. Brent looked into Arden's eyes and knew he was sincere. "I know it's only been one date, and uh, well, yeah...that other thing we did."

"Oh, you mean when you fucked me with your conjured lube after you blew me?" Brent asked, stepping forward. Arden adjusted his legs, which made his bulge poke out even more.

"Yes, that," Arden said, almost blushing. He was being playfully coy, and then his eyes darted to the house. Brent turned and could see the curtain close.

"Ahhh..." Brent realised and turned back to Arden.

"I want you to know I am here for you. Whatever comes next, we'll face it together. You're not alone in this."

"That's pretty much what Pax said," Brent replied with a smile then looked between Arden and the living room window behind him where he could see Pax peering through the sheer curtains. "Okay, I'll meet with Dr. Frost."

Arden nodded back. "Good. I'll inform Dr. Frost. In the meantime, try to get some rest. We have a lot to unravel, and you need to be in the best shape possible."

With that, Arden walked past Brent, leaving him to contemplate the storm of revelations that had erupted in his life. Brent remained outside, the weight of the day pressing down on him. Now, to top it off, a psych assessment was added into the mix. He was in desperate need of a shower to wash off the day.

He watched Arden walk away until the end of the street when a blue flash occurred, and he disappeared. Brent walked to the house and closed the door behind him. He stood still in the entrance hallway of his house. For a moment, he felt a sense of isolation. The world as he knew it shifted, and now he stood at the crossroads. After a deep breath, Brent walked through the hallway into the main part of his home. The warm glow of the lights filled him with the familiar comfort they always did.

Inside, Pax and Victoria, who had been peering through the curtains, shifted to sitting on the couch and turned their attention away when Brent entered.

"What was that about, Dad?" Victoria asked, clear concern in her voice.

Brent ran a hand through his hair once again, struggling to come up with something to say, except for a tired sigh that escaped him. "It's complicated, Tori."

Without waiting for a response, he headed towards his bedroom, leaving Victoria and Pax exchanging uncertain glances. In the bathroom, Brent stared at his reflection in the mirror. The lines on his face looked as if they were deeper than a week ago. Thoughts of defying Arden and not going to a therapy session with Dr. Frost crept in. Brent shook his head and tried to rid himself of these inner voices. He turned on the faucet and let the water flow over his hands as it heated. Once it was his desired temperature, he quickly undressed and got in, hoping that the cascade could wash away this whirlwind of emotions.

As he scrubbed his body, flashes of the video with the much younger Seraphina replayed in his mind, her confessing the truth. He let the warm water wash over him and tried to remember better thoughts of his past. Brent closed his eyes, allowing the memories to flood back.

He had never known his biological parents. The circumstances of his arrival at the orphanage were still shrouded in mystery. A single image of a cloaked man, a stranger whose face he couldn't recall, had left him at the doorstep of the orphanage. Brent could still remember the way his hands felt, rough but with a firm grip. Despite the longing to know his origins, Brent had grown up with a sense of gratitude towards the man, seeing him as some sort of guardian. This was as far back as his memory went. He was barely five. Now, thirty years later. It all began to unravel.

Life in the orphanage had been lonely, marked by a sense of detachment from the other children. Brent had always felt like an outsider, never quite fitting in with the bustling energy of the orphanage. It wasn't until the matrons discovered his innate magic abilities that his life took a drastic turn.

Spellford, with its towering spires and bustling streets, had been a world away from the quiet simplicity of the orphanage. Brent had felt both exhilarated and apprehensive as he stepped into the new chapter of his life as a student at the academy. The same place he met Pax, where they bonded over being orphans. Pax never knew his biological parents either and was raised by a human couple who adopted him.

Brent stood under the shower and hoped it wouldn't end. The memories of his past mingled with the uncertainties of the present. The revelation of his true identity as Subject B, a Monarch Child created by Seraphina, had shaken him to the core. Yet, amidst the turmoil, Brent clung to the hope of uncovering the truth, as he had longed to do since the day he arrived at the orphanage's doorstep. The answers began and would end with Seraphina. He had to find a time to talk with her.

Brent stepped out of the shower, his mind still swirling. He found himself lost in a haze of contemplation. The steam from the hot water lingered in the air and he wiped the mirror down to look at himself one last time. Pushing his wet hair back, he attempted a smile, but the corners remained downturned. He reflection stared back at him with a solemn smile that looked more like a frown.

"Not getting any younger there, are you, boy?" he said to himself. With a towel wrapped around his waist, he emerged into the hallway, then went to his room to change. The sounds of voices from the living room drew him out of his reverie, reminding him he was not alone.

Once dressed, Brent made his way to the living room, where he found Victoria waiting for him, her expression a mix of concern and curiosity. He sat down on the couch like he had many times before and offered her a small, reassuring smile. This time it was he who could do with some guiding words, but he didn't know how to even discuss it, let alone think about it.

"Hey, Tori." Brent spoke softer than usual, yet still with the loving tone he would usually use when addressing his daughter.

"Hey Dad, Pax went to get dinner. His shout, he insisted." Victoria rolled her eyes and chuckled to try to lighten the mood. Brent didn't offer a laugh or even a noise.

Instead, he looked at her plainly and asked. "How was your day?"

Victoria smiled back at him and regaled him with the details of her afternoon at Chrono Pier but noticed he was not really paying attention and stopped speaking mid-sentence.

Brent stopped nodding and could see a flicker of apprehension in her eyes. "Everything okay?" he asked, shifting on the couch a bit.

"Yeah, just..." Victoria's story could wait, she asked her dad what was on her mind. "I was wondering what is going on between you and Arden. It seemed pretty serious out there."

Brent sighed again, and scratched the back of his head, his hair still damp. "It's complicated," he admitted, his gaze shifted to the floor and inspected the curls of the rug. He wondered what it would be like to shrink down to the size of an ant or even less and burrow his way through the rug like a thick jungle. He could really do with a getaway.

"Dad...?" Victoria's voice came back into focus as he pulled himself out of his thoughts.

"Sorry, yeah... Look, it isn't something you need to worry about, just work stuff," Brent said. He wasn't ready to tell her he was potentially seeing his boss.

"You sure?" she asked. Brent appreciated her checking in and placed a hand on her knee, he squeezed it a little like he would when she was younger.

From outside Brent and Victoria could hear a shuffle, signalling Pax's return. He bustled back into the house, laden with bags of food from Chrono Fried Chicken. Brent felt a pang of gratitude for his friend's steadfast presence. Despite the chaos swirling around them, Pax's unwavering support provided a sense of stability in the tumultuous storm of uncertainty.

With dinner set out on the table and the comforting aroma of fried chicken filling the air, Brent settled into his seat. The weight of the day momentarily lifted by the warmth of companionship and the promise of a shared meal with those he cherished most. He swore he would tell Victoria soon, but not until he had definite answers.

***

Brent stood outside a local night market, his restless mind had made it impossible to sleep, and he found himself on a late-night walk hoping it would help. The bustling atmosphere provided him a welcome distraction as he strolled through rows of stalls, the vibrant lights and lively chatter of venders and citizens momentarily eased the weight of his thoughts. He wandered aimlessly, browsing the eclectic array of goods on display. Handmade crafts from the Ilathier region, exotic spices from Suncrest and even street food delicacies from Iron Helm.

He meandered through the crowd, his senses alive with the sights, sounds and smells of the market. Brent finally felt his mind at peace. Grabbing a box of freshly made doughnuts from the Iron Helm stall, with their hard chocolate exterior and soft fluffy interior, the name Armour Doughnuts was truly accurate. He placed the box in the bag of other goodies he bought himself, he was almost ready to go home. Brent reached in to sneak one doughnut when his gaze caught sight of a figure slipping into a dimly lit alleyway.

He watched from a distance as he kept his hand perfectly still. Their movements were furtive and suspicious. Intrigued, Brent's curiosity overcame him. He made sure the doughnuts remained in place and followed, silently walking as he trailed the shadowy figure into the depths of the alley. The narrow passage remained cloaked in darkness. The only illumination came from the occasional flickering light of a distant streetlamp. Brent moved with caution. His senses on high alert as he also balanced the rustling of the bag in the breeze. His pulse quickened with anticipation, while his mind told him to turn back.

He drew closer to the figure ahead, and Brent's instincts told him that something was amiss. He couldn't shake the feeling of unease that gnawed at him, a primal instinct warning him of danger lurking in the shadows. But fuelled by a mix of concerned interest and determination, Brent pressed on., If there was any truth to uncover behind the mysterious figure's actions, Brent had resolved to find out.

The figure split into two separate individuals as they stopped dead in their tracks. Their presence exuded an aura of ominous foreboding, sending shivers down his spine.

"Who goes there?" Brent called out. His voice echoed faintly in the shadowed alleyway. "I am an investigator of the Mage's Union, show yourselves!" He stood his ground, his curiosity overcoming his fear.

The figure closest to him turned and stepped forward into the light, revealing a pair of piercing eyes gleaming from beneath the hood. They wore a mask that covered their mouth, similar to the one he saw Marquis wore.

Muffled, the cloaked figure spoke. "The Weaver demands the one you call Victoria, and they dislike being kept waiting for you to hand her over."

"What do you want with her?" he demanded, his hand subconsciously forming a magic sign as his instincts took over. The assailant noticed and held out their own hand. Purple runes formed around their wrist and Brent's hand was forced upwards above his head. The bag fell out of his other hand as he struggled against their power.

"We pose you no harm," they said, with deep emphasis on the word "you."

"Really?" Brent winced. "You almost pulled my shoulder out of its socket."

"Consider it a warning." The other one spoke, stepping forward. "Bring Victoria to the Weaver or we will be forced to take action."

With that ominous warning, they lowered their hand, and Brent's arm was free. The figures melted back into the shadows, but not before he noticed a shiny strand of red hair falling out from the hood. Before he could call out to them, they were gone, leaving Brent alone in the alley. His mind once again swirling with more questions and uncertainty.

He picked up the bag and turned around to head home. Victoria was safe, Marquis couldn't touch her. As Arden had gone over many times, if he could, he would have captured her already.

His eyes widened as he realised the missing link. Marquis was in league with the Code Weavers. The advanced Magic-Tech they possessed all made sense. Brent recognised the wrist-tech they wore from a project the two men once worked on. But what had led Marquis to this point? Another mystery upon all the others Brent was trying to solve.

He promised he would tell Arden about this second warning as soon as possible. He began to ponder why they were trying to force Brent to hand her over as some form of sacrificial lamb for slaughter, as opposed to capturing Brent and using him as bait. He shook his head. His walk was supposed to clear his head but all it did was provide him with more unanswered questions.

CHAPTER TWENTY-THREE

DR. ASHTON FROST

B rent sat outside Dr. Ashton Frost's office in the DMW department, his leg bounced nervously as he waited for him to arrive. He glanced around the waiting area, trying to distract himself from the anxiety building up inside. The sterile white walls and soft hum of the air conditioning did little to settle his unease.

He ran a hand through his hair, feeling the weight of the recent events pressing down on him. Discovering the truth about his origins, the threats against Victoria, and the looming presence of Marquis—all of it weighed heavily on his mind.

Brent didn't even want to be here, but he knew it was necessary. He needed to clear his head, gain some perspective, and figure out his next move. Still, he couldn't shake the feeling of impatience, the desire to get this over with and return to the investigative work that felt more urgent than ever.

While he sat there, lost in his thoughts, Brent couldn't help but wonder what Dr. Frost would make of him. Would the psychologist be able to help him make sense of everything that had happened? Or would this just be another frustrating detour in his quest for answers? The idea of undergoing a magical psychological assessment was daunting, to say the least. He fidgeted with the hem of his jacket, trying to push aside his nerves.

The door to Frost's office creaked open, and the psychologist emerged, his presence exuding a calming aura. Brent forced a smile as Dr. Frost approached him.

Despite being older than Brent, he possessed a timeless quality about him that made it difficult for Brent to discern his exact age. His well-groomed beard was just like it was a few days ago. Keeping his eyes on Ashton, Brent could not help but feel a magnetic pull.

"Ah! Brent, please come in," Dr. Frost said, his voice carrying a subtle enchantment that soothed his frayed nerves. Brent followed him into the office, taking in the warm and inviting atmosphere. Brent watched Ashton walk to his desk, his impeccably tailored suit stressing his athletic build. Dr. Frost took a seat while Brent quickly glanced around the room, trying to hide that he had been staring at Ashton's physique.

Dr. Ashton Frost's office felt like a sanctuary of serenity. Imbued with enchanting ambiance, Brent could feel it as soon as he stepped through the door. He had been enveloped in a warm golden glow emanating from the walls, suffusing the space with comforting radiance.

Soft, plush carpets lined the floor, muffling footsteps and creating a sense of hushed reverence. In the centre of the room, a large, polished oak desk, its surface adorned with various magical artifacts and arcane symbols. A crystal ball rested in one corner, shimmering with ethereal light, while a stack of ancient tomes and scrolls sat nearby, filled with the wisdom of ages past. Large windows would normally allow for natural light to filter into the room, however, today had been plagued by a dreary storm. Heavy rain pelted the windowpanes and made Brent tired.

"We can do it here or..." Frost spoke from behind his desk. "Move over there and start our session." Ashton pointed to the cozy alcove with comfortable looking chairs and plush rugs. Brent chose the alcove.

"Have a seat." Dr. Frost gestured to the chair opposite his own and smiled, the creases around his mouth covered by his beard. Brent obliged, slinking past Dr. Frost and was greeted by the intoxicating aroma of his cologne. For what felt like a millennium, Brent let the fragrance fill his nostrils as he sunk into the plush cushions and allowed himself to relax the best he could.

"Now, let's delve into the reason for your visit," Dr. Frost began, his eyes shimmered with a faint magical glow. "What brings you to seek a magical assessment today?"

"Arden sen—"

"Let's focus on you, shall we? Why are *you* here today?" he asked again, leaning back and resting one muscular leg over the opposite knee.

Brent took a moment to collect his thoughts before launching into his reasons for the assessment. Before he knew it, he was telling Ashton everything. It rushed out like water from an open tap. Brent spoke of the recent upheavals in his life—the revelation of his true identity, the looming threats against Victoria, and the overwhelming sense of being caught in a web of destiny beyond his control.

A subtle energy filled the room, as if the very air hummed with magical resonance. Dr. Frost listened intently; his expression thoughtful as he absorbed Brent's words. He jotted down notes as Brent spoke, which Brent tried not let distract him.

"Well, Brent, you've certainly encountered some rather extraordinary challenges, not only recently but in your life leading up to this point," Dr. Frost said, his voice soothing and calm. "Magic has a way of revealing truths hidden in the depths of our souls."

Brent nodded, and felt a glimmer of hope stir within him.

"Now, Brent, I want to undertake an exercise with you. It will let us delve into the depths of your psyche," Dr. Frost said, his gaze piercing yet gentle. He reached over and played a song from his phone, the soothing melody filled the room and created a low humming that perfectly scratched Brent's brain. "Close your eyes and let your mind drift back to the memories and emotions that have shaped your journey thus far."

Brent closed his eyes and followed the instructions by Ashton. Sinking back into his chair, he let his body relax and his mind submerge into a state of deep relaxation. With each breath, he felt the weight of his burdens lift. Dr. Frost spoke softly, guiding him through the exercise, allowing for Brent to feel comfortable as well as in a place of trust.

"I'm going to stand and place my hands in front of your face. This will allow for me to channel your Leyline connection and hopefully give you temporary severance from the things plaguing you."

"Alright, now take a slow, deep breath." Brent followed the instructions. "And release..."

That concluded the session. Dr. Frost returned to his desk and jotted down a few more notes before he raised his eyes to study Brent once more.

"Great work today. Shall we quill you in for another session next week?" he asked, and Brent nodded. Dr. Frost wrote down the next session date on a slip of parchment for Brent and handed it to him.

"You really prefer the old ways of admin." Brent pointed to Ashton's use of a quill and parchment instead of a lexicon.

"I find it allows me to be more...connected, to my work, and less distracted by Magi-Tech's temptations. Such as that damn Vicious app," Dr. Frost said vehemently of the gay dating app. "And as for the session today, my apologies for getting so...close, I find it allows me to connect better, read your thoughts more clearly." He looked at Brent with a warm but coy smile suggesting he knew that Brent had been checking him out.

"I, uh..." Brent stammered.

Ashton waved his hand. "The next few sessions won't be as hands on. I will ensure it remains professional between us in this room." Ashton shifted in his seat. "Arden informed me you both had gone out recently?"

"We have had a date," Brent admitted, feeling his face go hot and his pants tighten at the memory of being in Arden's office.

"Well, he is one lucky man for getting to you first," Ashton said under his breath. Brent didn't quite hear and asked him to repeat, "Oh, sorry it was nothing. Go on, you are cleared for duty," he dismissed Brent and smiled. "I will see you in a week." He looked down at his parchment, continuing to take notes as he shifted his legs.

Brent didn't move. Did Dr. Frost just hint at being attracted to him. Brent wanted to ask him what he meant, he wanted to ask why. Both Arden and Ashton were incredibly handsome, rugged, ripped. Brent had a dad bod. Was out of shape for what he used to be, so why him? Why this attention from the both of them.

Ashton looked up from his parchment through his eyebrows. "Is there something else I can assist with, purely work related of course?"

"I, eh...no, just, thank you for your time." Brent forced out. Now wasn't the time to wonder on the laws of attraction, he had enough on his plate as it was.

"Pleasure was all mine," Ashton said slyly, and Brent slunk out of his office and closed the door. Before he walked down the corridor and out of the DMW office, he readjusted his underwear that had shifted from the pressure building as Ashton had subtly hit on him.

Brent headed out of the department and made his way back into his office, where Pax had been working on a report of the previous field duty.

"So how was it?"

"Arousing," Brent whispered.

"What?" Pax exclaimed a little too loudly.

Arden bolted out of his office to see what the noise was about. "Grim-tusk, you alright out here...oh!" Arden spotted Brent and continued out of the office towards their desks. "Brent you are back, well, so you are all cleared then?"

"Yup, nothing wrong up in this mind." Brent pretended to knock on his skull.

"Good to hear, because we have our next assignment," he said, tapping the top of Brent's desk. "What's your availability this Flintasday?" he asked.

"Should be okay, what do you have in mind?"

"Um, we are chaperoning Victoria's excursion, remember?" Pax spoke up, reminding Brent, who felt terrible he had completely forgotten.

"Oh, right," Arden sounded disappointed. "The Dragon Sanctuary, well that would be cool. Maybe I could tag along?"

"I don't think that would be a good idea. I want to be focused on my daughter," Brent replied firmly, his thoughts were already preoccupied with ensuring Victoria's safety during the field trip, especially with all the impending warnings. She would be out of the confines of Spellford Academy's protection, and he did not want Arden to be there as a distraction.

Arden nodded, understanding Brent's priorities, but looking completely disappointed. "Of course, family comes first." He tapped the desk loudly and stood up. "Just keep me updated on how it goes. I will be here all weekend monitoring the city," he said before retreating to his office.

Brent let out a sigh of relief, grateful that he had avoided any further complications. He turned to Pax and spoke in a hushed whisper, "I don't think he is all too pleased about that."

"Well, he can deal with it, besides you and me are enough protection for Victoria and the rest, we took on the freakin Behemoth for Tutelary sakes." Pax sighed before he broke into a smile, the points of his tusk hitting his cheeks. "So, tell me more about your session with Dr. Frost." He raised his eyebrows up and down a few times "What was so arousing about it?"

Brent rolled his eyes and moved closer to tell him in detail what had happened. They both laughed it off, but secretly Brent was a little disappointed that Dr. Frost didn't make a move. He wondered if any more flirtation would happen in future sessions. It didn't have to go anywhere, but it was flattering to get the attention. Turning back to his desk, he looked up at Arden in his office and their eyes met. Arden smiled weakly at him.

Brent looked at Pax, who was busy with his work then back to Arden. "I'll be back," he quickly whispered.

Pax nodded with a smirk. "Chrono's after?"

"Fine, but I'm getting a salad," Brent sighed, poking his belly.

"I like you pudgy," Pax said and Brent smiled at him. He always knew how to make Brent smile.

Brent skipped into Arden's office and shut the door slightly behind him.

"What's up, Abernathy?" The use of Brent's last name was like a dagger in his heart.

"I just wanted to check and see if you would like to come over for dinner, seeing that we won't see each other for a bit?" Brent asked, trying to return to the casual nature they once had.

"Uh, I would like to, but I was planning to go see Seraphina tonight, pay her a visit after, well, you know…" Arden said.

"Oh, okay, why don't I tag along?"

Arden looked up. His face took on a stern look. Speaking in a clipped tone, Arden said, "Actually, I think it would be better if you go and take Grimtusk with you. I am sure she would like to see you both after you stormed out so rudely."

Brent paused. He didn't just say it that way? Brent was not about to put up with it, no matter how handsome Arden was. Or if he was his boss.

"I would like to see how you would have handled learning your entire past was a lie in that split moment?" Brent responded just as sharply.

Arden's eyes widened. He stood up, his chair pushing into the wall a little too roughly. He stared at Brent with a mournful look and leaned his fingertips against the desk. "Sorry, I was…I don't know what I was thinking. I was more upset I had forgotten you had plans already this weekend, and if I am being honest, I didn't truly comprehend how much you were involved with Victoria's life." He stopped and Brent knew there was more he wanted to say. "She is seventeen, after all."

Brent stood silently. He didn't know what to say. He had guys leave him on dates the moment they learned he had a child. Or not even write back in messages. But here was a man expressing jealously over a seventeen-year-old.

"Victoria will always be my number one priority. If that is going to be a problem, we should not pursue whatever this is," Brent said firmly.

Arden lifted his gaze to him. With his lips pursed, he silently conveyed his disapproval. Just how Elwin would, with a mischievous twinkle in his eye. Brent felt Arden's blue eyes dissecting his every thought and emotion. This used to leave Brent defenceless, but not anymore. He had become so immersed in his own life, focused on raising Victoria and being independent, that no one could change his perspective. He stood as still as a statue, unmoving and rigid.

"So, what you are saying to me is—" Arden started, but Brent held up a single finger.

"I will stop you right there," Brent said, knowing exactly how this conversation was about to play out. He approached Arden's desk, mimicking his pose. Their eyes meet. Brent wanted to reach out and kiss him, but also slap him at the same time. This man before him was being foolish, and he wanted some way to make him understand. He hoped his next words would.

"What I'm saying is…Victoria is my everything. My reason for living. She comes first. And always will. Even if you were Elwin, who I loved with all my heart, it would not matter. She always comes first. Is that clear?"

Arden didn't hesitate. "Like a soothsayer's crystal ball."

There was a brief silent exchange, and then Arden smiled warmly. Brent wanted nothing more than for Arden to walk around his desk and wrap his arms around him. To kiss him. But they were at work.

"You are what I want," he said after what felt like a century long pause, "and if I get it only fifty percent of the time, because you are handling things in your life with Victoria or even Paxton, then I am fine with that." He dropped his head and sighed. "Sorry I was being foolish. I blurred the lines of our work relationship and personal one."

"It is fine," Brent said gently. "But you really want me?"

"Oh, absolutely," Arden replied. He threw his head back and chuckled. Brent felt the electricity spark between them. He longed for Arden to take him again in this office, but he behaved. "So, will you go see Seraphina?" Arden asked.

"Yeah, I think I need to talk it all out with her."

"Do you want me to come?" Arden asked.

Brent wanted to say yes, but he knew Paxton would be the better supporter. He had been there with Brent nearly his entire life.

"I will take Pax like you said."

"Smart decision. He knows you better," Arden admitted, and Brent chuckled, agreeing with him. "Before you go, I want to say…"

But Arden was interrupted. The Opticon alarm sounded, and Pax rushed in.

"We have an alert down in Encanto Village."

"Alright, I will handle it. You two go see Seraphina," Arden responded, shuffling them out.

"What if it's—" Brent started, and Arden held a finger to his lips.

"I'll be fine. I have Cyrus and the recruits to call upon," Arden reminded Brent.

"Okay, I will see you later then?" Brent asked, but Arden waved him off without giving a response.

CHAPTER TWENTY-FOUR
THE SILENT SAGES

"Who can tell me why we call it The Molotov Cockatiel?" Professor Silas' voice boomed in the Creature Studies classroom, causing Victoria to jump. His eyes twinkled with enthusiasm as they always did. His true enjoyment came from teaching the small class about all the wondrous creatures in Arcanum.

The afternoon sun beamed through the giant arch windows. Victoria was one of six students who had taken this optional subject. No one responded to his question. Victoria looked around the classroom, hoping to not have to volunteer yet again as she was the only one who had answered any of his questions.

"Last lesson I asked you all to read chapters thirty through thirty-eight, Arcanum's Avians. Surely, one of you knows." He sounded exasperated and looked to Victoria. "Abernathy, will you indulge me and answer?" He smiled.

Victoria stood. "They named the Molotov Cockatiel after years of exposure to the natural Augmenti wells throughout Arcanum. Closely related to Phoenixes. It has flame-like features flicking atop its head, resembling that of a candle." She smiled as Silas nodded and urged her to continue. "Mostly found in the volcanic landscapes of Iron Helm, the indigenous people of the land used them as explosive bomb-like weapons before they became imperilled," she said, sitting back down. Professor Silas looked around the class.

"Thank you, Victoria, for once again displaying your knowledge of these wondrous creatures." He walked to the front of his desk and sat on the edge. "Naturally, in modern society, the Arcanum Avian Protection Authority, or AAPA, has implemented national decrees to provide extensive protection for most of the Avians. However, for a time, the Molotov bird came dangerously close to extinction."

Professor Silas quickly changed subjects to discuss other Avians, from the Leyline Finches that populate Spellford's skies, to the Earthbound Röc throughout Valtoria.

"Giant flightless things, but they have strong, muscular legs for running," Silas muttered to no one in particular and drew by hand with chalk a picture of the bird. The class shared in a soft chuckle at his depiction, but he was undeterred.

"Alright, class, as it's nearing the end of our lesson, for homework I will assign you all an Avian and you will need to report on each. Extra marks if you can get a real-life picture of the bird. Abernathy I'll assign you...the Leyline Finch, Stonier the Frostwing Owl..." Silas trailed off assigning the students a bird each.

The class departed but Professor Silas dashed out of the room and hailed down Victoria. She followed him back into the room and dreaded what was to come.

"Ah, Abernathy, sorry to keep you," he started.

"No problem, Professor. What can I help you with?"

"The chaperone slip for your father has come through, but I will need you to get one for, what is he to you, that man at the shops...Paxton?" Silas appeared to be nervous, a sheen of sweat on his brow.

"He is basically an uncle. You can call him that if you want," she replied, shuffling her books in her arms.

"Alright, your Uncle Paxton, if you would get him to contact me, I will arrange for a verbal confirmation."

Victoria nodded and motioned to leave, but then recalled the day at the shops. "Don't you already have his number?" Victoria asked slyly. Silas' face began to flush.

He looked like he meant to reply but instead dismissed her so she could be on her way. Victoria made her way in the direction of Professor Nia's office. Her stomach dropped as she approached. Apprehension gnawed at her. She had missed two of their tutoring lessons, and now she felt sheepish about showing her face. With a deep breath, she knocked softly on the door and hoped that Nia wouldn't be too upset with her absence.

"Come in." Nia's voice called from inside her office. Victoria slowly pushed open the door.

Inside the office, even though it was warm and inviting as always, she felt a hint of coldness in Nia's posture. "Victoria it is good to finally see you." Her voice was gentle. Victoria still felt as if she was hit by a frozen pike, perhaps a result of her own guilt. "Please, have a seat." She held a handout pointing at the free chair opposite her.

Victoria nodded and took the seat, feeling a knot form in her stomach. She knew she had some explaining to do. Slinking into the chair, she dropped her bag by her feet and looked up at her professor. Disappointing her father was one thing. She was used to the struggle of wanting to escape his overly protective grip. But to disappoint someone she admired. The pit in her stomach grew ten times its size.

Victoria launched into an apology. "I am so sorry for missing our last two sessions." Her voice was filled with sincere regret. "I've been dealing with some personal issues, and it has been difficult to focus on my studies."

Nia examined her for a moment, her jade eyes thoughtful.

"I can see how attending the Chrono Pier with your friends can be incredibly difficult, especially when it is the first time they are all meeting, but if you are going to lie, next time do it better," Nia said sternly, not shifting in her chair.

Victoria could feel her heartbeat race in her ears. How did Nia know? "Am I in trouble?" Victoria's voice croaked softly after some time.

"Why would you be in any trouble?" Nia settled her shoulders and face. "These sessions are only for your benefit. If you see no need to attend, we can end—"

"No!" Victoria stood up, the chair moving backwards sharply, an ear-splitting screech emanated from its legs when they scraped against the wooden floor.

Nia observed Victoria with a knowing look. "Ah! There is the girl I know," she remarked, rising to her feet. With a flick of her wrist, the furniture vanished, leaving the room empty. "Now that you're fired up, let's try a few defensive spells, arms up, and summon a shield."

Victoria hesitated, unsure of what to expect. Before she could react, a small bolt of yellow energy struck her squarely between the eyebrows, knocking her back a few steps. Stunned momentarily, she rubbed her forehead, feeling the tingle of residual magic.

Victoria noticed smoke trailing from Nia's fingertips. "You're Aphonic, too?" she asked, adjusting her stance after recovering from Nia's strike.

"I come from a long line of Silent Sages. My father taught your father how to hone his gift, and now it's my turn to pass on his teachings to you." She stretched out her hands and settled into a focused stance. "It's through our actions, not our words, that we show our strength." Nia swiftly twirled and then swapped her own stance.

With determination, Victoria mirrored Nia's stand, her hands poised to channel her magic. She focused her mind, summoning her inner spark as she prepared to defend herself against her mentor's onslaught.

The attack came swiftly, a surge of energy crackled through the air as she unleased another yellow bolt. Victoria, much more prepared this time, reacted instinctively, conjuring a shimmering shield of energy to intercept the attack. The shield absorbed the impact, dispersing the lightning harmlessly around her.

Impressed, Nia nodded with approval. "Good work, but don't let your guard down," she cautioned with a firm voice. Appearing next to Victoria, she gripped her arm wielding the shield "Stay focused and expect my next move."

"Like this?" Victoria swung her other hand around for a direct attack into the stomach and shot out a ball of magenta light, forcing Nia to stumble back, letting go of Victoria. Victoria raised her hand as it seared with a burning white pain, it was surrounded in the same magenta light. Her skin had changed, her hand contorting as she performed the enchantment.

"Smart...girl," Nia panted, winded and holding her stomach. "You pick up...quick."

With renewed determination, Victoria maintained her defensive stance, her senses alert for any sign of Nia's next attack. As the tension mounted, she braced herself for whatever challenge her mentor would throw her way.

The practice battle raged on. Victoria's confidence grew with each passing moment. She could feel the strength of her magic surge through her, empowering her to stand her ground against Nia's formidable attacks. With every spell she cast, though, the pain in her left hand grew as her hand contorted further.

After what felt like an eternity, the duel ended. Both combatants rested to catch their breath and assess the aftermath of their confrontation. Despite the physical exertion, Victoria felt a sense of accomplishment wash over her. She had held her own against Nia, proving her skill and determination as a Mage.

"Can I take a look at your hand?" Nia asked after she noticed Victoria flexing and shaking her hand. Victoria offered up her hand for Nia's inspection. She carefully analysed its every angle, rotating Victoria's arm around. "Your body is trying to gain control of this transformation, but with each spell cast it is a losing battle." Green light emanated from Nia's hands. Victoria's entire arm, from the shoulder down tingled. "I've placed a block on it, but it is only temporary." She released her arm and flicked her wrists once more. The furniture returned to their spots. The two women took a seat. "If your hand contorts again, come see me straight away so we can keep it at bay."

"What if I transform again?" Victoria asked, flexing her hand and fore-arm muscles. She rolled her fingers into a fist and pulled it in tightly, they felt brand new.

"That's what the block is for," Nia said with reassurance.

"Did you learn anything in Suncrest about my transformation?" Victoria asked. Her heart began to slow after the mock battle. She wiped a trickling bead of sweat from her brow and was hit with a small wave of fatigue.

Nia sighed. Her expression clouded with frustration. "I am sorry Victoria, but I have found no new leads yet. The information I gathered in Suncrest was inconclusive, and I could not uncover any further clues since then."

Victoria's heart sank at the news, a sense of disappointment weighed heavily upon her. She had hoped that Nia's investigations would yield some answers, but it seemed their search for the reasons behind her transformation would continue. She looked down at her left hand and sighed.

"But I won't give up," Nia continued, her voice infused with determination. "I'll keep searching, exploring every avenue. My father might have something in his notes, care to accompany me?" Nia stood up and glided past, picking up Victoria's backpack with a graceful dip and handed it to her.

"Of course, I'd be happy to help," Victoria readily agreed, eager for the opportunity to delve into Nia's father's notes for clues.

On their way out of Nia's office, Victoria's Rune-Phone vibrated. She dove her hand into her pocket to see who was contacting her, expecting her father or Emily. She glanced at the screen to see a message.

> Don't forget, group project!

Lirien was right on time and reminded her about their upcoming project meeting.

"Oh, shit!" Victoria said, reading the message. "I forgot. Hector and I have a group project meeting with Lirien. Is it okay if we raincheck?" Victoria tugged on her bag straps.

"Well as I am the professor on the subject, I would be remiss if I took you away from this project. Go have fun and study hard so you have something amazing to present." Her jade eyes glistened as Victoria thanked her. "If you need anything, please reach out," she called down the corridor as some other students gathered.

Victoria made her way down the steps of the school, her mind already racing with thoughts of the group project.

> Hey Lirien, I am on my way to the station now, keep your lil gay elf ears on!

> Homophobic!

> I can't be homophobic, I'm Bi babes!

> Well, we both know that's a lie!

> Me being Bi? Who's the bigot now? Biphobic!

> No, you being homophobic, you witch!

Victoria chuckled to herself. She appreciated the candid relationship she had with Lirien, he was always able to turn her mood around or settle her mind. It was perfect timing, too. She needed to be clear headed so they could get a head start on the project and ensure they received top marks.

CHAPTER TWENTY-FIVE
EMPTY CHAIR AND SCORCH MARKS

Evening was drawing in as Pax knocked on the door of Seraphina's home. No answer. He knocked once more.

"Maybe she didn't hear?" Pax gave a nonchalant shrug of his shoulders. "She is old, after all."

Brent descended the porch stairs, cautiously peering through the windows. "Lights are out. Has she perhaps gone to bed?" Brent threw out what felt like a plausible reason. "Hello again, Mr. Grimtusk. Ah! And Victoria's father." A man spoke from behind and startled them both. "To what do I owe the pleasure of finding you two skulking around my grandmother's house?" Silas Evergreen stood before them with his red beard shining in the later afternoon streetlights.

"Ah, you see..." Brent started.

"Seraphina is our colleague at the Union. We were paying her a visit to brief her on an important matter," Pax quickly blurted out.

Impressed with his quick thinking, Brent beamed behind Pax. Maybe watching too many Mages Union Glimmer Dramas on the vision orb had it's benefits.

"Ah, here on business. Well, she sometimes falls asleep watching the vision orb. Here, I have a spare key." Silas dug around in his pockets and fished out a set of keys.

Silas inserted the key into the lock, turning it with a slight click. The door swung open, revealing the dimly lit interior of Seraphina's home. The air inside felt stale. An unspoken tension lingered.

"You gentlemen are welcome to step inside," Silas gestured, holding the door open.

Pax exchanged a quick glance with Brent before they entered the house with their guard up. Various artifacts and curiosities adorned the hallway as they walked through each memento of Seraphina's long life. Flickering light could be seen from a room in the distance, casting dancing shadows across the entrance. The atmosphere felt welcoming, but a sense of foreboding was in the air.

"She usually falls asleep in her chair," Silas explained, leading them further into the house. "Let me check upstairs, you two can check the living room and see if she's there." Silas pointed to a room beside them before he proceeded upstairs.

Pax and Brent slowly approached the living room. A sudden chill permeated the air. The chair near the fireplace was empty, but the fireplace roared as if it had recently been lit. The quiet ticking of a clock on the wall echoed throughout the room, only adding to the feelings of unease.

"She's not here," Silas stated as he entered the living room, his brow furrowed with concern. He stroked his beard. "That's strange. Her study is empty. It's as if she vanished."

Brent's mind raced, connecting the dots between Seraphina's disappearance and the cryptic revelations they had uncovered about the Monarch Children Program. If someone had taken her, Marquis had to be the one.

"We need to find her," Brent declared, determination etched on his face. "Silas, do you know if she had any enemies, anyone who might want to harm her?"

Silas shook his head. "My grandma is respected in the magical community. I can't imagine why someone would want to hurt her."

Pax glanced around the room, his senses on high alert as he sniffed the air. "If she's not here, do you know where else she could have gone to?" His voice laced with concern.

Brent began to consider every possibility. Just when he thought he could get answers, that he could make amends after his abrupt departure at the lab, it looked like his chances might be dashed. He couldn't let that happen.

"We need to keep searching. She may have left a clue behind, something that could tell us where she went," Brent said.

Silas nodded in agreement, his expression grave. "I'll check the study again," he offered, turning out of the room and back up the stairs.

Brent and Pax began their search of the living room. Brent combed through the dust covered bookshelves while Pax inspected every piece of furniture. They examined every nook and cranny for any sign of abduction. Minutes ticked by. The tension in the air got thicker. There was no sign of struggle, no residual magic energy Pax could sniff out. A sense of frustration gnawed at Brent's insides. The desperation to talk to her and apologise only grew.

"Where could she have gone?" Brent muttered, frustration clear in his tone.

"Hey, you two, I've found something." Silas called. Brent and Pax bounded up the stairs, their footsteps landing softly on the carpet.

Silas had turned the study upside down. He was crouched down in front of the desk, looking at the floor. There was a black scorch mark surrounded by a few scattered remnants of burnt parchment. Silas carefully reached out to touch the remnants, feeling the faint warmth still lingering in the air.

"Careful," Pax warned, squatting down to look while Brent hovered above.

Silas traced the mark on the floor, ripping his hand back as his fingertips began to spark. Silas pulled his index finger to his mouth and sucked on the tip. The residual energy left behind had burned it.

"Shit," Silas said, still sucking his finger. "What do you make of this?" Silas asked. "It looks like something was burned here."

Brent made to answer but Pax had already begun tracing it himself. His Orc immunity to some magics allowed for him to be an astute inspector.

Pax frowned, his mind racing with possibilities. "Could it be a spell gone bad? A ricocheted attack?" He wondered aloud.

"Maybe someone tried to destroy evidence?" Brent's jaw tightened at the thoughts of what happened.

"Either way, it is clear this is no ordinary mark," Silas said with the same concern in his voice and looked over the scorch mark once more. "We are above her bedroom, could you go down and look?" He turned to Brent and asked, "I would, but I don't want to exactly go into my grandmother's room, what if she is changing?"

"Sure, send me down," he laughed off nervously.

Bounding back downstairs, he traced the location with his mind and entered the room across from the living room. He pressed firmly against the door, and it opened with no resistance.

Brent cautiously stepped into Seraphina's bedroom. A shiver ran down his spine that sent prickles of unease rippling across his skin. He was greet-ed with chaos and destruction, a stark contrast to the serene atmosphere of the rest of her home. Remnants of a once tidy and orderly bedroom was now in disarray. Furniture overturned and belongings scattered haphazardly across the floor. The air was thick with an ominous aura that Brent couldn't shake. Like some unseen presence lingered in the shadows, watching. Waiting.

But it was the sight of the ceiling that truly chilled Brent to the core. Above him loomed a massive scorch mark, its twisted, gnarled shape resembling a monstrous handprint. The charred outline seemed to pulse with a sinister purple energy, casting eerie shadows across the room.

Brent's heart hammered in his chest as he took in the sight. His mind raced with dark possibilities, but whatever had transpired here it was no ordinary occurrence. A violent malevolence had snatched Seraphina from her home, right out of her bed, but she put up as much of a fight as she could.

Drawing upon his magic, Brent summoned a small ball of fire in his hands to illuminate the room. His senses on high alert as debris from the shattered mirror crunched under his boots into the carpet. Every nerve tingled with a primal instinct warning him of impending danger. Despite the gurgling fear that threatened to consume him, he pressed on, investigating with a sharp eye like Silas had upstairs. Brent was determined to uncover the truth, no matter the cost.

His phone dinged. He pulled out his phone and his blood ran cold as he read the message.

> "You have forced my hand, Abernathy. If you want to discover your past, bring me your future."

The words seemed to leap out at him, each letter dripped with malice. A thousand thoughts and fears swarmed his brain, all the pain of what Seraphina was enduring. But one thing was obvious. Marquis had made his move. He was behind Seraphina's disappearance. His sights were set on Victoria more than ever.

Pax entered the room while Brent stared at his phone.

"Making a habit of entering a woman's bedroom, is there something you need to tell me?" Pax's attempt at humour died in the air when he took in the state of the room and the damaged ceiling. "Oh—what in the infernal hells!"

"The scorch bled through," Brent said pointing at the giant mark on the ceiling. "But that's not all." Brent held up his phone and showed Pax the message. He could tell that the pieces hadn't clicked and had to spell it out.

"Marquis did this, he knows about Seraphina and is using her to get to me. To get Victoria," Brent said slowly.

"Marquis, as in Nia's father?" Silas asked, looking between them. "What would he want with my grandmother?"

Pax and Brent exchanged a quick glance.

"You see, umm, Seraphina was involved in…" Pax scratched the back of his head. "Uhhh, Brent, I don't know what to say here. Help me?"

"Seraphina was involved in an experiment that artificially created children and tested on them to push the boundaries of magic," Brent said directly, not wanting to skirt around the issue. He didn't care what his punishment would be from telling a civilian highly classified information.

"That's preposterous," Silas said with a laugh but stopped when Pax and Brent weren't laughing. "You're joking? My grandmother? You must have the wrong—"

"We don't. We have seen the evidence." Pax tried to keep a warm tone. He moved toward Silas in what Brent took as an attempt to comfort him, but Silas took a step back.

"It doesn't matter what she was involved in, though. What matters is we need to call Arden and get you home," Brent said.

"But what if they come after me next?" Silas asked with clear concern.

"Whoever is doing this isn't after you."

"I can't go home and be alone. I will, I'll…" Silas' breathing became laboured, his concern turning to distress. He grasped his chest. Pax approached and placed his hands on the outside of his shoulders and gave a firm but consoling squeeze before he rubbed his arms, trying to calm him down.

"Shhh, it is okay. You can come stay at our place tonight, right Brent?" Pax confirmed.

Brent nodded before he stepped out into the corridor and dialled Arden to fill him in as Pax continued to steady Silas.

"Brent, how is Seraphina?" Arden chirped in his ear.

"Uhhh, well…when Pax and I arrived at Seraphina's we stumbled upon a scene we didn't expect. You better head over ASAP."

"Are you okay?" Urgency filled Arden's voice.

"Yes, just come here quick," Brent replied. As he hung up his call, he felt something materialising behind him.

The air in the corridor shifted. A portal opened behind Brent and Arden stepped through.

"What's happened? Is she okay?" Arden's tone was firm. His eyes darting around looking for answers.

"Seraphina's missing," Brent divulged the news. A look of shock washed over Arden's face. He pushed past Brent and rushed into Seraphina's bedroom. Brent made to follow when another ding chimed from his phone.

By sundown tomorrow your time ends, come to where it all began.

Brent's jaw tightened. Had the threat become far greater than he imagined? Brent's once peaceful life was being torn apart by unseen powers lurking in the dark. He mouthed the words "come to where it all began". Did it mean the laboratory in Erimosia, where Elwin fell? But no one else knew about that besides Pax. Or could it mean the lab where Brent himself was created? He was pulled from his thoughts as Arden hurried around him.

Not missing a beat, Arden went straight into investigator mode. He began to take photos, collect evidence and called on the help of Cyrus, who had finished in Encanto Village, and arrived with a portal. Cyrus began to document everything on his lexicon while Arden continued to crane his neck and contort his body into all sorts of shapes to investigate the bedroom.

Feeling in the way and without much they could do, Arden dismissed Brent and Pax, saying he would finish up here.

"Oh, and Abernathy, be vigilant tomorrow at the Sanctuary," Arden added with a wave as Brent stepped through his own portal home. He needed to focus on Victoria's excursion after all.

CHAPTER TWENTY-SIX
DRAGON SANCTUARY EXCURSION

Victoria had been looking forward to this excursion for months. The monorail hummed with energy over ash coloured soil and rocks scattered underneath the rail line which lent an air of solemnity. The sleek, silver carriages glided effortlessly through the desolate Drakor Valley. Onboard, Victoria and her classmates from Creature Studies were all buzzing with excitement. Victoria's own heart fluttered with giddy anticipation She was eager to witness up close the majesty of the dragons her class had been studying.

Inside the carriage, students chattered excitedly, their excitement clear in the gleam of their eyes. Victoria focused on her father, who kept stealing glances at Professor Silas.

"You okay, Dad?" she asked quiet enough for only them to hear.

"What?" he asked after pulling his gaze away from her professor.

"If you like Professor Evergreen so much, what don't you talk to him?"

"I don't like him," Brent whispered. It wasn't the time to explain the intricate nature of his and Silas' relationship, especially because it had to do with work.

"Okay then..." Victoria rolled her eyes. "If it's not that, then what is it?"

"It's nothing," Brent lied, stretching his arm behind her and resting it on the seat. He flashed her a false smile. Brent wasn't only stressed that they had no leads in locating Seraphina as it pertained to his and Victoria's saftey, but guilty as well.

When they approached the outskirts of the gate to the Dragon Sanctuary the landscape began to shift. It grew more untamed and rugged. The monorail passed through the vast, stone archway, adorned with intricate Draconic carvings, that marked the entrance to the Dragon Sanctuary. The world outside transformed into a completely different realm. Towering trees with lush green leaves surrounded them. Soft rays of sunlight filtered through the dense canopy, casting enchanting patterns onto the monorail's windows. With a gentle deceleration, the monorail navigated through the heart of the sanctuary. The carriages offered panoramic views of this hidden paradise, designed to ensure the dragons' safety and well-being.

All the students had run up and pressed themselves against the glass, taking in the majesty of the giant dome structure. Pax had wiggled his way in between students, towering over them. Nestled amongst the trees, expansive platforms stretched out, serving as comfortable observation points for visitors. It was on one such platform that the monorail came to a halt. Excitement sounded in the air as the students disembarked, accompanied by the chaperones and their professor.

A chorus of dragon calls echoed above them when the group stepped onto the platform. Victoria's heart raced. She could hardly contain her joy as she caught her first glimpse of dragons soaring gracefully through the skies. Pax grabbed Brent's arm and pointed upward, following its trail. There was a collective gasp as it flew directly overhead in all its majesty. Victoria looked up in awe at her father, pure joy in her eyes. Brent smiled in return, glad he got to witness her seeing the sanctuary for the first time.

Brent tried to refocus his energy, reminding himself of the purpose of the visit, but his mind was in so many places. Between Seraphina's disappearance and the warning messages from Marquis last night. Arden reassured Brent that nothing would go wrong, and for extra measure they stationed some additional Mage's Union members for security.

The group stood in a semi-circle around their designated tour guide. Brent looked to Pax whose excitement might have trumped the students.

"The sanctuary is equipped with advanced magical surveillance, ensuring the utmost safety and security for all its Dragons, patrons and staff." The tour guide pointed up at the sky. "We don't need to worry about the dragons getting loose this way." The guide faked a laugh, and others nervously joined in. He handed out passes with their names. "Now please hold on to your nametags and follow all instructions you are given. Just because we've provided the dragons with a safe place to roam, it doesn't mean they aren't dangerous."

"Okay, class!" Professor Silas' deep voice sounded off, getting his students' attention.

"We have an exciting itinerary planned today as we explore the wonders of the Dragon Sanctuary. We'll start with a guided tour of this platform level and the outer area of the grounds, where you'll get a glimpse of the magnificent dragons from a distance." His dark auburn hair showed streaks of silver throughout, as it fell in waves to his shoulders. The top part tied back in a styled but loose ponytail.

"Next, we'll venture into the heart of the sanctuary, where you'll have the unique opportunity to observe and interact with various dragon species. Please remember, dragons are highly intelligent creatures, even in their youth, so be respectful and approach them with caution if offered the chance."

Pax couldn't hide his clear attraction to the man. Brent laid a hand on his shoulder to speak to him telepathically.

"How did last night go?" Brent asked.

"He is a lot more settled. I stayed on the couch and promised him we would find her. Not that I could guarantee, but we have never failed before, and I wanted to soothe his fears."

"Let's hope we can beat the clock," Brent said, and they both returned their focus on Professor Evergreen.

"During the afternoon, we'll split into groups for a special educational session. You'll learn about dragon behaviour, their diets, and how to identify different dragon species based not just on their scales but also their droppings. As the saying goes, 'judge dragons not by the colour of their scales but by the content of their droppings'." A handful of students grimaced or squirmed at the thought of sifting through dragon dung.

"We'll conclude the day with a thrilling dragon-riding demonstration by the skilled dragon riders, with a sneak peek of the set of *Dragonfire*. You might even witness some daring aerial acrobatics!" The group of students went off, cheering their enthusiasm for the day's events and the chance of seeing *Dragonfire* contestants.

Brent watched on, his heart full of joy at seeing Victoria in her element, clapping along with all her classmates at the thought of seeing Kiera and Garnet.

"Now, I know this will be an unforgettable experience for all of you. So, let's proceed with the tour and get ready to discover the true magnificence of these incredible creatures!" Professor Silas concluded.

With a warm smile, Professor Evergreen signalled to the tour guide to begin the adventure, eager to share his knowledge and passion for creatures with his students. Silas waited as the students all filed passed him until Victoria, Brent and Pax came up.

"Victoria, you can go on ahead. I need to have a quick word with your father and Pax here." He and Victoria exchanged a smile, and she stepped to the side to join some of the other students.

"Thank you for yesterday, Mr Abernathy. Paxton reassured me last night that you would do all that you can to get to the bottom of this. Let me know if there is news as soon as you can." He laid a tender hand on Pax's forearm.

"Don't stress, Silas. Best focus on the day ahead, hey?" Brent pointed at one of the eager students who was leaning over the ledge of a bridge. "And you can call me Brent."

"You're exactly right." Silas turned his attention to the student and ran off to scold him. "Shawn, get down from the ledge!"

Brent and Pax trailed after them. The tour guide led the group through winding pathways that crisscrossed the expansive grounds, each turn revealed new wonders around every corner. They passed by habitats of various dragon breeds, each carefully designed to resemble their natural environments in the outside world before they were taken in. Some dragons soared overhead with impressive wingspans wider than Brent had ever seen, while others lounged near bubbling streams, their scales shimmering in brilliant colours.

The guide provided intriguing facts about each dragon species they encountered, sharing details about their behaviour, diet, and magical abilities. She emphasised the importance of maintaining a safe distance and respecting the dragons' space, as the creatures were powerful and deserved to be treated with care. Only those who were trained could approach them in these parts of the sanctuary.

After leaving the open wild areas, they wandered towards a small dome building situated off on its own by a smaller wild area that imitated the surrounding ones. It was the dragon nursery.

"Okay, students, please remember to keep your voices down in here. These hatchlings aren't used to loud noises," Silas said and held the door open as the students filed in.

They walked through an enclosure, tiny hatchlings playfully tumbled around above while practicing their elemental abilities under the watchful eyes of their caregivers. The sight of the adorable hatchlings captivated the students, some couldn't resist giggling at the dragonlings' antics.

"Where are their mothers?" one student asked in a whisper. The tour guide looked on with a smile that had a lot more to it.

"These hatchlings have no mothers to raise them, the eggs were rescued. They were hatched and raised by Dragoon Corp, here in the sanctuary."

"Oh, that's sad," the same student replied. "They won't know their mum or dad," She sighed.

Victoria looked awkwardly at her father for a moment before turning her attention back to the hatchlings. She never felt more related to something than these poor orphaned hatchlings. The enclosure was segmented into different environments around the middle, where they all continued to watch from above. Most of the students looked on at the more playful, energetic dragonlings. Victoria, however, was drawn to a group of young dragons who rested on rock beds in an environment that simulated nighttime. Their iridescent wings shimmered like rainbows in the fake moonlight.

"These are Moonlit Seraphims," Professor Silas stated leaning forward against the rails alongside Victoria. "They are my favourite, with their gentle nature and ability to create mesmerising light displays in the night sky. Some even say that the northern lights originated from a Seraphim who perished."

Victoria felt an instant connection to these graceful creatures. "They are stunning," she breathed.

"You know, they say the dragon you are most drawn to says a lot about your personality," Silas stood and signalled to the class they were to continue on with the tour.

Brent looked on as he watched Victoria and Silas interact. He waited for them to finish speaking and for Silas to move ahead before he walked over. Victoria was looking down into the Seraphim pen when she began to wave. He paused once more to let her have this moment and smiled. All he could see was the innocent, yet strong willed young girl he and Pax raised.

"Having fun?" he asked with glee in his voice. "I noticed you looking at the Seraphims."

"Yeah, they are gorgeous."

"So, are you over the Emberflare?"

"No, Emberflares are still my favourite, but Moonlit Seraphims are definitely stunning." She hugged her father's arm, rested her head on his shoulder and thanked him for coming.

Throughout the tour the students learned about the sanctuary's conservation efforts and the ongoing research conducted by experts to ensure the well-being and harmony of the dragons. Professor Evergreen elaborated on the delicate balance between humans and magical creatures, stressing the importance of preserving their habitats and understanding their role in the ecosystem.

Victoria expressed to Brent that her fascination grew with each dragon she encountered. He found himself lowering his guard about her wanting to join the Dragoon Corp, but he kept it to himself for now.

Brent sat down, exhausted from all the walking while Pax and Victoria went to get their lunch at the cafeteria before they headed to the *Dragonfire* set. Brent had to restrain Pax from the many gift stores along the way after he found Pax in one, looking at all the dragon statues, his arms filled with boxes. Brent hated to be the one to burst his bubble but had to be the voice of reason and talked him into leaving with only two.

***

After lunch, they were allowed into the set of *Dragonfire*, the atmosphere was electric with anticipation. This is what Victoria had truly come to see. The colossal stadium spread out before them, its impressive architecture a testament to the grandeur of the event. Rows upon rows of elevated stalls surrounded the main arena, the students found themselves seated in a prime location to witness the upcoming spectacle.

The lighting was dim, which cast an air of mystery and excitement all around the arena. Hushed whispers and excited murmurs filled the air as the student body enthusiastically awaited the start of the show. Victoria's own restlessness was palpable, her legs bouncing with nervous energy. She felt her father's arm wrap around her in a comforting gesture rubbing her upper arm.

"I wonder how they will reveal them," Pax said to no one in particular, his voice on the brink of letting out an excited squeal.

The room went silent as the lighting gradually brightened and revealed the intricate set and vivid hues of the stadium. The crowd erupted in collective applause and cheers. Even Brent was impressed by the sleek fusion of ancient and modern elements and let out his own boisterous round of cheers. Towering spires and ethereal decorations surrounded the outer rims and upon careful inspection you could see scorch marks from the fire-breathing dragons.

Tension in the air rose as the audience went silent once more. Victoria took hold of both Pax and Brent's hands with a tight squeeze. From the centre stage erupted a burst of fire-magic, drawing everyone's attention.

"Please give a warm welcome to this year's contestants of *Dragonfire*!" The host's voice boomed through the audience stands and the crowd erupted into applause. Victoria recognised the host from the show, Elysia Emberheart. She wore a gown that seemed to shift and shimmer like flickering flames, adorned with elaborate patterns representing dragons in flight. From as high up as Victoria was seated, she could see her vibrant blue eyes sparkled with excitement. Elysia's voice carried a commanding yet warm tone, captivating the attention of everyone in the arena. Her presence and charisma set the stage for the thrilling dragon riding show that was about to unfold.

From the midst of the fiery display, the contestants of *Dragonfire* emerged, each riding astride their dragons. The dragons themselves were a stunning array of colours and sizes, representing various breeds. Their presence alone sent shivers of excitement through the crowd.

And then there she was–Kiera. Victoria's favourite. Astride her resplendent Emberflare, Garnet. Victoria's eyes widened with awe. Her heart raced as her favourite dragon rider took her position centre stage.

"There she is!" Victoria leapt from her chair, pointing out Kiera to her father and Brent.

Kiera's fiery mane of hair flowed in the wind as she commanded Garnet's attention with grace and confidence.

Elysia began to list and introduce the ten contestants to the over excited audience. When they got to Oren, even though he was her least favourite, she still cheered along. He sat atop of his Infernus, Ignis. Ignis brandished his fangs, looking displeased with all the noise. His rider matched his muscular structure. She let her gaze fall upon many others that caught her eye. There was Thorne, dressed in all dark armour riding Shadowscale, Obsidian and Linnea, whose partner Solstice was a Sunfury, a blinding yellow and white dragon that was uncommon even in the sanctuary.

Without hesitation, the riders took off one by one into the air. The dragon's wings spread wide as they soared across the entire sky. The riders undertook a very choreographed, but still wondrous, flight display. The spectacle continued as the contestants showed their dragon riding skills. Performing intricate manoeuvres and breathtaking aerial displays. Victoria clutched the seat back in front of her and gasped on a few of the closer calls.

The arena resonated with the powerful roars of dragons and the collective "oohs" and "ahhs" of the audience. It was a mesmerizing showcase of the magical bond between humans and dragons.

As the show reached its climax, and the dragon riders settled back down to the ground. Elysia announced there was a special twist for the day's show, an opportunity for one lucky audience member to experience the thrill of dragon riding firsthand with the rider of their choice.

"Would the person sitting in seat number thirty-six, Row F please come forward!"

People scrambled, double checking for their seat numbers. Victoria looked down to her left. On the armrest was the number that was called out, but it was Paxton's seat. The initial excitement that flickered over her face began to dwindle until Pax looked over at her with a large smile.

"You take this win, Tori. I know how much this means to you." Pax handed off his ticket and forced her to stand with an encouraging hand.

"We have a winner! Come on down!" Elysia called out over the crowd that was a mixture of excited chants and some groans from those who wished it had been them.

"No, Pax, I couldn't..." she whispered, trying to hand the ticket back.

"Go before I change my mind," Pax gave her a wink and rose to his feet, calling out that she was the winner, solidifying that she'd be the one to claim the prize.

All eyes turned to Victoria as she walked down the stairs toward the stadium. She felt like she was about to vomit as the nausea of nervous anticipation reached her throat, but she pressed on, ignoring the stares from her classmates. As she shuffled through the aisle, she overheard her dad and Pax talking and smiled.

"That was a very nice thing you did, Pax," Brent whispered, their shoulders brushed when he moved closer. It was gestures like this that made Brent sometimes think about how great of a partner and father Pax would have been if they weren't best friends. Perhaps in another life.

"You would have done the same." He clapped his hands with the crowd and kept his eyes ahead, not wanting to miss a thing.

The anticipation was intense as she stood at the edge of the platform, about to fulfill a dream that she'd spent countless hours hoping would come true. She was about to ride alongside a dragon rider—an experience that would forever etch itself into her memory.

"Tell the audience and the contestants your name and a little about yourself!" Elysia stood next to Victoria, her voice booming through the stadium once more.

"My name is Victoria Abernathy," she said shakily. Both Brent and Pax let out a loud cheer, which filled Victoria's heart. "I am here with my school, Spellford Academy, and when I graduate, I want to join the Dragoon Corp and study dragons."

Brent let out a loud whistle and shouted out from the top of the crowd. Pax roared with exhilaration and the crowd around them joined in.

"I wager that man is your father?" Elysia spoke to the audience. Victoria gave a nervous laugh and nodded. Brent felt a heat rise up his neck and toned it down a little bit.

"Such a supportive man!" Elysia's flirtatious tone got a rise out of the audience. "Now on to the task at hand, because I could go on about supportive fathers all day! Who do you pick as your rider?"

"Kiera!" Victoria shouted without hesitation.

"Kiera and Garnet, come forward!" Elysia drawled with elation followed by an eruption of enthusiasm from the crowd.

Kiera directed Garnet to walk closer to the platform where Victoria and the host stood. As the dragon got closer, Victoria admired its scales, like ruby gems shimmering in the sunlight. She summoned every ounce of reserve she had to not burst into tears. She reached out to stroke Garnet's body. Victoria was surprised when her scales were cool to the touch, expecting extreme heat from a fire-based dragon like Garnet.

"Hello there, Victoria. I am Kiera, and this wondrous beast is Garnet." Kiera gave Garnet's side a gentle pat. Garnet let out a snuff of air from her nose and Kiera held out a leather gloved hand. "Come on up!"

Victoria grabbed her hand. She felt the strength that Kiera possessed as she lifted her with ease behind her.

"Shall we go up?" Kiera asked Victoria, who managed to nod despite her heart feeling like it might pop out of her chest.

Victoria's heart raced with a mix of excitement and trepidation as she sat with Kiera and Garnet, ready to take to the skies. The moment Garnet's powerful wings beat against the air, lifting them off the ground, Victoria's breath caught in her throat. The world below shrank, and a rush of wind whipped through her hair, exhilarating and liberating.

Garnet's scales glowed with an intense, fiery brilliance as she ascended, spiralling gracefully upwards. Victoria clung to Kiera's waist, her grip tight, but her eyes were wide with wonder as the landscape unfurled beneath them.

"How ya' holding up?" Kiera shouted as the air whipped them across the face.

"I feel amazing!" Victoria shouted back, and truly meant it. The sensation of flight was unlike anything she had ever experienced before.

Garnet soared through the air, dancing gracefully across the stadium's grounds. Victoria rested her head against the middle of Kiera's back and committed to memory every second of this experience.

"We will have to head down soon," Kiera said to her, patting Victoria's hand.

"Oh, really? Already?" Disappointment rushed over her.

"I'm sorry, I know it was too fast, but have to stick to the rules." Kiera stated with a roll of the eyes and a certain smile that said she wasn't a fan of following protocol. Victoria got the impression the two of them would have a lot in common.

"Either way, this was aweso—" Victoria was cut off as Garnet dipped down through the air, her wings tucked in and soared like a javelin thrown by a soldier through the air.

"Hold on tight, this part is the best!" Kiera squealed with delight. Victoria gripped on tightly as Garnet barrel rolled through the sky and then swooped with grace, making a soft landing, the ground crunched slightly beneath her claws.

The crowd was on their feet when Victoria departed from Garnet with Kiera's help.

"You did amazing." Kiera pulled Victoria in for a hug and ruffled up her hair, revealing her pointed ear.

Victoria pulled back and adjusted her hair in a rush to cover it up.

"Oh, I am sorry, Victoria. I didn't mean to..."

"It's okay," Victoria said even though she felt like she was standing naked in the arena, exposed for everyone to see.

"You know my grandmother had an ear like that," Kiera said, leaning down to her and whispered. "I've never seen another like it." Her smile was warm, but her eyes narrowed in curiosity.

Victoria's interest was piqued. Could this be some connection to who her biological parents were? Before Victoria could ask any further questions, Elysia walked over and directed Victoria back down to the stands, where Brent and Pax were waiting. Victoria turned back at Kiera, who stood waving at the crowd but looked intently at Victoria, her gaze thoughtful.

"How was that, kiddo?" Brent pulled her in for a tight hug.

"You were amazing up there. We could see on the Cam-Mera Screens," Pax beamed, nudging her shoulder.

"It was fantastic! Thank you both!"

The crowd began to depart from the stadium, people flocked past Victoria, engaged in excited conversation over the show. Victoria, however, had questions that continued to bubble to the surface of her mind, lingering like a persistent itch she couldn't scratch. A part of her wanted to run back and talk to Kiera. She said her grandmother had a single pointed ear, same as Victoria. It wasn't a typical Half-Elf trait, and Kiera didn't look Half-Elf either…or did Victoria for that matter. In fact, she wasn't even sure if she was Half-Elf, her pointed ear was not the same kind of point as an elf's.

She pondered if there was a connection between them, or was it just a mere coincidence? Maybe wishful thinking on her part.

***

The class all clambered back on the monorail as the excursion drew to a close, their minds full of memories from the thrilling experience of the afternoon. Brent could see that Victoria's thoughts were preoccupied. She laid her head on her father's shoulder, exhausted from the day.

Brent wondered if he had judged her desire to be a dragon rider a little too harshly. She handled herself well around the majestic creature, and the pure enjoyment on her face couldn't be missed. He promised himself to have a real open and honest talk about her future heading toward Dragoon Corp. If she was this happy, how could he refuse?

He looked down and could see her eyes grew heavy as the carriage moved along, she closed them, and Brent let out a contented sigh. For the first time he really felt like a good father.

CHAPTER TWENTY-SEVEN
MUGS AND MEMORIES

Brent was on edge. His twenty-four hours was up, but nothing had happened. Nothing on the news, no update from Adren. Victoria had put herself to bed as soon as they got home as all three were exhausted from the long day.

"Don't tell Tori, but she is snoring up a storm in there," Pax snickered into his hoodie. He joined Brent in the living room, taking a seat beside him on the couch. "What a brilliant day we had."

Brent chuckled, "Yeah, I can't blame her, she is wiped out. I am feeling it, too." Brent couldn't control the yawn that escaped his mouth.

"You sure you're okay?" Pax leaned back and placed an arm over the headrest.

"Yeah, why wouldn't I be?" Brent tried to lead the conversation in a different direction.

"Well, with Seraphina's disappearance, and Marquis' threats..." Brent took his eyes off the orb and looked at Pax. "I just need to know you are okay, that's all." His tone shifted to one of concern. "Not that I want to bring up the past, but when Elwin died, you were a wreck," Pax continued when Brent remained quiet.

Brent knew Pax's heart was in the right place, but those words cut deep. Brent was already defensive and irritable with the stress he carried over Marquis' looming presence that this was not the conversation he wanted to have tonight. He jumped to his feet in clear frustration and waved a dismissive hand before he strode off into the kitchen. Pax wasn't deterred and followed behind him.

"Look, all I am saying is you have a tendency to escape your problems, and I know you said you weren't going to anymore, but you've said that before. Every anniversary I had to build you back up again. I want to make sure my friend has his head on straight if we are to have a major battle, I need him at his best."

Brent paused and stared into the fridge. He knew what Pax was saying, but it wasn't registering. He told himself to be calm and stay quiet. Maybe Pax would take the hint. He grabbed a bottle of Pep-Up and went to grab a cup. But something by the sink caught his eye, something that should not be there. Something that should not have been touched.

"Are you listening to me, Brent?" Pax pressed him.

Brent walked up to the counter, slamming the bottle down next to the intricately designed cup that had sat in the cupboard untouched for sixteen years.

"Who took out Elwin's Mug?" Brent grabbed it in his hands and whipped around to face Pax.

"I don't know, I was with you all day. I have been in my room since we got ho—" Pax stammered, but Brent cut him off.

"Why the fuck did you use his mug?" Brent's shrill voice reverberated off the walls.

Pax recoiled, taken aback by Brent's sudden outburst. He raised his hands defensively, his expression a mix of confusion and concern. "I didn't touch it, Brent. I swear." Pax's voice tinged with pain at the accusation from Brent. This reaction over such a small, insignificant thing only confirmed what Pax suspected. Brent was not okay.

"Well, someone must of as it has been sitting on the top shelf for years, and you are the only one tall enough to reach!" Brent's grip tightened around the mug, his knuckles turning white with the force of his emotions. Memories of Elwin flooded his mind, each one a bittersweet reminder of their time together. The mug was a cherished keepsake—a connection to a love that had been tragically cut short. Brent hung his head, his hand still gripping it tightly.

Pax's expression softened. His own grief mirrored in Brent's eyes. He reached out a hand, hesitating for a moment before gently resting it on Brent's shoulder.

Pax sighed internally before he spoke. "I miss him too," Pax said softly, and squeezed Brent's shoulder.

"You do?" Brent looked at him, tears swelled in his eyes but refused to drop.

"Well, yeah, he was my friend, too. He got me into Dragon Hoarde, remember?" Pax took the mug out of Brent's hands slowly and placed it back on the counter with a light clang.

"That's right, he did. What a bloody idiot he was, so reckless..." As the words left his mouth, he felt relief.

"If I remember correctly, both of you were reckless, just going gung-ho putting your hand in that cradle." Pax poured them both a glass of Pep-Up and handed one to Brent.

"If I could go back, I would—" Brent stopped himself and lifted the cup to his lips. Could he say it out loud?

Pax leaned against the counter next to Brent and smiled. "No, you wouldn't. You have Victoria, and you wouldn't change that for the world."

"I...what I was going to say is I wouldn't change a thing. I hate to admit it, but him falling into the void may have been the best thing to happen to me..." Brent's voice was so soft, laced with guilt but also truth. He lifted his face to Pax who clicked his tusks.

"I wouldn't go that far, mate. But you have been rewarded a blessed life. Perhaps...maybe it is time we both move on completely. What do you say?"

"What? Throw the mug away? Oh God no, that's too—" Brent paused, staring into his drink.

The realization settled around him, Brent had held onto a mug from a different life. He had gotten so angry over someone moving it. He was holding onto his past and refusing to let go or move forward. His life had been at such a standstill since Elwin died. Sure, he had Victoria, but his entire life revolved around raising her and ensuring her needs were met, while his own were pushed aside. That was the sacrifice he made to become a father, and he had come to terms with that early on.

But now, Victoria would be leaving for school soon enough. He had been so apprehensive to support her future desires, to accept that she was growing up, because it meant he would have to finally face his own problems, instead of burying them in being a father.

As Brent contemplated Pax's words, a weight lifted from his shoulders. Holding onto Elwin's mug wasn't about honouring his memory—it was a way of clinging to the past, to a time when things were simpler, albeit tinged with tragedy. Life had moved on, Victoria would soon move on, and it was time for Brent to do the same.

Setting down his glass, Brent reached for the mug once more. His fingers traced its contours. He took a deep breath, steeling himself for what he was about to do. With a determined expression and a smile, one of acceptance, Brent looked to Pax.

"You're right, Pax. It's time to let go," Brent said, his voice resolute. "Elwin wouldn't want me to be stuck in the past. He'd want me to embrace the present and look toward the future."

Pax motioned to speak, but Brent had flung the mug into the middle of the air. With a quick flick of his wrist, it disintegrated into a fine powder. With a small surge of magic fuelled by the remaining allotment of grief he had inside, he had destroyed one of the last memoirs from Elwin.

"I didn't mean destroy it." Pax poked his head out from under his arms as he shielded himself from the blast.

"Well, too late now," Brent chuckled, knowing this was exactly what he needed. He flicked his wrist at the bin and the lid opened, with a flick of his other wrist the powdered mug pile flew in, and the lid dropped closed.

Dusting his hands, Brent smirked. "Dessert? My treat!" Pax almost tripped over his feet rushing next to Brent when he opened up the Witches Wagon app and searched for a suitable dessert for them both.

"Should we wake Victoria?" Pax glanced over his shoulder in the direction of her bedroom.

"Let her sleep, we will keep this treat between us." He bumped Pax's shoulder with his own. Pax returned the nudge and then with a giggle, they scrolled through the dessert options.

***

The next morning, Brent awoke not to his alarm but the sounds of finches cooing outside in the yard. He sat up, extended his arms overhead and yawned, his legs shaking slightly as he stretched the sleep off. It was the first weekend in a long time where he felt like nothing could go wrong. Sunlight streamed through the windows above his bed, casting warm hues across the built-in robe. He replayed his meltdown the night before and remained content in his decision to destroy the mug.

Brent heard the faint sound of the vision orb from the lounge room. Shroudasday morning shows Victoria loved to devour would be consumed along with what smelled like one of Pax's breakfasts. Brent flung himself out of bed, pulled his robe off the hook on the door and fastened it around his waist. He placed his hand over the handle to leave but before he opened the door, he glanced over his shoulder to where Elwin's photo sat. He darted across the room to pick up the framed picture with a smile.

A rush of bittersweet memories flooded his mind. He traced the outline of Elwin's timeless face with his fingertips. His heart heavy with longing for a lover's embrace he would never feel again. For lips he could never kiss again. For a mind he could never pick or the best friend he couldn't annoy in the early hours of the morning.

"You'll exist in my memory forever, El," Brent whispered softly, pressing a gentle kiss to the photo.

With a steady hand, Brent placed his palm over the image of Elwin. It was now or never, and after last night, he knew it was time. He closed his eyes and summoned all his resolve. In an instant, a brilliant burst of light emanated from his hands, the grief he had held onto for all these years poured into his magic as it worked its way through the foundations of the frame, causing it to glow.

The frame got hot before it shattered into a thousand sparkling fragments, dissipating into the air like dust. Brent watched in awe as the remnants of the frame vanished, leaving behind only the memory of Elwin etched in his mind and the love he had for him. With a sense of closure and a broad smile, he left the room and headed directly to the kitchen.

"What smells good?" He took in the air and burst through the room, gaining the attention of both Victoria, and Pax, who slaved over the stove.

"Pax is making us Flan-cakes," she said, returning to her shows.

"Ah!" Brent replied joyfully. "Hey, come help your dad set the table."

"In a sec, let me pause." Victoria sat up and waved her hand instead of using the remote.

"Someone is getting better with her magic," he praised. He pulled her in for a side hug, Victoria turned into him and hugged him properly. Brent leaned his head against the top of hers and took in a silent whiff. Though she was nearing adulthood, he could still remember the smell of her head as a baby. "Studying with Nia seems to be paying off."

She recounted some of the techniques Nia had been teaching her as father and daughter set the table together. Brent looked at her and smiled. The simplicity of this moment was one he wanted to remember for the rest of his life.

"Breakfast is ready," Pax called out as he flipped the last of the Flan-Cakes onto a separate plate. He unwrapped the apron from his waist and brought the plate over to set on the table. "Don't forget the tea."

Victoria rushed to grab the teapot and looked at the mugs laid out. "Where's that mug with the Mirewood finishing?"

Brent and Pax froze and exchanged a glance but remained silent. Brent cleared his throat and forced himself to form a sentence. "I, um, I don't recall seeing one."

"It was a gift from Emily, I swore I left it next to the sink," Victoria explained. Pax's eyes darted towards Brent before landing on the bin.

Brent swallowed down hard. Had he mistaken that mug for Elwin's? He shuffled over to the bin while she was turned away.

"Ah, you see Victoria, the thing is—" Pax started scratching his head, while Brent silently rummaged in the bin.

Victoria opened the cabinet and flicked her wrist, pulling down a mug that was clearly like hers. "Oh, this one is similar, but not like mine." Victoria turned it upside down. "The label at the bottom states it's made in the Sylvan Territory." Victoria looked at Brent. "Dad, what are you doing?"

Brent pulled his hands away sharply and snapped around. "Nothing," he replied too fast to not sound suspicious. She tilted her head and gave him a look. Brent sighed. "Okay, you see, last night your mug was left on the counter, and I mistook it for that one in your hands and evaporated it."

Victoria narrowed her eyes. "And why would it matter if they are similar?"

"That is one of the last things of Elwin's that I kept." Brent lowered his head and sat down. The feeling of dread returned.

Victoria's gaze softened to one of understanding, she knew the hurt he felt, and the guilt over destroying her mug. She took a deep breath, "It's okay, really. It doesn't matter. This mug is better. Can I, have it?"

Brent raised his head in disbelief. "Umm, sure. Please go right ahead, might need a wash," he chuckled and sighed with relief, feeling at ease once more. If there was anyone who should have this beloved heirloom, it was Victoria.

Victoria came back with the tea, admiring the mug as she took a drink. Pax dished out the Flan-Cakes. Brent was about to take a bite when his phone vibrated on the table. He ignored it. This breakfast was way more important, but then it vibrated again. And again.

He gave a remorse filled look to Victoria. She nodded her head toward the phone signalling she understood it was most likely important.

> Abernathy, I know it is the weekend, but I really could use your help on a case.

> Could you come in today?

> Paid overtime, it is a private matter. Come Alone.

Brent eyed the messages. It wasn't like Arden to call him in without more details, let alone without Pax. A feeling of uncertainty washed over him, but it was work, and he had no real reason not to trust this. He replied he'd be in shortly.

"Arden?" Pax confirmed.

"He wants help on a case."

"Ah, well, let's finish up and get going." Pax sounded a little too eager to go to work on a weekend.

"He said the matter is private."

"Oh! Private, right. Hey, I get it. That's all good. You better hurry up to get working on the 'case'." Pax added air quotations and joined in when Victoria started to giggle under her breath.

"You happy to stay and keep watch of the house?" he said in a stern tone, sucking the humour from the room.

"Yeah, not a problem. I will get some painting done on my models."

"Oh, Dad, I have Lirien and Hector coming over today to work on our group assignment."

"That's right you mentioned that. If you guys get hungry, order some food for yourselves, anything you want." He handed his bank card off to Pax whose eyes lit up. "Just don't go crazy."

"Perhaps you should give that to me then." Victoria held out her hand and Pax sighed and handed it over.

Brent dressed in a rush and was on his way out the door when Victoria stopped him. "Do you really need to go today?" Victoria asked in a borderline whiney voice.

"Unfortunately, but one day you'll understand when you get a job and your own place." Brent gave her a thoughtful smile, now seemed like the perfect time to tell her. "If you fill out the Dragoon Corp Cadet forms, I will sign them when I get home."

"Are you serious?" She perked up, her tune changed immediately. "I'll leave them in your room!" Victoria called out and ran to her bedroom.

"That should buy you a few months of unbridled affection," Pax muttered as he came to close the door.

"Just keep your phone on you," Brent said as he ensured his belt was placed right.

"You sure I shouldn't come?"

"No, Victoria's safety is our highest priority. Only let her friends over, no one else," Brent confirmed with Pax. He stepped outside, locked the door and opened a portal, his destination Sanctum.

CHAPTER TWENTY-EIGHT
ARDEN APPREHENDED

Brent strolled through Sanctum's corridors, his destination the Strategic Department. He saw the door was ajar as he turned the corner and skidded to a halt. He approached with caution, keeping his steps light. He heard muffled voices inside.

Brent's footsteps faltered when he neared the door. His curiosity piqued, he strained to catch snippets of the voices emanating from within. Not sure if he should proceed and knock to make his presence known, his thoughts were disrupted when a shuffle sounding like an attack reached his ears, followed by what could only be described as a punch.

A sense of urgency raised in his chest, but he didn't want to barge in unprepared. He would be no good to anyone if he was caught. He crept along the wall, pressing his back firmly against it. He peeked his head through the cracked door to peer inside. The room was dim, the soft light of a desk lamp cast shadows throughout the space.

He listened to the attacker speak, but didn't recognize his voice.

"Callahan, we won't ask you again, where is Abernathy?"

Brent's heart thudded in his ears. They were after *him*.

"You expunged his records from the Union's systems. You can make this easy and tell us what we want to know, or we can beat it out of you, your choice."

Brent's eyes adjusted to the dark. Arden was tied to chair, two hulking figures loomed over him.

"You sent the messages. He should be here any moment." Arden spat blood from his mouth that splattered across his office floor. "But I should warn you," Arden's eyes darted to the crack in the door, "he is a handful." Brent wondered if this was Arden giving him a silent message that he thought Brent could take on the attackers. Brent crouched down and snaked his way through desks to hide his position. He would need to time his attack perfectly. The door swung open a moment later.

"Go wait at the entrance, he won't be far off." A voice boomed from inside. The two who had stood over Arden rushed out and past Brent without notice. There was a third person in the office that Brent had not been able to see. With two of the perpetrators out of the way, Brent was in the prime position for a rush attack. He edged his way back to the outside of the office to listen in on what the last perpetrator said to Arden.

"So, when did you suspect I was not the real Arch Mage?" A man spoke, it was Magnar's voice.

"The day Seraphina and I returned from the academy, when you relieved her of her temporary role after the loss of the previous Director and appointed me," Arden said with a mouth full of blood.

"You are clever Callahan, that's why I wanted you close. He and I needed loyal subjects for this to work."

"Have I not been loyal to you?" Arden responded. Brent froze.

Was Arden a double agent?

"I ensured Abernathy was a member of the Union. I brought him here to set up your plot for his daughter. I even took him down to the underground upon your wishes."

Brent's heart beat wildly in his chest as he listened to the exchange between Arden and the imposter Magnar. He couldn't believe what he was hearing. Arden, his trusted confidant. His boss. The man he was developing feelings for, the first person to make him feel something he hadn't felt since Elwin...had been playing him.

As the weight of Arden's betrayal washed over him, his mind raced, trying to make sense of it all. How had he been so blind to the man in front of him? Blind to his intentions. Was his returned affection all an act? Did he use Brent to get to Victoria? Surely, he would have suspected it earlier, or was he blinded by personal feelings? Arden must be playing along to buy time, Brent thought and hoped he was right.

He remained hidden, unwilling to reveal his presence yet. There was still too much at stake. He needed to gather as much information as possible before making his next move. He continued to listen in on the conversation, straining to catch Arden's response. Brent tried to decipher the cryptic exchange, and hoped Arden gave him a reason to believe he wasn't on the side of the enemy. A reason to burst in to rescue him.

"You have proven to be an unruly confidant in this operation," the other person added. "Where is your loyalty? Is it with Abernathy?"

Arden's voice, though muffled, carried a note of defiance as he spoke. "I have loyalty, but not blind obedience. I serve the Union and the people of Spellford, not the whims of a power-hungry imposter."

Brent's pulse quickened at Arden's words. He was clearly working on uncovering the truth. It was clear Arden's motives were to thwart the imposter's plans and protect the Union and Spellford. With a surge of resolve, Brent pushed open the door, his presence like a sudden storm breaking the tense silence.

The imposter's eyes widened in surprise, his hand instinctively reaching for a concealed weapon as he moved to strike. But Brent was quicker, his reflexes only enhanced by the adrenaline that flowed through his veins. His years of adventuring returned to him as he shifted with a swift motion and conjured a volley of fireballs, unleashing them with precision towards the imposter. Fiery projectiles streaked through the air, leaving trails of blazing energy in their wake.

The man scrambled to evade the onslaught as he dived across the room but not fast enough. He staggered backwards, his false façade crumbling in the face of Brent's ferocious onslaught. With nowhere to retreat except through Arden's office window, he found himself trapped in a maelstrom of flames. Brent's unwavering determination exposed the imposter's own deceit.

Brent stepped forward, overwhelmed when he recognised the man in front of him. "You're Nascien, Marquis' son!" Brent revealed the attacker's identity.

Nascien stood tall, unphased by being exposed. He was the spitting image of what Marquis once was. Nascien exuded an aura that attracted you to him like a moth to a flame. You could not take your eyes off him for long. He had strong angular features. A prominent jawline and high cheekbones gave him a distinguished air. His smile, so charming it could disarm even the most untrusting individual, turned to a scowl now that he was caught in Brent's fiery hold. Piercing blue eyes that held a hint of mystery and intrigue, hinting at depths of knowledge beyond his years. Marquis had chosen a good person to imitate Magnar.

"It is good to see you again, Brent." Nascien stood defeated with no way out of Brent's trap, the treachery now a cracked false mirror. "Father always said you were good at pitching a fireball. I didn't believe him, looks like I should have."

"Fathers tend to know best." Brent spoke down to him like the child he was. He glanced toward Adren. "You alright?"

"Never better for having you here, but what took you so long out there?" Arden strained against the ropes, trying to wiggle his way free. Brent rushed over and untied them. "I was keeping them talking as a distraction. You could have rushed them any moment."

"I was...waiting for just the right moment to intervene." Brent didn't want to let on to Arden that he'd been sceptical of whose side Arden's allegiances were in line with. Brent wiped Arden's bloodied lip with this thumb and then their eyes locked. Brent's earlier fear evaporated. He appreciated the man before him, for the unwavering loyalty he'd shown to The Mage's Union, and Brent hoped he would receive it, too.

Arden turned to Nascien. "Now, what to do with you?"

"Where is the real Magnar?" Brent asked, stepping forward, and Arden murmured in agreement.

"Like I would tell you anything." Nascien stood proud, committed to his cause.

"We have ways to extract the information, Beaumont," Arden threatened. "With the Arch Mage gone, Spellford's protection falls to the Elder Council. I don't suspect I would face a hard battle convincing them to agree to it." Arden narrowed his eyes, his face held true to the words. It was a side of Arden Brent hadn't seen yet, and he'd be lying if he tried to say he wasn't the least bit aroused.

"You can torture me all you want, but you'll need me to find him," Nascien warned, a devious smile spread to his lips.

He was right. They would need Nascien's cooperation to find Magnar. Arden weaved his hands in a circle. He conjured bindings around Nascien, constricting his arms tight to his sides. Brent lowered the circling flames to allow Arden to search him.

Arden patted him down across his broad shoulders and Brent tried to ignore the way Nascien's eyes traced over Arden. Arden crouched down, he squeezed his muscular calves and pulled up his trouser leg to reveal the concealed knives hidden beneath. He disarmed Nascien and continued his search back up his legs, stopping short of his crotch.

"Want to search anywhere else?" Nascien smirked down at Arden, his words full of innuendo.

"He's clear," Arden cleared his throat and willed the slight blush in his cheeks aware. He tossed the knives and what he could only assume was a vile of poison on his desk.

"Good." Brent stepped forward. "Now, maybe we can strike a deal?" Brent offered to Nascien, who stared at them with darkness in his eyes.

"From where I am standing, you need me more than I need you." Nascien's smile stretched wide across his face in an unnatural grimace. It made Brent want to shed his skin. When had this child become so cold?

"And why is that?" Brent questioned while Arden checked the weapons for curses or enchantments.

"Because without me you, you won't find Magnar, and you won't find my father..."

"You've alre—"

"Or your daughter..." Nascien revealed with a menacing tone.

"Excuse me?" Brent demanded.

"You daughter ought to be captured by now."

Like a flash of wildfire, Brent went berserk. He lunged at Nascien and landed a blow square in his jaw with his fist. Blow after blow connected as Brent could not control his rage.

"What have you done with Victoria?" Brent growled. He realized through his anger that his hits didn't seem to do any damage except to strip his own knuckles of their flesh.

Arden flew to Brent and struggled to pull him off of Nascien. "Come on Brent, leave it! Control yourself!" He tried to reach him, but Brent wanted nothing but to kill the man.

"I give it to you Abernathy, I almost felt those blows, but you're better off sticking to your magic," he sneered from his place on the ground. Brent pulled from Arden's grasp, ready to strike that smug look from Nascien's face.

"Brent!" Arden pulled Brent's face in line with his own. "Calm down." Arden held his hands out to place his fingertips on his temples, but Brent swatted him away, blocking his attempt at a calming charm.

"I'm fine!" Brent shouted and stepped backwards. "Deal with him." Brent's heart pounded so out of control he didn't notice the hurt look on Arden's face as he reluctantly turned away. Brent dug around in his pocket and pulled out his phone.

"Call Paxton!" he shouted and placed the phone against his ear. Pax didn't pick up. Brent grew frantic, trying multiple times but each went unanswered.

"Fuck the council, we haven't time." Arden stepped closer to Nascien and flicked his wrists, performing a magic Brent had not seen used by anyone before.

A swirl of turquoise smoke poured out of his fingertips like water rushed over the falls as it billowed out. It engulfed Nascien and entered his body through his nostrils, causing him to convulse. He stopped shaking when the smoke had invaded his entire body. Nascien opened his eyes, they were no longer that beautiful shade of blue, but dull and cloudy as if he was in a trance.

"Talk!" Arden demanded.

Nascien spoke in a monotone voice under the effect of the smoke. "My father was very clear in his instructions. We needed the right time to pounce. Nia's protective charms had worn off Victoria, leaving her vulnerable again. I needed to lure Abernathy here, away from Victoria. If it weren't for Emily, none of this would be possible."

"Emily!" Brent cursed loudly, and flew out the door, only one destination on his mind. Home.

"Brent! Come back!" Arden called out, desperately trying to reach him, but Brent had already conjured a portal, using his emergency rune. The portal closed behind him. Arden turned to Nascien once more.

"Sleep!" he barked and Nascien fell to the floor in a heap.

CHAPTER TWENTY-NINE
NULLIFYING MAGIC

"Lirien and Hector shouldn't be far off," Victoria called out to Pax, who wandered around the house. He kept sticking his head behind the curtains, darting his head back and forth as if he was expecting someone other than her friends. "You alright, Pax?"

"Yeah, well, no…I don't know," Pax said nervously. Victoria had never seen him like this. "What?" he asked as Victoria stood there with a watchful eye.

"Something is up," she said, with a raised brow.

"Okay, fine," Pax started. "The message Brent received felt odd."

"What's odd about it? It's just work, right?" Victoria asked, slinking onto the couch. Pax joined her.

"Well, yeah, but you see, there is…there is this case and it doesn't seem likely that Arden wouldn't have called me in—" Pax was cut short when the doorbell rang.

"They're here! We'll chat later." Victoria sprung up, before she headed toward the door she paused. "Pax, do you think you could go in your room? I know it's just working on a school project but…" Pax looked from her to the door and sighed.

"It's okay, I get it. Don't need me hovering like a babysitter. Call out if you need anything." Pax let his eyes fall to the door once more. He sighed then wandered over to his room, leaving the door open a crack.

He listened to the muffled voice of Victoria as he sat down at his desk to continue painting his Dragon Hoard figures. He was setting up his paints when he heard a glass shattering out in the kitchen and a scream from Victoria. His stomach dropped, his chair flew across the room as he leapt toward the door in a mad rush, pulling it off the hinges.

He bound around the corner into the kitchen only to find Victoria sweeping up a glass while Emily stood above her.

"Emily?" he asked, "I thought…?"

"They are running late," Victoria scoffed as she stood, finishing up her task. "I accidentally knocked the glass when I went to—" She looked at Emily and blushed with a smile. "Never mind."

"It is good to see you again, Paxton, sorry for disturbing you." Emily offered a forced smile that didn't sit right.

"Good to see you, too," Pax offered as a formality. The two stood there awkwardly while Victoria shuffled around to the bin and deposited the shards of glass.

"Well, nothing to see here, sorry I startled you. Didn't mean to take you away from your models." Victoria dropped the subtle hint that she wanted him to leave.

"Yes, I guess I best be back to—" Pax was cut off again when there was a knock at the door.

"Can you put this away." Victoria shoved the dustbin into Pax's hands. "And then…" Victoria whispered and nodded her head in the direction of his room dismissing him from her little study group.

Pax put the dustbin away and glimpsed the two boys as they arrived. He pulled out his Rune-Phone and used one of the apps to help him fix his door, getting it back on its hinges.

Perhaps his worries were unjustified, he'd built them up into something larger than he should have. The first time he met Emily, he took her as a good person. He wanted to believe that all of Arden and Brent's worries about her were nothing more than being overprotective and cautious. But the more things progressed he had this unspoken feeling that she couldn't be trusted. There was a nefariousness to how quickly Victoria met her and fell for her.

Pax fixed his room quickly and got to painting. He heard the kids chuckles outside the room and his anxious mind settled. Brent would be home soon from whatever Arden needed, he just had to keep it cool until then.

His phone buzzed on his desk. It was from Silas.

So…when you going to show me those statues?

Pax's heart leapt to his throat. It was the first time in a long time a man paid him extra attention and followed through when he said he'd call.

You could come by tonight?

Pax initially typed out a winking emoji, but then thought better of it and left it out.

> What if you come over for dinner?

> Bring your favourites? ;)

Silas on the other hand, didn't hold back, and included the winking emoji.

> Really? You going to cook for me? ;) ;)

Pax asked with a few winking emoji's back but removed all but two.

> Of course. Can't deny a hot Orc boy his dinner. See you around seven?

Pax's heart fluttered. He wanted to yell from the rooftops. Finally, a guy was chasing him. He started to look over all of his figurines. It didn't take long to decide which ones he would take tonight. He settled on the *Ancient Guardian Drake, The Stormwing Rider* and *Captain Flameheart*. His three oldest figurines, two of which were bought by Elwin. He was excited to tell Silas everything about how he started collecting and why he still collects them now. He hummed as he packed them silently in his room. He couldn't remember a time when he was this happy.

"Emily!" Victoria screamed from out in the lounge room. Pulling Pax from his wave of joy. "What are you doing?"

Pax dropped everything once again and lunged at the door. Grabbing the handle, his hand singed, it had been cursed to burn on contact. Pax banged against the door with his shoulder, trying to break through as he heard the shouts coming from the lounge room. The sounds of magic buzzed through the door, shots echoed throughout the house, he hoped Nia had taught Victoria enough that she could hold her own.

The door whipped open. Lirien had managed to remove the curse. "She...just attacked us..." he huffed, winded from the fight.

Pax wasted no time. He rushed around Lirien to find Emily standing in the now destroyed lounge room. Hector was crouched behind the couch. Victoria stood behind the wall between that room and the kitchen, flinging magic bolts toward Emily in defence.

"Paxton, watch out!" Victoria cried. He looked up to see Emily, arm raised, shoot a bolt of magenta magic. Pax raised his own arms to shield his body to defend himself. It absorbed most of the damage of the blow, but was still powerful enough it pushed him backwards into the kitchen cabinets.

"Ah! Fuck!" he groaned, lifting himself off the cabinet with his elbows. He stretched his neck and shoulders from the attack.

"You can't protect her!" Emily shouted and raised her arm again, but Victoria was too fast and flung her own magic. Emily did not flinch. "You should have come with me when I asked." Emily's demeanour had changed, her voice held a sinister undercurrent. On her arm, a Rune-Tech armlet was fashioned, shining with random symbols Pax could not easily decipher.

"We are not joining the Code Weavers!" Victoria called out. Pax raised an eyebrow. Is this what they were discussing when he was in his room?

"Stupid girl!" Emily shouted. "The Code Weavers were merely a pawn in a much larger plan." Emily aimed her armlet towards Victoria and shot a concentrated beam once more.

Victoria dodged it and squealed. A scorch mark burned its way through the paint. It looked exactly like the one at Seraphina's house.

While Emily remained focused on Victoria, he needed to act fast. He scanned the room and remembered that Brent always hid a collapsable Rune-Tech shield in one of the kitchen drawers.

"Your resistance is impressive. I see Nia has taught you well!" she taunted. Soley concerned about Victoria, she paid Pax no attention when she closed in on Victoria.

This was his time to act. He quickly darted over to the left side drawers and rummaged through it, finding the collapsable shield. He was about to deploy it when Emily tightly gripped Pax's hand. She had appeared out of nowhere.

"You'll find defending yourself is useless! This Rune-Tech has expanded my magical prowess beyond normal human limitations." She pointed to the armlet. Pax looked down at its marvel. "All thanks to the Weaver's genius."

"You expect a little arm bling will stop an Orc's rage?" Pax grasped hold of the armlet in a swift move and pried Emily's hand off of his wrist. With his free hand he grabbed hold of the collar of her shirt and lifted her up in the air.

Emily bashed at his tightened fists and arms, trying to set herself free. When that failed, she opted to kick with her legs. Pax weaved his head around each kick. He rushed over to the carpeted floor and slammed Emily into the floor twice. Her body went limp as she passed out. He dropped her to the ground like a rag doll and stood up.

"Pax!" Victoria cried out. He turned to look at her in a daze of confusion. Victoria leapt over the overturned couch and peered down at Emily, whose shirt was ripped, the shreds in Pax's hand.

"Oh, shit..." Pax dropped the piece of cloth to the floor and took a few steps back realising what he had done.

"Well, you beat the crap out of her." Lirien cleared the silence in the air. Victoria gave him a look and smacked his shoulder.

"Is she...?" Victoria's voice fell away as she turned back to Emily.

"I'll check on her, Lirien go check on Hector," Pax instructed. He knelt and held his fingers on her wrist checking her pulse. "She is still alive. I'll go get some rope. We need to restrain her." Pax stood and headed towards the back door when he felt an energy surge behind him.

Emily had rose to her feet and grabbed Victoria by the neck, holding her up from the ground like Pax had done with her.

"Orcs truly are dumb. Never turn your back on your enemy," she taunted, then raised her wrist with the armlet and pointed it at Victoria. "One wrong move and I will blow her pretty little brains out!" Victoria whimpered, trying to free herself. Lirien stayed hidden with Hector and shot Pax desperate looks to help save them all.

He was powerless. He had no magic, and his rage was all a farce. Pax was no superhero. Just a beefy geek who collected figurines as an adult. He hung his head in shame at not being able to help his best friend's daughter. If only he could get that armlet off, she would be powerless. A low rumble hummed from his room, his phone vibrating on his desk.

"What is that?" Emily demanded.

"My phone, what else?" Pax lifted his head and gave the sarcastic retort.

"I put a field around the house that wouldn't allow any communication in or out. How is this possible? What are you?" She narrowed her eyes and regarded him with suspicion.

"I'm a Half-Orc." Pax shrugged and stared at her sincerely confused.

"Liar! I've never seen this kind of nullifying magic before!" Emily had panic in her eyes. The confidence she had exhibited before cracked and Pax saw she was in over her head.

"Why don't you let Victoria go, and we will let you leave in return." Pax took a different approach, maybe she could be reasoned with. He glanced to Victoria who continued to whimper in Emily's hold.

"Quiet!" Emily shouted causing Victoria to cower in front of her.

"I can't let her go, he—" Her eyes darted around as if someone was watching her. She looked scared, in way too deep with no way out. "I...I have to bring her back."

"We can work together. Just tell me where he is, and Brent and I will find a way," Pax pleaded.

She looked from Victoria to Pax. "I'm sorry Paxton, in another life we could have all been friends, but..." She closed her eyes as she let out a small burst of magic. Victoria let out a scream before her head flopped forward.

Pax felt the heat rise in his face. Victoria was like a daughter to him. All the years he helped raise her alongside Brent flashed before his eyes. Something inside of him snapped, and it was a rage unlike one he'd experienced before.

"You'll regret that!" Pax roared, his body overheating, as it filled with fury. Moving faster than he ever had, he made a beeline directly toward Emily who was too slow to react. She pointed her armlet in his direction and shot out a bolt of magic, but Pax absorbed the blow. Her Rune-Tech was useless against him in this heightened state of pure anger.

"Hand her over!" Adrenaline surged through Pax's body. He had not felt this powerful in years.

"My magic might be useless against you, but there is something it can do that you can't," she sneered, gaining back some of her earlier composure.

"What's that?" he called out, trying to not lose his fury. She laughed; a piercing squeal that made Pax's ears hurt. She flashed a wicked grin and made to speak when the front door burst open.

"Pax? Victoria?" Brent's voice rang throughout the house. He flew into the lounge room and skidded to a halt. "What the fuck is going on?"

Emily reacted on impulse, opening a portal behind her before she pivoted on the spot and aimed at Brent. A concentration of dark purple magic fired from the armlet. Pax whose body still rushed with fury had a choice to make, seconds ticked by that felt like hours, but he let his instincts take over. He sprinted across the room and deflected the concentrated beam of magic which burned its way through the ceiling, debris fell around them. He leapt across the lounge room floor as Emily backed into her swirling portal, he landed a firm grip on her ankle and shouted back to Brent.

"Your phone!"

Brent stood there, frozen amidst the chaos around him. He feared Victoria would already be gone; he had not expected to walk in on the scene that unfolded around him. Lirien reacted fast and chucked Pax his Rune-Phone. Pax caught it just as he was sucked through the portal, along with Victoria and Emily.

It felt as if his entire body was set alight as it was being shoved through a tiny, plastic straw. Unstable, the portal discharged with such dark magic it stung at Pax's flesh. His eyes closed as he swirled around in circles making him nauseous. Emily continued to kick at his hand, managing to knock him off during the teleportation and sending Pax through a separate wormhole. He hit the ground with a thud.

Pax rolled over and crawled his way to his feet. He stood and took in his surroundings. His heart sank when he identified where he had landed. The dilapidated ruins of Erimosia took form around him. His eyes continued to adjust to the dark chasm, up above he could see a swath of sunlight. Pax slapped his phone a few times, trying to get some reception, but no bars appeared. He was truly alone here.

CHAPTER THIRTY
THE TRUE MONARCH CHILD

Arden arrived shortly after Pax and Victoria disappeared. Teleporting both himself and Nascien into Brent's home. They sat him, still bound, on Brent's couch, with Arden keeping a watchful eye. Hector was so worked up over the fight and Victoria being swept away in a portal that Brent encouraged him to lay down in Victoria's bed to help calm himself as the rest of them figured out what to do.

"Tell me everything once more," Brent directed Lirien with a firm but kind tone. He needed to know every detail. He stood beside the chair where Lirien sat, his fingertips pressed into the backrest but tried to hide his true emotions.

"It was like I said. We were all chatting about our group project and asking Emily questions about Acanthus's theories, because, you know, she is studying that herself. Then she offered to show us how it works practically." Lirien paused and sheepishly looked between Brent and Arden. "So, of course, we wanted to see it. That's when she showed us the armlet and how it worked. We were all so impressed, but then she went into some weird speech about joining the Code Weavers to get our own Rune-Tech just like hers."

"And what was Victoria's response?" Brent had his eyes closed and was rubbing his temples. His breathing quickened as he tried to maintain his composure. His only solace was that Pax was with her, even though he could use Pax's support here, too.

"She was adamant against it. Emily didn't take it well, clearly." Lirien waved his hands around, pointing out the damage to Brent's home. "Something struck me as odd, however."

"Yeah, what is that?" Brent pushed.

"Emily said she laid some sort of communication blocker around the house, but Pax's phone was still able to receive messages and calls. We heard it vibrating in his room." Brent's eyes sprang open at what Lirien said, and he left the kitchen.

"Uh, Brent..." Arden's voice faded away as Brent walked though the house towards Pax's room.

"Just give me a second!" Brent entered the room of his best friend. Greeted by row upon row of figurines, both painted and unpainted, stationed on his shelves and desk. His phone rested near a paint set that was slowly drying. He grabbed the phone, ready to rejoin the others but stopped short when a photo on Pax's bedside table piqued his interest.

The photo was taken a few years ago, it was of Pax and Victoria. Brent remembered the moment fondly, as he took the picture. In a mirror that hung behind them, you could see Brent's reflection, he was making a hand gesture to get Victoria's attention. Brent's heart swelled, the immense weight of how much these two people truly meant to him. At how much Victoria meant to Pax, not even related by blood, but bonded just the same. He put the photo down and tried to swallow down the intense emotion that gripped him over the prospect of losing both of his favourite people.

"His last messages were from Silas, and a bunch of missed calls from me," Brent announced when he walked back into the kitchen. Only Arden and Nascien remained.

"The kid went to check on his friend," Arden relayed, "but not before he told me something along the lines of Pax having potential nullifying magic. Did he ever say he had that ability to you? Or that he even suspected it?"

"Nope, never," Brent said plainly unable to stop himself from smiling. "But that means nothing, he probably wasn't even aware. It would make sense though," Brent chuckled to himself, "he was so bad at magic growing up, why would he suspect now that he'd have some sort of magic ability. App-Magic was the first time he truly felt like he could utilise any form of magic."

"It is highly unusual for someone with no magic prowess to develop anti-magic skills late in life," Arden surmised. His brow furrowed. It was the first time Brent had seen him stumped.

"What has he been eating?" Nascien piped up suddenly, causing Arden to jolt.

"What do mean?" Brent stepped forward and placed Pax's phone onto the kitchen table.

"Well, some studies have shown that those who consume an abundance of food cooked with magic can absorb the residual Augmenti. Sort of like

how we consume food for nutrients like essential minerals and vitamins..."
Nascien explained what he knew but his eyes became fixated on the scorch
marks left over from where Emily had teleported.

"Are you suggesting that Pax's insatiable lust for Chrono's has caused
him to develop magic abilities?" Brent couldn't believe what he was hearing. It was true there was a lot about the world he didn't know, but residual
Augmenti within food changing one's biological make-up was preposterous. Wasn't it?

"I'm not suggesting anything. I am telling you what I believe has happened based on the anecdotal evidence you have presented to me," Nascien retorted with a smarminess to his tone. Brent wanted nothing more
than to punch him, but he had to refrain after what happened last time.
Especially since despite throwing his all into every punch it did nothing to
harm Nascien. Arden assumed his skin was impenetrable by some means
of magic enhancement, by the hands of his father or some other means.
Nascien refused to confirm or deny it.

"Well, whatever the reason, his newfound skill will come in handy,"
Arden replied, turning away from Nascien. He moved closer to Brent,
taking hold of his hand. "We haven't talked, and I know it's a silly question,
but are you okay?"

"No...how could I be?" Brent's voice was shaky as he tried to hold back
his emotions. "I...what if I can't find them?"

"We can't think like that right now. We just have to hope that Pax
contacts us," Arden replied, resting Brent's head on his chest and stroked
his hair, lending Brent a moment of comfort.

"Are you two lovebirds done?" Nascien interrupted and Brent stood
tall. "If you are going to keep me captive, at least make me a drink? Emberflare Whiskey, no ice."

Arden scoffed, Nascien's smug attitude was grating on everyone's patience. "You won't get shit from us. You can stay there until I decide what
use you can be to us." With a click of his fingers Nascien fell back to sleep.
Arden turned around and walked over to where Nascien flopped on the
couch. "That should buy us some time. Keep watch as I scan his mind."

Arden's level of magic prowess left Brent in awe. It was one thing to be
adept in a single school of magic, like Brent with instinctive magic and
fireballs. It was another to have such a keen ability to force someone to
sleep with the snap of his fingers. Arden would make for great Arch Mage
material one day.

"Monitoring of the mind is meant to approved by the Elder Council," Brent reminded Arden calmly, but given the circumstances it needed to be done. Brent just didn't want to break all the rules he'd lived by most of his life. "So, make it quick," Brent sighed.

Arden knelt down behind the arm where Nascien's head rested. Placing both palms over Nascien's temples, he closed his eyes and took in a few deep breaths. "I couldn't breach his mind before, but maybe I can this time."

Blue lights formed in his palms, they connected to Nascien's temples. Arden groaned as he struggled once again.

"You know this would be much easier for you if I was sedated, better yet stilted." Nascien spoke calmly, keeping his eyes shut. Arden froze, as did Brent.

Arden got up from his knees and strode off to the kitchen. "Where is your whiskey?" he asked, looking in cupboards.

"I don't have any," Brent said. If we was to drink, he preferred it to be wine.

"Oh, fuck it." Arden clicked his fingers, and a bottle of Emberflare Whiskey manifested before them with a glass. "If you tell a soul, I conjured alcohol..."

"I won't. Believe me, it is awkward enough that they decreed it illegal." Brent rolled his eyes. Also, thinking back to the time he conjured lube. The rebellious side of Arden was a turn on, but Brent couldn't let his mind go there and shook it off. "Thankfully, you didn't hack the App-Mag Network for it."

"Well, I am not a Technomancer, but Beckoning, it was one of my core competences in Iron Helm," Arden added and poured a glass of Nascien's desired whiskey. Waving his hand, he forced Nascien's body to sit and held the glass in front of his face.

"What am I to do with that?" Nascien asked, turning his head to face Arden. "I can't use my hands." Nascien motioned with his bound arms behind his back and wiggled his fingers near his legs.

Arden waived his hand once more, forcing Nascien's head to fall back, and his mouth open. Arden poured the drink into his open mouth, but some of it ran down his chin and onto Brent's couch.

"Ah!" Nascien had swallowed the drink in one go without even flinching from the burn. "That is a good one, must be a vintage collection." He smacked his lips and looked to them both. "So, tell me Brent, why did you and my father have a falling out, he never would say," Nascien asked, sinking back into the couch.

Brent stared at him with disdain; he didn't like this man. He wanted him out of his house. Nascien represented everything he had hated about Marquis in the end. The smugness, the contrived personality. Everything about Nascien reminded him of Marquis. But in his eyes, there was a glint of something else. He couldn't perceive what it was, as this man was an expert at deflection.

"We held different ideals," Brent said softly, thinking back to the day he entered Marquis' study with baby Victoria in his arms to introduce the two. He should have known back then that Marquis was up to something when he wanted to perform experiments on an infant.

"And what ideals were those? Because you both seem pretty similar to me," he quipped with a wide smile.

"I am nothing like him!" Brent gnashed out the spiteful words then hung his head. It wasn't Nascien he was lying to but himself.

Both were fathers. Both loved their children. Both enjoyed the rush they felt when using their magic. He experienced it firsthand with Marquis many times. Brent had always aspired to be a father like him.

"Part of that is true," Nascien said, pausing Brent's spiral as he counted all their similarities. "You actually love your child and want her to succeed where you didn't. He...he only used Nia and I as pawns for his ultimate goal."

"What goal was that?" Brent asked. It was as if it were only Nascien and himself in the room now.

"He wanted to become a True Monarch, even now. Something more than the tutelary. His lust for power after being rejected by the council only manifested further from that day. It is why he needs Victoria. Her powers are, well, you should know, you're her father."

"I know Victoria is brilliant, but I didn't think she was anything beyond a normal teenager even with the Aphonic skills like mine."

"She is much more than brilliant. Why do you think he warned Arden to bring her to him? She is an enigmatic anomaly, a paradox. She shouldn't exist, and yet she does. One half of you and the other half your fallen lover." Nascien did not take his gaze off of Brent. "Elwin and you created her with the Erimosian Cradle. She is the True Monarch Child."

Brent allowed his eyes to close then cast his mind back. It was still so clouded with grief. He did not want to revisit it, but Nascien left him no choice.

"You pulled her from the original cradle, did you not?" Nascien pressed Brent for answers. Brent flinched as the memory flooded back to his mind.

"Yes, but we didn't—"

"Victoria is yours and Elwin's biological daughter. That's why she has the single pointed ear. She is not a child born but created from two halves. Two hearts who loved one another. Born from your grief and Elwin's dying breath, quite poetic when you think about it." Nascien paused, he regarded Brent with a careful eye when Brent failed to reply. "You remember now, don't you?"

Brent nodded. His eyes welled up as the memory of the ground crumbling under Elwin's feet flooded back into his mind. Elwin's fear-stricken face. His eyes going wide. And Brent, a blood-curdling scream forced from his throat as Elwin descended into the abyss.

His grief was now unlocked. He looked into Nascien's eyes as if they told the story of Brent's darkest moment. The newly created baby Victoria had cried out for someone to hold her and Brent was set free by The Cradle, allowed to rescue Victoria, but not his husband to be.

"The Cradle chose you, by fate, to bring Victoria to life. But now your fate is tied to my father, who is trying to twist this for his own power gain," Nascien spat.

Brent stood there as Arden and the rest of the room came back into focus.

"There is no need to enter my mind, Arden. I will help you find them all. I am tired of chasing after my father and his delusions," he replied softly.

Brent walked over to Nascien, bending down in front of him. Nascien looked at him with a weak smile. The façade had been dropped and Brent saw the young boy that he once knew. Brent pulled him in and hugged him around his shoulders. "Thank you," he whispered.

"How about taking these binds off," he joked, trying to shrug off the hug.

Arden stepped forward waving his hands. Brent stepped aside, and they unwound gracefully until he was free. "You try anything, and I will kill you myself," Arden warned, holding his exposed palm directly in front of Nascien's face, who only smiled back.

"Are you coming on to me Arden?" Nascien teased and Arden sneered in response.

CHAPTER THIRTY-ONE
PAX'S ADVENTURE

The ruins of Erimosia stretched out before Pax. A maze of crumbling buildings, weathered structures, and ancient artifacts lost to time. Time itself seemed to warp and shift around him, adding to his sense of disorientation. He moved cautiously through the deserted streets and kept a wary eye out for any signs of danger.

His priority, communicate with Brent. Unfortunately, the ruins had been sinking into a chasm for many years now and the residual arcane energies interfered with conventional Rune-Tech communication methods. With no way of reaching the Leyline, Pax was stuck with a Rune-Phone whose signal was non-existent, no magic to defend himself, and no way home.

Stashing the phone, he pressed on, frustrated but determined. He scanned his surroundings for clues, but there was nothing he could discern that would assist his escape. The air was heavy with an eerie stillness, broken only by the occasional whisper, echoing the past that lived on through the ruins.

In the distance, a strange high pitch giggle could be heard. Pax darted around, trying to find where it was coming from. He remembered this same giggling from when he was last here. Memories burned into ruins, manifested like a repeating record. Cursed to play over and over. He followed the giggles down a side street that felt familiar.

He moved with caution, his mind fraught with worry for Victoria. Then a voice he recognized called out to him. Pax spun toward the sound.

"Pax!" It was Brent's voice, as clear as day. Pax dashed ahead, calling out to Brent.

"Oi! Paxton, come out already!" Pax stopped on the spot, skidding hard on the rubble path. This voice was also familiar, but he had not heard it in over sixteen years. Standing as still as he ever had, a haunting vision from the past glided in front of him.

There, before him, stood a shimmering silhouette. A memory he could remember, etched into the very fabric of Erimosia's ruins. A scene from his youth, and a pivotal moment he never thought he would witness again.

Brent, Elwin and he had journeyed to these ruins in search of knowledge, under the instructions of Marquis. In the ghostly tableau, Pax watched as the ethereal Brent and Elwin stood side by side, their faces illuminated in a soft glow of teal magical energy. They were deep in conversation, but he remembered their voices carrying on in the still air.

Brent turned to face him and smiled. That same ridiculous half-smile he always gave, but with no beard to cover his upper lip. He was young. His eyes lit with excitement at the journey they were undertaking together. It was their last quest. Hindsight is always a beautiful thing, right?

"Pax, there you are, up here!" Brent's voice echoed through the ruins and stirred memories long buried in his mind.

With a mixture of awe and trepidation, Pax approached the spectral vision, drawn inexorably toward the familiar figures of his friends. As he drew closer, the memory seemed to solidify, enveloping him in its bitter-sweet embrace.

As if he was transported back to that moment, Pax felt lighter and younger, full of energy. He reached up to his scalp and there was a full head of long, luxurious locks of hair. His arms were toned as well, and his stomach tight.

Brent stood tall and resolute; his gaze scanned the horizon in search of something elusive. Next to him, off slightly to the side, stood Elwin, his expression more guarded. His features etched with a hint of scepticism. Pax could sense a subtle tension between them, a lingering undercurrent of unresolved conflict.

Pax knew now what it was about. The couple had fought about Brent wanting Pax to live with them, to allow him somewhere to stay while he got back on his feet.

"Look at this, Pax." Brent gestured toward the city with a mixture of awe and excitement. "Isn't it incredible? An entire civilisation long forgotten, waiting to be rediscovered."

Pax blinked and played his part exactly as he was meant to. Nodding in agreement, his eyes traced the intricate patterns of the ancient architecture.

Despite the desolation, there was a strange beauty amongst the decay. Pax admired the ingenuity of those who had built them.

They neared the part Pax was dreading. He turned to Elwin and could see his chilly demeanour. A barrier that seemed to have erected between them. Elwin's gaze was distant, his focus elsewhere.

"Elwin, look how wonderful these ruins are," Pax chimed, but sighed internally, if only he could prevent the next chain of events from hitting him so hard.

"It's...impressive, I suppose," Elwin said, his words measured and cautious. "But let's not forget why we are here, we have a mission to complete, so if you two could stop messing about. We can't afford to get distracted."

Pax felt that same pang of disappointment at Elwin's coldness. His gaze fell as Brent began the descent down the hill towards the previous location of the laboratory, which in his vision was not yet an empty chasm.

"Elwin, I'm sorry," Pax whispered, going off script as he watched Elwin begin his own descent.

"What are you talking about?" Elwin offered him an unusual look, his shimmering form starting to glitch.

"Nothing..." Pax waved his hands in front of his face. "It was nothing. Proceed—"

"You are old..." The memory of Elwin broke in and approached him. "Much older than I remember." Elwin raised his hands and looked at his body, then looked up and did not shift his gaze off Pax's. "What has happened to me?"

Elwin's pupils went dark. His once handsome features shifted, replaced by a gaunt image with protruding cheek bones and sunken eye sockets. His stare hardened; his head twisted to the right as he spoke. "You shouldn't have come here Orc!" Elwin shouted at him from the hilltop and Pax twinged when he said "Orc" in such a demeaning tone. "You are not a denizen of the Memory Void. Be gone you foolish Oaf! You were nothing but trouble for Brent and me. Always mooching off of us," he shouted at Pax.

Pax clasped his hands to his ears and shook his head. The movement caused him to lose his footing as he stumbled backwards, falling out of the memory's warm embrace and down into the dirt and rubble of the ruins, cutting his hands on sharp rocks. The shimmering silhouette of Elwin glided towards him, but as if a barrier were between them, it could not proceed. It shouted and pointed at Pax, but he could hear nothing it said.

Pax jumped to his feet and ran in the opposite direction. He glanced over his shoulder to see the vision of Elwin still yelling after him.

Once he was far enough away, he stopped to catch his breath. He stood hunched over, only to fall to his knees and release the tears he had tried to hold back. Tears for his friend, for what Brent went through. Tears for himself. If he had known how Elwin felt, he wouldn't have agreed to move in. But it changed nothing. Nothing would bring Elwin back. Nothing could. He was lost. Forever.

Wiping his face, mud smeared across his cheeks, he stood tall, dusting the front of his pants and tidying himself up. He was rubbing at his eyes, sore from crying, when a glimmer of light caught his attention from the corner of his eye. It emanated from the base of a crumbling tower, catching a ray of light from above. Pax traced his eyes upwards.

He ran towards the tower, squinting as he tried to navigate through the blankness. Orcs could naturally see in the dark, but with age, the other half of his lineage was winning in terms of eyesight. Pax smirked as he remembered words Brent would say to him about his eyes buried in the vision orb and that one day it would come back to haunt him. He couldn't wait to get back home and share a laugh with Brent about how he'd been right.

Pax crossed the threshold of the now crumbling tower and darted his eyes around to find the source of the light beyond the reflection. His eyes adjusted to the dim light of the tower. He scanned the shadows for any sign of movement.

The air, thick with dust and the scent of decay, clung to his skin, and there was something else that lingered in the air. Never in the past could he sense a magical presence, but since the attack in the lounge room, he had felt...different. Pax felt a chill, it caused an intense shiver to run down his spine. There was something in the tower with him.

He saw a faint glimmer down below. Pulling out his phone, he illuminated the surrounding space with its light and his breath caught in his throat. Before him was a large hole in the floor. One more step and he would have tumbled down multiple floors.

"Where are the stairs?" Pax asked out loud, not taking his eyes off of the glimmering object for too long. He shifted his gaze and used the light from the phone to seek out the stairs, spotting them on the other side of the hole. He approached a small ledge he could shuffle along to get to the other side.

"Okay, you can do this, Pax." He summoned his courage and kept the phone illuminated to guide him along.

One foot after the other, he balanced his weight on his heels and shuffled across. He was almost across when his right foot slipped, and he lost his footing. Stumbling like he was in some form of an animated glimmer, his arms flailed, his phone flung out of his hands, and he went flying downwards through the darkness. He let out a terrified roar as he tumbled further down until he felt himself come to a cushioned landing, then bounced onto his feet.

He searched for the phone. A faint light came from the floor where it had landed face down. He quickly checked to ensure it was undamaged and gave a sigh of relief. It was his only way to communicate with the outside world once he could find a functioning Leyline. He pocketed the device and turned his attention to the source of the pale light below.

Descending cautiously, he shuffled along ledges until he made it further down to the lower levels. He approached the illuminated area. With each step, the air grew colder, the chill running up his spine again.

Finally, he reached the bottom of the chamber. His eyes widened in sheer astonishment as he took in the sight before him. Nestled in the shadows was a creature unlike any he had seen. A strange amalgamation of scales, feathers and a set of glowing green eyes that seemed to pierce through the darkness.

Its eyes connected with Pax's, and he stopped dead in his tracks. The creature regarded him warily, its gaze shifting from Pax to the fallen orb at its feet. Pax drew nearer and could see that the orb was cracked, its light flickering weakly, as if it was on the verge of extinguishing.

"Hi," Pax uttered softly, holding up a hand in a gesture of peace. "I mean you no harm."

The creature observed him for a moment longer, before emitting a low, rumbling sound, a cross between a wolf's growl and a cat's purr. It cautiously approached Pax, sniffing the air as if assessing his intentions.

Pax remained still. His heart pounding rapidly in his chest. The creature's fangs glistened in the dim light; it looked like he was about to lunge for an attack. Pax winced but to his surprise, it brushed the ridge of its head against his outstretched hand, its rough scales warm to the touch. Pax ruffled the feathers that protruded from the back of its neck, down its shoulder hackles. It let out a loud snuff of air and chirped at the contact.

"You're just a little sweetheart, aren't you?" Pax said scratching it behind its ears and it purred and chirped once more. "What are you doing down here all alone?"

The creature pointed at the orb at its feet with its nose. The crack down the centre was not deep, but was draining the orb of whatever magic was harboured within.

"I can't fix it here," Pax said truthfully. The creature looked at him and then the orb analysing what he said. "If you can find me a way to the surface, I can fix your orb," Pax offered.

The creature regarded Pax with intelligent eyes, understanding what he said. It let out a low rumbling sound, like a purr of gratitude, and nuzzled against his hand once more. Pax kept rustling its mix of fur and feathers, feeling the warmth emanating from its body. It was a comforting presence in the tower's darkness.

Pax began to ponder how to escape the tower and find a way home. His eyes landed on a narrow passage behind the creature, leading upwards, however it was obscured by rubble. It seemed like a potential route to the surface, albeit a challenging one for someone his size.

With a determined nod, Pax made his decision. He gestured to the creature, showing the passage before them. "Come on, let's see where this leads," he said, but the creature did not move. "What is wrong?" Pax asked, gently bending down. He noticed it motioned to the orb again. "Ah!"

Pax reached down to pick it up. He barely placed his fingertips on its surface when a flash of emotions electrified his mind, leaving him momentarily paralysed. A voice in his mind spoke to him.

"Orc, this Aelaris belonged to a dear friend of mine. Please hold on to it and keep it safe." Pax realised the voice was not coming from the orb, but from the creature. He was speaking to him telepathically. "I am Dracornis, but please call me Drac. Follow me. I know how to get you back to the surface. Keep my friend's Aelaris safe."

Pax opened his eyes and held the cracked orb, or the Aelaris, in his hands. "I understand," Pax said to Drac and smiled. "I am Paxton Grimtusk, but you can call me Pax." Drac chirped in response then took off through the narrow passage.

It was a single straight passage that slowly raised towards the surface. Pax kept close behind Drac, who bounded on all four legs. In the dark, he could just make out Drac's body. He had the legs of a dragon, the body of a wolf, which was covered in fur and feathers. His head and jowls were a mix of a dragon with a wolf like structure and the beady eyes of an owl. They were bright green, similar to ones you would see on a Jade Serpent. Two horns protruded from atop his skull, and he had pointed ears like a wolf.

The passage became a tighter and tighter squeeze as they proceeded further up. Pax crouched down as far as he could, but Drac had no problem being much shorter in stature. After some time, Pax was forced to crawl across the ground. He could hear Drac barking up ahead calling for him. Pax kept his pace as fast as he could, ensuring the Aelaris was safe.

"Hey Drac, how much longer do we have?" It was silent. "Drac?" Pax called out. He couldn't see anything in the intense darkness of the passage, but knew Drac had not left him behind when his face was covered by a slobbery tongue that licked his face. Pax laughed and patted Drac. "Good boy!"

Once Drac stopped licking him, Pax's eyes fully adjusted, and he realised he was outside, but not just outside of the ruins, he was in the wilderness of Arcanum. The night sky illuminated his surroundings. Pax rose to his feet and looked around. He stood near the outskirts of a nearby village. Small patches of trees and a lake could be seen. Smoke pillowed into the air from a nearby inn. The tavern was lively with its patrons. And atop the hill, the Orphanage where he grew up.

"You've brought me to Leown Village?" Pax asked quietly and looked down at Drac with a smile. Reaching down, he patted him gently and began his walk into town. "Come on, I know a place, we can call Brent from there."

Drac looked up at Pax, confused at the mention of Brent, and tilted his head. Pax laughed. "Don't stress. I will tell you about all my friends." Pax smiled as Drac followed him along the path through the village where he grew up.

CHAPTER THIRTY-TWO
VICTORIA'S RESOLVE

Victoria's heart beat wildly as she struggled to make sense of her surroundings. She had lost track of the time spent here. The metallic clang of the cell echoed in her ears, sending shivers down her spine. She fought against the paralysis of fear, willing her limbs to move, but they felt heavy and unresponsive. Each breath was a struggle, her chest tight with anxiety.

Memories of the torturous experiments flooded her mind, each one a nightmare she couldn't escape. Emily had dragged her into this nightmare, a painful betrayal she struggled to come to terms with. Although only knowing her a short time, Victoria thought she could trust her and had started to develop feelings for her.

The thought of facing more of the Weaver's twisted simulations made her stomach churn with dread. Tears streamed down her cheeks, her thoughts racing with uncertainty and terror. She was trapped here, no way to communicate with the outside world, and only a sliver of hope that her father or Pax were coming to rescue her.

But as the moments dragged on, doubt crept into her mind. Would they find her in time, or was she destined to be a prisoner of The Weaver's cruel experiments? Or worse. Dead.

The doors to her cell opened and panic struck her down once more. Before she could react, they were shut as fast as they opened, followed by a loud thud of someone falling to the ground. Victoria scrambled backward, her eyes wide with fear. Who was this person invading the false safety of this cell. Was it another test by the Weaver?

"Could have let me walk in gently, assholes!" The woman's gruff voice resonated around the room. She pushed herself up but struggled to gain her footing. Victoria had a distinct feeling that she knew this woman but could not quite place it. She took in the woman's tousled hair, weary eyes and noted how her skin was like a wrinkled leather bag.

Victoria cautiously scooted off the bed and approached her. "Are you alright?" she asked, her voice barely a whisper.

The woman looked up, her gaze filled with a mixture of relief and exhaustion. "I...I think so," she replied, her voice trembling. "Thank you for helping me up." She grasped Victoria's hands and got to her feet. Victoria couldn't shake the feeling of déjà vu.

"Have we met before?" she ventured.

The woman shook her head. "No, I don't think so. Help me to the bed, child, would you?" Victoria held out her arm to assist the older woman while she hobbled over to the bed. Once she was seated, she let out an alleviated groan. "What is your name, child?"

"Victoria ma'am, and yours?" she asked, sitting next to her.

"Many people call me Elder, and I guess at my age I am, but you may call me Seraphina. It will foster some sort of balance as we co-exist in this prison."

Victoria didn't respond. The name sounded familiar, still she was unsure why she felt familiar. Before she could dwell on it further, Seraphina spoke again.

"I've been...forced to assist him," she explained, her voice heavy with regret. "But I'm not only here for you."

"That man has you under his control too?" Her eyes widened in realisation.

Seraphina nodded; her expression pained. "Yes. These bindings..." She gestured to the intricate magical restraints around her wrists and one around her neck. "If I were to disobey him, they'll..."

"Kill you, yeah. She said the same thing."

"Who did?" Seraphina asked, tucking her clothes back into place.

"Emily..." Victoria's mouth filled with vitriol as she said the name. "I...I was silly to think she actually liked me." Victoria hung her head in despair.

"Ah, the pretty redhead? Sucks darling, she is a looker, but take it from an old fool, there are plenty more people out there who won't backstab you and bring you to some maniac warlock to perform experiments on you." Seraphina granted her a warm but short-lived smile. "Speaking of, I need to ensure you are in fighting shape for the next round." Victoria's heart sank even further.

***

Victoria felt betrayed by everyone around her, even if it was beyond their control. Seraphina was only there to restore Victoria back to full health, before she'd be thrown back into another experiment. Emily had captured her and played her for a fool. She stood awaiting the next experiment, arcane machinery surrounded her. The air was thick with the fog of magic. The Weaver stood behind a panel that was below the pedestal she was chained to. His eyes gleamed purple from under the hood with a tested sense of anticipation.

"Monarch Child..." he spoke to Victoria through a microphone, his voice dripping with malice. "It is time to unleash your true potential."

Victoria couldn't stop to breathe before he flicked his wrist. A series of complex spells were activated, weaving them together in a sinister violet pattern. The air crackled with intensity as the magic surged through the chamber and enveloped Victoria in a pulsating aura of power.

The energy wrapped around her arms like pythons constricting its victims. Piercing her skin, it coursed through her veins, causing Victoria to scream out in pain. The sensation building within her, the raw magic of her essence awakening in response to the Weaver's manipulations. She looked down at her arms, raised out before her, prickling with energy. The fine hairs all over her body stood on end and she could feel the transformation beginning to take hold of her once more.

The powerful magical force was completely absorbed into her body, like a paper towel absorbed a spill. The Weaver studied her from underneath the hood of his robe. They were all alone, and she feared no one was coming to rescue her.

Intense energy continued to surge through her body, she threw her head back, a piercing wail escaped past her lips that even the Weaver couldn't stand. He clasped his hands over his ears. A sudden jolt of force, generated a small tornado of wind around her, causing Victoria's body to contort and shift. Her bones cracked as they grew and morphed. Her flesh felt like it was on fire, and all she could do was cry out in pain as the forced transformation was complete.

Wings unfurled from her back first, causing blood to splatter across the surrounding floor. The wings shimmered with an iridescent light; the rest of her skin followed. It became taut, and like paint spilled across canvas, a deep magenta colour washed over the remainder of her flesh. Her hands grew into dark, elongated claws while her legs lengthened, and talons emerged from her feet. Her eyes glowed with an otherworldly energy, and the chains around her body ignited in pink flames, melting them to liquid and running off her body.

The Weaver laughed triumphantly as he beheld the sight before him. Revelling in the power of Victoria's new form. Eager to witness the full extent of her potential, he ordered her to show her newfound abilities.

Forced to obey his every command, Victoria unleashed a barrage of magical energy towards the targets he had arranged. With clear precision, she hit each one. The Weaver was impressed. But even as she complied with his demands, a fire burned deep within her, a fierce determination to break free from his control.

She channelled her resolve, and his control wanned through his gleeful cheers, too distracted to notice. Victoria turned her sights on him as her next target. With his back turned, she made quick footwork and lunged towards him with her shimmering wings, closing the rest of the distance. She took hold of him with her claws and didn't hesitate to rip him to shreds with her talons, tearing him apart like a piece of paper.

She threw The Weaver's body to the floor and let out an almighty roar at having defeated her captor. Her scream resonated around the room. She took flight triumphant in her victory. The energy was too much for her to control, she needed to burn it off before it ate her up.

The sound of clapping hands came from below, The Weaver stood, fully formed and unscathed. Each clap echoed around the room. How could she be so blind to his illusions? This transformation was more beast than it was brain. The concentrated energy determined to eat her alive if she couldn't burn it off. If only she could harness the power and keep her mind functioning.

"Very good, V!" He smirked under his hood. Victoria wanted to rip his mouth off his face. "Come on down before you burn out."

"*No!*" Victoria let out an ethereal screech. She flapped her wings rapidly as the transformation wanned. Frantically, she clawed the air, trying to maintain her position.

Her wings were the first to shift back, disappearing in a shattering flash, her entire body returned to normal shortly after. In a tremendous fall, she was knocked out cold when she landed on the ground with a thud.

"Evergreen!" The Weaver snapped his fingers and Seraphina hobbled up behind him. "There you are. Check on Subject V. Get her ready for another round in three hours." The Weaver disappeared through the chamber and left Seraphina to tend to Victoria.

Rushing over as fast as she could, Seraphina placed two fingers on Victoria's neck to check she was still alive. "Listen Victoria, I have a plan to get us out of here, but you need to listen carefully." In her post transformation daze, the room swirled as Victoria tried to maintain a focus on what Seraphina was telling her.

Seraphina pulled a mask away from her face, revealing the face of someone Victoria did not expect. Emily had come to her rescue. She scooped Victoria up in her arms. "Let's get back to the cell and get you sorted," she said calmly, reapplying the mask once more.

The two departed the experiment chamber, an unknown plan in place that would hopefully ensure her safety. Victoria wanted to ask more questions, but she could not stay awake any longer. Her body, now depleted of all magic essence, caused her to pass out as she was carried back to her room.

CHAPTER THIRTY-THREE
POEMS FROM MARQUIS

Four silhouettes could be seen conversing through the dimly illuminated windows of Professor Nia's unit from the academy dormitory's ground floor.

Brent, Arden and Nascien had arrived unannounced to seek Nia's guidance. One look at her brother and she dragged all three inside, not by her hands but by the magical force of her mind. Nascien was thrown into a chair roughly, while Nia swung her hands sideways, one closed the door and the other pushed Brent and Arden to take a seat on the desk beside him.

"Tell me again, why should I help you Nascien?" Nia spat. She jabbed her brother in the chest, untrusting of his motives, regardless of his willingness to help Brent and Arden find where Victoria was being held captive. Nascien remained silent, seated on a chair, his legs spread apart. Nia placed a foot between them and wrapped her hand around his neck, impatient with brother's insolence.

"Because of Victoria!" Brent interrupted before Nascien could make a sound. Nia turned to face Brent and let go of her brother's neck. Brent could tell by the contempt in Nia's eyes that he would need to provide more in order to get Nia's help. "Paxton too, and Seraphina. I am sure countless others are under his control or captured. Nascien told us Marquis is pursuing a way to become a True Monarch and seek revenge on the Mage's Union for denying him a seat at the elder council." Brent felt like he was pleading a case that should be obvious.

"Yeah, what he said," Nascien replied arrogantly rubbing his jaw. Nia didn't hesitate and slapped him with the back of her hand, the sound echoing in her living room. Nascien didn't move an inch, but the red mark across his face radiated brightly. He did not take his eyes off his sister. "We need you in order to stop him," he began, his voice steady despite the obvious tension in the air. "We cannot do it alone. You know that as well as I do."

Nia's gaze hardened, there was a flicker of uncertainty in her eyes. She couldn't deny the truth of Nascien's words, even if she was loath to admit it. She also had no reason to mistrust Brent.

"And how do I know I can trust you?" she demanded, crossing her arms in defiance. "You have been gone for years. In fact, I think the last words I said to you were that if I ever saw you again, I would kill you myself." She pulled her foot down and stepped back, dropping her shoulders. She sighed, lowering her guard.

Nascien's jaw tightened, a shadow passed over his features as he lowered his head. "The truth is you have no reason to trust me, none of you." He looked up, his gaze shifted from Brent to Arden and back to his sister. His voice was tinged with regret. "But I am still your brother, and I cannot stand by and watch him tear Brent's family apart. What of you?" He spoke with a martyr's conviction.

Brent and Arden exchanged a knowing glance. Silently, they acknowledged the complexity of the situation. Brent hoped Nia would be more helpful, but Nascien warned him it had been quite a while since they had seen each other. They not only needed Nascien but also Nia's help if they were to have any chance of rescuing Victoria from Marquis' clutches.

"We have little time," Brent interjected, his tone tinged with urgency. "If there is anything you can tell us that might help," Brent paused and looked between the siblings, "now is the time to speak up."

"This is much harder for Nia. She was always dad's favourite," Nascien explained, noticing her apprehension.

"That's rich coming from you." Nia ignited fast again, approaching Nascien. "Do you know what it was like living in the shadow of our father's successes? Mother was right." She turned back, feeling scorned. "I should have cut ties much earlier and followed my own path." Nascien shifted at the mention of their mother.

"How is she?" His tone was hesitant but inquisitive.

"She is doing well. I travel to Suncrest every other weekend."

Brent was aware Marquis' wife was unwell, but he never knew the nature of her illness. Nia noticed the look of curiosity on his face and began to elaborate.

"Mum has aphasia and is being treated in Suncrest with Speech Therapy Mages. She has kept moments of clarity with me, but her flow of magical energy has been disrupted permanently. For Silent Sages, this disease is detrimental, and she struggles to translate her thoughts into magical actions, sometimes to devastating effects. This could lead to the loss of her own life, or the lives of others." Nia remained stoic.

"We should never had let father attempt to treat her," Nascien spat under his breath. Arden jolted forward.

"You mean he tried to treat her without the proper facilitation of medical magic?" Arden questioned.

"He performed illegal magic and failed?" Brent prodded, and both Nascien and Nia nodded sombrely. Brent pressed on, hoping to lead the conversation in the direction he needed. "If facing your father is too much for you, I understand, but please know my daughter looks up to you so much. You are like a mother figure to her. I don't think there had been a day I haven't heard her mention you at least once."

Nia's eyes connected to Brent's and they welled up with fresh tears. "You know this is something I'm going to struggle with and yet you still ask," she stammered. "I know to you he is a villain, but to me he is my father, he is still a good man."

"And she is my daughter, she is my entire life. Your father kidnapped her and is performing fuck knows what experiments on her!" Brent raised his voice at the end. He ran a hand through his hair and urged himself to calm down. "If you can't do it for me or Victoria, do it for your mother who needed someone in her corner to prevent Marquis from his insanity," Brent pressured Nia, his voice stern, as he leaned forward pleading with her. "Marquis is not well. He needs all our help. I don't think you want to see another parent institutionalised or worse, dead, because you chose not to do anything." Brent reclaimed his composure.

The room went silent as Nia contemplated his words. "I know you are right, and while I don't want to betray my family, it is evident from what you've said that my father has gone too far..." She slunk against the wall. Nia's introspective thoughts took formation on her face as she felt the weight of his words. She straightened her posture and smiled, albeit weakly. "Where do we start?"

"Well, we need to find a way of tracking him down" Arden looked between them. "Nascien has expressed he doesn't know where Marquis or the Code Weavers are, just that he was placed at Sanctum and did what he was ordered to do."

"Unfortunately, I have not been in contact with him for a while. The last message he sent—" Nia's eyes widened, and she darted to her bedroom only to return a second later with her phone, scrolling through to find what it was she remembered.

"He messaged me the week before he was announced missing, but I never told the Mage's Union because I didn't think it was relevant." She pulled up the message and handed her phone to Brent. Arden stood next to him, eager to read it as well.

"It's a poem?" Brent looked perplexed.

"Yes, he wrote poetry a lot, and sent me some from time to time," Nia expressed.

"Read it out loud," Nascien said, leaning forward, resting an elbow on one knee and his chin in the same hand. Brent cleared his throat and read the poem.

> *In shadows deep where secrets sleep,*
> *A plan unfolds, its roots running deep.*
> *Monarch's children lost and found.*
> *Endless power through their essence bound.*
> *With every step and every breath,*
> *I draw in closer; I court their death.*
> *For in their veins, the magic thrums,*
> *The key to power, of angelic hums.*
> *They deny me a seat in the place of might.*
> *But it is I who rise, with the power of silence.*
> *Through darkness vast and shadows grim,*
> *I'll rise again. My vengeance Erimosian.*
> *So, heed this warning, o'council unfair.*
> *Your end draws near, my love sklayre.*
> *For in the heart of nights embrace.*
> *I'll claim my throne, my rightful place.*

Silence echoed loud around the room; the words buzzed in their ears as they quietly tried to decipher what was written.

"Father always wrote poetry that was sort of anti-establishment, but I saw it as nothing more than him expressing his emotions," Nia said, cutting the silence.

"That feels much worse than just expressing his emotions," Brent said, handing back the phone to her, committing the words to memory the best he could. Brent had an idea what it meant based on the last message he received from Marquis, but they didn't have the time to guess and be wrong.

"Yeah, he clearly states he was upset with the Elder Council decision, so he is going to make them pay," Arden added.

"I will not debate poetry at this hour. Based on the knowledge you gave me, the overall message is clear, this was his way of telling me." Nia put an end to the discussion.

"Like I said, you were his favourite," Nascien muttered once more.

"Then why did he choose you to impersonate the Arch Mage?" Brent asked.

Nascien sighed, "Look, I am not proud of it. I was just happy he was speaking to me after years of being a disappointment to him. I jumped at the chance to help when he needed me."

"So where is the Arch Mage? Is father holding him?" Nia asked.

"Father never said," he replied.

"You two really were way too trusting of your parents," Arden snapped in clear agitation.

"This isn't the time to argue over the past, I think I might—"

Brent's pocket vibrated cutting him off mid-thought. He reached in to pull his phone from his pocket. The screen read a number registered in Leown village.

"Hello?" Brent stood as he answered the call.

"Brent!" Pax's voice came through. He switched the call to loudspeaker.

"Pax!" His voice filled with relief. "Where are you?" Brent cried out as the other three exchanged concerned looks. "Where's Victoria? Is she okay? Wha' 'bout you? Wha' happened?" he slurred his words. His heart was pounding in his chest so rapidly it was hard to get out the words.

"I'm so sorry Brent, Emily kicked me off when she was transporting us..."

Arden's eyes darted to Brent. He reached over and snatched the phone. Brent tried to protest but was denied as Arden turned away. "Grimtusk, it's Callahan. Do you remember what the portal was like?"

"What's that got to do with anything?" Nia whispered to Brent, who shrugged.

"The portal reflects both ends of transport. It may have some clues," Arden added.

"Arden, I am happy to discuss all this, but wouldn't it be better if it was in person?" Paxton asked.

"Where are you then?" Arden asked, already preparing a portal wide enough for all four of them to enter.

"I'm in Leown Village, the Orphanage at the end of Mulbury," Paxton explained. A whooshing sound of a portal closing could be heard from outside.

Before he could hang up Arden held the front door open with one arm so Brent could be the first to walk through. Pax placed the phone on the receiver and ran over to them. Drac sat up and bounded off the chaise lounge he was resting on. The pitter patter of his enormous claws echoed in the empty house. Pax made to stop him, but it was too late.

Brent caught unaware, fell to the ground, narrowly missing hitting his head, as Drac sprung up and licked his face. "Hello, little guy," Brent laughed as the tongue slobbering tickled. "What is your name?"

Brent laughed and patted Drac. Pax was just relieved and happy to see his friends again. He chuckled along with Brent then scooped his arms around Drac and pulled Brent up with an outstretched hand. "Seems he likes you." Drac wriggled in Pax's arms as Brent stood up.

"You remember Victoria's teacher, Nia Beaumont," he nodded to where she stood beside Arden. "Nascien is her brother, he...well... You know what, let me..." Brent trailed off and placed his hand on Pax's shoulder.

Brent's attempt at a mind-link failed. A heavy silence settled between them, thick with unspoken emotions. Pax's expression mirrored Brent's own melancholy. They shared a moment of mutual understanding outside of the confines of their minds. For years, they had been connected, only requiring a hand on the shoulder for thought transfer. Their bond forged through many years of shared experiences and unbreakable friendship.

Through every stage of his life, Pax was there, hovering around inside Brent's mind. Now, the absence of the connection left a void. Like a part of each other was stolen from them. Brent swallowed hard and tried to push back the wave of sadness threatening to overwhelm him. He couldn't afford to dwell on this loss now, not when Victoria still needed to be rescued. With a deep breath, he forced a smile and pulled Pax in for a hug.

"I'm so glad you are okay," Brent said into Pax's shoulder with a sniffle, glistening tears formed in his eyes.

"Of course, Brent, I'll always be here, even if—" Pax couldn't bring himself to say it. "It'll take more than a bunch of teenaged, manipulated Tech-Mages to stop this Orc!"

Brent pried himself off of Pax's hulking shoulder, regaining his composure. "Sorry, everyone…" Brent trailed off, there was no way to easily explain so he moved on. "As I said, this is Nascien, Nia's brother and Marquis' son.

"Looks like you two have been busy." Pax spoke directly to Arden and Brent. "When Emily kicked me off, I found myself in Erimosia. I landed in an old memory, a painful one…" Pax trailed off.

"Marquis has her at the lab in Erimosia. He had given a cryptic clue about where this started, I didn't know if he meant my past or hers."

"Well, it stands to reason that he would take Victoria to the place she was created, father was always sentimental like that," Nascien replied.

"He legit said it in the poem, why did we not think of it?" Arden mumbled aloud but to no one in particular. He seemed to be frustrated he hadn't figured it out on the spot.

"Well, that settles it, we go to the lab." Nia interjected. She wasted no time, turning on her heel and heading back outside where they could conjure a portal. Brent made to follow when Arden held up a hand to his chest.

"Brent…" His tone shifted. "Don't take this the wrong way, but I think it best you and Pax stay behind. You are too emotionally invested, think of how you lost it on Nascien. We can't have that happen; we need to sharp if we're going to defeat Marquis."

His words hit Brent like a tidal wave. His entire stomach fell to the ground before the anger rose in him. He wanted to punch him. Push him out of the way and tell him to get fucked. But…this was exactly Arden's point. Brent wasn't thinking clearly, and the last thing they needed was him to ruin their attempts at saving Victoria.

"I know you're right, bu—"

"I knew you'd understand." Arden effectively cut him off and strode off toward the door before Brent could finish his thought or give a rebuttal.

He stood and watched them leave to Erimosia. Where he should be.

CHAPTER THIRTY-FOUR
UNLINKED UNCERTAINTY

Brent sat gazing out the windowsill of Paxton's old orphanage bedroom. He counted the many moths that fluttered through the night sky, dancing around streetlamps as they courted each other on the last of the summer nights. Leown was silent, almost a ghost town, one of few villages that had remained behind once Spellford had expanded many years ago. He pondered what a simple life in a country town would be like, had he himself never moved to the city.

The other three had left for Erimosia less than hour ago. Brent wrestled with the confusion building in him. Arden wasn't entirely wrong in his reasons to leave Brent behind, but still it was his daughter that needed to be rescued. He was the one that had been to the Erimosian Lab before.

Did Arden have a different reason for telling him to stay behind? It made no sense!

Rage ignited within him, he needed to break something. Hurt someone as much as he was. He regretted having stood there like a stunned mullet. He should have pushed back. Brent slammed his fist down on the windowsill and instantly regretted it as a sharp piece of wood splintered into his hand.

"Ah! For fucks sake!" He winced, pulling the splinter out and sucked on the wound to relieve the pain. There was a knock at the door. He didn't bother to turn when it opened. All Brent could focus on was devising a plan of his own to find Victoria. He needed her safe, and in his arms, once more.

Brent wanted to tell her all the things he regretted. The things he never said. Like how much he loved her. How much she reminded him of himself at her age. How much of Elwin he saw in her. He wanted to tell her all the secrets he kept bottled up inside. Even the ones he only recently learned. He never wanted to keep anything from her again. He just wanted her safe.

"Drac has gone peeps and poops," Pax said in a playful, almost triumphant voice when he entered through the door after Brent hadn't acknowledged him.

Brent murmured something unintelligible and continued to stare out the window without looking back. Drac bounded onto the bed behind him, then circled around like a pup trying to find its place to sleep. With a few scratches he had made his own nook and curled up, readying himself to sleep.

Pax slunk himself onto the bed behind Brent, giving Drac enough room to sleep between his legs. "I know you are upset you aren't out there with them, but maybe Arden's right, maybe you are too emotionally connected." Brent knew Pax was trying to reassure him, but it just felt like a dagger in the back.

"I couldn't give a shit right now, Pax. So, if you don't mind, I am busy thinking, you know, that thing you never do," Brent said with malicious intent. He wanted it to hurt. He was mad and needed someone else to feel his pain. He wanted Pax to feel the ache Brent had in his heart, and now that their mind-link was gone, how else could he share the load of anguish on his mind?

"You know what..." Pax stood up sharply, accidentally causing Drac to roll onto his back. He flapped his ears with a huff. "I have had it with this sulking act you do every fucking time something doesn't go your way." Pax's voice filled with a stern venom. It was so potent it could have peeled the paint off the walls.

Brent whipped around with wide eyes. Pax had never shouted at him before.

"You have everything in life, a job, a daughter who loves you, a house, brilliant hair, men throwing themselves at you. You were labelled the 'Hero of Spellford', got all the glory, while everyone pushed me aside like I wasn't the one who gave you the chicken piece in the first place!"

Brent made to interrupt, but Pax snapped his tusks forcing Brent to keep quiet.

"And although I know how hard it was when you were going through depression after Elwin died, you still did not once think to ask how I was doing. He was my friend, too. He's the reason I am in love with Dragon Hoarde, did you know that?" Brent stammered a "no", but Pax continued.

"It has always been about you and your self-centred mindset. Like you are the main character, but you aren't Brent, this is *all* our lives. We all matter! I am hurting as much as you are for Victoria. She may be your flesh and blood, but I raised her, too. When you were too grief stricken, it was me changing her diapers, feeding her, and ensuring she had everything she needed. Where were you?"

'The love of my life just died...I was—" Pax interrupted Brent again by snapping his tusks once more.

"You don't get it, and I don't think you ever will. You are too self-centred. It was much easier when we co-existed in our thoughts, and I was your lackey. But these few hours without that niggling thought inside of my head has given me clarity on these emotions I have felt for a long time."

"So...you have been feeling like this even before we lost the mind-link?" Brent asked and Pax stood firm. "Then why didn't you fucking say something sooner?" Brent aimed a punch into Pax's chest. "Would have saved me the hassle of dragging you around all the time!" Brent chose the words he needed to purposefully hurt Pax.

"I know you aren't angry with me." Pax lowered his tone.

"Well, I don't have fucking anyone else to yell at now, do I?" Brent's eyes filled with tears, and his throat choked up with emotion.

Drac had enough of the two fighting and trotted towards the door. He whimpered to be let out.

"And another thing, you aren't bringing a pet into my home, especially not one like that! You can forget about it!" Brent lashed out once more because he didn't know what else to do.

"He needs a home!" Pax defended Drac who was innocently pawing at the door.

"Well, you can go find him one," Brent paused, his next words formed in his mouth before he could stop them, "and go live there with him. A couple of lap dogs, you two should get on fine without me." He turned around sharply.

"I know you don't mean that Brent. I know you better than anyone else. You are angry at yourself for sitting here and doing nothing!"

There was a long, silent but heated exchange between the two. Brent with his back turned and Pax standing in silence. Pax had enough. He moved toward the door, opened it wide to allow Drac to trot through. He stood there, holding onto the door handle, contemplating his next move.

Brent's muscles began to shake, adrenaline coursed through him. Pax had never confronted Brent like this before. Was it because they were unlinked? Perhaps it was Victoria's capture getting to them.

"I'm going now," Pax said softly. Brent did not respond. The hurt in Pax's voice stained the air.

The click of the door latch was followed by Pax's heavy steps trudging down the stairs. Brent's heart sank. He wanted chase after Pax, but his pride was too strong to let him. He knew where his anger was coming from and as the front doors slammed of the orphanage, Brent was finally alone.

But he didn't enjoy it like he thought he would. In fact, the silence was deafening and disorientating. It was weird not being linked with Pax anymore. He was unsure how to...be. He groaned. He had to apologise. Brent was in the wrong, and it didn't matter how upset he was.

Hee kicked his foot against the leg of the bed as he stumbled to rush from the room. His tunnel vision to locate his friend blocked out any pain. Yanking the door handle as firmly as he could, he almost pulled the aged door off its hinges. Bounding down the stairs two at a time, he didn't take any care and fell down the last few. He managed to regain his footing and bounced off the wall. Brent rushed through the orphanage entrance and burst through the double doors into the cool air of Leown's streets.

Darting his eyes around, he could barely see Pax in the distance, walking with Drac by his side. Brent took off, tripping on his feet again, realising how unfit he truly was.

"Paxton!" Brent called out, catching up to him. "You're not seriously going to go on foot?" Brent slowed down, his breathing heavy. Even Drac didn't pay him any attention and continued to trot next to Pax.

"Don't pretend to care about me now," he replied coolly, the hurt still in his voice.

Panting, Brent looked up at him and could swear he saw tears forming. He had never seen Pax cry, not even once. "Look, I'm sorry. You are right, I took you for granted."

"And?" Pax asked, goading more out of him.

"And..." Brent stared guiltily at his feet. "I never cared to ask you how you were. I was self-centred and assumed you were okay with how things were."

"That's a start," Pax replied coldly.

'Fuck, I don't know Pax. When we were linked, everything was easier and in these last hours, everything has become such a mess. I want my best friend back. I fucked up, I am sorry." Brent stopped and bowed his head, hoping for forgiveness.

Pax turned and placed his hand on Brent's head, ruffling up his hair.

"Things are changing fast." Pax released a heavy sigh. I accept your apology, but you better not talk to me like that ever again. There is still much to be said, but right now we need to remain united if we are to have any hope of finding Victoria. So, what do we do now?"

Brent stood upright and readjusted his hair. He took a minute and considered Nia's words from earlier in the evening. Marquis had always been a reasonable man. Perhaps Brent could talk to him, make him see reason now that he knew a little more of the story.

"We are going to defy Arden and go down into the lab," Brent stated.

Pax raised an intrigued brow. "Good to see you thinking like yourself again. I think it's time we get our daughter back."

"She is basically our daughter, huh?" Brent laughed.

"Well, she gets her kind-hearted ways from me, she gets her sassy cunt ways from you." Pax jabbed him in the ribs.

"I deserved that." A grin formed on Brent's face, illuminated by the warmth flickering from the streetlamp. Brent deserved much worse. He was remorseful and would make it up to Pax once Victoria was safe.

"What should we do about Drac?" Pax's expression was full of silent pleading.

"We can't exactly leave him here on his own. Where did you find him again?" Brent asked.

"He was down in Erimosia. I don't know, maybe I could...no, probably not..." Pax went back in forth out loud. It didn't take a mind-link for Brent to know his thoughts, years of friendship also had its strengths.

"Silas?" Brent asked and Pax nodded. "So, what is going on there?"

"We are..." Pax almost giggled like a smitten teen. "It's not established yet, but it was where I planned to go when you rudely said Drac, and I were no longer welcome." Pax poked and Brent had to wear it. "I will call and see if he can help."

Pax avoided giving Brent a straight answer, and in the past, he would have been able to search his mind for potential clues. It dawned on Brent that maybe this was why Pax never branched out for a relationship with anyone else. Brent was finally understanding his best friend, more so than when they were linked.

He stood watch over Drac while Pax made the call to Silas. Drac kept looking back at him as he sniffed around. Something about Drac's eyes felt familiar to Brent, but he couldn't put his finger on it. He took in the night's chill air and waited for Pax to finish up his call. Drac happily chased around fireflies. Brent bent down and picked up a stick.

"Probably just happy to be out above the pit, aren't you?" He spoke to Drac. The creature looked from Brent to the stick and turned his nose away. Brent chuckled, "You don't want the stick?"

"Well, he isn't a hound, Brent," Pax said, approaching them. "Silas is on his way, you don't have to stick around and wait, Victoria is more important."

"She is, but so are you. I need you with me," Brent said with blatant honesty.

Brent's phone vibrated in his pocket.

He yanked it from his pocket to see Arden's name on the screen. He placed the receiver to his ear.

"Ah, Abernathy, glad you picked up." It wasn't Arden, but he recognised the voice in an instant. Marquis' distorted voice cracked through the phone as he struggled to inhale. "Sending someone else to do your dirty work won't do, I made quick work of them before they even got inside, I'm afraid boy. Face me like a man, you coward." The phone hung up.

Brent looked down at Pax. "He has the others now, too," Brent said through gritted teeth, his eyes wide with renewed determination to take Marquis down.

CHAPTER THIRTY-FIVE

BETRAYED AND BRUISED, BUT NOT BROKEN

Victoria awoke in her cell again. This time aware of where she was. Seraphina was off to the side snoozing away. Seated on the floor, crossed legged, was Emily, but her face was obscured. Victoria wanted to leap forward and strangle her, anything she could to make Emily feel the pain she felt.

But she couldn't. Her body was too weak from the forced transformation.

"You're awake?" Emily spoke softly. "I know you aren't happy with me right now."

Victoria glared at her. "You're damn right I'm not! I trusted you, and you were conning me the entire time!" she spat, turning away to hide her tears. "Was any of it real?" she asked with a sniffle.

"I can't answer that." Emily hung her head. By her tone, Victoria could tell Emily was being truthful. But she needed answers.

"What do you mean? We kissed! And not just an ordinary kiss...it meant something to me." Victoria hated to feel vulnerable, but this was what caring for someone did to you.

"The Emily you met isn't the real me." She rose and walked closer; her face illuminated in the light. This person's face was similar, but older than the Emily Victoria knew.

"You look like her. Are you her older sister or something?" Victoria asked, not entirely convinced.

"No, more like her mother, in a sense. She is me, and I her, but we are not each other," Emily explained, but Victoria couldn't make sense of it.

"I'm sorry what?"

"I'll explain it, but it isn't easy to grasp," she started.

"Try me, I have seen my share of crazy."

"I was copied, cloned. Marquis, he, somehow, altered The Cradle to allow for copies to be made. Thrasha, Sama, we were all copied. Those clones had their memories altered and were given orders to follow until Marquis deemed it fit you were ready for him."

"So, he wants to clone me?" Victoria asked, her body still restrained by the invisible binds that were her fatigue.

"Worse," Emily warned. "That Emily and I are still connected, but I don't think she knows it yet." Victoria's head was swimming. She was in too much pain both mentally and physically, to deal with this amount of information. "What I gleamed while in stasis, is that Marquis means to drain you of all your essence and absorb your powers for his own."

"That's fucking insane!" she barked a laugh, it became uncontrollable. All of this was wearing her down, her mind felt like it might fracture. "It's not that I don't believe you, I have been tortured enough in the last few hours that the news isn't a shock." Victoria spoke truthfully. She heard herself say it, but it still didn't feel real. "I still find this so unfathomable. Why?"

"Why would a respected and celebrated Sage do this?" Emily asked bluntly, and Victoria nodded. "I don't know, but I don't want either of us sticking around here to find out. How are your legs? Can you walk?" Victoria made to stand but couldn't support her own weight.

Seraphina stirred in her sleep. "We need to get her out, too," Victoria demanded.

Emily pondered for a moment. "Marquis has a portal he uses to travel between here and Spellford. If we can reach it, all of us will be home free. But..."

"But there is the problem of me still not being able to walk..."

"I'm still rusty, but here." Emily took off her gloves with her teeth and laid them on her lap. Shuffling forward, she outstretched her hands in front of Victoria. "I wasn't always the best at healing augmentum, but I can transfer some of my strength to you."

Victoria was apprehensive, but Emily urged her on. Victoria took hold of her outstretched hands, and a cooling burst of energy generated. It enveloped Victoria from within, like a glass of ice-cold water on a hot summer's day. She wiggled her toes and fingers as her energy seemed to return.

"Thank you," Victoria whispered, and slowly stood up. Emily kept hold of her hands and helped her stand. Victoria's heart fluttered. If she was the real Emily, and her feelings were for the fake one, then why did she still get the same jittery butterflies in her stomach? She shook her head and focused on the issue at hand, their escape. "Alright, let's wake Seraphina and get out of here."

***

"Fucking Marquis," Seraphina grumbled loudly as she shuffled slowly behind Emily and Victoria. "He took my caster, and it was an herbal mix for my health." Without her ECC, she was withering fast.

"You alright back there, Grandma?" Emily asked and Victoria shifted her gaze between them.

"That's Elder to you, Elder Evergreen." Seraphina spoke in an unsteady voice. Victoria stopped in her tracks.

"Evergreen," Victoria started and linked an arm with Seraphina's, helping her walk along. "Do you have a grandson named Silas?"

"Why yes, I do," she coughed, a deep rumbling cough which sounded like she had ingested gravel. "Why do you ask?"

"He is my Creature Studies Professor," Victoria said gently, slowly hobbling along with Seraphina towards Emily, who was leaning against a wall waiting for them. "I suspect he and my Uncle Paxton, are dating or have a thing."

"Pax! You know him? Wait, uncle? You don't look very Orc, more Half-Elf." Seraphina pointed towards her ear. "Though I have never seen a Half-Elf with ears like this."

"He and I aren't related, but he helped my father raise me," Victoria said. Her eyes grew when she remembered where she had seen Seraphina from. "You were there at the academy, the day of the Behemoth and so was Arden!"

"So, you're Brent Abernathy's daughter." Seraphina's tone shifted. She began to emit an aura of warmth and gave a look only a grandmother would give.

"Adopted, but yes," Victoria corrected her and shifted her gaze away, her cheeks flushed red with an unknown feeling. She wasn't sure if it was embarrassment or not.

"Ah, well you wouldn't know it upon first glance." Seraphina smiled "And to answer your other statement, yes, we both were there." She let go of Victoria's arm to cough as they caught up with Emily.

Victoria began to piece the puzzle together. It appeared Marquis had involved everyone and anyone who was connected to her father and herself. The only solace she could take was that she wasn't alone.

"Coast clear?" Victoria asked.

"I, er…" Emily scratched the back of her head. "I don't know. Never been in this place before, I have been wandering aimlessly if I am being honest."

"Fat load of good you two are," Seraphina coughed hard into a handkerchief. As she pulled it back, blood splatters were formed. Victoria closed her hand over it.

"Let's find your ECC."

"Unless you can materialise one without App-Magic, I am afraid—" Seraphina said, but was interrupted as Victoria was compelled to hold out her hands before her.

Seraphina paused and watched as glistening colours of purples, blues and yellows swirled around in a pattern. An object formed in Victoria's hands. It was rough, as Victoria created it from memory, and had seen them only a few times in her life.

Seraphina's eyes lit up as the object materialised in her hand. Victoria had somehow created an ECC out of thin air. Going against the very laws of magic and creation that Seraphina was taught. Victoria's magic had created something from nothing.

"Where did you learn to do that?" Seraphina asked, impressed by the talent of Victoria.

"I…I don't know, it just came to me to try it out. You said you needed it, so I made it." Victoria shrugged, handing the crudely crafted ECC to Seraphina.

Seraphina snatched it up to inspect it with a keen eye. Pulling the mouthpiece to her lips, she took a drag. "Seems to work fine."

"You reckon?" Victoria asked, beaming.

"I'll give it a shot. I always keep some of the essence close to my body." Seraphina dived under her robes and dug around in her bra. Pulling out a small vial of green vapour with silvery floating hues, she opened the ECC and poured the contents inside. Bringing it to her mouth again, it activated, working but silently. There was no crackling like her other one.

Seraphina held the vapours in her mouth momentarily, then let them out in a big bursting cloud. The cloud hung in the air, generating fireworks and lightning bolts. Seraphina released a slight cough before she took in the cloud she generated.

"Wow, this is better than the shit that's on the market, it made the essence burn off so clean, too. There is no weird after tickle in my throat," Seraphina said, rubbing her oesophagus.

She leaned over and patted Victoria on the back. "When we get out of here, I will take this to my friends in the Union. We need to get it patented."

"Are you two done?" Emily pushed herself from the wall.

"Sorry, your *highness*," Seraphina quipped, walking past her. Victoria noticed Seraphina give Emily a quick wink.

Emily took off behind Seraphina. Victoria made a small jog to catch up. They continued to wander through this dilapidated laboratory. Emily stated she had a vague idea of the way, but Victoria was not so certain. Wanting to remain hopeful and not let her mind spiral into negativity she tried to fill the silence.

"So, why did Elder Evergreen wink at you?" she asked. Emily's face went white but kept her line-of-sight forward.

"You really don't know who I am, do you?"

"What am I supposed to know?" Victoria asked.

Seraphina let out a little chuckle before she took another puff of her ECC.

"Spellford Academy clearly does not teach its students about its neighbouring nations, or perhaps the clueless adolescence is as it has always been." Emily let out a sigh. "You know me as Emily, but my real name, the name I only go by when in Suncrest, is Queen Emilia Aurelia Selunarta of the Moonchild Clan, ruler of the Sunfolk and Protector of Lune's Light. But please call me Emilia." Her tone changed when she revealed her true identity, carrying with it an air of authority that commanded attention.

"You know what?" Victoria laughed. "I can't wait to tell Luminia I kissed royalty. She is going to freak!" Victoria jumped around in joy. Seraphina and Emily shook their heads, unamused by the silliness of the teenage girl.

"I see you are taking my reveal with ease."

"Are you kidding me!? This is amazing!" Victoria stopped jumping and took Emilia's hands in hers. "Can I turn you in for the cash reward?"

"You most certainly will not!' Emilia snatched back her hands and turned to Seraphina. "Can you help me calm down Vic—" Emily looked up; her face went paler than it had before.

Victoria turned around. Seraphina stood motionless, still looking toward them with the ECC in her mouth.

"What's up?" she smirked, taking in one last puff of her ECC. The corridor was silent. Seraphina took in the horror on both the young women's faces and followed their line of sight.

Looking down, a blade, emanating a purple aura, had pierced her stomach all the way through. She gazed at her own reflection on the side of the blade. Her arms dropped lifelessly to the side, along with her head. The ECC fell from limp fingers to the ground.

The owner of the blade kicked her. She fell into a heap, blood spurting forth and pooling on the ground. The sound of Seraphina's bloodied wound sliding off the blade echoed in Victoria's ears. All she could do was stare on in silent terror.

She had seen murders in Glimmers many times, but never in real life. Fury boiled deep within her, layered in fear and deep sadness for a person she admired, but only just started to get to know. Silent tears trickled down her face as Emilia held Victoria back.

Behind where Seraphina stood, the other Emily blocked their path, blade in hand.

"I see my true self escaped. Pity you both will have to die today!" Emily hissed.

How could she stand there and not care about what she had done? All the rage and fear buried deep inside Victoria bubbled up. Taking heavy breaths, she could not control her anger anymore. Emilia tried with her might to pull her back, but her hands started to singe. Victoria was transforming again, but this time it was of her own volition.

Victoria's transformation was awe-inspiring and terrifying to behold. Her once-human form was now enveloped in a radiant white aura, tinged with magenta highlights that danced along the edges like flicking flames. Her eyes blazed with a brilliant white light, reflecting the intensity of the Augmenti running through her. As her body changed, it flowed seamlessly. Each movement graceful and fluid, unlike the previous chaotic distortions of her forced transformations.

Gone was the unrecognisable shape of a human or beast, replaced instead by a sleek and slender form that shimmered with otherworldly energy. Victoria's limbs elongated; her skin took on a pearlescent sheen set aglow from within. Despite the ferocity of her stare and the raw power she emanated, there was a haunting beauty to her new form. A testament to the depth of her inner strength and resolve.

As she floated there, transformation complete, she turned her attention to the clone Emily before her. She exuded an aura of both danger and majesty. She was no longer just Victoria Abernathy, but something far greater. Something ethereal and unstoppable. And she knew that she was more than capable of facing Emily and even Marquis head on.

CHAPTER THIRTY-SIX
MALEVOLENT DARKNESS

Amidst the ruins, Brent's determination only grew stronger. With each step, he drew upon the memories of his past adventures with Elwin, seeking clues and connections that might lead him to Victoria and the others. Brent felt fearless and, with Pax by his side, he had a firm resolve that he would return victorious, hopefully with no lives lost.

"Do you remember the way?" Pax asked as they wandered aimlessly in the streets.

"Sadly, I don't, but I can feel we are getting close. The laboratory was in the centre of the city, which..." Brent nodded, his brow furrowed in concentration as he navigated the twisted streets of Erimosia. "We are almost there."

The city, once a place of wonder and magic, had become a maze of broken memories and crumbling structures. The air was heavy with the scent of damp earth and ancient enchantments, a reminder of the powerful forces that had shaped the city's fate. A fate he did not want to share.

As they ventured deeper, the surroundings grew darker, the light of the sun barely filtering through the gaps between the buildings. The distant echoes of their footsteps reverberated off the walls, creating an eerie symphony of sound in the empty streets.

"We must be cautious," Brent forewarned, his eyes scanned the surroundings. "There could be remnants of old spells lingering here. We don't know what might have been left behind."

Pax nodded in agreement, his senses sharp. Despite the desolation, there was an underlying tension in the air, as if the very ground beneath them held its breath, waiting for some long-lost secret to be unveiled.

They continued their trek through the dark streets, guided by Brent's intuition and the faint pull of forgotten magic. After what felt like hours of searching, they finally stumbled upon a familiar landmark—an ancient arch adorned with intricate runes. Brent's eyes lit up with recognition holding an orb of light near the weathered arch.

"I remember this place," Brent said, his voice filled with relief. "This was the arch that Elwin and I walked under. The laboratory must be close by."

The air crackled with residual magic, leaving an electric charge in their senses and the hair on the back of their necks standing up. Something was here with them. They continued forth, keeping their wits about them for any sudden movements.

As Brent and Pax approached the laboratory, the air grew thick with anticipation. The once-grand structure, now a dilapidated relic of forgotten experiments, loomed before them. Brent held out his hand and processed the residual energy left behind.

The remnants of twisted magic clung to the very essence of the place, creating an aura of malevolence that hung in the air like a shroud. Brent stepped forward and a crumble of rocks could be heard ahead.

A grotesque figure emerged from the shadows, a warped embodiment of rage and wickedness. The creature, once a being of immense power, was now a contorted and tormented entity. Its form was gnarled and distorted, its features barely recognizable as human. Its eyes glowed purple with an otherworldly fury, its movements jerky and unnatural.

The ground beneath the creature's feet quivered with its sheer evil, causing the ash and debris to crinkle under its weight. It let out a guttural growl. The sound sent chills down Brent and Pax's spines. The very air seemed to tremble in the wake of its presence, as if the very fabric of reality recoiled from its twisted form.

"What is this?" Pax asked Brent, standing his ground with a slight tremble.

"It feels like..." Brent closed his eyes with his palm out ahead of him "It can't be..." He attempted to breach the creature's mind, but it was too far gone. It was rabid and beyond saving, but he captured a glint of who was trapped inside.

"Nia, Nascien and Arden never made it inside. The beast devoured them," Brent said, his voiced laced with horror.

Pax snapped his gaze to Brent. "What do we do to free them? Surely if we kill it, we will kill them, right?"

"I don't plan to, but I will need you to cover me." Brent removed his cloak and threw it to the side; the thud made the creature uneasy. It cocked its head in their direction. It became clear it could not see in the dark, but it certainly could hear. Brent rolled up his sleeves, this would be a battle he needed complete focus for.

There was a surge of dark energy as the malevolent creature lunged at the two friends, its contorted limbs moving in unnatural ways. Brent reacted swiftly, summoning a protective barrier of shimmering light around him and Pax. The creature's attacks collided with the barrier, sending shock-waves through the air.

Pax, armed with no weapon but his brute strength, countered the creature's onslaught by deflecting each strike. Though the creature was blind, its attacks were precise and powerful. Despite the creature's malevolence, Pax's fortitude and expertise shone through as he parried and countered, never once allowing fear to cloud his focus. He was doing this for Victoria. For Arden, Nia and Nascien. For Seraphina and for the entirety of Spell-ford. Pax dug his heels into the ground and when the creature lunged, he took hold of its limbs and gripped tightly.

"Now Brent!" Pax shouted to Brent who had stood back just enough, biding his time to launch an attack.

With a wave of his hand, he conjured bolts of radiant energy and fired them directly at the creature. Pax wrenched the creature around so that the bolts pierced through its back with unerring accuracy. The bolts of light seared through the darkness that enveloped the creature, causing it to recoil in pain. Its flesh burned and singed as it leapt away from Pax. Running around like a chicken with its head cut off, it contorted, trying to relieve the pain.

The creature didn't take long to recover before it charged at them. The air sparked with the clash of opposing forces. Pax as a sentinel shield and Brent the radiant Mage. It was almost comic book like. Their attacks were coordinated with precision that spoke of years of their bond of friendship and trust. Brent fired more bolts of light and even evoked a holy chain in which to bind the beast to one spot. Swinging it around, Brent aimed a radiant lasso and awaited the opportune time to capture the monster.

Pax pushed the creature back a final time and Brent leapt into the air, swinging the holy chain around the beast and tugging on it tightly. The chain burned at its flesh, and it fell to the ground with a loud thud. The malevolent creature, fuelled by rage and desperation, unleashed a barrage of dark tendrils that snaked through the air, surrounded by red lightning, seeking to ensnare Brent and Pax, but they dodged them with ease.

The beast writhed in pain as the chain added more pressure, burning deeper into its flesh. Not wishing to let it suffer any longer, Brent's final attack would purge the creature of any evil, but there was the risk of killing the people within. Without hesitation, Brent charged a fireball in one hand and a radiant ball of light in the other. He merged the two, joining his wrists together, and threw the ball of holy flame directly at it. The wicked beast let out a terrible scream, its twisted form writhed in agony as it pushed against the chains before it withered to the ground.

And then it was silent. Brent had done it. He vanquished the creature. The shadowy form melted from its body.

In its final moments, the dark energy dissipated into shadows, overcome by the combined might of Brent and Pax. The air, once heavy with malice, cleared, and a sense of victory washed over them.

Panting hard, they both checked themselves over for wounds. Minus a few scratches, the two men came out pretty unscathed, much to their surprise. They embraced in a victorious celebratory cheer.

"Did you see my bolts?" Brent exclaimed.

"How did you do that?" Pax asked.

"I don't know, it just—" They were interrupted by gurgling and moaning. Amongst the dissipating shadows, Arden, Nia and Nascien were lying hardly conscious. Brent and Pax rushed over to check on their companions. Arden opened his eyes first.

"Took you long enough," Arden said through a cough. Black ooze still dissipated around him. Despite his state he peered up at Brent with one eye open and mustered a slight smile.

"Yeah, well, be happy I arrived when I did." Brent crouched down on one knee and overlooked the three.

"Can someone please get me out of here!" Nia flung her hands free from the ooze over her and Pax sprung to life holding out a giant green paw, yanking her out. Nascien climbed out of the hole that was left behind by the creature.

"You think you can stand?" Brent held out a hand to Arden who grasped it tightly so Brent could pull him to his feet.

"What was that thing?" Nascien asked, scanning the area to ensure it wasn't about to reanimate.

"I am uncertain, but it felt like centuries of emotions built up, manifesting into a creature of pure evil," Nia responded.

"It doesn't matter, it is gone now," Brent reassured.

"Okay, now what, what's our plan?" Pax asked.

"We find our way in and make Marquis pay for taking my daughter," Brent ground out; eyes filled with determination. "Are you all okay to go on?" The three shook their heads and indicated he should lead the way.

The small troupe followed behind Brent as they made it to the ruins of the collapsed laboratory. Brent's heart skipped a beat. It had not changed at all over the years. Within a chasm, it was wedged at an angle within the hole, upright enough to be semi-stable. Brent was shocked that it had not fallen through over the years. The chasm below looked endless, foreboding. He pulled himself back and took in a sharp breath.

"You alright?" Arden gripped on to Brent's hand. Brent turned to face him, feeling the warmth in his body return emanating from Arden's hand.

"I have to be. Victoria needs me," Brent replied.

"Well then, it's a bit of a jump, how do we—" before Arden could finish, Pax came charging through, splitting them apart.

Pax, pushed off one foot, leaping into the air. He soared across the chasm as if aided by some unknown magic before landing on the body of ground that was supporting the lab.

"How did he do that?" Arden asked, perplexed. He turned to find Nia with her hands still raised.

"Silent Sages are full of wonder, Mr Callahan." She offered a smile. "I will use my magic and get you all over the chasm, but I will stay behind."

"Sister..." Nascien started, and she shot him a look.

"I am not as brave as the rest of you. He is my father regardless of what he has done. But to see it..." She hung her head. Silence permeated the air.

Brent placed a hand on Nia's shoulder. "It is okay, you brought me here, and for that I am grateful. I will handle the rest."

"Bring him back alive, please," she whispered. When she looked up, tears were falling down her face. "And he will face a trial for his crimes."

Brent hated this as much as she. Marquis was his mentor. A father figure and a role model.

They awaited Nia's signal and then Nascien, Arden and Brent were lifted with Nia's magic, allowing them to leap across the chasm like Pax had. Soaring across the hole, Brent looked down into the chasm. A glint of blue light emanated from below. He shook his head and focused on his destination.

Brent felt the effects of Nia's magic wane as the laboratory came into view. He braced his legs and made a soft landing, taking a few steps forward as the momentum wore off.

"What took you all so long?" Pax teased. "Where is Nia?" he asked confused, glancing back across the chasm to find her standing alone.

"She stayed behind. She is not ready to face Marquis," Brent explained and Nascien scoffed.

"Do you have something to say?" Arden interrupted, pushing past Brent and Pax, attempting to grip onto Nascien, but he darted out of reach.

"No. It was my sister's choice to stay behind," Nascien dismissed

Arden narrowed his eyes, but let it go. "How do we get inside this place?"

"Last time, the door opened on its own for Brent," Pax divulged.

"Well, by all means, Abernathy." Nascien turned and motioned Brent forward with his hands.

Brent approached the door with slight apprehension, but like before it creaked open of its own volition.

"How?" Arden looked on both disbelieving and impressed.

"I am not sure, but let's not question it, shall we?" Pax patted Arden on the back then stepped forward, crossing the threshold between the laboratory and the sunken city with Nascien right behind him. Arden lingered behind.

"Look, Brent, I need to say something," Arden stammered.

"Can it wait?" Brent asked. "I kind of want to rescue my daughter."

"No, no, you are right…" Arden waved his hands and shook his head into a smile. "I'll tell you after. Come on."

Brent smiled at him, and Arden proceeded ahead. Brent looked back at Nia. A reminder that the next steps he took would forever change both of their lives. Whether for better or worse, was yet to be seen.

CHAPTER THIRTY-SEVEN
CHILLED AIR

The air inside the lab felt heavy with forgotten memories and trauma. Each step he took echoed through the dim corridors. The tiled floor cracked under their feet from the many years spent underground. The outside was exactly how he remembered but once he stepped inside it was not the image he had in his mind.

Or was it his grief that shielded him from remembering the truth? Was the truth in his memories lost for good?

Dust mites danced in what little light filtered through the cracks in the walls and shattered windows that cast eerie shadows on the walls. The scent of old technology and ancient magic were a reminder of the experiments and secrets hidden within the laboratory's past. Brent's senses were on high alert as he navigated the labyrinthine corridors, his footsteps muffled by the layers of dust and debris.

"We are going to have to head down." Nascien pointed. "I can sense something much further below."

"Is Victoria there?" Brent asked eagerly.

"I can't say for certain, there are multiple energies...but don't let that deter you." He gave a crooked smile. Something about it didn't sit right with Brent. He wasn't completely sure if he could trust him, but Nascien was his best bet to bring Marquis to justice.

Nascien took off down the corridor while Brent, Arden and Pax followed behind. The further they descended into the depths of the lab, the more ominous the atmosphere became. Brent felt a bead of sweat trickle down his back. His mind filled with thoughts of the last time he was here. Flashes of the past unlocked from where they had been buried in his mind while he traversed through the halls. Elwin getting them lost. An energy or aura swelled around them causing them to argue. Pax finding the way to The Cradle Chamber. Elwin and Brent entering the chamber and then…Victoria.

Nascien and Pax were a way up ahead of Arden and Brent, who could not maintain his focus on anything. He kept moving forward only to stumble, planting against the wall at an angle and slipping down.

"Brent, are you okay?" Arden rushed to his side, his footsteps echoing through the corridor. He pulled Brent around by his shoulders.

As Arden came into view, Brent could only picture Elwin's face. A face he was so desperate to see again. "Elwin?" Brent slurred. He watched Elwin's mouth move but could not make out the words. "I have missed you…" Brent pulled the man before him towards him and planted a kiss on his lips. "Never leave my side again…" he bawled, and then pulled him back. "I love you, Elwin…" Brent swayed on the spot.

"Umm, you two…guys! Come quick!" Arden called and looked at Brent with concern. His eyes rolled into the back of his head. Brent's legs collapsed beneath him, and Arden helped ease him gently to the floor.

"Elwin. Why are we on the floor?" Brent asked, still slurring. "Where are we? This place looks like shit…"

"What's wrong with him?" Pax pushed Arden out of the way and sat in front of Brent. Nascien continued on without them.

"Oh, Pax…" Brent smiled. He sounded overly jovial like he had been drugged. "You're here, but you look different! You're much…balder…what happened?"

"He is suffering something…but there is nothing in the air. I don't know what it could be," Pax said, taking a sniff of the air.

"Stress?" Arden asked.

"Maybe, but he has never shown symptoms like this," Pax responded, looking at Brent with concern.

The air grew colder and as Arden exhaled, he could see his breath misting in the frigid air. His skin prickled with goosebumps and despite the coat, he was zapped of all warmth.

"Did the heat just drop in here?" Pax looked around, not taking notice of the cool air but seeing it on his breath. Arden wrapped his arms around his body attempting to keep warm and made a murmur of agreement.

From the shadows of the corridor where Nascien had been, high heeled footsteps click clacked along, making their way closer. The floor froze beneath their feet with every step. A woman approached them, her icy eyes glinting with malice.

The woman's clothes matched her icy persona. She wore a form-fitting bodysuit crafted from shimmering silvery fabric, its sleek lines stressing her lithe figure. The bodysuit was adorned with intricate patterns that resembled circuitry in the shape of snowflakes, glowing with a faint blue light that pulsed with her magical energy. Atop her bodysuit, a thin, silky robe clung to her as she glided into view. Arden knew whoever this woman was, she posed a formidable threat.

Her voice cut through the frigid air like a shard of ice as she entered, her words were laced with a chilling certainty. "Only two things can survive Frost," she declared, an ominous finality echoed as she spoke. Her gaze swept over the three of them with steely determination. Her piercing eyes locked onto her adversaries with unwavering focus.

With a flick of her wrist, she summoned a swirling vortex of icy energy. The air around her crackled with frost as her powers surged to life.

"The first," she continued as Pax stood tall, "is the unyielding resolve of a woman scorned." Her gaze lingered on Pax as he stood before her. "Those with fire in their hearts can withstand the icy grip of my power, but none yet have been able to stand the test of the ice age I can summon." She paused a moment, letting the weight of her words sink in before she continued.

"The second..." Her voice dropped to a low, ominous whisper. "Is death."

With that chilling proclamation, she raised her hand and unleashed her frigid magic upon the three of them. A blizzard blasted its way across the room, its icy tendrils reached out hungrily towards its targets. As the chill reverberated across the corridor, a barrier of warmth and resilience formed around Pax. Despite the howling winds and freezing temperatures, he stood firm. His towering figure was a bastion of the storm.

The blizzard raged and roared, but it could not penetrate the protective aura that had surrounded Pax. His newfound nullifying magic had activated out of the instinctive need to protect himself and his friends and proved it was an impenetrable force.

"How?" she demanded. "My frost can freeze even the hottest lava!"

Pax was as surprised as she, but he needed to remain focused. He stepped closer and pushed back against the icy onslaught, creating a pocket of calm amidst the chaos. With each step forward, Pax showed his strength and determination, refusing to be swept away by the blizzard's fury.

She summoned more strength and let out a scream as she focused more of her energy into the blizzard storm, but she was no match. His presence alone was a challenge to the very essence of her power. As he edged closer, panic gleamed in her eyes.

Pax gripped her wrists tightly, and the storm stopped raging. The warmth returned to the room. Arden leapt to his feet and skid across the ice sheet that had formed on the floor. As he slid to his knees, he landed beside the woman. She struggled under Pax's grip, but he would not let go, his powers nullifying her abilities.

"I'm sorry, my dear. In another life I would celebrate your powers, but for now." Arden paused, standing up and taking in a deep breath he, raised his hands around her head. She furiously shook her head and begged them to reconsider. "Lights out," Arden said, and she fell unconscious into Pax's arms.

Pax gently lowered her body to the floor.

The two men stood and looked over her body. Arden turned to Pax and placed a hand on his shoulder, like Brent always had. "So, this is your new power? It's damn impressive."

"I guess so..." He flexed his hands and forearms, amazed by his own powers. "I have no control over it, though," Pax replied sheepishly. "We should probably check on Brent..."

"Check on me for what?" He approached from behind, stopping to look at the women on the ground. "Who's that?"

"Long story, come on we will tell you on the way," Pax said, chittering his tusks at having finally received a compliment from Arden.

***

They reached the lower levels. The corridors had become more claustrophobic, growing narrower with each step. Pax had to crouch down to walk through. Brent awoke after his friends had battled off a worthy adversary with no memory of falling to the floor or his incohesive ramblings. He would feel fine, however, he could not shake the feeling of dread that gripped him tightly, like invisible hands squeezing the air out of his lungs.

His anxiety only heightening, he thought it odd they had not run into any other signs of life, that Nascien disappeared. Strange symbols and sigils adorned the walls, remnants of long-forgotten rituals and experiments.

The dim lighting flickered ominously, casting eerie shadows that seemed to move and shift in the corners of their vision. Brent could not help but feel like unseen eyes were watching them, following their every move.

Pax came to a sharp halt. Brent's head smacked directly into the back of Arden's, causing Brent to stumble backwards after both men crashed into Pax.

"What the hell, Pax?" Brent rubbed his nose and blinked furiously, trying to regain his footing.

"Look." Pax pointed to the ground and illuminated his phone to reveal a puddle of blood pooling around the corner.

"Blood!" Arden exclaimed, pulling his shoes up and following the trail in the darkness.

"What?" Brent pushed forward, following the trail. The corridor's lights had gone out. Brent pulled out his phone and ignited one of the light runes.

Holding out his phone, he pointed it forward and moved a few steps until he saw a shoe, attached to a body that lie unmoving on the floor. He raised it slowly, hoping beyond all hope it wasn't Victoria.

It wasn't his daughter, but his heart sunk anyway as he realised who the body belonged to. Blood rushed to his head, as he dropped his phone, the light swirled and illuminated the corridor.

He rushed over to Seraphina's limp body. Dropping to her side, he placed his fingers on her neck to check her pulse. She was alive, but barely.

She groaned softly, keeping her hands over her stomach. "Brent..." Blood gurgled in her throat. "It is good to see you," she coughed hard, lunging forward.

"I'm here!" Brent pushed strands of hair out of her face.

Arden picked up Brent's phone and shined the light over the two of them. The sight that came before him snatched a near inaudible gasp from his lungs. Pax stood rigid, shock coursing through his veins.

Her once vibrant eyes were now dulled with pain and exhaustion. Her breaths shallow and laboured. Blood stained her clothes, seeping from the wound in her abdomen. The smell of iron and torn flesh flooded Brent's nostrils. His heart ached as he looked at Seraphina. His mother. Her face contorted in agony, yet still bearing a sense of her rebellious nature.

"Seraphina, we're here," Brent said softly, his voice thick with emotion. He gently cradled her head in his hands, his fingers trembling against her clammy skin. "What happened? Who did this?"

Seraphina's lips parted, her words nothing more than strained whispers. "It...was...Emily," she rasped. Her voice was barely audible over the distant echoes of their surroundings. "We were trying...to escape with Victoria," she coughed, blood dribbling down her chin. Brent wiped it away. "She's alive...but..." A pained expression flickered across her face as she struggled to convey her message. "Emily, she's not who you think," she coughed again. "She's a clone...of Queen Emilia...Suncrest..."

Brent's mind reeled with the weight of Seraphina's words. Victoria being alive was all he needed to hear. He felt a surge of anger and determination welling up within him, fuelling his resolve to rescue his daughter from Marquis' clutches and put an end to this once and for all.

Brent looked to Arden. "Can we stop her bleeding?"

But as Brent returned his eyes to Seraphina, her strength waned, her gaze locked onto Brent's, a final flicker of urgency ignited in her eyes. "You have a sister," she whispered, her voice barely audible amidst the echoing darkness. "Tell Silas who you are." Brent's heart clenched at her words, the weight of her love and her sacrifice settled heavily upon him.

"I will." Brent paused, a frail smile met his lips. A long, stroking drop flowed down his cheek. He quickly wiped it away. "I promise." His voice trembled with emotion. An emotion even he wasn't sure he understood. He had barely known this woman. Sure, she was revealed to be his mother, but he didn't truly know her. So why was he crying?

Arden rushed to her other side; Seraphina turned her head. "You were one of my greatest employees." She smirked. "It is a shame what state our office has turned into after I left..." she let out a pained laugh.

Arden's eyes lit up. "Look, I can stop the bleeding, but I don't know for how long. We will need to get you to a Cleric."

Seraphina's lips curled into a faint smile. "It's okay, you can let an old lame duck die, the future is for you."

"You're not dying here!" Brent exclaimed, tears still flowing.

"Brent, step back. I will try my best," Arden said, offering a warm smile.

As he held his hands over the wound, Brent shuffled backwards and watched on. Pax came up behind him and placed a comforting hand on his shoulder. Brent raised his hand and gripped Pax's tightly. The green light forming around Arden's hand was a similar magic Brent had witnessed before. A healing magic. The light shone brightly, illuminating the corridor completely. Exposing the amount of blood she had lost.

Though he had only got to know her briefly, there was a bond shared between them. She was his mother, and he did not want it to end this way. Her breathes grew shallower with each passing minute. Brent gently stroked her leg to let Seraphina know he was there. That they were all there for her.

Arden pulled his hands away. The green light faded to a dim glow and stayed over the wound. "I have done all I can to stop the bleeding, but it is only a bandage or sorts. She will need to be looked at properly." Arden shuffled backwards on the ground.

"Why couldn't you leave me here to fucking die? I have lived long enough!" she croaked.

The three men let out a brief chuckle which was short-lived.

Two sets of footsteps approaching in the distance pulled them out of their moment of relief. The group turned their heads to the darkened corridor. Arden sprung to his feet, readying to defend them.

The shadowy figures came into view, a woman was dragging a hobbling Nascien behind her.

"Callahan?" The woman raised her voice in shocked disbelief.

"Your highness?" he exclaimed, squinting his eyes. "Emilia...I was wondering when we would bump into each other."

Brent looked between them. The woman looked so familiar; it took only a second to place it. She looked like Emily, well, a much older version of her. Could it be her mother? What was the connection?

Pax relieved Emilia from the weight of Nascien, taking it upon himself to help the injured man stand. She then rushed into Arden's arms with a warm embrace. Like two long-lost friends reunited, they planted a kiss on each cheek.

Emilia pulled back and looked at him fondly. "I see you're caught up in this too?" she asked, placing a hand on his face. "I have missed those eyes, my friend!" She ran her hands through his hair, ruffling it up. "It's been too many years." She looked around and saw Seraphina still breathed. "My goodness! How are you still alive?" she asked, rushing over to her side.

"Well, it's no thanks to you!" Seraphina called out. "Arden has patched me up."

Emilia looked up at Arden. "If we were in Suncrest, she could get the help she needs," Emilia quickly said, looking between them all and back to Seraphina.

Arden turned to face Brent and smiled. "Emilia, this is Paxton Grimtusk." He pointed to Pax, who adjusted Nascien under his shoulder and then to Brent, who had not moved from Seraphina's side. "And this is Brent Abernathy, my boyfriend," Arden said with no hesitation.

Brent's stomach flipped. Did he actually hear those words out loud?

"Ah, so you are Victoria's father?" she asked in a slightly sombre tone.

Brent could not get over how alike she and Emily looked and had so many questions. "I know my appearance has probably raised a lot of questions, but time is of the essence. Victoria chased after my, uh, how do I explain it..."

"Clone?" Brent supplemented the answer. "It's okay, Seraphina informed us."

"I am truly sorry for leaving you," Emilia apologised to Seraphina.

"Can you get me to Suncrest?" she asked.

"I thought you wanted to die?" Brent said softly.

"Well, if you are going through all the effort to keep me around, I might as well make the most of it," she snapped.

"Emilia, you have been missing for a while. If you return to the Palace, won't it raise alarm bells?" Arden questioned. Emilia squeezed Seraphina's hand, then got to her feet.

"I will be fine. But we need a portal. I know Marquis has one in this place."

"It's okay." Arden dug around in his pockets. "I have enough juice left for the trip." He pulled out his phone and handed it out toward Pax. "Grimtusk," Pax aped to attention. "I want you to take Nascien back to his sister, and then wait there, Emilia will get Seraphina to Suncrest from there."

"But I could—" Pax started, but he could tell by his face it wasn't up for discussion.

"That is an order. I have another important task I need you for." Arden disclosed with a quick smile.

"Okay, and what is that?" He twisted his lips to the side out of curiosity.

"I don't think either of us will be strong enough to take on Marquis," Arden said, and the corridor's temperature shifted. "I am just being honest."

"So, what do you propose?" Pax asked.

"Nia is the key to stopping him," Arden said.

"I think I understand." Pax smiled widely with his tusks.

"Can you stand?" Emilia asked Seraphina, who nodded. She held out two hands, and Emilia helped her up, groaning as she lurched upright. Arden watched on, hoping his magic was enough.

"Your magic better hold Callahan!" Seraphina warned him.

Arden handed Pax his Rune-Phone. "If all goes to plan, we will see each other soon." His smile was light-hearted, even if there was worry behind his eyes. Pax adjusted his hold on Nascien and was about to open the portal when Arden shouted out.

"Grimtusk!" he exclaimed, and then his tone changed. "Thanks for this, we're depending on you."

Brent and Arden stood together as the portal closed. They turned around, heading towards a destination they did not know if they would return from.

CHAPTER THIRTY-EIGHT
POISONOUS SMOG

Brent travelled alongside Arden in silence, their hands clasped tightly. There was a trail of destruction in their path. Multiple bodies of unknown people laid on the floor. It looked like a magic that had never been seen before, but the residual signal left behind screamed of his daughter, of Victoria.

The two men gave up checking for pulses after the first few had been confirmed dead. They kept looking for a sign or whisper of where Victoria might have got to.

"Were these The Code Weavers?" Arden asked.

"I don't think so."

"Wonder what did this to them?"

"I'm not sticking around to find out," Brent replied and picked up his pace.

"Brent," Arden whispered, suddenly stopping as he picked up a trace of magic further ahead.

"What?" Brent replied in the same hushed whisper.

"Listen, do you hear that?" Arden put a finger to his ear. Brent shook his head.

"I hear nothing, you're just maki—" A loud crashing noise came from further in the distance and interrupted Brent. They exchanged a glance and without saying a word sprinted towards the noise.

His heart pounding, Brent kept running, placing his feet squarely in front of him. Whatever it was, he was determined to rescue his daughter. She was too young, and she had so much more life ahead of her. Everything that had happened to her was his fault. He needed to make it up to her.

Brent and Arden raced down the corridor; the tension hung heavy. Each step brought them closer to the source of the commotion. The anticipation built with every passing moment. Finally, they turned one last corner and reached the entrance to the testing chamber.

Sounds of a fierce magical battle reverberated through the double doors and then a loud thud, as if someone had fallen from high in the air. There was a scream followed by a strange swooshing sound. Brent's heart thumped louder as he placed his hand on the door, preparing himself for what lay ahead. With a shared nod, he and Arden charged into the room, kicking the doors open.

They had entered what appeared to be some sort of training facility with a raised platform in the middle. No one appeared to be there, so what or who was making the sound? Brent noticed a body in the middle of the platform as he walked further into the room. Victoria laid there unconscious.

"Victoria!" Brent didn't hesitate to break into a sprint, rushing up the stairs and sliding across the ground to be by his daughter's side. She was unresponsive. He gave her a few lights taps on the face and shook her gently, trying to rouse her.

"Hey baby, wake up, come on!" he cried out. Arden approached slowly behind him. Cradling Victoria, he kissed her forehead and kept repeating the same words, trying to awaken her.

While Brent desperately tried to reach Victoria, a sudden silence fell over the chamber. The air crackled with tension and the hair on the back of Brent's neck stood up. Brent turned around, his heart thumping, and then froze at the sight before him.

Standing at the far end of the platform, Marquis towered over them, his black cloak billowing in the otherworldly aura that surrounded him. As he stepped forward, dark lightning generated around his boots as the pressure of his presence created cracks in the platform's surface. His expression was unreadable as he regarded Brent with a cold, calculating gaze.

Arden attempted to leap up the stairs and lunge an attack at Marquis from behind, but it was futile. As if in slow motion, without a word, Marquis raised his hand and Arden was instantly immobilised, frozen in place by some unseen force. Brent's eyes widened in shock as he watched Arden be thrown across the room with ease. When he landed, the curse took hold of him, rendering him rigid and lifeless. Brent looked back at Marquis. His eyes filled with rage.

"Marquis!" Brent shouted. His voice trembled with fury and his arms shook while he held Victoria. He placed her down gently and stood, facing Marquis. "What do you want with my daughter?" he demanded.

Marquis did not immediately respond. Instead, he curled his lips into a cruel smile and took a quiet step forward, his hands now placed firmly behind his back. His gaze did not shift from Brent.

"Ah, Abernathy," he replied, his voice saturated with malice. This was not the Marquis Brent remembered. He had been corrupted. "I believe you already know the answer to that question." He stepped to the left of the platform and bounced on his heels, clicking them together and then standing still. "Victoria is special, the first true Aesir and human hybrid born from The Cradle. She possesses many gifts from yourself, a Monarch Child, and her other father, Elwin. A man with a long and ancient celestial lineage."

"So, what? She isn't some test subject for you perform experiments on!" Brent roared back at him, his mouth full of poison for his once admired mentor.

"She is unlike any other Mage I have come across. Not even those Monarch Children under Spellford could compare to the likes of her potential." He did not move from his spot and Brent dared not take his eyesight off him, even refusing to blink. "Her power could change the course of history itself and I intend to harness her power for myself." His face changed to a sombre look. "To return them to me!"

Brent looked on and could see the very reflection of himself in Marquis. This man was aching from unending pain. Grieving from the loss he had experienced. The only difference was his wife was still alive. She was unwell, as Nascien and Nia pointed out, but she was alive.

"But Marquis, she is alive..." Brent pleaded.

"Don't talk to me as if you know anything of what I am going through!" he shouted. Brent stayed silent. Their eyes met for a moment, Marquis lowered his guard and Brent could see he was still in his early stages of dealing with this loss.

"I have been unfair to you," Brent started softly. "I have had my entire life to deal with losing Elwin, but your loss was so sudden."

His words hung in the room's air. It was a rare moment of vulnerability between the two. Marquis remained silent, his expression a mixture of pain and resignation. Brent could see on his face that Marquis knew he was telling the truth, yet the weight of his grief was not allowing him to believe it. Marquis' eyes fell to the floor.

"I understand your desperation to save her," Brent continued, pleading with the man he once admired as his teacher. The man he modelled himself after for a father figure. "I'd have done anything to bring Elwin back, but Victoria is not the answer. Stealing her powers will only bring more suffering."

Marquis lifted his gaze back to Brent. His eyes, bloodshot, tears welling in the corners. "Do not talk about this like you understand!" he bellowed, creating a small gust around the room, generated from his aura. "I lost them. I was meant to protect them, and I couldn't. But I refuse to give up," he declared, raising a hand into a fist. "Even if it means sacrificing the entire world!"

Brent sighed and hung his head. He could see he was beyond reasoning. Their paths had diverged forever, and the rift between them seemed wider than ever. Yet, deep down, Brent could not help but feel pity for the man standing before him. Consumed by his grief and blinded by desperation.

"Please let me leave with Victoria and the others and I will put this all behind us," Brent begged one last time, a final plea. "We can help each other like we once did." Marquis looked up, a glimmer of hope in his eyes. "With the help of the Mage's Union," Brent finished.

Marquis tilted his head, his eyes glowed bright, like white fiery flames.

"I won't ask again, let us all go," Brent shouted, and he aimed his hand directly at Marquis, conjuring a ball of fire and launching it at him. Marquis dodged the fireball, de-materialising in front of Brent only to pop back up before him.

"Now, Abernathy, you are definitely going to need to do better than that," he mocked him.

Brent didn't take a second to react and conjured a sphere of radiant energy into Marquis' face, narrowly missing him as he disappeared and reappeared again.

"Oh!" Marquis chortled, taking enjoyment in the battle. "Turning up the heat, are we?" He toyed with Brent.

Brent had outsmarted him before, but would he fall for the same trick twice? There was only one way to find out. As he attempted to land multiple hits on Marquis, he kept a watch on Victoria, hoping she would stir, and they could make a run for it. He attempted blow after blow, but Brent was too slow and too distracted. He missed every shot.

"Maybe I spoke too soon. For a Monarch Child, you are pretty pathetic, whereas I, well here, why don't you experience it yourself!" Marquis held out his hand, a dark black bolt of magical energy pulsated, cracking and juddering through the air at all angles towards Brent. The dark magic landed its blow directly at Brent, flinging him off his feet and sending him flying across the ground. He went skidding toward Victoria.

Marquis floated around the testing stage erratically as Brent darted around to keep his focus on him. Marquis was too fast, his eyes couldn't keep up, Brent struggled to stay on top of him, firing rounds of fireballs in all directions, hoping one would land.

"Come on, this is the best you have?" he asked out loud. "I expected much better. Consider me very disappointed."

Brent leapt to his feet. Hearing the last words incited the rage in him further. Brent let out a puff of hot air from his mouth as the fire burned in his belly.

Conjuring the same radiant magic from before he flung it towards Marquis'. As it flew, Brent made to sprint sideways and started firing rounds of magic bolts, leaping from side to side and throwing them above Marquis' head. Round after round he conjured them, and they hung immobile in the air. Either Marquis didn't pay any attention to Brent's attempts, or he was too overconfident to care.

"You missed every shot!" Marquis cackled.

Brent returned to his spot and stood tall, he had mere seconds to enact his plan and attempt an escape.

"My turn!" Marquis had a glint in his eyes paired with a wicked smirk.

Marquis charged toward him. This was Brent's moment to strike. With adrenaline coursing through his veins, he took in a deep breath and raised his hand. He waited for the opportune moment when Marquis reached the middle of the platform and then Brent lowered his hand. The balls of radiant light rained down onto the platform, searing the metallic structure like it was acid rain. Pouring like a torrential storm, Marquis attempted to dodge them all one by one, but they pelted unmercifully towards the ground.

Marquis' attempt to dodge one, resulted in another sphere hitting its mark, making impact with Marquis' back, pushing him to the ground. Brent released the rest of the radiant rounds. Marquis groaned in pain from the pummelling. Dust swirled up as the attack got fiercer. Round after round they fell, creating a small torrential storm of holy rain.

The attack ended, and Brent stood tall, panting from burning into his energy reserves on the attack. He didn't want to admit it, but Marquis might be out of his league.

As the dust settled, Brent squinted through at the black form standing on the opposite side.

"You cannot defeat me, Abernathy!" Marquis called out to Brent, who was still catching his breath. "It will be only a matter of time before your magic will wane!"

"And by that time, we will have escaped!" Brent exclaimed through a pant.

Marquis smirked and dematerialised from view, the air crackling around where he disappeared from. Brent darted around; panic striking him hard. He scoured every corner of the room.

"I admit you have done well." Marquis' voice whispered around him. Brent darted up and looked around, but he could not see him. Echoes of his voice clung to the surrounding air. Taunting Brent and making him unnerved.

"Show yourself!" Brent demanded.

"As you wish!" he cried out from behind him.

In his peripherals, Brent could see Marquis propel himself off the wall and conjure the same dark bolts from before. This time they were dark, sharp, jagged tendrils, acting like extra limbs. Brent attempted to duck down, but Marquis was too fast for him. One tendril caught him and scooped him up like a spider hunting its prey. Marquis's shadowy bindings caught Brent, suspending him in the middle of the air on a dark cloud. Brent fumbled on the cloud and released an ear-piercing scream as one tendril pierced through his back like a spear.

"Perhaps some venom will shut you up!" Marquis called out. The tendril gurgled as it forced the shadowy substance into Brent's body.

Where the tendril pierced through Brent's skin, the black venom trickled down mixed with blood falling to the floor. Writhing in pain, Brent cried out louder. In his mind, all he could think of was how he failed Victoria and Arden, Paxton and the rest. He had failed them all.

The pain seared both hot and freezing cold at the same time. He could feel the venom invading his body and as much as he wanted to resist it, his body went numb. His arms fell to his sides and his legs went limp.

Marquis let out a sinister laugh, which pierced through the air, causing Victoria to stir. She opened her eyes, still blurred at the edges, she struggled to see the scene playing out before her.

Her senses gradually returned to her. The first image that came together was a blurry vision of her father. For a split moment, she was happy. He was here with her now. She wasn't alone. Her eyes fluttered closed and she remembered exactly where she was. Her eyes popped open. Above her, Brent was suspended in mid-air on pike like tendrils through his back. Marquis floated upwards, each tendril extending from his body, pumping a black smog substance into him.

"Dad!" Victoria screamed out. Marquis cast an unaffected glance in her direction before he scoffed and continued.

Victoria's heart pounded. The horrifying spectacle before her made her sick to her stomach. She tried to move, to intervene, but her body felt heavy, sluggish and weak. Her memories were hazy. She felt as if she had transformed again. Panic surged through her veins, she struggled against her own limitations. Desperation clawing at her mind.

Her gaze locked onto her father suspended above her. His body wracked with agony, and he cried out in pain. Marquis's tendrils pierced deeper into his flesh. Tears streamed from her eyes as a surge of helplessness washed over her. She couldn't bear to see her father in such torment. To witness his suffering at the hands of this vindictive enemy.

She felt her heart thump louder and before she knew it; she was standing upright. With a rush of fortitude, she forced herself to push past her own physical limitations. Drawing upon every ounce of her strength, she reached deep within herself. Into her magic, focusing on her energy and breaking free from the restraints in her mind that held her back. Her body was ablaze with determination to save her father.

Her breathing became strained as the heat rose in her body when the intensity of her power surged forth.

"You are too late to save your father, stupid girl!" Marquis snarled at her.

A brilliant shimmering light enveloped her, illuminating the surrounding chamber, ricocheting off the metallic walls. The tendrils that held Brent suspended above began to weaken and fray under the force of her magic, their dark grip loosening with each moment the light shined. With a last burst of effort, Victoria let out an ear-piercing scream, shattering the tendrils, completely freeing her father from their hold.

Marquis let out a painful groan as the dark energy retracted. Ignoring the protests of her exhausted body, she willed her body forward, her mind singularly focused on reaching her father before he crashed into the ground.

Marquis' attention turned towards her. His eyes filled with lustful malice realising the level of threat she posed. Victoria was undeterred. She glided with ease, like a graceful ice skater, she sliced across the surface of the platform and with every movement she drew closer to her father. Her resolve was unyielding. Marquis had caught up with her, he reached out his hands to grasp her, but when touched her skin, his own flesh singed like he had been branded with a white-hot poker.

He could not touch Victoria. He attempted to lunge at her once, but she pivoted quickly, gripping hold of his face with her bare hands and refused to let go. Marquis cried out in agony as his flesh burned. Her hands were a holy flame of radiance, gifted from the unknown. Her powers no longer required complete transformation; they came instinctual. She could hurt her adversary with a simple touch.

Victoria summoned her energy, focusing it into her hands and pushed them forwards, sending Marquis flying across the room. She dashed around in a blink of light, throwing out her arms as she skidded across the ground taking hold of her father's limp body. The dead weight caused her to crumble forward.

Marquis continued to cry out in agony, gripping his smouldering face, the skin bubbling into large, painful blisters.

Victoria lifted Brent's head. He opened his eyes weakly. They were bloodshot and dull. Brent had been zapped of all energy from within. Dark veins protruded to the surface around his temples and weaved their way to his eyes. Whatever Marquis had injected him with was killing him. Fast. He forced a smile and reached out to stroke her face.

"My everything..." His words were weak, barely uttered before his eyes rolled into the back of his head.

"Dad!" She shook his lifeless body, cradling him in her arms. "I need you, Dad. I can't do this on my own..." Sorrowful tears fell down her face onto Brent's. As they did, they began to shimmer and glow. Through her clouded eyes, Victoria blinked. Did her tears hold an unusual mystical radiance in them that could purge Marquis' venom?

Victoria placed her thumb where the tear fell and dragged it across his face, along his arm, to his palm. Then she placed her other hand on his heart.

"It's okay, Victoria," Brent groaned, his eyes half shut, gripping hold of her hand. He was smiling. He always smiled at her. Why did he have to smile at her in a time like this? He was in so much pain. Couldn't he show that to her, be vulnerable with her? Instead of always trying to show strength, to be an unbreakable father.

"Before I go, there is something you must know..." His breathing was shallow and laboured, unable to keep his eyes open long.

"Shhh, Dad, no don't..." She didn't want to say goodbye, her voice filled with grief. Tears filled her eyes as the weight of his body increased in her arms.

"This is important, you are *my* daughter..." he said.

What a dumb thing to say. Of course, she was his daughter...she replayed the words, how he emphasised *my,* it clicked. He didn't mean adoptive. It all began to make sense. How her abilities were like his, why they looked so similar, her one human ear. Why did he hide it from her for so long?

"What would I do without you?" she asked him, tears falling down her face.

"What you always have done, make me proud." He smiled once more before his head fell to the side as he passed out. Victoria refused to believe this was real.

Victoria's eyes darted around the room. Arden remained motionless in the corner. Marquis had stopped screaming in pain. She was alone. There was no one else that could help her.

"Heal my father!" she demanded to no one. To the cosmos. To whoever had the power to grant her wish. She closed her eyes and focused her powers on her desired result. Just like when she showed off levitating the statue in her school, this was the same. But she was so tired, she didn't know how much she had left in her. She pushed all her energy into her palms and syphoned it into his chest, trying to restart his heart. Nothing happened.

Victoria hugged her father and sobbed as his body became cold. The life draining from him.

Marquis' footsteps echoed from behind her as he could no longer float across the ground. Victoria turned her head and looked at him. She raised her hand to send a blast towards him, but nothing came. She had nothing left in her reserves. An empty well, whose bucket was just scrapping the bottom of the muddy surface.

Marquis laughed a low, rumbling snicker. It echoed in Victoria's ears. "He is dead. Everyone who will ever protect you will die Victoria, don't you see?" he said, edging closer. "Give me your power and I can revive them all."

Victoria contemplated giving up her powers. She was tired and wanted the suffering to end. She hung her head and gave into the inevitable. They had tried but Marquis was too strong for them. She had failed to protect her family.

The doors to the room were thrust open. "Get away from her, Marquis!" Pax roared, bursting through the doors. He rushed through the room like a charging rhino and his target was Marquis. Victoria felt the breeze rush past her as she sprinted after him.

There was one other person in the room, close behind Pax. Nia. Victoria's heart raced, filling with warmth, the helpless expression on her face began to fade. She could wonder how Nia got here later. Victoria was just glad to see her.

"Victoria! Thank goodness, you are alive!"

Victoria's tears blurred her vision, but she smiled hearing her voice.

"Oh no, Brent!" The look on Nia's face brought back the dread in Victoria's heart. "What happened?" Nia's voice remained calm even with the problems they faced.

"Marquis, he...injected my dad with...something," Victoria stammered.

Nia held her hand on his chest, closing her eyes, she inhaled silently. As she exhaled, she opened her eyes. "He is still alive, but barely." She turned around while her hand was still placed on Brent and looked over to the side. "Arden, he's...?"

"Petrified, or dead...I am not sure." Victoria said in a rush, she was frantic and losing the ability to control herself. "I'm losing everyone around me," Victoria sobbed loudly. Nia pulled Victoria against in a tight embrace.

"I need you to be strong for me," Nia said. She held Victoria's face in her hands wiping the tears from her eyes.

Nia felt like the sister Victoria never got to have. Someone to look up to, to admire. The type of person she would strive to be. Nia smiled and looked beyond her to where Pax and Marquis were struggling. Pax had Marquis in a chokehold, but Marquis turned to smog and slithered free.

"I am going to put an end to this," she said, her jade eyes ignited with a deep flame. "Like I should have years ago." She rested her hand on Victoria's shoulder and got to her feet.

Nia glided slowly over the platform past Victoria, turning back, she conjured a shield around Victoria and Brent, extending her fingers in a circular motion. A circle of yellow light illuminated around Victoria as the shield came into existence. Nia's Silent Sage magic felt as powerful as she remembered from their training. Victoria could kick herself. Had she trained more, resisting the temptation to spend time with Emily, she would have been better prepared. In hindsight, it was her biggest regret. The warmth of the conjured shield encompassed her surroundings. She gazed down at her father, who was slowly breathing.

"Hold on dad," she whispered and kissed his forehead.

CHAPTER THIRTY-NINE

THE VOID KING

Nia moved with a grace like Pax had never seen before. She appeared to his side while Pax struggled to fight and hold on to Marquis. Pax had Marquis cornered using shields he conjured with App-Magic.

"I'll take it from here, go check on Arden." She pointed in Arden's direction.

Pax leapt off the platform and down into the chamber, running towards Arden. He skidded along the floor, rolling his body over Arden's.

"Hello Grimtusk, I knew we would see each other again." He tried to force a smile, but his body below his neck remained rigid. "Help a boy up, won't you?" Pax held out a giant hand, and Arden gripped it. Upon Pax's touch the curse faded, and Arden's limbs became mobile. With a groan, he was able to stand but was still a little unstable. "I'll be fine, just give me a second."

Pax looked back to Nia who stood in a stand-off with her father.

"Nia," Marquis said, his voice croaking.

"Where is my father?" she asked.

"I am right here," his voice cracked.

"Whatever you are, you are not him. My father would have sensed me arriving, so I ask again," Nia paused, her eyes narrowed, "where is my father?" She remained calm. Much calmer than she expected she would be.

"You are clever girl." Marquis' voice changed, his body shifting, contorting and changing form. "I'll give that pathetic, desperate old coot something, he was right. He told me you would be a problem."

Nia's eyes widened. She didn't recognise the voice, but she remembered the face. It was a Fae of by the name...

Oh! why couldn't she remember it?

"Cyrus?" Arden croaked from the opposite side of the room.

"You are the last king of Erimosia!" Hearing the name, Nia was hit with the realisation of how she knew this Fae.

"You are your father's favourite for a reason," he replied, vitriol in his voice. His eyes were red and bloodshot. His face badly burned. The attack by Victoria had left scars, his skin was cracked, leaving dark crevices, as if his face might detach from itself.

"Where is my father?" she demanded again.

"Oh, he has been out of the picture for quite some time. I got bored with tormenting him while I moved all the pieces into place. When I murdered the original Arch Mage and absorbed his powers, I got an insatiable lust. Marquis promised to find me a suitable avenue, but the street rat children weren't enough!" he spat.

"What did you do?" Arden asked, adjusting his footing as he shuffled up the platform with Pax.

"It was all Marquis, really. He came looking here for more information about The Cradle Technology and I called out to him from the void." Cyrus' skin glistened from the shifting form. The translucent shimmering glow moving as he did. "He removed the firmament that prevented me from entering this realm, and then I made a deal with him. In exchange for his service, I would find him the means to bring his wife back."

"So, you lied to him?" Nia asked, trying to understand what was happening while also stalling for time. The shield she had generated was replenishing Victoria of her energy. Nia knew she couldn't fight and win, but with Victoria's potential, Nia believed Victoria could if she was pushed far enough.

"It was simple, he led me to Abernathy," he exclaimed loudly. "Marquis had studied the Monarch Children for ages, his knowledge was delicious." He licked his lips "But it was only when I read the reports about Abernathy's daughter...your reports. That is when things changed."

"Me? What did I do?"

"You gave the Mage's Union information about the girl's potential." Cyrus gave a sly smile.

"I follow protocol, always," Nia replied sternly. "I mandatorily reported her status as a powerful Mage."

"And that little report was all I needed to know she was my next target. She is the true Monarch Child that would help me unlock the void, but I needed to bide my time. Her powers were still dormant, so I pushed her a bit, played with her to get them to activate."

"Why did you do all this, though?" Arden begged, moving forward on his own. He stalled behind Nia, there was a pressure between them. He could not penetrate it. Arden focused and realised it was an energy transfer. The shield she had generated was a clever disguise.

Pax crouched down beside Brent and Victoria. He stroked her hair as she sobbed. Arden's heart ached to see Brent barely holding on to life, but he could feel a small energy signal coming from him. It was faint, but he was fighting to stay alive. But like a candle flickering in the wind, one big gust and it could go out. They needed to act quickly. Arden gathered his resolve, garnered from the rising anger of seeing those he cared for hurt.

"Where is the original Magnar?" Arden asked through gritted teeth.

"Dead, like Marquis. Once I was done with them, I chucked them to the void." Cyrus threw his hand out and imitated dropping something. "But to answer your other question, Callahan, it was simple. I needed power. Power to free the others from the void. I am their king, and a king must lead their people home."

"Home? This reality is not yours anymore," Arden stated.

"On the contrary, my dear, naïve man, we are in their home right now."

"What are you saying?" Nia asked.

"This is Erimosia, is it not? When the void opened that day, we were all sucked in." Cyrus said simply.

"So, Nia was right—" Arden was cut off.

"Yes! I am Erimosian. The Last King. We have all been wandering lost in the void for years with no way out. But it wasn't until that man entered, that Aesir..." Cyrus grew sombre. "His..." Cyrus pointed at Brent and Arden knew he was referring to.

"Elwin?" he asked.

"I don't know the name, he never said, but I knew when he fell in that we could step out," Cyrus said.

"You've been gone for decades, centuries even. Why return now?"

"Wouldn't you want to bask in the light after being in the dark for so very long?" Cyrus asked him simply, holding his arms out beside him. "That man and Abernathy created a child in this very room with The Cradle. She is the essence of all Erimosia's citizens, created from Augmenti! When The Cradle activated, creating the girl, the magic was unstable, sending him into the void, but when he fell...it opened the path for us. I stepped through, time exists differently across the threshold you see. But all that time in the void had drained me of natural magic, I needed power. I was a mere husk. Marquis restored me and he took me to meet the Arch Mage. I played along, and that's when I turned on them both," he explained. Nia and Arden stayed silent, knowing they needed to bide their time.

"The power she possesses, her energy and potential, it is unlike any Erimosian before her. She is our saviour. She can open the void and bring my, *her* people home. Is that so wrong?"

"You mean to kill her, Cyrus, and I will not allow it!" Arden shouted. "You have hurt countless people in your quest for power. I refuse to allow you to get your hands on Victoria!"

"You played us all for fools the entire time!" Pax roared, looking up at Cyrus. He did not know what came over him. He dropped Victoria's hand, stood and shifted through the shield barrier. It glitched as he walked through, shimmering around him.

"Well, obviously," he sneered. "And what credulous fools to play. Her potential, her energy are unlike anything I've ever encountered. I will swat you all like flies and bring my people home. I will let Abernathy live on with his grief, like the benevolent God I am."

Nia's heart raced. She knew she had to keep Cyrus talking if the energy transfer was to work, just like it did the evening she found Victoria passed out from transforming. Every moment was precious, allowing Victoria to gather her strength.

"So, you would kill her for that? Take a life and for what?" Nia demanded. The hurt of knowing her father was dead bubbled up underneath. "Not much of a God if a teenage girl holds you back!"

"For my people, I would sacrifice anything," Cyrus said coldly. "Life is there to be used. You cannot comprehend the suffering we have endured in the void. We are a people lost to time, stripped of our home, our legacy. Victoria's power is the key to our salvation."

"You are wrong." Pax spoke again. "She is the legacy of your people, don't you see? The last living remnant of Erimosia!" He didn't even know what he was saying, but it sounded convincing.

"There has to be another way," Nia pleaded, her voice growing desperate.

"There is no other way!" Cyrus roared, his form flickering with unstable energy. "The void demands a sacrifice. It craves the life force of Erimosians. Of the Monarch Children. Her death is inevitable, it is destiny!"

Nia felt a flicker of fire in the back of her chest. Victoria's energy was peaking. She hung her head and looked back at Cyrus, her eyes filled with a mix of pain and determination. "You say you are their king, Cyrus. A king should protect his people, not sacrifice innocent lives. If you were truly a king, you would find another way."

Cyrus's eyes blazed with anger, the cracks on his face deepened. "You know nothing of kingship! Of the burdens I carry!" he spat at her. "This is the only way!"

"Then, I pity you," Nia said. Stepping backwards towards Victoria.

"Pity? Me?" Cyrus said and then noticed the white aura building around Victoria. "Wait, what have you done?" he asked, panic in his voice. Nia stripped the shield away and knelt beside Victoria.

"Your turn, I will take watch of your father," she said, caressing her cheek.

Victoria's body raised out of her control.

Pax pulled Arden backwards, scooping up Brent as he walked past, pulling them a safe distance from where Victoria and Cyrus stood. Nia backed away slowly, following Pax's lead. "Your plan better work. Brent won't take lightly to you using Victoria as a puppet."

"I'm not. She is completely conscious. You have my word."

Victoria's body was surrounded in powerful, flickering white aura. She turned to Cyrus, the power within her stronger than she had felt before. Her eyes glowed with radiant power. She blinked the shields around Cyrus shattered in a burst of magic. The force of the blast from a simple flutter of her lids sent him reeling. He quickly scampered to his feet. His eyes filled with pure rage.

"You cannot kill me!" Cyrus bellowed, gathering dark energy in his hands.

"I don't intend to." Victoria's voice echoed through the room. "I will un-write your wrongs and return you to the place you came from! You reign ends here Weaver, Void King, Cyrus. Whatever pitiful name and path you choose in the next life. Choose one of peace!" Her voice echoed with a metallic tinge as energy flowed through her.

Cyrus charged forward, black energy crackling with purple lighting following his path, but Victoria was too fast. She could see everything. Every atom of existence. Every bit of time as it played out. She could shift amongst it seamlessly and play its chords like heaven-sent music. She was the legacy of the Erimosian people. She slipped out of reality and dived through time, revisiting her favourite moments, her saddest ones too. The time sped from her fingertips and pulled her all the way to the beginning of her life. The Cradle's hatch opened and there was Brent's smile face before her. She could hear herself crying out. She had just been born by the love of both Elwin and Brent. Brent pulled her out of the cradle and then handed her to Pax. Her spirit dashed out of the baby's body and she watched on from above as her father was calling out into the void.

She floated down and gently rested a hand on her father's shoulder, whispering words of love and encouraging him that everything would be okay. She wanted to stay with him forever. Watch over him. But she had to move on. Go back and save them all from Cyrus. But, she halted for what felt like forever. She had a thought. Victoria sped past Brent and dove into the void. Plunging deep into the darkness, she moved fast, gliding through the emptiness like a comet in the night's sky. She saw a man tumbling and went to him. She took his hand in hers and instantly felt the warmth of an Aesir. They locked eyes.

"I recognise those eyes, that pointed ear...you are my daughter!" he said proudly and smiled at her. In the darkness she could not quite make out his face but his blue eyes were visible from the aura of Augmenti still flowing through him. And his smile, it was like hers.

"You know who I am?" she asked in the challenging way she would with Brent.

"An Aesir can recognise their own kin, even if that one is Erimosian made." His eyes glowed again. Elwin began to speak in a language foreign yet entirely familiar to her. Like song lyrics she had forgotten he sang it out to her and she recognised and understood what he said.

ᛏᛁᛘᛁ ᛁᛋ ᛏᛁᚹᚹᚹᛁᚱᛁᚼᛏ ᚹᚨᚱ ᚢᛋ ᛘᛁ ᚹᛉᛁᛚᛏ ᛁ ᛋᚨᚾ ᛁᚨᚾ ᚹᚨᛘᛁᚨ ᛘᚨᚼᛁ

ᚹᛁᚨᛏᚢᚱᛁᛁᛋ ᚨᚹᚨ ᛒᚾᛏ ᛁ ᚱᛁᚹᚾᛋᛁᛏ ᛏᚨ ᚾᛁᛏ ᛒᚱᛁᚨᛏ ᛒᛁ ᚦᛁ ᚨᛏᛁ ᛏᚨ ᚹᚨᛁᛁ ᛒᛁ

ᚹᚨᚨᛏ ᛏᚨ ᛒᚱᛁᚨᛏ ᚹᚨᚱ ᛘᛁ ᛉᛁ ᚢᛁᛚᛁ ᚼᛁᛁᛏ ᛋᚨᛘᛁᚨᛁ ᛏᚨ ᚱᛁᚾ ᚨᛏ ᛏᚨᚾ ᚦᛏᛏ ᛁ

ᛏᛘ ᚹᚨᛁ ᚹᚱᚨᛘ ᚦᛁᛋ ᚱᛏᛘ ᛁᚨᚾ ᛏᚱᛁ ᚦᛁ ᛚᛁᚹᚨᛘᛁ ᚨᚹ ᚨᚢᚱ ᛚᚨᚾᛁ

Victoria's eyes began to swell with tears. He pulled her close and gently placed his forehead to hers. All she could think was how he should be saved. How she wished she could decree it. But she couldn't change this moment in time. No one could. Not even the Tutelary. She finally felt that missing piece in her life, her missing half, the father she never got to meet, except in this brief moment. And it was being pulled from her as fast as it arrived.

She wanted to stay there forever and ask him all the questions she always had on her mind.

But she could not...he smiled one last time and then let go. Plunging forever into the darkness of the void.

With a blink, she was pulled back to the present. Back into the action. Cyrus charged in her direction.

"I'm sorry King of Erimosia, your time is done!" Victoria raised her hands, and a barrier of shimmering light enveloped Cyrus, trapping him in place. "You are not worthy of returning to your people." She shifted forward, leaning in, looking him over. "What to do..." The barrier tightened, squeezing the dark energy out of Cyrus.

Cyrus screamed in fury and pain as three gold threads were purged from his body, pulsating out at different angles. One floated towards Brent and Pax made to swat it away but Arden stopped him.

"No, this is his energy, Victoria is undoing everything," he explained. "Lay him down."

Pax did as he was told, and the gold thread connected to Brent's heart. He jolted as if he had been shocked by electricity.

Two other threads spread out, they began to take shape, each of them forming a body.

Cyrus continued to scream out in pain. His form violently flickering. "No! You cannot do this! I am the King of Erimosia!"

Nia stepped forward, her heart pulsating with adrenaline. Arden watched the gold threads weave together the very fabric of a human form; their identities slowly became recognizable.

"Nia, that's your father!" Arden pointed toward the ethereal form of Marquis taking shape on the platform.

"Dad!" Nia cried out.

"My dear, Nia." His normal voice a comfort to her ears. "Stay back, let Victoria vanquish this evil."

"I will expunge you of all darkness, Cyrus," Victoria breathed. He attempted to break free, the barrier weakening enough for him to pull an arm free. Cyrus conjured a beam of dark energy, shooting it directly at Nia. Victoria's emotions took over. She could not stop the beam and Cyrus all at once. It was a written moment in time, just like Elwin's death.

Pax rushed forward. "Nia, look out!" He pushed her out of the way and took the full force of the blast.

"Pax!" Victoria cried out, but no audible words came out of her mouth. She lost control, her emotions unstable. She threw her hands down, and the barrier squeezed even tighter. She took hold of his free arm and ripped it right out of its socket. He cried out in pain, but no blood spurted forth, instead black smog emptied into the air. Whipping it around, she walloped Cyrus with his own arm before she dropped it. She stared him dead in the eyes. "Perish!"

Panic rose in his eyes. He shook his head. "No, no don't!"

"Your reign ends here. You are not king, just a husk of what you once were!" Victoria snapped her fingers, and the barrier squeezed him one last time as white flame engulfed all around him.

With a final, desperate roar, Cyrus's form disintegrated into a burst of bright light. A blast wave from his energy dissipated into the air, sending everyone in the group backwards, except for Victoria, who floated through it with ease. She hovered towards Pax's body. He was cold.

The room went silent as the echoes of Cyrus's screams faded away. Touching between Pax's brows, Victoria imbued some of her energy into him, reverting the damage of Cyrus' blast that had been too strong for his newly discovered nullifying magic.

Pax gasped for air as life returned to him. "*Ow!* That fucking hurt."

Victoria laughed as she returned to her normal state, her eyes still glowing with residual power. "Are you okay?"

"I am thanks to you." Pax reached up and stroked her cheek.

Victoria released a sigh of relief, but he wasn't the only one she needed to check on.

"Dad?" Victoria said softly.

Brent sat up with ease, having returned to the state he was in before Cyrus attacked him. "I'm...fine," he said in disbelief, inspecting his hands and touching his face. He felt normal.

"Good, because I—" Victoria's voice cut out as she fainted. Pax caught her. Brent stood up, shakey at first, and then looked at Pax with a smile.

"She is fine. Just passed out," Pax said, looking her over for any sign of injury.

"She's been through a lot," Brent replied.

"We all have." Arden came up beside him and grabbed his hand.

The ethereal form of Marquis had not disappeared with the demise of Cyrus. Nia stood with him, the two spoke in hushed tones, the air around them emotionally charged. There was no telling how much time they had left.

The other ethereal being wasn't clearly recognisable. It looked like Cyrus, but not as damaged.

"Wait, is that...no it can't be...Magnar?" Arden exclaimed, dropping Brent's hand and rushing over.

"Watch over her," Brent asked of Pax before he followed behind Arden.

"We're not going anywhere," Pax chortled, his eyes forming tears. "Thank God you survived Victoria," he whispered to her and stroked her hair behind her pointed ear. "I couldn't handle your father alone." A smile formed on her face as if she could hear him.

"We have little time, but Magnar, this is Brent Abernathy." Arden gave a quick introduction when Brent approached.

"Brenton?" Magnar asked. "You look young again. What happened?"

"No, no." Arden shook his head. "This is Seraphina's—you know what, it doesn't matter. Where will you go from here?"

"Not sure, I've never had my soul, my essence, drained by a Void King before." Magnar's reply held a hint of humour. He appeared happy. At ease. It comforted Brent. "We never got to know each other, but I can tell I am leaving this world in the right hands." He smiled and closed his eyes as his form disappeared. Arden looked to Brent, who had a tear form in his eye.

"Are you crying, Brent?" Arden asked, pulling him closer.

"I am exhausted and overwhelmed. I feel relieved but also so much sorrow. I know it will get better, but I can't help but be emotional," Brent said quietly. Brent made to turn, but Arden pulled him back and looked at him like he never looked at him before.

"There is something about you, Brent. You ignite my world in cherry blossoms and glitter. I feel so elated when I'm around you." With a tender gesture, Arden pulled him in for a lingering kiss, and Brent reciprocated by staying close. Brent felt comfort in Arden's arms.

"Did we actually win?" Brent asked when he pulled back from their kiss. His head was spinning, but he wasn't sure if it was from the battle or the kiss he and Arden shared. "And with minimal casualty?"

"Seems that way," Arden replied.

Brent looked around the room at the small group that had defeated Cyrus. Nia stood beside her father, who began to disappear.

"Take care, Abernathy," Marquis whispered, his voice echoed around the room. Brent smiled, chills running all over his body.

Nia stared with remorse at the spot where her father had stood. Everything had changed for them, as Brent predicted. The life in her face drained as she realised her father would no longer be there for her.

CHAPTER FORTY
RED LIGHTNING

The experiments that Marquis, now revealed as Cyrus, the King of Erimosia who entered through from void, had subjected Victoria to had taken a bigger toll than any transformation could. Though the final transformation healed her physically, her mental health had taken a toll. Many nights after they returned from Erimosia, she had nightmares that kept her up. Flashes of her taking innocent lives as she slashed through corridors in her other form. The scars of the betrayal by Emily lived on within her. But she kept it all to herself. She knew it would pass if she gave it time.

Victoria meandered through the Mage's Union grounds. This wasn't her first time, but it was the first time on her own. Her father had organised for her to meet with one of the Psycholomage's. She agreed as she felt she could use the help in dealing with all the trauma. It had been a month since they all left the Erimosia ruins, but the scars ran deep.

It fell on the same day as the public memorial service for the fallen Arch Mage Magnar and Marquis Beaumont. Seraphina had remained in Suncrest but was officially the Elder for international affairs on the Spellford Council and arranged everything for her fallen comrades as the Mage's Union tried to recover from the damage caused by Cyrus.

Victoria followed her father's instructions, on a poorly hand-drawn map, to his office. Since the kidnapping and almost losing him, she had cut him some slack at how he treated her. Victoria was grateful for everything he offered her. They came to an understanding that he would work on being less overbearing and she would try and not be so hard on him. Realising that he only wanted the best for her

As she wound around the last corner, the doors to the once called Magic Strategic department, now called Magic Anomaly Investigation Unit, or M.A.I.U as Brent called it, were at the end of the corridor. She walked up and stroked the name plate with her finger.

"Director Brent Abernathy," she mouthed and smiled. She was proud of her father's achievements, especially in such a short time. The Mage's Union undertook a massive restructure, and they needed to put people in place they could trust.

She knocked on the door and opened it gently. Hearing the ancient wood creak gave it more of a humbling, homey vibe. She took in the large panels of the Opticon, the magic-tech thoroughly impressive. Professor Nia's words echoed in her brain about the ethical nature of something so invasive on people's privacy.

Brent came rushing out of his office, his hair a little messy from running his hands through it. "Ah! Victoria, you are a little early."

"No, Dad, I am on time, you are running late." She smirked.

Brent flicked his wrist and looked at his Rune-Watch. His eyes opened wide. "Shit, we got to get you to the Psycholomage, and I got to finish this report before we—" Brent spoke in rapid clipped tones.

"Dad! Dad!" Victoria gripped his shoulders and made him look at her. "Breathe, it will all be okay, let's just go."

"You are right again. Sorry it has been a hectic month, and I am short listing for positions. Cyrus did a number on this place."

They wandered out of the office and headed towards the Department for Magical Wellbeing. As they approached it, he looked at her and smiled. "I shall get us a coffee. You won't be too long. It's the first session."

"Okay, see you soon," Victoria said, watching her father wander off around the corner before she entered the department.

She wandered into the office, and a heavy lavender aroma instantly assaulted her nostrils. Instead of feeling calm, she felt a wave of panic. What was she doing here? She was fine! A few nightmares were normal, right?

"Ah! Ms. Abernathy." A female Psycholomage stepped out of the side office, Victoria's request. "I am Dr. Blackthorn, are you ready?" Victoria nodded, and Dr. Blackthorn motioned with her hand to enter. She took one step and was rushed by a flood of memories flashing through her mind. She froze where she stood.

Her surroundings became enveloped in a heavy smoke and the room shifted and changed around her. Was it a dream? She didn't know. They had all felt so real. She turned around trying to make senses of her new surroundings, a person in a dark cloak appeared before her at the end of the corridor the room had shifted into. She recognised this cloak from Cauldron and panic entered her system.

The person held out a hand and launched towards her. Victoria screamed but could hear her father call out her name. She followed his voice and snapped her eyes open. Sweat trickling down her neck was the first thing she remembered, and then the room came back into view, the heavy lavender scent still in the air. Brent's worried face hung over her as did Dr. Blackthorn's.

"Are you okay?" Brent asked.

"Sorry, I must have fainted," she said, shaking her head and rubbing her eyes.

"Does this happen a lot?" Blackthorn asked.

"Not that I am aware," Brent answered honestly.

"I suggest we get her re-assessed."

"No more tests!" Victoria burst out loud and the room went silent.

After a short period of awkward silence, Brent looked at Blackthorn. "Thank you for today, I'll be in touch." He helped Victoria up, and they wandered out of the room.

"Oops, I almost forgot our..." Brent turned, and Blackthorn had their coffees in her hands. "Thanks." He smiled and handed Victoria hers.

"May I?" Blackthorn motioned to speak to Victoria and Brent stepped out of the way. Victoria looked up at her weakly. "This is an offer from me, and I don't do it often, but why don't you and I meet somewhere you choose for our first official meeting by the end of Nightveil? I will be un-available during Winter Solstice unfortunately. Perhaps we were pushing too soon?" She spoke calmly, and Victoria already started to like her.

"I would like that." Victoria smiled, taking her own advice, she'd allow herself to be more willing to accept the help from others, as well as hearing out their point of view.

They made plans to have Victoria contact Blackthorn's private office at a later date. Besides the small episode she experienced, Victoria's heart and mind were less burdened today. She and her father wandered the grounds for a bit before finding a bench.

"Still a bit too early before we head there," Brent said, sipping his coffee and wrapping an arm around Victoria, who snuggled into her father. They sat in silence for a while. Watching guests slowly arrive.

"This is not normal, is it?" Victoria asked.

"What isn't?" Brent asked, taking in another sip.

"Going to a public memorial for your old mentor, and an Arch Mage you never met."

"No, it isn't, I am afraid," he answered. "Victoria, my life has been nothing but the abnormal, and it seems like it caught up with you as well," he paused momentarily, "I need to apologise to you."

"What do you mean?" she adjusted in her seat and looked at him.

"I know we've talked about it, but I was too harsh on you this year. I told myself if we got out of that awful situation, I would be better about trusting you to make your own choices. And I plan to hold true to that promise. I meant what I said, from now on I will let you make your own decisions, but I am always here if you need to talk it out."

"It is okay, Dad. It's not like you were an Ogre!"

"Acts of Ogression aren't covered in our insurance plan, remember?" Pax called out from the side. Standing next to him was Silas, both men imposing frames in formal attire.

"So, are you two officially dating now?" Brent asked, sipping his coffee slyly.

Pax laughed and then sheepishly shrugged while scratching the back of his head.

"Yes, Uncle. Do you have a problem with me dating an Orc?" Silas asked, his deep voice booming across the way.

"Well, I mean, Pax is only half an Orc, the jury is still out on what the other half is." The three men shared a laugh. Victoria remained quiet; her attention was on the guests filing in. As Brent and the others turned, they could see Queen Emilia walking up the procession line. The Mage's Union employees greeted her. Victoria's heart skipped a beat. She had not seen her since Erimosia.

Brent looked at his daughter, and she caught his line of sight. With a reassuring smile, he gripped her hand and mouthed, "I'm here."

"If you forgive me, I am greeting guests. My grandmother put this all together and I got roped into helping." Silas smiled and patted Pax on the hand. Pax planted a kiss on Silas' cheek and then he was off.

Brent and Victoria shuffled over so that Pax could sit with them.

"So, did they ever find Emily?" Pax asked. Victoria uncomfortably shifted in her seat.

"The Arch Mage ordered scouts to scour Erimosia and the laboratory, but when they arrived, it was empty," Brent said.

"How is Arden taking on the new role?" Pax asked.

"You know him," Brent said with a sly smile.

"Chaos?" Pax raised a brow, and the two friends began to laugh.

"So, did you think about what we discussed?" Brent stood, as they should begin to make their way for the memorial.

"Yes, and I think it is a great idea, but for now, let's keep things the same for a little longer." Pax stretched his back and looked at the clouds forming above. "Hope this rain holds off."

"I'm sure it will pass," Victoria dismissed after she took a look at the sky. She jumped to her feet. "Come on, let's go grab a seat."

Brent filed in with Victoria on his arm. Pax had rushed forward to sit where Silas would be seated. Brent had requested seating at the back as he wanted to respect those who Magnar and Marquis knew in their illustrious careers.

Victoria held Brent's hand, not letting go the entire proceedings. Nia took to the pedestal alone. Brent craned his neck and spotted Nascien standing towards the back. Brent leaned into Victoria and whispered an apology in her ear, but he needed to go to the toilet.

Nia regaled everyone in the room with stories about Marquis and his many achievements. Seraphina walked up to the podium and handed Nia the medal they retroactively awarded Marquis for his service to Spellford.

"So, you didn't want to say anything?" Brent whispered to Nascien, bumping his shoulder.

"I never made amends with my dad." He hung his head.

"I get it, but don't let that stop you from reaching out and fixing things with Nia," he replied.

"You are as nice as always," Nascien replied sarcastically. Brent knew Nascien hated how kind he was towards him.

"Thank you for coming clean about it all for my investigation. I promise you will be reimbursed for your time."

"What about the job? Still hiring?" Nascien asked.

"You interested?" Brent asked. Nascien pushed himself off the wall and brushed past him.

"Not in a million years, but keep asking, maybe one of these days I'll say yes." He smiled, his golden eyes welling with tears as he walked out of the room. Everyone clapped for Nia in respect for her father. People came up in troves talking about Magnar and Marquis.

Arden was hosting the public reception after the memorial service. As Arch Mage, it was his duty, so he said, but he kept stealing glances with Brent. They had seen little of each other in the past month. Brent went outside and stood on the balcony overlooking Sanctum grounds, with a plate of food in his hands.

"How are you holding up?" Arden asked, walking out onto the balcony holding a plate of food he barely touched.

"Yeah, fine." Brent did not turn around.

Arden stepped up to his side. They shared a private smile. "We're good, right?"

"Why wouldn't we be?" Brent asked.

"This is the first proper conversation we have had in weeks," Arden added.

"With all that's happened, Victoria's recovery and us in new roles, I don't think there is much time left for romance," Brent said truthfully.

"Maybe when things settle, we can pick it back up again?" Arden placed the plate down on the balustrade. He turned Brent around, fixing his jacket collar. "I have about half an hour before I am required anywhere. Perhaps we could go back to my office and—" Arden stopped when he saw the look on Brent's face. His eyes sceptical as he stared into the distance up into the sky.

"What are you looking at?" Arden went to look.

"What's that?" Victoria's voice came from inside. She rushed out on the balcony and pointed at the dark, ominous cloud forming above Spellford. Red lightning juddered out of the sides as it grew in size, almost ready to burst.

Brent rushed to Victoria's side and held her by the shoulders. "Stay here alright and keep everyone inside."

"Wait, I want to—" Victoria tried to say something, but Brent had already opened a portal on his RuneWatch. Both Arden and Brent leapt over the balustrade, entering their own portals and waved as it closed behind them.

Their portals opened on Marquis' old building's balcony. Still closed for renovations as it was being sold off.

The cloud above them continued to grow in size. Arden scanned it with the new technology they had in their watches. "I can't get a reading," he shouted. The winds were picking up this high off the ground.

Suddenly, the lightning burst and the sky turned red and black. From the sky, a towering pillar of scarlet lightning burst from the cloud and fell between the buildings, shattering the road beneath it. Arden and Brent swayed as the lightning strike caused an earthquake throughout all of

Spellford. They rushed over to the balcony ledge and looked down. Standing up tall, a giant man extended his legs, growing to a staggering height. He was half the size of the building, his bulging muscles rippling. His long dark hair and beard whipped in the wind. Sparks ignited from his glowing red eyes.

"Where is the thief who stole my Storm Hound?" the gigantic man bellowed, causing the winds to form a cyclone. "Where is Brent Abernathy?" Brent turned to Arden, who was as confused as he was. Running forward, Arden and Brent leapt into battle, ready to defend Spellford from the new threat looming above. Brent's life would never be quite the same ever again. But at least he had one thing he could count on never changing—his *Dad Magic*.

THE END...of book one.

The Monarch Children Saga continues in Scarlet Rex

ABOUT THE AUTHOR

Benjamin Twigg is a fantasy and romance writer from Australia. As a queer author, Ben strives to write stories that have authentic representation, queer joy and a sense of wonder.

As a child, Ben dreamed of being a fantasy author and dived into those books, devouring the stories and world they created. As an adult, his love for fantasy world-building continued with role-playing video games, and he has racked up hundreds of hours of gameplay, immersing himself in character stories with amazing arcs.

Benjamin now also writes paranormal MM romance featuring monsters, ghostly boyfriends, ghoulish gays and sad-bois desperate for connection under the pen name B. J. Twigg

You can find Ben making whimsical memes and reels on

Instagram or spending time with his beloved dog, and his partner.

ACKNOWLEDGEMENTS

When I started this book, I didn't know if it was going to be just like the others. A finished WIP or an actual finished published piece. I have struggled for years trying to get a finished novel and "Dad Magic" was a story that once it started, I couldn't stop thinking about it or writing about it. I spoke to everyone and anyone who would let me talk or listen to me. I was obsessed. These characters were breathing, living people. The culture of the world I created and how magic functioned was something that excited me. I am still excited to share this world with you, the readers.

I had returned to the heights of excitement that I felt as a seventeen-year-old boy who wrote his first big story. I still have that book and it is currently being reworked, so I can't divulge just yet,

When I think of this story and the two years I took to write it; I look back at all the people who helped me along the way. Whether it was small as sharing in my excitement as I posted my updated word count or as big as reading my drafts or being my brain's trust in ideas that I might incorporate. These moments mean the world to me in the process of finishing Dad Magic.

One very important person who must be named. She provided me a critical overview of my first version of Dad Magic book and brought it to the place it needed, is **Liz Leiby**. I met her through an Australian Podcast, Toni and Ryan Podcast.

We are both super big fans of. Our friendship has grown over the twelve or more months and I am so happy you reached out to me. Liz is an amazing writer herself–go check out her books.

To **Toni and Ryan**! Thank you for the support and many shout outs. It is, in fact, Toni writing her book that spurred me to return to writing. Her determined, albeit with sometimes comedic effect, attitude to trying anything. And doing the things you are afraid of. Thank you for the constant laughs and happiness you bring. Ryan, you were the first to see my book cover, did you know? I respect you both so much! You gave me the nickname Big Twigg, but I still wager my hair is taller than yours Ryan. Thanks for all the brain breaks over the years!

Without **Lane Cox**, CodeWeavers would be completely different. Probably dare I say not even exist as they are? Lane is one of those guys who tells it how it is. He is forth right in how he feels but always willing to share a smile, a laugh and have a good time. He doesn't take a lot seriously, unless it comes to animals. I bonded with Lane instantly about our dogs and a strong friendship was formed. Thankyou for being the kind, thoughtful person you are, as well as providing me advice I needed for dog matters and even the Code Weavers. Maybe there will bea giant in a potential sequel inspired by you? Congratulations on the birth of little Harper!

To **Lauren**! My hive mind queen! Thank you for your guidance and skills! Your keen eyes, wicked wit and wonderful, brilliant and beautifully crass humour. Our shared love of big dudes with big–never mind. You know what I mean. Anyone reading this, please just don't! Thank you a million times over for your friendship! I don't know how I could ever repay you.

To **Thomas Anthony Lay**, my constant fantasy and writing inspiration. ***NAEISUS! HAMMERS! DUDE!*** How and why did you ever comment on my threads post that day? It has ruined all expectations of what online friends can be. You have set the bar for my future friendships with Cis-Het men. I believe you are one of the greatest, and you deserve all the success in the world. Thank you for cheering me on through this entire process.I cannot thank you enough!

To my Writing Girlies! You Dark Romance *QUEENS!* I love you! You are all wickedly sickening and fantastic. Your sense of humour and ability to just embrace me and let me fly my freak flag! Everyone should go out and buy your books! Thank you all for the advice and friendship! I love you all! **Jessica Carrasquillo, Poppy Fitzgerald, Addy O'Brien, Allie Oleander, D W Brooks, Jessuer Sutherland, Katie A Perez, Kelly L Clarke, Layna James, Madison Diaz, Tember Sapphire, Varsha Chitnis, Vanessa Stock, Krista Renee. THANK YOU FOR YOUR GUIDANCE. THE LAUGHS AND GOOD TIMES!**

A very special thank you to **Des Devivo**. Your companionship and guidance throughout the entire year has truly meant the world to me. You are stuck with me now. Thank you for always speaking your mind and truth, and be willing to shoot the shit with me about pretty much anything. You are my vocab, purple prose inspiration! I wish to write like you oneday! P.S. Priest Detectives is all I am thinking about now.

To my editor! My fellow Chaos Coveness! **Sara Burton** – Words cannot express how much you mean to me. You brought the magic out in me and my work. You challenged me in ways I didn't know I needed, and you made me the writer I wish I always was. A billion"thank you's"I whisper into the night, so that you could feel the gratitude that I have for you. I know you will hear it as well, as you and I are linked, just like Brentand Pax are. Or were now... Sorry we may be unliked like them now? LOL!

<u>To the most important people in my immediate life:</u>
Without **Desmond**, Pax would not be the lovable geeky,

balding Orc he is. Des, without you I would not have had someone cheering me on every single chapter and providing me amazing feedback to get me to the end. We have known each other for years now and I would say our relationship/friendship is intimate enough that I can express my love and appreciation for everything you do for me. You are one of the greatest people I know, and I thank you for reading every chapter and support throughout this process.

Aleks, the love of my life. You saved me in ways none can imagine or even put into words. You are the hardest working man I know. Everything you provide for us is beyond something a person is lucky to get in life. I cherish you more and more everyday. Your support on the sidelines and allowing me the space to write this story, being a constant inspiration to work hard on my dreams and all the video games and narratives we have shared over the years have brought me to this point where I can comfortably say, you are my other half that makes me whole and without you, this book would not exist. We have gone through a lot in our life, losing friends and family who wish not to speak to us anymore for whatever reason, but the only constant in my life has been you. You are my life, my love, and my everything, and I will say it now. **I love you the most** (*kidding, Venus; I love you the most!*)

To the most important relationship, minus Aleks, I have ever formed in my life. **Venus**, my love, my life, my everything. Though nothing in the world will make you understand what I am saying here, and even though these words you cannot understand, I know you feel it every day when I walk inside the front door, and you are waiting for me tail wagging and jumping up to see me with a smile on your face. (*Yes! dogs can smile.*) Venus, you mean the world to me, and I will immortalise your existence and moments in my life through this story, and every story after, forever until your last breath. I know your time will be shorter than mine, and for that I hate myself for ever allowing myself to fall so deeply in love with you, because the hurt is coming, and I am not prepared for that day. BUT! when I look in your eyes, when you sit on my lap and gaze into mine, I forget any apprehension or doubt that I have not loved you enough. When I see you, my world lights up. You taught me so much about love and life. You take every day as a new opportunity to live it to the best and enjoy life's best moments. I will miss napping with you and your nacho cheese paws. Whoever sent you to me, I hope they read this and tell you how much I love you, and when you finally pass on, I know you will wait for me to take me along on the next journey.

To all my mum and dad, my family, followers, co-workers, supporters, ARC Readers and people & connections I have met along the way, thank you for supporting me small or large.

If you are reading this, it means you have purchased the book. Unless someone sent you a screenshot, in which case I say go out and buy this book, you won't regret it. I worked really hard on it.

Thank you for reading Dad Magic and I hope you enjoy Brent, Victoria and Paxton's stories for many years to come.

Now I must go nap. I'm **<u>fucking</u>** exhausted from writing this book.

Ancient Aesirian Language

"Time is different for us my child. I saw you coming many centuries ago, but I refused to let him be the one to fall. Be good to him for me. He will need someone to rely on now that I am gone from this realm. You are the legacy of our love."

"Erimosian Are Monarch Children"

www.ingramcontent.com/pod-product-compliance
Lightning Source LLC
Chambersburg PA
CBHW020254120726
47904CB00001B/202